I'll Look
For You
Everywhere

I'll Look For You Everywhere

CAMERON CAPELLO

FOREVER

NEW YORK   BOSTON

Forever
Hachette Book Group
1290 Avenue of the Americas, New York, NY 10104
read-forever.com
@readforeverpub

Originally published in 2024 by Macmillan, an imprint of Pan Macmillan, The Smithson, 6 Briset Street, London EC1M 5NR
First Forever Edition: January 2025

Forever is an imprint of Grand Central Publishing. The Forever name and logo are registered trademarks of Hachette Book Group, Inc.

The publisher is not responsible for websites (or their content) that are not owned by the publisher.

The Hachette Speakers Bureau provides a wide range of authors for speaking events. To find out more, go to hachettespeakersbureau.com or email HachetteSpeakers@hbgusa.com.

Forever books may be purchased in bulk for business, educational, or promotional use. For information, please contact your local bookseller or the Hachette Book Group Special Markets Department at special.markets@hbgusa.com.

ISBNs: 9781538771358 (paperback), 9781538771365 (ebook)

Printed in the United States of America

CCR

10 9 8 7 6 5 4 3 2 1

To my Little Women, thank you for letting me imagine.

1

MAGDALEN

I watch the wine in her glass tremble with each laugh, the liquid edging toward the rim, wanting to escape, no doubt, but inevitably sinking back into the glass. I watch this for fifteen fucking minutes.

My eyes zone out until the clear edge of her wine glass becomes blurred and, abandoning my sense of sight, I see the party through what I can hear. People I don't know crowd around our tiny flat. Heightened laughter from someone attempting to flirt, the gentle tug of a cork, someone dropping their keys. A cough pulls me out of the trance, and I stretch my ankles until they crack. Watching this girl with her wine reminds me that the fullness of my left hand is not from a similar glass but, instead, a letter. It's too heavy to be a simple piece of paper, purposely eggshell in color and thick with feigned importance. But it is important, isn't it? I've turned into a bitch at my own party.

I press the cardstock corner hard into my finger, the sharp pain causing me to look down. I watch the skin around it swell with agitation and feel disappointed that I can't draw blood. The corner simply folds inwards, limp and lame. I want the letter to hurt me; maybe it'll be an excuse not to read it. To scream at my mother, *Your letter hurt me so I couldn't possibly return a reply.* But I realize the wine girl has asked another question that draws my attention away.

"*Chivasso,*" I repeat, already knowing she will ask me, for the third time, the name of my hometown.

"I'm sorry," she slurs, "can you repeat that?"

Her face is flushed the same shade of burgundy as her wine, and I can tell she is far past the point of being gracefully drunk. Not entirely irredeemable yet, I'll give her that. Perhaps a glass of water and a strong *caffè* can at least subside the inevitable headache tomorrow. She rubs her nose with the back of her hand, staring, waiting. I can tell her mind is projecting kaleidoscopic, spinning images of my face, and based on how her eyes shift from my eyebrows to my mouth, I know there are three of me in front of her. *Wait till you try grappa*, I want to say, but of course I don't. Instead, I remain seated, quietly waiting for her to condense the three of me into my singular self.

A sonata by Liszt echoes from a speaker in the kitchen, followed immediately by Billy Joel. I roll my eyes. His voice streams in as the new Oxford graduates mingle and compare, melodically commanding us to *slow down* because *we're doing fine.* But I already feel particularly slow tonight, and I'm unsure whether I've ever been fine.

Emily must be behind this. I love my roommate but I can't forget that she's also an Oxford student. Only the pretentious would transition Liszt to Billy Joel at a party. My eyes drift back to this girl, and the word *stupor* comes to mind. I stifle a smile, happy and sad at the same time. She is in a cozy, drunken stupor. She licks her lips, chapped from excess alcohol, and her eyes are half glazed with the inability to remember her name, let alone the name of the town I was born in. But she blinks slowly and patiently waits for me to repeat it. It's a ritual for Oxford students to get shit-faced at the end of term. A compressed period of overzealous indulgence to counterbalance their years of late-night library runs and thesis writing.

I sigh, "*KEY-VA-SO*," deliberately enunciating every consonant, elongating every vowel. I tuck myself further into the leather armchair, drawing my knees up underneath my chin. The letter I've been carrying around all afternoon slides to my hips, pressed tightly between my stomach and the front of my thighs, safely protected from any partygoers with slippery fingers. On second thought, maybe it would be better to hand it to one of them. A free summer in Italy for the small price of attending my sister's wedding. I take another sip of my beer and wipe my mouth with the back of my hand like a lonesome cowboy in an old Western movie. The credits will roll. Life will move on. A sequel will be in the works. When will my movie begin? Looking around the flat I've spent the past year in, I find myself disinterested. Not wanting to remember it, wanting more to avoid looking at anything. Surely that's not normal twenty-year-old girl behavior.

There is an antiquity about Oxford that is beautiful. No one can deny that the rich know how to decorate. The walls are steeped in dark history, held together with powerful columns of academia. Faces of brilliant men are carved into the ceilings. Women buried underneath the floor. Success always looks different for young girls.

The worn-out wood of library floors is a nice reminder of the presence of brilliant minds running to and from bookshelves. And I am here. My footsteps are etched into the very same floors; my empty ink cartridges lie underneath the mahogany benches of the lecture halls. Oxford is dusted in an almost violent intelligence that can sometimes overwhelm you.

But it's not home. Although it had been for my mother, Vittoria, and my father, Claudio. I take another sip and see that I'm empty.

The sun can never really find its way here between the ornate buildings. And no matter the season or clothes I'm wearing, whether I'm in a hot bath for an hour or running around the campus, I've always felt a coldness chasing me. It's like the memory of a rain-soaked sweater that I can never really get rid of—a permanent, melancholic mildew following me around.

Before I have time to feel blue, the drunken girl tries to get up too quickly from the opposing leather armchair and it makes a terrible squeaking sound and I look up.

"*Oh! Kayvazso!*" Her eyes try to light up, but her drunkenness only allows a dull head nod. Plopping down on the armrest, I smile as I watch her eyelids succumbing to the weight of the wine, so at peace, so unafraid.

"Kayvazso!" she says again, slapping her hand to her forehead comically, becoming confident and radiant with knowledge. Something about the name's vowels and structure strikes her as very Italian, and she leaps to conflate all the knowledge she has assembled about Italy into the name of my hometown. This happens at Oxford; even in intoxication, people are always on the hunt to prove.

"I love Italy! I went abroad last semester and it changed my life. Like really, like, the culture there is so . . . different . . . so open, you know? Like from here, I mean British people can be so . . ."—she pauses, trying to find the right word—"*depressing*." A giggle bubbles out of her, proud of her boldness. Impressed that she said such a racy and unorthodox thing, she giggles again because she, herself, is British.

"Maybe Italians are too open?" I weakly say, hoping that would be enough for her to take over the conversation. Picking up my empty beer, I start to scratch the moist label off my bottle in the discomfort. Looking at her, how the lines around her mouth are relaxed and faded, how her mascara is smudged but she's young and fun so she doesn't care—my blueness creeps up without warning.

My inability to relax my shoulders and join her in a drunken stupor infuriates me. I want to be silly! But I am also drunk and still painfully aware of the condensation that falls on my finger. Aware how the right side of my hair is tucked behind my ear, but the left side hangs in front of my face, mindful of the freckle that sits above my eyebrow, wondering if she has noticed I have a freckle, wondering if anyone has ever noticed that I have that freckle. I glance at the kitchen to see if there's any more beers left on the counter. Oxford is not home.

My gaze finds its way back to her wine. I take a breath in, closing my eyes, the smell of alcohol making me fifteen and back at the museum in Torino. Anika and me sitting on the marble tile underneath the statue of Isis, a bottle of wine open between us, her MAC lipstick tattooed on the rim. If I really focus, I can hear her dad, Dexter, in the hidden office behind the third-floor gift shop, rustling papers with sub-tle frustration, frequently reminding us to behave ourselves. That he's always there and can hear everything.

We used to love staying after hours in the damp darkness of our museum, as it really was *ours* when the CLOSED sign was hung up each night. Faces of unknown statues looked down on us, shaking their heads, whispering, *No, no, no, it'll always be ours.* The backs of my thighs shifting against the cool floor, wanting to find relief from the heat of the museum, in an unbearable Italian summer.

"The statues hate the cold," my papa used to say. "It makes them remember their death."

Personally, I just think Italians are too cheap to buy an aircon. I stifled a groan of discomfort, wishing to feel that coldness if just for a moment. The warm effect of the wine mingled with the unforgiving heat, the back of my neck dampening to my hair. I looked up into the eyes of Isis and thought being conscious of your mortality seemed far worse than briefly remembering your death. Anika shrugged her shoes off and placed her bare feet on the base of the statue, looking up at Isis.

"She wants to fuck me," she sighed and grazed her big toe against the carved foot of Isis with intimate slowness. "I just know it."

We laugh. Anika describes her latest sexual encounter. I listen and know her father is also listening and feel weird but don't say anything.

Lost in the memory of my youth, I feel the letter slip from my hand. I jerk off the chair, scrambling to pick it up off the floor. It is not the first one she has sent. Three identical envelopes sit unopened with only dust to respond, nestled between my winter knits.

My sister's wedding.

Arguably something I should want to attend. But something about this party makes my fingers twitch. The hazy memories of crawling barefoot in the museum with Anika come back. My skin feels tight as I realize what is happening— I'm considering going back.

No! my subconscious screams. *Oxford is your safe haven. Remember why you left. Who you left. Think of how long you felt sad.* I sigh. Maybe I just don't like parties. I tend to be my most melodramatic in social settings, so it's difficult to tell when I mean what I think.

Scooting up further on the chair, I look around the flat again. The scratched hardwood floors, the chipped corner of our kitchen countertop from when Emily cracked a beer bottle over the ceramic. The memory makes my eyes

7

involuntarily search for her. Wild curls sway around her as she argues about simple nothings with the man she is in love with. A professor, tricky. But he's very charming and seems to listen when she speaks. Usually, this would make me smile. But I look at all of these things from outside of myself. Seeing them but feeling nothing.

My ribs burn. The drunk girl is still rubbing her nose until it's flushed with red irritation. She is nameless, happy, and free. *Give me some of that!* my mind screams. I want to reach out, grab her carelessness, swallow it, and tread in her stupor. But I can't.

I think of the walls of Chivasso, permanent and profound with age. Running away has done nothing but drag my blueness to another country. My sister shouldn't pay the price for something I should have worked out years ago. The air becomes heavy with sadness, and I feel burdensome. My fingers dig into the letter.

Why am I always left behind? So afraid of everything and so tired of being afraid.

A deep exhale escapes me, feeling like my skin itself is deflating from the loss of breath. I have no dress. No shawl for my potentially exposed shoulders.

I feel my heart constrict so tightly I think I'm dying. I wait a moment, trying to feel the action of breath. Waiting for a pulse through the skin of my wrist. My ears fill with white noise as I look down at the letter.

But then I feel it; the rush of blood settles in my fingertips, letting me know I'm not dying, just being a pussy.

My nails slide through the hardened wax seal, fingers

gripping the invitation, feeling the raised lettering of my sister's name, feeling selfish for not wanting to go in the first place.

So I shove my melodrama back into the envelope and seal it shut.

I have a wedding to attend.

2

MAGDALEN

It's a week later and Emily is still furious. My roommate fucking the professor, angry with me! We have already purchased tickets to backpack across Peru, and she cannot fathom why on earth I would want to go back *home*. She says "*home*" with disgust, bitter and resentful of a word that has the potential to mean so much. But not to her.

Emily had her annual falling-out with her mother five months ago, and this trip guaranteed another three months during which she didn't have to see her again.

"Ask Professor Cal," I giggle.

"Stop calling him that."

"What? He should be proud of his education. Are you not making him feel proud, Emily?"

"I'm making him feel things, all right." She winks.

"Gross. It's too early to be this gross!"

She falls to her knees in front of the leather chair, still sticky from last week's spilt alcohol, and grabs my face in her hands. "Ugh, men. They disgust me!" Her black hair spills around her face in wild curls, casting shadows across our walls.

"You and home." Her eyes search mine and she sighs. "I don't get it with you."

My cheek warms in her palm as I lean into her touch. "You and me both, sister." I shrug. "I'm complex."

"You're secretive."

"I'm not! Remember when I told you about the spot on my ass?"

"The only reason you told me was because I had to pop it."

"Gross again, Emily! Too early for gross."

Emily pinches my cheek and pouts, standing. "No way I can convince you, Maggie? Peruvian boys, Peruvian wine, Machu Picchu? Enlightenment?"

"I haven't even met an English boy yet and you're already handing me over to the Peruvians?" I laugh, relieved that she has forgiven me. It is always so easy with Emily.

"What you mean to say is that you've never had any boy, Maggie dearest. Which, I will never bloody understand. You just have to get it over with, like the flu shot." She pads over to the kitchen, searching for a bottle of wine to open, despite the noon chime minutes away from ringing. "You're so fucking beautiful, and smart and you know, and I bet you'd fuck like a—"

I inwardly cringe. "Ah, *sta' zitto! Shut up!*" I bury my face in my hands, absolutely hating the rush of compliments, or any compliment, ever. I blame it on my mother.

Emily looks at me and laughs. "You can't hide forever." She smiles, hopping onto the kitchen counter to try to reach her secret bottle of wine. I follow her, hovering underneath the archway.

"Someone deserves to see how brilliant you are." She grunts, moving to stand up on the countertop. Turning

11

around to look at me, Emily's stopped smiling. It's like I can read her mind as she frowns, wondering, always wondering why I am the way I am.

My cheeks flush with embarrassment at her kindness; I fear I'll always hate being so seen.

"Why don't you and *Cal* come to visit me in Chivasso after your Peruvian hiatus? I'd be more than happy to show you around?" I pick at the chipped paint of the kitchen wall. I think we both know this will never happen but it seems important to ask.

Rolling her eyes at my skillful deviation in conversation, Emily pauses to think about my proposal.

"Fuck it. All right. I'll ask Cal. I'll have to break the bad news to dear old Mum." She carefully walks across the counter to get a glass and laughs bitterly. "She'll be so upset!"

Watching her stretch helplessly for the top shelf, my fingers twitch with the need to show her how much she means to me. In a rare and very unlike Magdalen Savoy manner, I lean off the archway and walk across the kitchen floor. The one stained with red wine and spilled nail polish. A floor that has absorbed the unstoppable laughter after Saturday nights out and the tears over term papers. I run to hug her but she's still standing on the counter, so I settle my arms around her calves.

"What would I do without you, Emily?" I am desperate and fervent, hoping my statement will be enough to show her how grateful I am. That without her, part of me would not exist. These are big confessions to make before noon. So

I settle with the silent heaviness of our hug, pressing my love for her between the space of our bodies.

Emily pauses a moment before bending down to try to hug me back. She tenderly squeezes my shoulders and then pats me gently on the head and sighs. "I don't know, but chances are you still wouldn't have gotten laid."

She pinches my sides, and I squeal. "You bitch!" I say and laugh. "You know I'm just waiting!"

She tilts her head back in laughter and attempts the ugliest Italian accent I've ever heard. "You, my dear friend, are waiting for da Vinci to roll out of his grave and rip your clothes off! You dirty, nast—"

"Do not even think about finishing that!"

She hops off the counter and begins chasing me around the flat, both of us squealing and laughing like little schoolgirls. I could never have survived Oxford if it were not for Emily, who I am certain God sent down to guide me.

I met her on my fifth day. I was looking for the closest bathroom to escape my isolation at a party thrown by someone I had never met. I'd forced myself to go after my mother had called and asked if I was going out in my first week, her voice ready to console, anticipating I'd say no.

"Yes, I am. I'm on my way actually," I had said while in bed, my pillowcase damp with tears.

"Oh, great then. I won't keep you." She hung up.

I accidentally ran into Emily with her underwear around her ankles, having loud and grotesque sex with a man much her senior in the bathroom. Clearly, she has a type. I was so stunned that I froze with sheer panic and just stared at their naked and twisted bodies in front of me, hypnotized but incredibly horrified. A victim of Medusa's glare.

"Do you want to take over from here?" Emily said, looking up at me. Her hair was plastered to her sweating face and she was breathing loudly out of her mouth, but her eyes were light with humor. *This was funny for her?* It was as if she had expected me to be there, never sorry or embarrassed for being caught.

"I warn you, his dick hurts like hell," she smirked and nudged the man behind her. He let out an uncomfortable grunt, which I assume was meant to sound like a laugh. I let out the breath I was holding and squeezed my eyes shut.

"No, no, you look like you are more than capable of finishing that off!" I couldn't help the laughter that was escaping me. "Maybe try the lock next time?"

I quickly shut the door behind me and clamped my hand over my mouth. She was not, for one moment, *ashamed.* Looking back, I still feel self-conscious. And I wasn't even the naked one!

But Emily is right. I am afraid of a feeling I have no name for yet. I can't even look at a man without acid rising up my throat. A brief flash of pain in my ribs. I close my eyes and let it pass. The thought makes me nauseous because deep down, I know, despite Emily's kind words of affirmation, no one will ever want to be so close to me. My issue is not entirely physical. Maybe I'm not considered ugly, sure. But I don't consider myself necessary. I am tall, possibly too tall, and was called flat-chested by Lorenzo in seventh grade, but I assume he actually liked me. My hair is long and brown but sometimes looks red in the sun. I don't mind my hair. And I've gotten thinner over this last year, I know Anika will say something about it. Several men and women have tried to seduce me through the dim and warm setting of Oxford's bars. And if it happens only after dark, does that count?

It seems my body is just feminine enough to allow people to find me attractive after midnight.

The truth? I feel unwanted.

How do you say that to someone without sounding self-deprecating, without it looking like you want their pity? I remember sitting by the window as a teen, watching Anika kiss some boy from town under the veranda and thinking that if anyone ever came near my face like that, I would scream.

And this is what Emily will never fully be able to understand, this *thing* that exists inside me, reminding me every day that I am always just a step behind everyone else.

So Emily came out of that bathroom, flushed and radiant ("I wasn't kidding, it was huge," she complained), took my hand ("Don't worry, I washed them") and asked, "Do you want to be my roommate? Mine's a fucking cunt."

Stunned, I didn't answer.

"I mean you've already seen me naked, so that won't be an issue for us." She stared at me, waiting, perhaps knowing I would say yes.

"Yeah, I guess." I blushed, pleased that she would find my brief company enjoyable enough to room with for an entire year. "As long as he doesn't join us."

She stopped walking and stared at me, and I felt my throat close up with embarrassment, a stupid joke too soon made. I didn't even know her last name.

As I was about to apologize, she threw her head back and laughed. "Oh, we will *never* see him again." Her body shivered at the thought of the mystery man. She locked her arm around mine, and without prompt, began talking about dreams, horoscopes and Russian literature. From that one moment, I felt I had worth at Oxford. Even if I failed my classes or never received another party invitation again. I had her. Emily, *Emilia* I'd call her in the Tuscan sun, my guardian angel.

3

THEO

Jesus fucking Christ, Theo. Just walk.

She stands there in a red top that shouts **ROME** pacing the airport baggage claim in search of me. For a moment, I feel like hiding, knowing that seeing her for the first time in all these years will change my course. Unsure, however, if this path is the dangerous, violent and regrettable choice or the one I should have taken seven years ago. I cough, loud enough for her to hear, and she responds without fail, her head jerking at the sound. She jumps up and down in frenzied excitement, clapping her hands and shrieking.

"Theo! We've been waiting forever! Come here, right now!" Anika leaps toward me, her arms outstretched, preparing for a hug.

I notice she is alone. The "we" she refers to is out of habit. I prefer *her* to *them* and expected my Houdini act would not be forgotten with the purchase of a fucking plane ticket. But I let myself feel it for one second; after seven years, just her left. Shit. This is going to be a long fucking summer.

"I missed you, too," I say, her force causing me to lose my breath. She smells of fresh sunscreen and fig perfume; my eyes close at the nostalgia that brushes over my skin, curls

17

the roots of my hair, and I breathe in deeply. She smells of home. Chivasso has been home since I was seven and my father took us out for ice cream and told us we'd be leaving Edinburgh. I remember the sound of Mamma's clapping. Her ice cream spoon clattering against the table. She was so excited to return home. To reunite with Vittoria.

"I can't believe you're real!" Anika squeezes her arms around my waist, gripping so tight it begins to sting.

"I'd forgotten how big you are!"

"Right," I mumble in her hair, enjoying but never revealing how much I love her missing me. I feel like a brother again, giddy and eager to impress.

"Haven't grown since I was seventeen. I think maybe you're just getting smaller?" I say to the top of her head. Anika is a foot shorter than me, making it easy to want to protect her. Although I would never fucking think about saying that to her.

"Shut up. Maybe if you came home every once in a while, I could have prepared for this gargantuan height!" Her tone is light, but within her words lies my abandonment. She has not forgiven me yet, either. Didn't think I'd get off that easy, anyway.

She lets go of my waist to look up at my face. Taking her hand, she squeezes my chin with two fingers, forcing my head to look side to side, examining and probing me like a lab rat.

"Since when did you become such a *stud*?"

I take her hand in mine and kiss her palm. "I came out of the womb a stud, Anika. Don't forget it," I say with a wink.

She snorts and slaps me on the shoulder. "Disgusting!" she screams, and then tries to pry the luggage out of my hand.

"The girls in Chivasso will have a field day with you, Theo. You better be careful, it's still a small town and if you fuck someone, I'll know in three to five hours after completion."

"Jesus, Anika. It's 8 a.m. Can we not make this the first topic of conversation?" I jerk my hand away so she misses the handle of my bag. "I can carry my own bag," I gruff, annoyed that she tried to take it in the first place.

I grab the handle with determination, feeling the need to prove that I have become a grown adult in the seven years she hasn't seen me. She rolls her eyes but drops her hand, letting me take the luggage handle.

"No way I'm starting shit with any girls," I clarify, wanting it understood that I really have fucking learned.

"I give you three days."

"Oh, come on. You haven't seen me in seven bloody years. I'm not a Neanderthal," I swallow, hoping if I say the words out loud, they'll be true.

"Fine. Let's make it four."

"Fuck you, Anika."

"And it's like you never left!" She prances ahead of me, spinning in circles, barging into airport employees and people waiting for their luggage who stare with disapproval. Her hair is much longer than I remember. Dark and black like our mother's, and it swings heavily as she trots away.

Within minutes, the tension from the plane ride dissolves.

19

Seven years away. Four in New York. Three in Connecticut. It was easier not to feel guilty when I couldn't see her face. But now? I release a breath.

This was the right choice.

I feel stupid for considering this the risky path. Stupid for not calling more often. How can life in Chivasso be regrettable if Anika is in it? My baby sister. My hand squeezes around the luggage handle. Guilt and regret sink into me, making my limbs feel sluggish.

An image flashes in my mind of a memory, hazy colors and hushed whispers and the sound of tearing fabric. I squeeze my eyes shut. What I really want is to show her that I am not *him*, that in adulthood, I will not become him.

She looks back at me, her smile big and proud. I'm not good enough to deserve this. But I look at her, realize my face mirrors hers, and immediately look ahead, suppressing my smile.

"Fuck off," I laugh.

When I've caught up to her, her hands are on her hips with disapproval. "Your accent has disappeared." She tilts her head and laughs silently, eyes light with amusement.

I pause our walk. "Tell that to everyone at university who can't understand anything I fucking say."

"All right, *va bene,* still a Scotsman." Anika throws her hands up in protest. Scottish, Italian, thrust into Ivy League America.

We pass through the sliding doors of Malpensa Airport, and the windless Italian heat overwhelms me. Looking around, feeling the gold and seductive air, a wave of sadness hits me. *Home.*

"I'm just saying, I'm noticing a little American in that Scottish, Theo! And your hair! *Che cazzo!* It's almost as long as mine! Is this why you're back? Yale couldn't get you a job with that hair?" Her arms are waving everywhere, and her cheeks are red with excitement.

"I've been in New York, Anika. Long hair is very in," I say, but unconsciously tuck my hair behind my ear, which I hadn't realized fell at my chin until just now.

"Oh, how could I forget! From that one five-minute phone call you made telling us that you were moving to New York fucking City." *Us, again.* She's always done this. Attached her feelings to theirs.

"*Tornerò su quell'aereo se non smetti di parlare,* Anika!" *I'm going to go back to that airport if you don't stop talking!* I bite, getting my Italian over with. The words feel rusty in my mouth. I wait for her to poke fun. My vowels are too long; my infliction is a beat off.

On cue, she rolls her eyes. "I will honest to god murder you if you so much as take a step toward that airport, Theo! There's no going back now."

"Fine," I say with a smile. Seeing my sister, it becomes excruciatingly clear that I can't turn my back on her now. It was never *her* I wanted to leave. She knows that, of course. But I try not to think of that now.

I follow her into the parking garage; the shade gives momentary relief from the unforgiving heat.

"Also, Theo, maybe it's best if you stick to English," she laughs. "I mean, Jesus, that was like nails on a chalkboard." Her face scrunches up in disgust. "Got to work on that, Theo! We speak *Italiana* with an English accent! *English!*" She imitates the elegant accent, winking at me. Anika was only three when we moved to Chivasso, so the only detectable Scottish thing about her is how thrawn she gets in the morning.

"Come, questo!" Like this!

"You realize, in the two minutes since I have landed, that you have insulted my hair, education, and accent?" I raise my eyebrow at her, teasing my loud-mouthed and forever opinionated sister.

She looks at me, and I expect a witty comeback, but she just stares, and her eyes, without warning, fill with sincere but unplaceable emotion. She is silent for a moment.

"Why now, Theo?" she whispers. "Why didn't you ever come back home?"

I swallow, and my tongue is heavy with an unanswerable response, hands suddenly weak as I retract the handle of my suitcase and open the car trunk, taking my time to place it inside the carpeted interior. Taking my time to think of something to say.

"I was at school." My voice comes out annoyed, as if her asking me why I haven't been home in seven years is somehow a nuisance. It is a lame excuse, and I know she can see right through me.

Liar, liar, liar. It's written in the furrow of my brow; you can hear it in my inhale.

"But I'm home now," I add, hoping this will be enough for her.

I shut the trunk, shove my hands in my pockets, squeeze them into tight fists, and walk to the passenger side.

Knowing I won't say any more, she looks at me for one moment longer, sighs again, and nods her head. Accepting for now, for now, that I won't talk.

Despite our four-year age difference, when we were young, Anika was determined to join me every time I left the house. My protests were always theatrical, conjuring up excuses I had watched older brothers on TV say to their little sisters. Never understanding why I wouldn't want to have her near. Always happy she even wanted to stay.

Even my secrets could never just be my secrets; they were always *ours*. Except for one.

My leaving was the first betrayal. I know it hurt her, severed a piece of that bond we once shared. It was the first time she didn't follow me.

But in all these years, she has never been angry, never blamed me for leaving. Part of her knows why I went, so she lets me get away with lies, but I think the other half will always wonder.

"That's right; you're home now. And I'm not letting you go this time." She ducks her head into the car and turns the key in the ignition. I take a breath and squeeze into her tiny orange Fiat. The ceiling is covered in enamel pins from concerts, holidays, and there are at least fifteen saying, "FLOSSING IS FUN."

Anika. I close my eyes as she pulls the car in reverse. *If only you knew how much I want to say. How badly I want you to know.* My throat burns. We exit the airport parking lot, and I stare out the window. *Welcome,* the blurring shades of green scream, *we thought you forgot us!*

4

MAGDALEN

I lie on the white linen sheets of my childhood bed, warm from baking in the afternoon sun. It is difficult to explain the sun in Italy. The light is different here; it radiates with archaic strength. Perhaps God loves Italians more. Flesh touched by the Italian sun seems irrevocably golden, penetrating into personalities as much as their skin. But the sweat that trickles down my temple is cold and, to distract myself, I pick at the chipping white paint of the frame, listening to my breath, sedated and pleasant, savoring the silence. Growing up in this house with three other siblings, quiet was a rarity. My siblings Joseph, Luciana and Dante, the adoring trio, were always good at taking up space. Joseph, the eldest and most serious out of the four. Eager to speak about the latest developments in the museum's marketing campaign. We tend to avoid any mention of our website if we don't want the latest analysis of his conversion rate optimization. Luciana is practically made of light. Radiant, intelligent, gorgeous. The only one who followed my father's footsteps as an archeologist and, for that, I feel she'll always be the favorite of the three. A seasoned world traveler. Unafraid of the dark. The girl doesn't even wear concealer! If it was anyone else in the family's wedding, I'm certain I could have skipped it. But it's Luciana! And in this family, her name carries weight.

And then there is Dante. It's impossible to think of him without smiling. Taking after my mother, Dante is blessed with the ability to talk about anything to anyone. Even the older ladies at the market stop him to chat. Tanned skin and too much hair gel. Despite being five years older than me, he is forever seventeen. Foul-mouthed and chasing his next dream. Last time I checked, he and Anika were planning on opening up a wine bar in the south of France. Anika and Dante are inseparable, possibly in love. But I'm not sure either one of them knows that yet. Who am I to spoil the surprise?

Thinking of my siblings, it's difficult not to feel my differences. When did it happen? Maybe as children, our heads all under that same christened water in the local church in Chivasso.

Chivasso is a small enough town to know the who, what and when of everyone the moment they stand in front of our *duomo*. We are nosey people, curious for details, lovers of drama. Our front door has no lock and people often walk into our house whenever the mood strikes. It is welcomed, never seen as an intrusion or nuisance. Conversation, the spontaneous and unplanned kind, is beautiful to these people; it is a blessing to communicate. And my mother is always home; with the door propped open with a battered textbook, she sits and waits for a stranger to knock on the door. She gave up her career when the four of us were born, but after so long away from work, her comfort suppressed her ambitions. The museum, which is where she worked, where my dad and Jo still work, and which the Sinclairs co-own, annually begs her to come back. To write another book. But she shakes her head and laughs.

If I close my eyes and concentrate, I can hear their laughter downstairs, despite being secluded on the third floor. You can hear everything in old houses, the soft pedaling of footsteps to the kitchen at midnight, a gentle creak of the gate at dawn, the drunken whispers of Dante and Jo arguing after a night out. Even if everyone is asleep in this house, there is never deafening silence, not when the house itself is awake.

My eyes shoot open against the setting sun and I realize I've drifted off. Shit. Dinner must be soon. I hurry to get off the bed. The bathroom mirror is waiting and, when I sneak a look, my forehead is pale and clammy and my lips are chapped. *Morte*, I poke my cheek. I look dead. Stripping in front of the mirror, I feel offensively naked. The bathroom mirror at Oxford was cracked and a few inches too high, meaning I haven't properly looked at myself in over a year. As I stare, it occurs to me that no one has ever seen what I see at this moment. I am confidential. Turning around, I examine myself fully, noticing the dimples and marks that trail up my body. Those pesky scars. It feels intrusive to look at myself so intimately. Do I want this to be a secret forever?

Thinking about it for too long makes me nauseous. How would I begin to reveal? My hair starts to stick to my neck and I look away from the mirror to find a hairbrush. When I look back, it's difficult to meet my own gaze. I settle instead on the ends of my hair.

5

MAGDALEN

"Ah, Eccola qui! La regina stessa!" Here she is, the queen herself!

I enter the kitchen, bracing myself for our neighbors from down the street or the vegetable vendor from the *piazza* with some homegrown *cime di rapa*.

I stand by the doorway. The kitchen is crowded with people: my mom sits at the table, chopping away, with Dante and Jo sitting around her. In the corner is my dad, who nurses a glass of *grappa*, and sitting on the counter is Anika. She is all I see.

"Anika!" I yelp, never expecting to see my sister, unrelated by blood but tethered by soul, sitting in my kitchen.

"Why didn't you tell me you were coming over?"

"It was supposed to be a surprise! I thought you were sleeping, I never would have come now." She wipes her forehead with the back of her hand. "I was supposed to change and look better than you!"

"You idiot, you look perfect!" I hug her tight, the warmth and nostalgic perfume making me realize just how much I had needed to come home.

"You look skinny, *non sembra magra?*" She squeezes my hips and I giggle, despite the pang of insecurity at her observation. I make a mental note to introduce Emily and Anika. It seems I am a beacon for the loud and confident—they need someone next to them, to absorb their excess so they don't drown in it themselves. I breathe deep, a tremor of anxiety surfacing as I take in the fact that I am the empty vessel in this scenario.

"It was finals, I was stressed!" I get out, hoping it's enough to stop everyone examining me. My dad's eyes flicker to my ankles and I subconsciously press the pad of my foot over the clear outline of my bones.

"*Lo fa, le ho detto che Oxford era troppo stressante per lei*." *You see, I told her Oxford was too stressful for her*, Dante chimes in, the cherub older brother who didn't see the point in university.

Anika winks and rubs my shoulders, trying to suppress her laughter. "You see, *perché non hai ascoltato Dante?*" *Why did you not listen to Dante?* She tsks mockingly while patting my head, as if making sure I'm really here.

"All right, I'm skinny and stupid now, *va bene*?" I roll my eyes and grab an apple. "Are you all happy?"

The chatter continues and Anika and I look at each other from across the kitchen, silently agreeing to sneak outside to talk. Our secret code, mastered from years of escaping weekly family dinners. It is an indistinguishable blink of the eye, a short breath in, a tap of the foot. We've had twelve years of practice, and by now it's become a science. I toss my apple in the bin and Anika fills her glass with more wine and we exit through the back door; the chatter doesn't falter.

"I can't believe you're home. It feels like years since I've seen you," Anika's Scottish accent is undetectable compared to the rest of her family. The Sinclairs are treasured in Chivasso, half Scottish, half Italian; they're the first outsiders to have ever stepped foot in this sleepy town and are protected by the old townsfolk down in the *piazza*. When they came here, they changed everything. Dexter Sinclair became co-director of the Museo Egizio with my father in Torino, transforming it from a museum you go to on a rainy day to an epicenter of tourism. Foreigners began to flood the city just to see the exhibits that Dexter assembled. My papa never had the knack for marketing, too busy stuck in history.

I stare at the moving pattern of leaves the afternoon shadow has created and breathe in. "I didn't think I would come home, to be honest."

"Do I repel everyone?" Anika groans. "First Theo and then you. This last year has been fucking torture."

"My poor Anika." I squeeze her knee and lean my head against her shoulder. "You're the one who brought us back, babycakes."

"Oh jeez, thanks. Only took Theo seven fucking years to miss me."

"But only a year for me! Does that mean you love me more than your brother?"

Anika laughs, leaning her head against mine so we're stacked on top of one another. "You're telling me you're not even a little excited for Lucia's big day?"

I sigh, considering her question. "No, no, I am. Her and I haven't ever been that close, you know? It's not like you and Theo."

"Lucia loves you, Maggie. Surely you know that she'd be fucking devastated if you didn't come."

It's easier to talk this way, head to head. "Of course, of course." I rush to change the subject: "Anyway, enough about me. How's everyone here?"

"Everyone's fine. My parents are always at the museum so they're never home, and I am still a disappointment, so really nothing has changed since you lived here!"

She takes a sip of her wine and then sighs. "And as much as I love to have you here, you were supposed to be in Peru." She lifts her head from mine, nudging me in the rib with her elbow. So much for the change of subject.

"It's Lucia's big day. I already didn't make the cut being maid of honor for my own sister, the least I could do is show up. Machu Picchu will still be there next summer."

"And maybe next time, you can invite me to meet this Emily girl."

"You hate planes! Last time I checked, you only do trains."

"Ugh, can you stop remembering everything I say! Your brain is freaky."

It's my turn to lift my head. "Because I remember that my best friend doesn't like flying?"

"You called me your best friend." Anika takes another gulp of her wine and wraps her arms around me tightly. "I missed you so much, freak," she whispers.

"I promise you, I missed you so much more." I squeeze her back, feeling safe in her embrace. "I was homesick."

"Homesick?" Anika detaches herself to look at me. "You decide to go to university in England and then decide you get homesick? *Madonna*, you could've stayed here with me and Dante! It's not too late! Don't go back!"

"If those are my two options, I'll go right back to England," I laugh. Dante, unlike Anika, is not good company for an extended amount of time. He and I were never close growing up. I think my shyness made him uncomfortable, and eventually he started hanging more around the Sinclairs' house than ours once Jo and Lucia left.

"Oh, fuck off." She shakes her head. "You've always been too smart for your own good, you and Theo both."

She pauses, looking up at the coming twilight, and huffs out, "What the fuck happened to me? I put salt in my coffee yesterday, that's what I did. Fucking salt! Jesus, the gene pool in this fucking family is rigged. So unfair."

I try to stifle my laughter but it comes out as a snort, and Anika whips around to slap me on the shoulder.

"Oh, fuck you then!" She stands up and begins to pace, taking progressively larger sips of her wine between each aggression. "Fuck Theo, fuck my parents and, for the hell of it, fuck your parents, too! Without you around I might as well run away and join a convent. You know how insufferable Dante is? I can't do this any more. He made me shave his back last weekend, Maggie."

She continues but my own laughter deafens her ramble.

Finally, she joins and I've fallen off the bench with one hand on my stomach and the other stretched above my head, fingering the cool grass. Listening to my heartbeat, I take a deep breath in and stretch, feeling a deep, sedated calm wash over me. The wooden gate behind me opens, but we don't hear it until soft footsteps begin to come up the gravel driveway.

6

THEO

My mum left a note:

> DINNER AT SAVOYS.
> BE THERE BEFORE EIGHT.
>
> MUMMY

It is 7:50 now; pushing it. I paced for a few hours, drank what was left of my dad's gin, took a cold shower; my cheeks feel warm and my nose is numb.

When I near the driveway, I hear laughter and can already tell one of the voices belongs to Anika, but the other is foreign, deeper than Anika's, but rich. How can I not place it? My seven years away slowly settles in me and I come to a standstill at the gate, hesitant to intrude on the life that's been built in my absence.

Going away to Yale, I left the Savoys just as much as my real family. And now my stomach drops at having to enter the house. I can already hear them saying, *"Long time, no see! Did you forget about us?"*

But I fear most the "*I've missed you,*" because I know, with certainty, that I have missed them more.

I tug on my collar, feeling claustrophobic, and try to steady my breath. *Do not do it here, Theo. Do not have a fucking panic attack in the Savoys' driveway.* I try to count my breaths. I breathe in and visualize what will happen when I enter their kitchen. My dad will adjust his watch, he'll feign disinterest; if his hair is grown out, he'll keep smoothing it over with his right hand because his left will be holding a drink.

The sound of my footsteps against the gravel silences the laughter, and I briefly pause, not ready to be seen yet. But I realize, as they had heard my steps, they will hear my silence, so I continue forward, crushing into the gravel a little harder—an attempt at confidence.

"Who's there?" It's Anika's voice, serrated with defiance. My sister is always ready for a fight.

"Ehm, it's me," I reply awkwardly before I see anyone. My voice comes out rough, after so long not speaking, leaving me sounding strained and unimpressed. I duck beneath the tree and stumble forward at the movement, the gin guiding me. When I lift my head to check for my next step, it is not Anika I see. A girl is lying in the grass, her skin bronze in the hushed blue light of the coming night.

"Hi, Theo," she says.

"Theo, you're here! I thought you would have passed out!" Anika blurts from the background. She's sat on the outdoor bench with raised arms in an air hug, but she sees I'm too far away and immediately drops her arms. It doesn't take me a second to realize she's drunk.

"*Devo fare pipi!*" *I have to pee*, she mumbles and stands up to leave, swaying for a brief second.

I look back down.

"Hi, Magdalen, I almost didn't recognize you."

It's Magdalen, my Magdalen of childhood. Suddenly I'm unsure of where to look and seem only able to stare at her bare feet. Her ankles are sharp and delicate. She wears a pair of linen overalls that are unbuttoned and hang loosely around her hips, and the tiny white T-shirt underneath has rolled up to her ribs from lying down, but I tell myself I didn't notice that.

She laughs and I rub my eye with the back of my hand.

"I know, I grew four inches in one summer. It's been the talk of town. You look well," she says nonchalantly, approvingly. Her legs are impossibly long.

"Yeah, well, I don't feel it." My voice comes out curt. I look at her ankles again to avert from her thighs and feel formidable as she lies on the ground beneath me, so I take a step back in hope that she doesn't think I am in some way trying to intimidate her. Jesus Christ. Was I always this fucking self-conscious?

"I just came back home today, too, although my flight time wasn't as bad. You must be thirsty. Would you like something to drink?" She begins to get up and her shirt falls back down on her stomach, the waves of her thick hair falling around her face. When she stands up, she is almost as tall as me—Magdalen of my childhood, no more. Her comment about me being thirsty takes me off guard. Do I somehow look dehydrated?

Fuck's sake. I squeeze my eyes shut. *What is it about this country that makes me so sensitive?*

"Sure, thanks. Is everyone inside?" I kick an escaped rock back onto the gravel, hoping Anika is on her way back so I can fucking breathe.

"Yep, they'll be pleased to know you are here," she says while walking toward the back door, tugging down at her shirt as if just now realizing it was at one point rolled up. I still haven't really seen her face properly and somehow, it's a relief—I know that when I do, I'll wish I hadn't. I shouldn't be looking at her, my younger sister's best friend, with smug lust. It is villainous. Despicable. Anika's assumption of me fucking within the first week back nags at me and I try to think about what's waiting in that kitchen instead. But it seems far away now. Instead, my desire to look at Magdalen, at her skin, is so strong I dig my nail into my palm until I can't think of anything but the stinging in my hands. I focus on her words, yes, the sexless distraction of words. Excited, she said, thrilled, exhilarated, jubilant. I let myself smile, her accent elongates the "l" sound with a deep pressure, making the whole sentence conform and mold around the one word: *pleased*.

We've been speaking English since I can remember, even though the Savoys are native Italians. Something about Vittoria wanting a challenge of teaching. They say we still have a Scottish accent; my father's lilt combined with the summers in Perth have stuck.

"Sure, sure," I say and roll my eyes. She would never say that if she knew what happened behind those walls. We both have to bend to enter the small kitchen door, and the yellow light of the sconces makes me squint. Magdalen enters before me, almost like an unknowing shield for my fragile ego. I try not to look at her ass as she steps down into the room.

It takes everyone a moment to notice my presence. I swallow hard, waiting for the light to dull and their reactions to surface. When was the last time I was in here? The tile floors are still the same deep terra-cotta color. The cabinets, with rusted handles, remain a pale yellow. Bright red plastic chair in the corner. Time has stopped here.

"Theodore the fucking ghost." Dante speaks first and gets up immediately to greet me. He's a few inches shorter than me and looks as if his whole body is coated in hair gel. He just shines. And, when his head brushes against mine, I have to hide my laughter in his shoulder, at how hard it is. Not a strand moves out of place. He smells of cigarettes and an expensive cologne he's no doubt stolen, and as he squeezes me, I feel his heartbeat, fast and erratic, and squeeze him back the best I can.

I press my lips into his shoulder and mumble, "I'm back now."

"Yes, you are. Yes, you fucking are, baby."

7

MAGDALEN

Theo's presence has a triumphant effect on the families; even Dante is close to tears at the sight of him.

Dante and Theo share an inseparable connection, and when Theo left I could feel a part of Dante break. The skin on his cheeks, which were usually stretched in a smile, grew taut and dull. Theo was his light. And while I know it felt like abandonment to Dante, everyone in Chivasso knew that Theo was going to disappear one day. Granted, maybe not as abruptly. But his brilliance, in school, in sports, in fucking girls—it felt wrong to have all that stay in the one town he grew up in. He unknowingly made people self-conscious of their own worth.

When Theo Sinclair took a 4 a.m. flight to Connecticut without warning seven years ago, our world had shifted a centimeter; the clouds hung low as if trying to hold him in the sky, trapped above Chivasso forever. The fruit felt rotten, Anika was silent, and Cinzia Sinclair stayed in her bedroom for months. But, at the same time, it was also the most mundane thing that could have taken place in town that day, and so life went on without Theo.

I look at Theo now, 6 foot 4 and forearms corded with

muscle, and try to remember him all those years ago. As a child, he took an hour-long bus to Torino every morning to go to a specialized school for gifted students. The *genio* of our little town. He was also athletic, obliterating all the tennis tournaments, football and track matches in Chivasso and then again in Torino. He was watched and gossiped about daily from a young age. Even five years younger than him, I was aware he was different. Would he go into medicine? Become a lawyer? Play tennis professionally? But what we were all really wondering was the same, big question; how would Theo Sinclair change the world, and would he remember us when he did?

This is why I always assumed he ran away. It felt obvious. The pressure to be the savior of a small town drove him to find a bigger one with more than one *genio* to ogle at. I don't blame him for leaving; I followed his lead. Except my plane landed in England; closer to home. Whereas Theo made sure no one could come find him.

Theo cast a large shadow, and people who walked too close behind were bound to become lost. And maybe it's because I am a girl, or because people who are quiet tend to go unnoticed, but no one ever said anything when I stepped on that bus after him. For seven years, it felt like no one saw me enter the very same school. Or maybe it was because I could never kick a ball; these things are important to Italians.

Sitting in my family kitchen after seven years, Theo is immediately interrogated by everyone.

"Yeah, I did some research for the Yale Monastic

Archaeology Program in Sohang," Theo says, his ears red with embarrassment. I'm mesmerized. Watching him talk, I let myself indulge in just how beautiful he is. Tanned and husky; gray eyes. Thick dark strands of hair curling around his ears. How can someone so objectively perfect ever know the feeling of embarrassment? Even wondering that is unfair. I know nothing about him. What makes him embarrassed, what interests him. Theo's intelligence is in competition with his beauty. It's terrifying to think he is Achilles with no poisoned heel.

Looking at Theo like this makes me remember the first time I became aware of his reputation. Dante, Theo, Anika and I took the train to Torino—Anika and I following the boys like lost puppies. Sure, I'd been to Torino for school. But for fun?

Never.

Torino during the day is much like all Italian cities, expansive and cobblestoned, the buildings that now hold independent boutiques and *tabaccherie* once held Roman deities. You can't ever get over how old everything is here. But at night the young and the old flood the streets with vibrancy. Sidewalks are lined with cheap plastic tables; friends gather and dance in the street to music blaring from someone's car radio. Beers are tossed in the fountain. This is not an act of disrespect, but rather a ritual to keep the city eternally young; our cities survive so long because of the mystery of nighttime. Knowing how many secrets are in these streets can make a person feel very insignificant—*young*.

It was on a night like this when I first realized Theo's

reputation. I was twelve and had bought myself eyeliner for the first time that morning. Anika left a copy of *Lei Glamour* on my bed and Milla Jovovich stared at me from the cover, taunting me with her big blue eyes. After leafing through the pages of red lipstick and neon blue eyeshadow, I settled for some maroon eyeliner because the magazine told me that color would make my eyes pop.

At this stage in my life, I believed I could seduce men with just my eyes.

An older girl in Theo's grade called Titziana asked me if I could introduce her to Theo. "*Che bello!*" she had said. *How hot!*

The music was loud and seductive, and her question stirred a confusion in me. "Theo?" I replied dumbly. "*Voui parlare con Theo?*" *You want to talk to Theo?*

I asked this as if she had told me she was going to have sex with my brother and make me watch. Theo was synonymous with Dante to me, so the idea of someone finding him attractive was disturbing, and I had no desire to be part of her getting to know him. But thinking back on this memory, it seems so obvious.

I was afraid. With that one question, Theo had opened the door of boyhood, walked into manhood and locked the entrance behind him. I was afraid that if I told him that Titziana found him attractive, he would know that *I knew* he was now a man, and that word was something to be afraid of. I stirred my Coke Zero and looked at Titziana. "Sorry, I don't know him that well."

I later found out my refusal did nothing to stop Titziana;

they were caught having sex in the back of Dexter Sinclair's car later that night. This was standard behavior for Theo. Because I was twelve and too worried with finishing my summer reading or whether I'd need braces, I did not spend any time thinking of Theo as someone that other people would want.

He was Dante's brother, mine by proxy. But to the rest of Chivasso? Theo evoked desire in girls who had not yet been awakened; he was a centaur in a field of horses. It was at this point that I stopped talking to him. I was terrified he would think any interaction with me indicated that I desired him in *every* way. My silent avoidance of him was my way of saying: *I will never ask you to awaken me. I will never ask you to turn me down.* Whether or not this translated in my everyday actions is inconclusive, but somehow, I always felt it did.

Seeing him now, sitting in the ugly red chair in our kitchen, where he had sat just seven years ago, nothing has changed. He is still taller than me, but he's definitely grown up. Shoulders broader, hardened with muscles I didn't remember him ever having. Still beautiful. His face is tense, as if he is purposely trying to remain unread, except for his eyebrows, which furrow constantly, giving him away. When someone speaks, you can tell that he is actively processing what they are saying. Words are currency, and Theo cares about their value. Most people care only about their own. One strand of hair falls across his forehead and I forget I am staring until he is looking straight at me.

"Magdalen?" he says, as though this is his second time saying my name.

"*Scusa*, what did you say?"

"How are you liking Oxford?"

"Oh, well, it's nice. Hard but worth it. I like the material." I look away, unsure if my response is satisfactory.

He stares at the table and nods in understanding, "You always did like to read if I remember," and takes a sip of his drink that someone put in front of him. I think he is going to say something else but he doesn't.

"Yes, but hates to talk to people," my mother adds, and I look up. Her tone is contemptuous. Have I done something wrong? "What's the point in reading if you don't have anyone to discuss your books with, right?"

Anika's father is standing in the corner, looking into his glass as if he is searching for prophetic intervention. He clears his throat. "Well, at least our kids are back. It's been a while since the family was together. Magdalen, you have grown to be a beautiful woman. And, Theo, you've certainly grown your hair," Dexter says, laughing at his own words.

"I like your hair," I hear myself saying.

Theo turns to me, eyebrows raised in surprise. "Really?" Noticing the strand that's fallen, he quickly tucks it behind his ear. "It's a little fucking long, don't you think?"

"Long hair is very hot in America." My eyes widen when I realize what I've said. "Hot as in, trendy. Um, not saying you're hot or anything like that." *This is what I get for talking, Mum*, I want to shout. I call Theo Sinclair hot in front of every person I fucking know.

"Don't think I'm hot, Maggie?" Theo leans back in his

chair, nursing the drink in his hand. His eyes flicker with humor, daring me to take it back.

Before I have time think of a response, Dante interjects. "Ew, Theo. Don't make my sister call you hot in front of the entire fucking family."

My mother inhales sharply. "Dante, language."

Dante slams his hand on the table, clearly about to defend his right to curse, but Jo quickly interrupts him. "Since you're back, Theo, I'm sure the boys at the club will want to see you."

"Don't expect any of your usual girls to want you looking like that," Dexter snorts, finishing off his drink in one final sip.

It's a cheap joke and I politely smile, but debasing Theo to a humorless one-liner after so many years apart feels insensitive. I glance at Theo, who is not laughing; he is not looking at his father. His mother, Cinzia, smiles weakly but also seems tired by Dexter's words. A few years before Theo left, Cinzia resigned from the museum, leaving only my father and Dexter Sinclair in charge of operations. She looks smaller than I remember as she sits at the chair near the open kitchen door. The skin of her arms hangs loosely from her muscles, and I can see her hair is turning gray at the roots.

"Funny. Shall we, then?" Jo ignores Dexter. Tension has filled the room alongside the smoke of the open oven.

"Yup, that'll be fine," Theo briskly responds, finishing his drink in one large sip and getting up. I only realize now I wasn't the one to give him a drink, despite offering. *Must not get so distracted, Magdalen! He's only a man.*

46

"Bye, everyone," Theo says warmly. "Magdalen," he adds hastily, with his eyes flickering to mine for a split second, and then he is gone.

"Bye, fuckers," Dante bows, and my father and mother both suck in a breath. The warm cozy feeling that entered with Theo disappears. A trail of goosebumps covers my arm, and I shiver.

8

THEO

Each of us is afraid to speak on the car ride to Tirumapifort, the tennis-cum-nightclub outside of Chivasso. Jo is driving with both of his hands clenched tightly around the wheel as if to prove his focus is so entirely on driving that he can't start the conversation. This is fucking awkward. Jo, Dante and almost every member of the Savoy family are notorious talkers. Almost all of them. Dante sits in the back, preoccupied with a cigarette, but even the exhales of his smoke are off; cut short with tension.

"Is Matilde still fucking with those yellow wristbands?" I ask; it is the only thing I can remember about the club. Yellow wristbands, strapped so tightly around your wrists that your fingers begin to go numb after only a few minutes of her putting one on you. It is a silent force that makes people leave before Matilde has to kick them out.

"Matilde is a fucking cunt. I pray every night she falls and drowns in the pool," Dante says while rolling the window down and spitting.

"Fuck that old hag," adds Jo, who has relaxed to one hand on the wheel—progress. I lean into the cushioned seat while Dante laughs, feeling a bit lighter.

Silver Pozzoli blares on the speakers as we circle the club parking lot a few times. My eyes shut, trying to steady the anticipation as Jo tries to find parking in the full lot. The engine shuts off and Dante pokes his head between the seats.

"All right, fuckers, *il re e tornato!*" *The king has returned.*

Fuck me. Not this again. My hands itch for another drink.

The music we'd heard in the car seems faded by the time we reach the entrance. Everything is eerily the same; the red gravel is still as vibrant as it was the day I left. Without warning, Matilde appears, hustling toward us from the bushes behind; she looks like a witch as she waves the plastic bands frantically above her head, shaking her head with annoyance at us.

"Just because you little boys can't find another place to wet your dick does not mean you can enter for free!"

"Excuse yourself, Matilde. I'm a father now," Jo says. "There will be no dick wetting for me."

"That makes one of you," she huffs, looking now to see who's in our group.

She hasn't seen me yet. I brace for the impact. Matilde has known me since I was running around here with chocolate gelato dried around my mouth. I grimace. And she caught me fucking Chiara that one time.

"*Ma guarda,*" she shoves the bands in her apron pocket and a few fall to the gravel. "You came back to us!"

In no time, her face is inches away from mine so I can see the aging lines on her forehead, deep and creased with years of rushing about in the sun.

49

You forget about the people on the outskirts when you're rushing out the door. The ones you order coffee from each morning, the ones you see at the gym. I feel guilty for forgetting Matilde when she saw so much of me growing up.

I clear my throat. "Only for you, Matilde. Does this mean I'm excused from the yellow-band tax?" I say to lighten the mood. Fuck. Having anything to do with Matilde's sadness makes me want to punch myself.

Her voice is gravelly. Disappointed. "You should have stayed gone."

She gently pats my face and I flinch at the roughness of her palm or maybe how right she fucking is.

"Fuck off, Matilde, how much for your three favorite cherubs tonight?" Dante begins to unbutton his shirt, swaying toward her.

She looks at the three of us and then once again at me, her eyes watery and iridescent, and nods. Matilde might be God running a tennis club.

"For you cherubs, 100. Pay for Theo, too." Matilde winks at me, looking me over one last time before peering behind me at the forming line.

"Thank you, my love," I say while she straps the plastic band around my wrist. But it is so loose that with the slightest movement of my hand, the band almost slips off.

9

MAGDALEN

The hot candle wax hardens over my finger and I envision casting it over my open eyes as Anika talks. Maybe I've gotten too used to being by myself at university. No one cares if you lock the door and don't talk for six days. When Emily met Cal, the flat was empty most of term.

"Do you want to meet the boys at the club, Mag? Or go on a gelato run? What was the gelato like in England? Awful, I bet. But, anyway, Fiore is still trying to fuck me believe it or not, so I would rather we steer clear of there, if I'm being honest. Or we could smoke, because clearly, I can see what a weed-head you've become at Oxford. I mean you're practically foaming at the mouth for a hit. It's a shame," she continues, rambling, not needing me to speak at all to carry out the conversation. "You used to be so pure. It's always the ones you least expect."

"Whatever you want, Anika. Although the club is a little far, right? I'm pretty tired." This is a lie; it's the club's grimy dancing and tennis playing that I'm trying to avoid. Between the drunk grinding and swinging rackets, gambling and cannonballs in the pool, I can confidently say it's where I feel most out of place. It's the closest thing Chivasso

51

has to nightlife, yes, but for my first night back, it seems Anika is trying to make me miss England.

"It's okay, I'll drive. I don't mind!" She's so excited. I suppress a groan, not wanting to be the one to disappoint her. Without me here, Anika's outgoing personality has been wasted on strangers at the museum, where she works as a tour guide, and coffee dates with Dante, so I guess I can give her this.

"All right, all right, but I'll drive back. Don't really feel like dying tonight," I snub, unable to hold back my annoyance.

Anika is oblivious. "Oh, fuck off. You don't even have your license. And, I would like to add, I would never put your life in danger, Mag. Especially not when I just got you back."

Her honesty stings. *It's been a year*, I want to say. *I've come back for holidays! At least it hasn't been seven!* But I haven't called. Hadn't written a postcard like I'd promised. She wrote me one email and I took four weeks to reply. Am I a good person? Or do I only do good when someone is close to seeing I'm not?

"Fine, fine. And I told you not to bring up my license. You know I'm working on it."

"You've been saying that for five years, Mag. It's time to let it go. It's also time for you to put a bra on," she giggles.

I sigh and glance at the end of the table where our parents are huddled, smoking their cigarettes and laughing raucously over silly nothings. Dexter smacks the table loudly, causing everyone to gasp. My mother's hand stays glued to my father's forearm on the kitchen table, and his hand rests on top of hers. They are teenagers.

Why does it make me angry to see them like this? If anything, I should be happy they're having fun. With no way of explaining it, sometimes I feel like they've stolen my adolescent angst and I've skipped to being a bitter and reclusive old woman. They don't turn around when we get up, they don't ask us where we are headed off to at midnight; they just keep laughing among the smoke, and I stand up, waving at no one. Maybe I do need a drink.

I decided to ignore the bra mandate. I tie my hair up with a satin ribbon and spread a thick layer of strawberry-flavored lip-gloss across my lips. I feel Anika will appreciate this effort. I pace my driveway waiting for her car to pull up. The night air is cool, with silken moonlight lapping over my skin. Hydrangeas in full bloom, the wind guides their honey scent toward me, and I feel happy in a sad way. I close my eyes and absorb these few minutes alone and secretly wish the sound of her tires on the gravel will never come. Maybe she's passed out, or the engine broke down; perhaps there's been an alien attack on Chivasso. But, when I look up, her car is in front of me, engine off, and Anika is staring at me through the open window, tapping the steering wheel impatiently. She reminds me so much of Emily when she looks at me like that. It's worry and love and knowing you can't do anything but observe from a distance.

"Maggie, let's go. We've surpassed being fashionably late."

"Okay. But, just to let you know, I've set my tits free. They will not be imprisoned."

"Shocker."

53

* * *

"*Questa una festa!*" shouts Anika as the engine shuts off in the parking lot of Tirumapifort. *This is a party!*

The red gravel reminds me of a space-themed restaurant in Torino, where my father used to take me as a child, called *Marte 2121*. Tonight, we dance on Mars.

"I'm going to make someone want to fuck me tonight, and then spit on them!" Anika jumps out of the car and starts dancing in the parking lot as we hear the dull bop of disco through the speaker.

"You are so weird, Anika."

"Then, I'll force you to dance with someone."

"You will not."

"With those tits out? Honey, I'm going to have to barricade you from all the boys and girls."

"Anika," I groan, regretting my liberated chest. "Give me your bra."

"No way! My girls don't float."

"Shit." I cross my arms as we walk inside. "This is what I get for rebelling against you."

Everything is the same as I remember; the heat of the pool has created a mist around the entire outside perimeter, giving the club a haunted atmosphere. There are teens floating in the water and old men gambling behind beaded curtains in the lounge. Matilde comes forward, like a statue carved of hard marble.

"Maggie, *tesoro!*" She waddles toward us. "*Vieni, vieni, vieni!* Both of you back! What a treat." Does she mean Theo? I reach into my waistband to grab the money I've stashed but Matilde puts her hand out, stopping me. "*Stasera, i fantasmi ballano liberi!*" *Tonight, ghosts dance free!*

I frown at her. "What?"

"My ghosts dance for free tonight."

I try to smile but feel oddly exposed. Ghost? My skin prickles. Has Matilde become the guard between life and death? If I touch her, do I become transparent, forced to dance forever at *Tirumapifort*?

I grab her hand and squeeze, "*Grazie mille*, Matilde. I missed you, too."

My hand subconsciously reaches for my neck, feeling for a pulse. Okay, still alive. Still pumping blood. My dancing will have a curfew tonight, Matilde!

"You've become so beautiful," she calls out as we pass her. It is always the same reaction when people call me beautiful. An internal flinch of muscle. The rational part of me understands how silly being pretty is. How quickly it fades.

But the other part, the part of my brain dusted with cobwebs and self-doubt, wants to believe someone thinks I am.

"*Grazie*, Matilde. I'll dance for you tonight."

10

THEO

"Anika! You finally going to fuck me tonight?" Dante yells from the deep end of the pool, where he floats in his usual uniform of Diesel jeans and Lacoste polo, bobbing his head up and down in the chlorine illuminated by the tall lamps around the club. Not giving a single shit that he'll have to go home soaking wet. Only his hand remains high above the water level, elegantly fingering a cigarette that remains untouched by the water.

"My sister, mate," I remind him from the pool chair I sit on.

"Fuck, sorry." He looks down with mock shame. "Anika, baby, are you finally going to make deep, passionate, mind-altering love to me tonight?" Dante rephrases.

I laugh because I know Anika will take care of it. *In your dreams, D*, I say through my silence.

Almost every man is staring at Anika as she peruses the rows of pool chairs, the fabric of her dress providing the same security as cheesecloth, leaving every inch of her visible underneath that pathetic excuse of an outfit. I look away, both angry and impressed by her. There is no use fighting little sisters over little dresses.

"Dante, I would rather cut off that microscopic thing you call a penis and eat it before I ever fucked you," she says breezily, but there is less heart in it than usual. She is distracted. Her gaze is scattered as she searches around the pool, and it registers that she is looking for me. She nervously combs her fingers through the ends of her hair and sighs when the other brunette men she's tapped on the shoulder are not me. And it's like I can see what she's thinking: that I have disappeared again, throwing up a middle finger and speeding back to the airport without even a goodbye.

And then she spots me. "Brother!" Anika barrels over with relief, pausing to remove the stilettos that, unsurprisingly, interfere with her ability to run.

"These motherfuckers!" she mumbles, and grabs hold of an innocent bystander's arm and pulls the heels off. The guy's eyes drift to her chest and she winks.

"Anika, you look lovely," I lie.

"You liar." She rolls her eyes and sits next to me, and I cringe as her dress moves farther up her legs.

"Can I get you a drink?" I divert the conversation.

"How chivalrous! I sent Maggie to get one, but poor thing is probably too scared to go up to the bar. Are you not drinking?" She looks down at my cup of water with complete disappointment.

"No, not tonight. Jet lag and alcohol." I pathetically try to connect the two as reasons enough for my sobriety. I'm actually desperate for a drink. But the gin from earlier still settles in my stomach and, in truth, I'm afraid of what I may say under the influence. "I've never seen Magdalen here," I say, changing the subject, looking down at my cup.

Fishing a cigarette from her purse, she mumbles, "I had to drag her ass here. She's only been a few times after you left." She lights the cigarette and turns, looking at me. "You know, you should try to be nice to her. She's shy, uncomfortable. You two are more alike than you think. Both hot and annoyingly fucking smart. The only difference is that she isn't a raging whore like you. I forgot to get the update from her, but, if I'm not mistaken, she's still never even—" She shakes her head to stop herself and takes a deep drag of the cigarette.

"She's never what?"

Anika exhales from the side of her mouth. "Oh please, like Dante hasn't told you."

"Told me what?"

"Let's just say, she has enough innocence to save us all." She makes the sign of the cross and continues her rant. "Can you please go see where the fuck she went? I'm too sober to look at Dante's face and discuss Magdalen's sex history."

Dante's head jerks from the pool, cigarette slightly wet. "Heard that, cunt! Don't say that word when talking about my sister."

Anika forgets about me immediately, her voice piercing as she begins to humiliate Dante in front of every girl within ten meters of him.

It doesn't take any convincing for me to stand up and

find her. Following Anika's request, I make my way through the crowd, searching for Magdalen. Bathing-suit-clad bodies playing tennis, making out, dancing on top of tables. I squint, trying to see through the mist and disco lights, but she's not at the bar. I veer toward the DJ booth, thinking maybe she went out for a smoke. Does she smoke? I know fuck-all about this girl. I see her in the grass again, that shirt dangerously ridden up her stomach, and correct myself. Woman. Definitely woman.

I'm about to turn around and check the parking lot when I spot her. Her eyes are wide, and she wraps her arms around her body as if protecting herself, creating distance between the man she's speaking with and her. Something close to annoyance flickers inside me as he bends to whisper something in her ear. Magdalen cringes and rolls her eyes while he laughs obnoxiously into her shoulder. And as she tries to take a step away, he abruptly leans his hand on the wall, blocking her in. The flicker turns into something a little darker. Shoving drunk dancers out of the way, I pace until I'm right behind him. *Cool it, Theo.* But I look at her eyes, uncomfortable and unsure of herself.

She and I need to have a talk about how to tell someone to fuck off.

Once I'm close enough, Magdalen looks at me, her voice falsely bright. "You promised me a dance, Theo."

The man turns his head to look at me, and Magdalen's eyes close in relief, warmth spreading in her cheeks. When her eyes open, it's as if she's put on a mask.

"I was just on my way to find you. I remembered how much you love this song. We'll talk soon, okay?" She winks at him. "It was nice seeing you again, Antonio. Have a great rest of your night." No wonder the man won't give up. A bloody wink!

The man, Antonio, looks between us and turns back to Magdalen, bending down to her cheek to give a slow kiss, but she jerks her head, laughing his attempt away, and pats him on the shoulder. When she steps forward, her hand grips my wrist, hard. She stares up at me, her eyes screaming, *THANK YOU!* I nod, giving her a weak smile. Feeling angry that she was so uncomfortable. What would have happened if I hadn't been there?

But, then again, who the fuck sex-winks at someone they don't want to be around?

I lead her away from the dark exit and enter the flashing lights of the dance floor. In the middle of the crowd, the music surrounds us, the sticky heat of bodies pulsing happily. Stopping, I turn to come face to face with Magdalen, but her eyes drop to the ground.

"You don't really have to dance with me." Her hand is still wrapped tightly around my wrist, her fingers slender but firm, tipped with a dark red nail polish. Anger stops me from saying anything. When she parts her lips and stares at me with those green doe eyes, I understand why Antonio gave it a shot. Those eyes are dangerous. Slowly, my hands trace over her fingers; her skin is soft and cold despite the summer heat. Settling my palm over hers, I hold her hand in mine for a moment, enjoying the softness of her against me, and gently, I bring it to rest on my shoulder.

Anika's words tug at my subconscious. *Enough innocence to save us all.* "Dance with me," I shrug. "Make the fucker jealous." I dip my head to the side, trying to find her eye line, but she refuses to look at me.

Instead she glances in the direction of Antonio, who continues to watch us from the corner. He licks his lips and rubs the non-existent beard he has on his chin as if deciding whether to come over and interrupt. My jaw clenches. Can he not take a fucking hint?

I drop my hands to her waist, her eyes find mine, and we both stare at each other. Despite the darkness, those fucking eyes are glowing, and she chews her bottom lip in deliberation. Unsure. Afraid. *Interested.* Shades of each emotion so quick you would miss it in a moment. Without meaning to, my gaze slips to her mouth, colored lights from the disco ball casting strobes of violet and rose across her face, turning the pink of her lips a deep red. Dangerously shiny, her lips are candied in gloss and I can't help but wonder how sweet her tongue would taste in my mouth. Would she moan if I licked the fullness of her bottom lip? Whimper if I took a bite?

Fuck me. I close my eyes for a moment, hopelessly trying to erase the image. Was Anika right?

I come back to reality and there she is, looking at me with a slight furrow between her brows.

"Okay." She glides her other hand down my chest and

I swallow a groan; a strong need in the shape of her palm burns through me. I want those cool fingertips against my chest.

Music floods through the club, practically forcing everyone to dance. Even in dripping bathing suits and bikinis, no one's fucking missing a chance to hump each other. I laugh to myself, fine with blaming Tirumapifort for enjoying the slightest touch of my best friend's sister. Magdalen seems to be slipping into comfort with the music's rhythm, glancing at the girls grinding on their partners around us, eyes closed and succumbing to the bass.

"This music is terrible," she shouts, tilting her head back in laughter. The featherweight of her forearms press into my shoulders, as if she's given up trying to give me personal space and instead is enjoying the happiness that this twenty meters of dance floor can give you.

When she leans her head forward toward my chest, I murmur, lips brushing against the outline of her ear, "I'm a dangerous dancer, even to terrible music."

She angles herself so that my mouth grazes the tender, damp skin of her neck. "I can be dangerous, too."

Christ. Our bodies find a slow rhythm as we begin to dance. My hands snake around her hips, slightly dipping into the waistband of her skirt for better control of her body on mine. Because Dante is still in the pool, and there's a significant crowd between us and him, I press her tightly against me.

"Happy to be home?" I say, my face buried in her long hair. I breathe in despite myself; she smells delicious.

Magdalen doesn't answer immediately and my grip tightens on her. "Is that a no?"

"It's an, I'm not sure yet."

"Ah, I see. What part aren't you sure about?"

When she doesn't answer again, I look at her, squinting. "Are you not going to tell me anything?"

"I don't know you. It feels weird airing my dirty secrets in a nightclub."

"Tennis club."

"Irrelevant."

I spin her around and she yelps, grinning widely, her auburn hair splaying. Pulling her back in, I say, "What are you talking about? We grew up next to each other."

She lets out a sigh, and as her arms come around me again, her fingertips graze the nape of my neck, and I have to fight a shiver.

"So we were close physically, sure. But we never talked."

"Did you want to talk to me?" My voice is low, curious as I finger the silk ribbon in her hair.

"I was thirteen when you left. I was too afraid to even *want* to have a conversation with you." She puts emphasis on "want" and it settles in my stomach. It's odd to think this is the same lanky girl who used to make crab-apple pudding for faeries she and Anika were convinced lived in our backyard. They screamed for hours when they found out crab apples stain your skin and rushed to my mother for help with their bright orange hands. I was sent to the market to buy the soap.

"You mean because your haircut was so awful?"

63

Magdalen gasps and tries to bury her face in my shoulder but my hand comes to her chin, holding her face up so she has to look at me. Without meaning to, I brush the freckle above her eyebrow and smile. "It was cute."

Magdalen smiles—and is that a blush? My hand finds her chin again.

"It looked like I was drafted into the military."

Now it's my turn to laugh as I remember how short Vittoria used to cut her hair. Why was that? She was right: it was cut with military precision right above her chin.

"She loved a pair of scissors."

"She just didn't want my hair to compete with hers."

I frown. "You mean she was jealous of a kid?" The hand holding her chin now rests softly on her shoulder, my thumb between her jaw and neck, her pulse beating against my fingers.

"No, no," she says, but I'm unconvinced. "I don't know why I brought it up." Magdalen looks away and that's when we both spot Anika coming toward us. She lets go of me. I have to bite my tongue to stop myself asking her to stay for one more dance.

"Thank you," she whispers.

"Any time. Really." *Really, Magdalen. Give me one more dance so I can get this out of my system. We can dance the pasodoble, if that's what you want, march together side by side down the streets of Chivasso, I don't care. Just let me have music and you, for five more minutes.*

I still feel her skin underneath me and I'm worried for a moment by just how much more I crave.

Magdalen gestures to the bar and Anika nods her head. "I'm going to try to get drinks again. Do you want anything?"

"No, thanks," I say, my voice low. Still feeling her on me. She nods and turns to the bar. "Also, stop winking at boys who are trying to flirt with you, Magdalen."

Her head whips back around, eyes widening like she has no clue what I'm talking about. "I did not wink," she scoffs. "*I do not wink.*"

"Do you have some sort of flirting amnesia? You nearly had me on my knees with that wink."

"Well, wouldn't that be a sight." Blood rushes to her cheeks and I have to fight the urge to grab her head and lick those precious cheeks to see if they're as sweet as her lips look.

I shrug. "Just let me know when you'd like me below you."

Magdalen's eyes widen again and her lips part, clearly surprised. Adorable. Confused. I curse myself for taking it too far. "Noted," she says in a harsh exhale, and turns to walk to the bar again, this time staying on the opposite side of Antonio. "Goodnight, Theo. Thanks for the dance."

"Goodnight, Magdalen."

Once she's gone, I bury my face in my hands. "Fucking idiot," I murmur to myself, embarrassed, turned on, and unsure where to put this energy from talking to Magdalen. When I decide to find Dante again, I turn to see Anika right behind me.

"So?" she asks suspiciously. "What was that?"

"Fucking hell. How much did you hear?"

"According to my calculations, you lasted about twelve fucking minutes." She rests her hands on her hips with smug satisfaction. Behind us, two men start arguing loudly, so Anika grabs my wrist, pulling me to the corner of the dance floor.

"I know, I know. But to be fair, you could have told me that Magdalen grew up to look like a fucking angel. Really, when did that happen? Surely I wasn't gone for that long." My body feels desperate to turn around to look at her again, to pull that red ribbon out of her hair.

Anika smiles sadly, looking past me at Magdalen. "You can't, Theo. She's not into that."

"Into what, Anika?" I'm annoyed that Anika thinks I'm only capable of fucking a girl and running away after I come.

"Look, I get you both here for like, five minutes this summer. Last time I checked, you're not in the market for a girlfriend, and Magdalen is certainly not looking for a summer-time fuck buddy. Just cool it, okay? Call Chiara or something."

It feels like someone has blown hot air into me and pricked me with a needle. I'm suddenly deflated by Anika's assumptions and how true they are. I'm about to press further, wanting to know more about Magdalen even if I can't have her, when the loud crash of a table by the bar interrupts me. I hear a man curse and a voice, now familiar to me, scream out.

"What the fuck was that?" Anika tries to walk past me but I am steaming toward the crowd before I feel my feet begin to move. Pushing past bodies, people surround two drunken men beating the shit out of each other. It's clear there is joy in the watchers' eyes as they see the blood sprayed from one man's nose and hear the other's indecipherable swears. I roll my eyes. People love chaos from a distance.

But all I can hear is that familiar scream. My eyes search frantically for Magdalen, something within driving me to find her. To my right I see a few women hurriedly trying to lift a cracked glass table from the ground, and that's when I see her.

Magdalen's waist is pinned beneath the heavy metal frame of the table, shards of glass littered across her bare legs and the surrounding ground. Eyes shut with unvoiced pain. I watch her try to maneuver out from under the table. A petite blonde bends to ask if she's okay, and with an apology already in her eyes Magdalen bitterly nods, teeth clenched on her bottom lip. A victim of someone else's disaster and yet her face is burning red as if she's embarrassed, as if this is somehow her doing? Shoving the bystanders aside, agitated by their ogling, I tell the blonde to stand back as I heave the table to one side, releasing Magdalen.

"I'm sorry," she whispers as I bend down to examine her and again a fierce current of anger rushes through me. How the fuck can *she* think an apology is necessary?

Sitting up, she lifts her trembling hand from under herself and a trickle of crimson blood spills across her palm.

"I thought ghosts couldn't bleed," she murmurs with a faint smile. Her fingertips are wet with new blood and I'm worried about where the worst of her wounds are. If she has a concussion, I am going to beat the shit out of those men. I feel dark fury begin to boil inside me. For a girl I've only ever known through a hedgerow.

"Far from a ghost, Magdalen," I say, taking a deep breath in. As if she hadn't realized she spoke the words aloud, she blinks with surprise at my being so close to her.

My anger simmers, but I don't want to direct it at her, so I try to smile but my mouth fights back and I'm sure it comes off as a creepy grimace. Without warning, she quickly shifts her weight onto one side in an effort to crawl up but the motion is too abrupt, she crumples forward. Her forehead is creased with agitation, and she looks up at the group of women standing around her.

"Fuck," she whispers, and places her hand on her head. Blood smears her temple. I can see it's not the pain that makes her curse, but the people watching.

"I've got you." I kneel next to her and wrap my arm around her waist. Her shirt is ripped and my fingers brush against her bare skin, soft and warm.

"I'm sorry, fuck." Her face is still creased with embarrassment. "This is why I don't dance." Quickly checking her over, I see there is no glass inside her and feel relief for a moment. But it fades as I take in the cuts that cover her shoulder blades, and I know for certain there must be more underneath her shirt.

"Magdalen, please," I muster, and reach under her knees to carry her toward the exit, careful not to touch any visible wounds. The men, sweaty and drunk, still fight as I pass them.

"Anika will be upset." She closes her eyes but I keep my gaze straight ahead, toward the red gravel, toward the dark. "She loves to dance. And I was already being a bitch about coming."

"She'll understand." We pass the metal gate of the entrance, and people waiting to get inside the club watch us with interest.

"I hate men," she laughs to herself, and the red ribbon in her hair grazes my ear.

"Ouch." I hide my smile in the silky fabric, breathing in her heady sweetness that's now cut with the metallic tang of blood. I fucking hate men, too.

"You don't conform to my category of generic man." I can feel her breath on my shoulder and I fight the desire to look down at her.

"Liar," I scoff.

"You're Theo," she retorts, and unconsciously rests her head on my arm. She says my name like it means home. Her comment, innocent and complimentary, makes my bones heavy with disappointment. Those who know me now, know she is so wrong.

"Keep those eyes open, little one." I begin to feel anxious for this girl, who is both stranger and family and somehow must now rely on me.

Sets of footsteps echo from behind me, sharp heels and
sneakers clacking on the pavement, and I know it is them
before I turn.

"*Cazzo*, Maggie." Dante's eyes widen with worry as
he reaches out to examine her. Anika and Jo follow close
behind and immediately Magdalen is harassed for details.

"You can put me down now." She suddenly squirms to be
released from my grip and I place her feet on the ground, not
realizing how tightly I was holding on. She doesn't stumble
or falter, but appears eager to comfort their anxiety, pressing
her skirt down.

"Seriously, guys, I'm fine! Those two men were fighting
and I got pushed into the table!" She speaks with authority
and shrugs her shoulder like these things happen all the
time. You would never know her entire back is covered in
blood.

The trio look stunned, if not a little disappointed. Things
rarely happen in Chivasso, and to be so closely affiliated to
the spectacle, and receive such a boring response, their faces
fail to hide it.

"I am tired, though, and have blood all over me, so I
think I'll head home. But you guys go back in! Can't waste
a dress like that for just an hour, Anika." She smiles, but
her eyes are so tired that I have to bite the inside of my
cheek to refrain from stepping closer and holding her up.
Jo's shoes are already hovering over the ground, judging
when it is acceptable to return back inside. Dante reaches
in his back pocket for a cigarette and Anika is staring at
Magdalen.

"I swear, only to you would this happen." She shakes her head and grabs the cigarette from Dante and lights it up before Dante realizes it has even left his grip.

"But I'm not a bitch, so I will let you go without a fight. I know how you get. And, Theo, you're taking her home." She scowls at me, pointing her finger viciously, waiting for me to rebuke.

"Of course."

"Oh, that's not necessary." Magdalen becomes flustered with sudden agitation, and I can't help but wonder: *Does she not want me to drive her? Does she not trust me enough to drive?*

"I'll walk. Seriously, it's fine! So that you can keep your car here! You've done enough." She looks at Anika, silently begging for her to agree, as the unspoken judge, jury and executioner in all familial cases.

"Nope." She takes another drag and points at me again. "He will take you. He's been chugging water all night." She drops the cigarette on the ground and buries it in the red abyss with her heel. I think of its sudden fossilization, a reminder of blood and ribbons and dancing with this strange girl. A reminder of seeing Magdalen for what feels like the first time.

Anika's voice snaps me from my thoughts.

"I'll see you tomorrow, Maggie!" She waddles toward Magdalen in her stilettos and grabs her face tenderly, planting a loud kiss on her cheek. "Call me if you need anything, okay?" Magdalen gives a tight smile but Anika seems satisfied. Turning around to toss me the keys to her car, she narrows her eyes. "Take care of her," Anika says. "I mean it." Before I can respond, she trails behind Jo and Dante back into the tennis club, swatting Dante's ass as she passes him.

The invisible string that connects Anika and Magdalen snaps the second Anika turns around. Magdalen sags in place. It doesn't take a genius to see she's in pain, looking frail standing in the darkness of the parking lot. I watch as her knees tremble slightly and I silently reach for her arm and once again slip my hand across her skin. I try not to think about how soft she is, how badly I want to tighten my hands around her waist. I move us forward, toward the car.

"Sorry." Her eyes are closed but shadowed with shame.

"Please stop apologizing." My anger has not subsided but grows with each apologetic word.

"I've ruined your first night back. I think I'm granted the right to say sorry," she bites back, and turns out of my grip to walk to the car, her hand on the car door handle. My hands feel cold without her. I stifle a laugh at her choosing to be pissy, but falter as I catch a glimpse of her back. Blood. Everywhere. Her entire shirt is soaked through.

My voice comes out rough: "Magdalen, stop."

She turns to look at me, face pale but stern, shadows dancing across the hollows of her cheekbones. "What is it?"

"Your back." My jaw clenches. "There's so much blood," I choke out.

"Oh." She nervously chews her bottom lip. "Well, it'll have to wait until we get home. Just need to wash it off is all." Her voice is trembling.

"Fuck no." My annoyance comes back. "We have to go to the hospital."

Her eyes widen and she takes a step back. "Absolutely not."

"Why not?"

"It's late, I'm tired and it's just a few scratches on my back. I swear. It looks like a lot of blood, but it's nothing really. You know how pesky little cuts can be. Please, just take me home."

"No. Turn around."

Magdalen presses herself against the car. "I said no, Theodore."

"I'm not giving you an option. If I have to pin you down to look, I will. Now what's the fucking problem?" I take a silent step forward. "Spit it out."

"But, I'm not…" she groans, running her hands through her hair. The red ribbon remains untouched from the accident, the warm wind blowing it away from her face.

"You're not what?" I feel my patience wearing, knowing with each minute her back bleeds more.

She stares at her feet, which trace abstract shapes in the red gravel. Her voice drops to a whisper. "Fine! Oh my god. I'm not wearing a bra and if I take my shirt off, I'll have to, you know…" Her hands fly in front of her chest, gesturing to her breasts. "…take my shirt off."

I take a sharp breath in, my gaze lowering to her breasts that peek through her white tank top. The chilled air has caused a perfect outline of her to show through the translucent fabric and my throat seizes.

"Theo!" she gasps quickly, covering her boobs with her hands. "That wasn't an invitation to look!"

I blink, not realizing I was still looking. "First off, I could give less of a shit that you're not wearing a bra. I've seen boobs before, Magdalen. I can guarantee you that yours are the same as every other woman's. Second, if you think I and every other person here didn't notice your lack of bra prior to this moment, you severely underestimate the male gaze. And thirdly," I take a breath in, anger resurfacing in full force, "if you don't let me see your back in the next five seconds, I swear to fucking god I will rip that pathetic excuse for a shirt off your body."

A flash of hurt briefly touches her eyes but she quickly blinks it away and sighs. My heart rate settles, and I know I've won.

She rolls her eyes. "Since when did you get so demanding?"

11

MAGDALEN

Theo smirks and walks toward me with three quick steps. "I've been away a while, I don't expect you to remember all my amazing attributes." His tone is light-hearted, but a muscle feathers in his jaw and his fingers drum against his thigh. He's anxious.

I snort, and glance around the empty parking lot to make sure no drunk patrons come dancing to their car. God, I'm an idiot. Already, I can see my mother rolling her eyes when she finds out that I managed to only make it an hour in the club. I chew the inside of my cheek, a spark of anger flickering at both my own predictability and my mother's judgment. Looking around into the darkness, I feel myself on the precipice of tears. Why am I always on the outside? The blood is thickening on my back, soaking through my shirt with every second that passes. Anika, as always, was right. I should have worn a fucking bra.

Even the idea of him looking at my naked back frightens me. *Cazzo, I am seriously fucked up.* A groan of frustration escapes me; I feel pathetic and tired. Theo stands in front of me and slowly raises his hand to place it on my shoulder, silently asking me to turn around, or asking for permission to touch me. Am I that fucking frigid that he can't touch my shoulder without needing to ask me? If it were Anika, she'd strip naked and laugh, dancing until the blood dried. Emily would seductively unbutton her shirt and pour vodka over the cut without even flinching. I look at him for a moment; his eyes are stern and without compromise. He must be so bored with my foolishness. I sigh and turn around.

"I'm really sor—"

"Say it one more fucking time." His breath tickles my ear as he reaches for the car door handle behind me.

After an awkward and painful drive back to the house, Theo opens the gate and walks us into my family kitchen, holding my hand tightly as he guides us through the doorway. Just hours ago, it was me leading him in here, and now I'm hobbling pathetically behind him. I glance out the window, seeing the light on in the Sinclairs' kitchen, and know the parents have migrated there for the night. I remain quiet, partly because the adrenaline is beginning to wear away, but mostly because I've never seen Theo angry before and I'd rather not witness it tonight.

"I know you said not to say it again, but I need to apologize for this mess."

Theo's back stiffens.

"Last time, I promise," I mumble. I try to stretch my shoulder blades but the movement causes me to bend over with pain. Suddenly, Theo turns around and, with gentleness, he lifts me by the waist to sit on the counter, so our eyes are level.

"Hey." His fingers graze my bare skin and I flinch at the contact, my heart pounding. He smells of clean cotton and sunscreen and continues holding me, either not noticing my reaction or just ignoring it out of politeness. I can feel the warmth of him as he steps closer. Tentatively, his hands travel down my waist to rest on my hips, and he dips his fingers beneath my shirt to pull it up. The fabric welds to some dried blood and a sharp pain causes me to flex my hand on the wooden countertop to stop me from making a sound, not wanting to draw any more attention to myself than I already have.

Yet he briefly squeezes my wrist, knowing that it would hurt, and anticipating my refusal to admit it. I take a breath out, more grateful for his closeness than I should be. And then I feel his lips against my ear as he tries to get a better look at my back.

"That's it. Lift your shirt for me," he whispers, obviously trying to comfort me.

My throat goes dry. *He's just trying to help, Magdalen! Don't overthink it.* I tilt my head to look at him. "Can you do it? Everything's starting to hurt."

His eyes darken but he quickly blinks it away. Walking around me so he's facing my back, I hear him exhale and mumble, "Yeah, sure," while he lifts my shirt until it reaches the middle of my spine. But then I feel him stiffen behind me.

"No, I think there is a bigger cut farther up." I try to lift my arms again to instruct him, but a sharp, burning pain halts my movement.

Theo coughs awkwardly. "Yeah, I know." He shifts on his heels. "But I've reached," he clears his throat, his discomfort palpable, "an impasse."

Momentarily confused, I look down to see the shirt has ridden up below my breasts.

"Oh, I see."

"May I?"

A huff of annoyance escapes me. "Yes, Theo, you may." I roll my eyes at his formality, my discomfort turning into impatience. My tits have been referred to as an impasse, a problem, a fucking obstruction! This must be a new low. Wanting to go upstairs, to cry in the tub, to sulk in my bloody sadness, I swallow the lump forming in my throat and raise my chin. My cheeks burn with embarrassment, realizing he must look at me like a little sister as he touches me with clinical distance. This is all too much.

It's not that I want Theo to look at me as anything other than an impasse, but his hands are hovering over me as if touching me, even for a second, would be grotesque. At the club, for a second, I thought maybe . . . No. Not even going to humor that.

I exhale loudly, nerves spreading wildly in my stomach.

"Tell me if it's too much," Theo says deeply. "I can cut the shirt if it's painful."

"I'm okay."

"You're not. But I'll help you get there."

As he begins to lift the shirt, his fingers pause briefly and he sucks in a breath. I freeze, mortified when I realize he's looking at the burn marks. *Stupid! How could you forget about the marks?* I open my mouth to say something, my mind racing for an excuse. I think about jumping off the counter and running upstairs but I'm so tired that I think I'd only make it to the hall before he caught me. Resigned, I stay seated, frozen as his fingers outline each ugly mark like he's taking his time to learn them. Callused fingers stroke their shapes. *Don't ask, Theo. Please, don't ask.*

I fight a shiver at the lightness of his touch and, despite being behind me, I can hear him wondering. I know he wants to ask. His knuckles graze the marks one last time and he clears his throat, moving on.

I breathe out, grateful for his silence, and then he dips underneath the swell of my breast, trailing along the sides with my shirt with agonizing slowness. My heartbeat quickens again as his palm brushes the edge of my nipple and I hear him suck in a breath. He drops his hands.

"I'm going to get some antiseptic wipes for these." His voice is hoarse, a slight tremor at the end of his sentence, and I wonder if doing this has made him upset. Is this that weird for him? His earlier words about my boobs being nothing extraordinary are enough to confirm that he's not enjoying this. Certainly not fantasizing about my blood-covered breasts. Before I can tell him that he can stop, that none of this is necessary, he disappears into the laundry room attached to the kitchen. I self-consciously cover myself with my hands, even though no one is here to see me exposed.

Taking the moment alone to collect my thoughts, I realize how absolutely fucking absurd this is. Here I am, first day back in Chivasso, sitting on the kitchen counter with

Cameron Capello

my shirt above my tits and Theo Sinclair, a man I've barely spoken to my entire life, granted a relatively beautiful one, having to wipe up my bleeding flesh. A loud laugh escapes me, events of the past few hours reeling in my head like a fever dream. This is fucking ridiculous. It's fucking typical that the first man to get me shirtless in a darkened room doesn't want me shirtless and it's not even his room.

"Something funny?" Theo's voice startles me and my laughter slows.

"This is a first for me." I turn my head to look at him, a slight smile still on my lips, my hands still covering my breasts. But, when I meet his gaze, his lips are parted slightly and his eyes appear heavy. He hovers by the door, as if afraid to come any closer. He must be pissed he's spending his first night back like this. Suddenly uncomfortable with his prolonged silence, I straighten my spine and turn my head to look away, matching his silence with my own. My smile disappears. His footsteps are loud as I feel him behind me once again.

"Hold still, this will burn for a second," he says reassuringly, and begins to wipe the cuts and scrapes up my back. A sharp pain shoots up my spine, causing a moan to escape me before I have time to smother it. The grand attempt to suffer in silence gone. I curse myself for ever going to the club, for not speaking up as those men hurled their bodies into me. Theo rubs at a scabbed-over cut and fresh blood drips down my back, reminding me of how pathetic I am. Things like this don't happen to girls who can speak up. They throw drinks! They punch back! They don't end up

80

squashed under tennis club tables. But the relief I feel after knowing the worst is over lets me take a full breath in and sag at the relief.

"At least tell me you didn't wink at them after they threw you into a table," Theo says from behind.

"Of course not," I say with a sigh. "I was saving my wink for you."

He sucks in a breath, and I swear I can hear him smile. "Good girl. Now let's clean you up some more, yeah?"

Considering he is only five years older than me, I'm impressed with his ability to make me feel so much like a child. I lower the shirt back over my breasts, somehow feeling self-conscious as Theo calls me a good girl with my tits out. An image of him clad in leather chaps with a whip enters my mind and I squeeze my eyes closed to erase the image. Thinking about Theo doing anything remotely sexual does not help my already confused brain. And besides, Theo doing any normal task is already sexual.

He continues to clean up the blood in gentle strokes, stopping every so often to give me a reassuring squeeze on the shoulder. I can't help it, I lean into him, feeling warm and tired. With even breaths and a calm demeanor, I see that he is excellent in a crisis, the type of person you want around.

"You don't go out much, if I remember correctly," he says in the silence. It's not a question but I feel compelled to defend myself, to tell him he doesn't know anything about me, to remind him he left Chivasso before I did, and I could have turned into a raving social butterfly since then. But what's the point in lying? He'll find out eventually. And I'm too tired to lie.

"We're not all blessed with Anika's social skills," I confess.

The cloth touches one of the deeper scrapes and I flinch at the contact. A hand flashes to my ribs, fingers flat against my lower abdomen with an intensity I feel deep in the pit of my stomach. "I got you," he whispers.

As quickly as I take a breath in, he lets go. A mistake, I tell myself, an accident born from reflex. But the feeling of his skin on mine remains the entire night, imprinted on me with unwanted permanence. I try to calm my heartbeat, to remind myself that he is only concerned for my safety because it would affect Anika's happiness if something were to happen to me. I try to rationalize his reaction, but the heat of his phantom handprint pulses through my heart. He doesn't respond to my answer but continues to clean silently.

"I'll walk you to your room and then I have a few errands to run," he says without prompt.

"You have errands to run at one a.m.?" I pick at my nails, the disbelief clear in my voice.

He doesn't answer immediately, pretending to focus on cleaning the blood that I know is no longer there. "Anika shouldn't make you do things you don't want to do."

I shake my head. He's ignoring my question. Annoyed at his accusation of Anika forcing me to do things I don't want to do, I repeat my question.

"Theo," I straighten my back. "Where are you going?"

The only sound is the slight rattle of the ceiling fan above us. "They can't get away with this, Magdalen." His voice is strained, and I'm struck with the need to turn around and look at him. Slowly, I swing my legs over the counter so that I'm facing him. His knees brush against mine, but he makes no effort to move them.

"Of course they can. Just go to bed."

"I'm not tired," he whispers slowly.

"Well," I breathe, exasperated by his sudden need for heroism. I know it's just because I'm Anika's best mate; his protective instinct has nothing to do with needing to defend me. The realization makes me sad, as I take in that no one knows me enough to want to protect me; not even Dante or Jo seemed to care that much.

"Count some sheep," I suggest.

He dips his head and leans forward, breath warm against my neck, and a low chuckle reverberates through him. It's a beautiful sound. Without warning, he slides his hands to my hips and squeezes for the briefest moment. I suck in a breath, his touch somehow different this time. Warmer.

A friendly gesture, I tell myself.

"Oh, Magdalen." His voice is deep and sensual, and I struggle not to close my eyes at the sound. His lips brush my ear again and I feel him whisper in my hair, "There are no sheep in Chivasso."

12

THEO

I close the back door of the Savoys' house, and I feel my calmness disappear with it. Two hours' scrubbing blood, watching her shoulder blades contract with pain, feeling her breath stop with too sudden a movement. And all the while she spoke five sentences to me. *And* all the while the image of her shirt bunched up over her breasts is burned into my memory. *She has just been assaulted and you can't stop thinking of how her body felt beneath your hands?* I wipe my hands against my jeans, trying to rub off the feeling of her on my palms. Selfish and pathetic, I conclude. Maybe my father isn't too wrong about me.

"Get it fucking together," I mumble to myself as I walk back to the car parked in front of her house. The night is cool, and the slight wind is a welcome change from the heat of her skin. Stars blister from behind translucent clouds, the faint chirp of crickets following me as I walk across the gravel. My footsteps feel loud against the silence. There is only darkness and the sound of my footsteps and I remember what it feels like to not belong. To feel this intrusive.

I look at my house, maybe thirty meters from the Savoys', and think in disbelief about all the years I'd been so close to her. Yet I can't remember a moment she ever existed to me before today.

My mind tries to conjure up an image of childhood Magdalen, of a birthday we must have shared together, but each time only one memory appears. Three days before I left, reaching for a CD from Anika. Probably Madonna, knowing my sister's taste. The rest is a haze of color and sound, laughter, and mine and Dante's empty wine bottles rolling across cobblestones. Forever in my blind spot, I secretly thank whatever god there is for my ignorance, knowing that running away would have been harder if I saw her as I did tonight. Exhaling a shaky breath, I unlock Anika's car and sit in the darkness.

Olive skin and a red ribbon blowing against the breeze. She's fucking perfect.

A scream bubbles in my throat but I swallow it, burying this feeling so deep inside of me it presses on the edge of my spine. Turning the engine on, I back out of the driveway and steal one last glance at Magdalen's house. A faint yellow glow of a lamp shines from the farthest window, letting me know that she's in her bedroom. Groaning, I try not to picture her in her bed, but it's too late. A prickle of fear forms in my stomach. Fear born of desire. To follow her up those creaky steps and be the one she lets into her room. One day back and already I feel like I'm losing my mind.

Why couldn't she stay in England? She wouldn't be bleeding half as much and I wouldn't be supressing a hard-on for my best friend's younger sister. "God help me," I sigh. "You were not part of the plan, Magdalen." Looking again at her window before I back out of the driveway, I see her single light amid the night. Another disturber of the darkness. Perhaps I was never as alone as I felt.

When I get inside Tirumapifort, the tennis club remains crowded with sweaty bodies and short dresses.

I make my way through to the bar, people move before I ask them to, and when I look up I notice people staring. Examining. Jesus, this is creepy. A man I don't recognize, dressed in a white vest and gold chain, with more hair growing from his eyebrows than his head, squints as his gaze falls from my hair to my neck then finally back up to my eyes. He nods, approving and welcoming. Do I fucking know you? I try to think back on my time at the club, but all I remember is Chiara and empty beer cans discarded in the pool, and shiver at the memory. Hating who I was. *Hating who I am*, I correct myself. Best to be humble.

I try not to think about Chiara right now, but before I can stop myself my eyes search for the bathroom door on the far wall. Inside a stall she'd had her dress raked up to her thighs as she settled herself on top of me. No underwear. I can still smell the spilled cheap vodka and disinfectant. Her dress straps falling as she moaned in my ear, stale and practiced, knowing what I like to hear. We'd been fucking for two months at that point. I was too lazy to tell her I couldn't stand the sound of her voice. If I drank enough, nothing mattered. I blink the memory away. Looking back to the crowd, a complete path has been opened for me.

A short man with a stomach hanging over his trousers and an anchor tattooed on his bicep laughs obnoxiously and somehow, I know. It's him. The glass table next to him has been cleaned up, with only the frame pushed into the corner. Anger swells in my stomach. Watching him laugh is enough to set me off. I picture his elbow slamming into Magdalen's stomach; I see her fear. I tap his shoulder. Flashing a smile, extending my hand out in greeting. The man looks at me confused, but immediately takes my hand in earnest, shaking hard. His palms are slick with sweat, and he smells of stale clothes and tequila. *You have no idea what I'm about to do to you, fucker.*

All I can see when I look at him is Magdalen hurt, chewing on her bottom lip, accepting the pain as if it belonged to her. It was her need to hide her hurt before Anika saw, and the sight of her back. Her back, plastered with the same color as that fucking red ribbon. And the burns, years-old scars that made her body tense as I traced them with my fingers. *Enough innocence to save us all.*

Despite not knowing me, the man is eager to talk to anyone who shows interest, and he moistens his lips in preparation.

"Sorry to bother you, I just have a quick question."

"Ask away!"

"Didn't your mother teach you not to be such a fucking cunt?"

My hand hardens around his, and I watch as his eyes widen in confusion. He has the audacity to look like a victim! Like he's never committed a sin in his life. With no notice, I pull his hand toward me as my other hand connects with his jaw, watching with fire behind my eyes as his head snaps back, eyes shutting with pain. The fucker reaches for his face, blood pooling from his lip, eyes shining with fury. Innocence evaporated.

"You Scottish prick." He spits a combination of saliva and blood to the ground.

Ah, so he does know who I am. Calling me a Scot is an ineffective insult, and what he really means is something more sinister. There is no denying the Sinclairs' rarity in this small town, our accents thick, the hot shots who own the museum! A nerve in my temple begins to throb.

Before I can respond to the man-pig, a sharp pain strikes my leg and I fall to my knee. My bones crash into the concrete, small remnants of glass still scattered across from Magdalen's accident scrape my skin and I can already feel a gash on my knee. Our skin has been torn from the same glass and I briefly wonder if this connects us in some way. I jerk my head to see the one responsible but a crowd has amassed behind me, the attacker hidden among them. *Pussy.* As I turn my head back to face the bar again, a fist connects with my nose, causing my vision to darken. I touch my fingers to my nose and they come away bloody. The heady pressure of his punch fills my head, my lungs. My heartbeat steadies and I stifle a moan from the comfort of the pain. *Finally*.

Breathing a sigh of relief, I enjoy the dull throbbing in my nose for a moment. *Thank you*, I want to say. My mind clears. For once I'm not thinking about all the shit. I think only of the ache and feel better than I have since landing. My head bends low, watching my own blood hit the floor in even, measured drips.

"Shouldn't have done that." I slowly raise my head, a grin tugging at my lips. Spitting the blood toward his sandals, I watch his eyes widen above me. Recognizing his momentary dominance as he towers above me, the disgruntled man lets out a weak, "You really want to say that from down there, bitch?"

Shifting his weight from his right to left, flexing and fisting his hands, it's clear he's never had to fight before.

Growing courage, the man grabs my hair by the roots, forcing me to look up at him.

"Now that I think about it," I muse, my voice low, "you probably learned it from your mother, huh?"

In one quick motion I drag my knee to his groin in a casual arc. A loud groan fills the bar space as he bends over in pain, panting with exhaustion. Without hesitation, I stand up, my hand wraps around the back of his neck and pushes his face into the floor. An alarm rings in my head, a crowd of people materializing around us, all who know my father. Who'll be the first to tell him? Maybe I should stop. But the thought of my father only ignites my anger tenfold.

The man's gasps are muffled by the floor and he coughs aggressively. I know that this is over, he's learned his lesson; I've won. I bend down and flip him over, scratches from broken glass cover his forehead. I exhale loudly, knowing what I'm about to do is wrong, but all I see is how vulnerable my Magdalen looked underneath the yellow lamp of her kitchen.

This time I can feel the bone crack as I punch him in the nose; the wet sound of crushed cartilage creates a sickening noise that burns my stomach. My fist hovers above him again, the tantalizing lure to create pain is like a whisper over my skin. *Do it, do it, do it.* The more pain he feels the less you will.

"Are you crazy? What the fuck did I even do?" he yells, but it's far away, so easy to ignore.

With one hand curled around the collar of his shirt, I press my weight into his neck, causing a guttural choke to leave his lips. Finally, someone gets it. His shirt rides up his body, exposing his hairy stomach.

"Yes." My voice is unrecognizable even to myself. "You hurt her." I am lost to the anger, but this is now more than just about Magdalen. The years of hurt, from everything that happened in Chivasso before I left, creep too close to the surface. The muscle in my arm flexes as I swing again but before I can make contact a hand grabs the back of my shirt and tugs me away.

"*Cazzo,*" a familiar voice spits at me. I drop my hand and turn to find Dante staring at me, bewilderment in his eyes. Shoving me aside, he reaches for the man on the floor, muttering pathetic apologies to him. There's terror in the man's eyes as he looks at me one last time before huffing out his chest in exaggerated pain, performing for the crowd of onlookers.

"It's a broken nose, not a severed head," I yell as Dante guides him to the bar, signaling the bartender for napkins and a glass of bourbon. Every so often, the man steals looks at me. I flash him a smile, running my tongue over my teeth, and I taste the metallic warmth of blood coating my gums. The crowd, sensing the fight is over, begin to disperse with gossiping whispers.

Stranger. Their bodies are defensive, hardened by the realization that I am not who they remember me to be.

With fury, Dante is back and dragging me toward the exit, fingers digging into my bicep with surprising strength, and I stumble as I follow him.

"Hey," I spit, but then spot Matilde sitting perched on the lifeguard chair, watching the entire scene, her blue eyes visible even from across the club. And then she nods her head to me, as if...

As if she's congratulating me.

The air changes as we reach the exit of the club.

"What the actual fuck, Theo?" Dante lets go, but he remains too close to me. I shove him away and he stumbles a few paces back, looking down at his chest with disbelief, hesitantly touching the spot of my touch, determining whether it was real. That I could touch him in any other way than with brotherly affection disturbs him. *Might as well let everyone know I'm not who they remember.*

"You have thirty seconds to take that back," Dante challenges.

My mouth opens in apology, regretful of how selfish I am for hurting one of the only people in the world who cares about me. The crackle of unspent energy dissipates, draining through my fingertips until my limbs feel heavy and drunk. Disgusted that I acted so irrationally, my guilt threatens to choke me.

But as I stare down at the red gravel, the image of

Magdalen's white sneakers stained with her blood, limping across this floor, stops the apology before it reaches the back of my teeth. I replay the sequence of events. Table crashing, Magdalen's body pinned under glass, Dante reaching for a cigarette, Jo nervously tapping his foot until he could get back in the club again. Magdalen alone, Magdalen with me, Dante buying the man a drink.

He didn't even fucking check to make sure she was okay.

Dante, eyes rolling as Anika takes his last cigarette, did nothing to ensure his little sister wasn't hurt.

"Why would I take it back?" I take a step closer. A crash of thunder fills my ears until I can only hear the sound of my heart racing.

"Why would you?" Dante's voice is loud against the quiet night. "*Cazzo*," he repeats for the second time tonight. "What the fuck is wrong with you? Beating up men you don't know? You hitting me? Who the fuck even are you?" He runs his hand through his dark hair, eyes huge and afraid. I bite back a bitter laugh, remembering what a selfish prick he can be.

"Your sister's back currently looks like a bloody Jackson Pollock painting." I take a step closer. "She's your sister," I repeat, shoving my finger at his chest again. "And you're more concerned about fucking Anika than worrying about if Magdalen's all right?"

The night air stills around us, holding its breath.

"Magdalen's always been able to take care of herself," he falters, trying to avoid my glare. Shame overcomes him, staining his cheeks with red, but I can only feel disgust when I look at him. Drunk and whiny, absolutely pathetic.

"No one should have to take care of themselves in a situation like that," I hiss. Dante will never fucking understand. I begin walking away, my hands shoved so deeply in my pockets that I feel the seams scream in protest.

"Wait, bro. Let's talk about it. I'm sor—"

"Why the fuck are you apologizing to me?" I spit out.

Not waiting for a response, I turn back toward Anika's car and drive away.

13

MAGDALEN

Everything hurts. I get out of bed slowly, the old frame creaking as my feet hover over the edge, skimming the floor as though it were hot sand. Not ready to face anyone yet.

I stretch my limbs, testing the extent of my mobility. I can move my arms despite the stiffness, but the tenderness of my back is a reminder of what I let happen last night.

Theo Sinclair dissected my bloody back while my tits were out. My face heats with embarrassment, like flashes of a drunken memory rushing toward you at the first sip of coffee. I limp to the bathroom and check my reflection. Is this what Theo saw last night? My eyes are slightly too big, but green in the morning sun. I edge closer to the mirror, my heart giving an involuntary thud at the proximity. A lot of freckles. A brief flash of him touching the freckle above my eyebrow causes me to blush. Black eyelashes. Unruly eyebrows. One finger touches my cheek and I imagine the hand is someone else's. I trace the length of my nose where there is a slight bump in the middle—a Savoy family trait. I outline my mouth, the divot beneath my bottom lip.

Stepping back from myself, I turn the faucet on the tub and sit on the edge while the water fills up. Steam begins to fog the corners of the mirror so I strip off my shorts, and then my shirt. I look at myself and pantomime my actions from last night. Cupping my breasts and turning to the side to envision what Theo saw. My hair falls down my back in long, dark auburn strands and I'm struck with not hating what I see in the reflection. This is new. I see a woman. Sure, the burn marks are still ugly, especially in the bright light of the bathroom. My eyes close shut when I remember Theo's lingering fingers on the raised skin, but I calm myself knowing that he'll never have to see them again. Taking a deep, centering breath, I continue observing myself.

The curvature of my spine is alluring. If I didn't know better I'd say I almost feel content, and even if Theo found me unpleasant with weird burns and small tits, I think I could be beautiful all the same. Someone would be lucky to see me, I tell myself. Repeating the affirmations I'd heard from Emily and Anika. Someone would be lucky.

Well, Theo? Did you feel fucking lucky?

My mother is outside gardening when I'm finished in the bathroom.

"*Buon giorno, Mamma.*"

She doesn't turn around, just waves a hand in acknowledgment.

"How was last night?" she asks, but is so disinterested I roll my eyes.

Breathing heavily, she shovels dirt to make room for a new basil plant Cinzia gave her. Cinzia, Theo's mother, is everything mine is not. Quiet, reserved, and she rarely smiles, but, when she does, it's brilliant. Why the two of them are so close, I'll never understand. They've been inseparable since university.

For once, I am glad my mother doesn't turn around. A bruise has appeared across my right forearm and I'm too tired to come up with an excuse. Instead, I sigh happily as I take in the backyard. My mother is many things, and a genius gardener happens to be one of them.

Our garden is lined with almost every herb imaginable. Gravel walkways separate the rows of produce, creating a maze of rosemary, basil and thyme. Dotted among the leaves are small statues, in true Savoy fashion. Little cherub faces peek out behind a fig tree or a lavender shrub. I've been stealing bundles of lavender to make perfume since I accidentally fell into one shrub and realized how good I smelt. But under a veranda in the center of the garden sits the old wooden table. The table—unpolished and scattered with rings of condensation from wine glasses, flecks of wax dripping off the edges— has witnessed every Savoy and Sinclair birthday until Theo left. Every summer night, sneaky sleepovers underneath its wooden top. Sometimes if it was warm enough in October, Anika and I would tiptoe out to the veranda with thin blankets to sip wine and gossip about boys.

I love this table. I had my first kiss on this table. When our school put on a performance of *Romeo and Juliet* in grade six. I was cast as Juliet, with a boy named Stefano destined to be my Romeo. He told me he should come over to practice our kiss scene. For the play, he said, we didn't want to look silly. I mumbled something very stupid, saying, "Sure, sure. For the play."

I remember my heartbeat the most. Worried about how big my nose would look so close up. The throbbing of my heart raced up to my head, banging against the inside of my skull. He sat me down on the corner of the table and put himself between my legs. He'd said, "Hold still," as if he was going to perform surgery on me.

I said, "Okay," like I wanted him to kiss me.

With a quick breath out, he dove into my face. Cold and wet. I hated every moment of it; the smell of his breath had suddenly suffocated me. It was unbearable. He tried to open his mouth but I was so scared and disgusted that I kept my lips tightly shut, my body inverting into itself. He stepped back, with a loud and sloppy finish. His hands on his hips as if he was an artist, and I his latest creation. Trying to create as much distance between us, I scooted farther back onto the table, and that's when I saw it. Looking down, I saw the obvious impression of an erection in his trousers. My face drained of blood and a coldness swept over my body, my first realization that boys were so different from me.

That horribly wet and painful kiss gave him a boner. But that's not why I love the table.

I love the table because it's where Anika met me after Stefano left, rushing through the gate, tripping over her untied shoelaces and anticipation for my recount of the kiss. She grabbed my face, scanning to see if there was any physical change in me after being touched by a boy. There wasn't. Just a tremor of disappointment that lingered so long I can still feel it today. I felt cheated by *Romeo and Juliet*, realizing it was written by a man and now feeling that it must be an inaccurate representation of love. Because no woman would die for a kiss, if all kisses were like Stefano's. Anika shoved me to the side and sat down next to me, one hand patting my knee.

"Just wait until one of them fingers you."

I choked on the air and shoved her back, bursting into a fit of laughter. "You've been kissed once, Anika. How do you know anything about fingering?"

"I read books. I do my research."

"Jab, jab, jab, jab." She motioned her middle and pointer finger in a violent upward motion. "Men really can't do anything right. Especially Stefano." She threw her hands up in mock exaggeration and sighed loudly.

Giggling and proud of having now both become women, we lay down on the table, looking at the intricate pattern of vines that grew across the veranda, trying to find stars in between their weave.

Anika, usually so confident, turned her head to me. "It'll get better, won't it?" she asked shyly.

I turned my head to her, our noses almost touching, and squeezed her hand. "I hope so," I whispered back. "But, if not, promise that we'll marry each other and never have to kiss anyone again."

She squeezed my hand back and then, after a beat of silence, slapped my stomach. "Always, baby girl. I'll give us until forty." She hoisted herself off the table. "But for now, unfortunately, boysssss!"

And then she was off, back through the gate and to her

house next door, skipping loudly down the gravel path. Her laughter fading through the trees.

"You should go and see your father today." My mother's voice snaps me from my memory.

I stare at the back of her head; she hasn't turned around once since I've entered the garden, or since I've come home. Seemingly unimpressed with the version that showed up in Chivasso this time around.

"Of course." My tone is light. "I was on my way now."

14

THEO

I leave the house before my father wakes up. Too early for disappointment. The bald pig from last night managed to get a few punches in, leaving a slight bruise beneath my right eye and a cut along my nose. Not wanting to think about it, I shrug on a clean white T-shirt and jeans, careful to stay silent among the morning birds, and sneak downstairs. Passing through the kitchen to see slices of half-eaten toast and day-old fried eggs tells me Anika came home last night. I relax, annoyed with how preoccupied I was with Dante that I forgot to check up on her. But it wasn't just Dante that was distracting me, was it?

Anika's car sits in the driveway where I parked it last night so I get inside, shivering with the morning breeze. Deciding to drive to the museum before it opens, wanting to see what they've done to it since I left. The windows are fogged with the morning dew and the sun appears behind the terra-cotta buildings, creating a glow of amber around the neighborhood.

The museum has been the center of my life for as long as I can remember. It was my home before my house ever was. I'd always fought my want of studying Egyptology, not wanting to follow my father's footsteps so closely. But it was useless. It was my first love. My only love.

I'm halfway down the steep hill that our neighborhood is set at the top of when I see someone walking down, rotating her shoulder and kicking a pebble every so often. Ponytail swinging with each step. Despite me being fifty meters back, I can feel it's Magdalen. She wears a silk lavender top and a small white skirt, the light colors making her olive skin glow. Even at a distance she's fucking beautiful.

I slow the car when I get close enough and tap the horn a few times, hoping she recognizes Anika's car.

She doesn't, stumbling over the pebble she was kicking as her head turns to the car. Eyes wide and alarmed, she shoots a hand to her chest, panting in shock before she realizes it's me.

"*Cazzo*, Theo!" Bending forward, she rests her hands on her knees as she tries to catch her breath. I supress a groan as her skirt hikes up even further. "What happened to your face?" she gasps, coming closer to the window.

"Morning, Magdalen," I grin.

"Jealous I was the only one with an injury?"

I squint from the sunlight through the window shield. "Something like that."

She rolls her eyes. "How is it that in the thirteen years of living next door to you, I barely see you, and now within two days you're everywhere?" Her breathing is still uneven, but she snorts with laughter, shaking her head.

"Maybe it's fate." I smile but it quickly fades when I really take her in. The injuries from last night are brutal in the morning light. Bruises line the nape of her neck to the collar of her shirt; an abstract array of deep purples and greens creates a gradient across her skin. Lower down, I see another dark blue bruise covering the back of her forearm. My hands squeeze the steering wheel, trying to keep my temper in check. I should have smashed his nose off his fucking face.

Magdalen places her hands on her hips, tilting her head. Oblivious to my anger. "And where are you headed off to so early in the morning, Rocky Balboa?"

Without meaning to, my eyes trace her legs, long and tanned, covered only by the small tennis skirt that skims her upper thigh. God, those thighs are something. I swallow hard, focusing past her, on a dandelion growing between the cracks in the pavement. Not picturing my hands on her. Not at all.

"Running errands," I smirk.

"Do most of your errands involve physical altercations, or was that just a one-time sort of thing?"

"Depends on whether someone hurts you again." Her pretty smile fades and I internally cringe. Why do I have to keep making things so intense?

"You didn't have to—"

"You shouldn't be walking on your own in your condition," I cut her off, shutting down the engine.

"In my condition?" Magdalen scoffs. "What is that supposed to mean?" Her hands rest on the open window and I look down at her nails, still painted that deep shade of red. Even her fucking fingers are pretty.

I have to roll my eyes. "Do you not have a mirror? You're covered in bruises."

"Do bruises mean I can't walk?" She pauses. "Should I be scolding you for driving with a black eye?" She bites her lip to conceal her laugh, drawing my eyes to her full lips.

"Are you laughing at me, Magdalen?" My voice sinks deeper—enjoying this playful side of her. Wanting to see that smile more.

She releases her bottom lip, her eyes still bright with humor. My hands grip the steering wheel again, but this time to stop myself from running my thumb over her knuckles, over those cherry-red nails.

"I think I might be, yes." She nods her head, pretending to think about it. "I'll catch you later, Theodore."

And then she's off, leaving me staring at her ass as she saunters downhill. I blink and press my foot on the gas only to remain in place, forgetting I turned the car off. "Fuck," I whisper, clumsily finding the key in the ignition and following her like a bloody stalker. But I can't let it go.

"Let me give you a ride," I say in the moving car. She looks straight ahead, pretending I'm not there.

"I'm okay." She shrugs her shoulders but stops the action midway, her face scrunching with pain, revealing she's very much not okay. My stomach drops. I should've killed him. I should've beat him to a bloody pulp. "I like to walk." Her voice is strained and I almost stop the car; the need to make sure she's all right is so strong I feel myself tremble.

"There's time for walking when you're not in this much pain," I say cautiously, not wanting to spook her but also not taking no for an answer. "Those cuts are still fresh, Magdalen."

"Look, I appreciate the concern, I really do. Last night was a big help. Sorry you had to see my tits. But I'm a big girl. If I say I can walk down a hill, I mean it."

I blanche, her words automatically making me remember her cupping herself. "At least tell me where you're going," I croak, fighting off the image of her half naked and on display for me. There's no fucking way she's not getting in this car.

She huffs in annoyance and I have to hide my smile.

"No."

"Yes."

"Theo," she warns, and I feel giddy when she says my name.

"Maggie," I whisper back, enjoying this frustrated side of her. "I've got all day. I'm more than happy to follow you around if that's what you want."

"That is most certainly not what I want."

"Okay, so tell me where you're going and I'll be out of your pretty hair."

Magdalen stumbles a little, cheeks burning as she clears her throat and whips her head toward me again.

"All right, fine. But just because I'm telling you doesn't mean I want a ride. You're just annoying."

"Yeah, I know, I'm just curious." I tap my finger on the gear shift.

"I'm going to the train station."

My jaw almost drops. That's a three-kilometer walk along

the highway. If her bruises are this bad, I can't even imagine the shape of her back. Fucking hell, how is this girl even standing up right now? Her mother should have tied her to the bed.

"Magdalen—"

"What did we talk about?"

"Get in the car," I push and then cringe at my tone. There's no way she'll listen if I force her. I try to soften my approach. "Please? I'm headed in that direction anyway," I add, hoping this will help. Not understanding why I need to have her near me. Picturing her walking along the highway in pain sends a flicker of concern down my spine. There's no way I'm leaving without her.

She sighs again, looking back up the hill and then down again, as if judging whether it's worth the fight I'm willing to have.

"Fine. Jesus, you're worse than Jo." As she walks around the front of the car to get into the passenger seat, I find myself mumbling.

"Just for you, Magdalen. I'm only this bad for you."

15

MAGDALEN

The car ride is silent and uncomfortable as we descend the craggy hill to the train station. I don't know whether to make a comment about the potholes that ruin the road. I think about how much my cheeks jiggle from the impact.

"Thank god we're not holding eggs!" I would say. But then I realize how awkward that would be, so I stay silent instead. What do you even say to a shit joke like that?

Theo makes no motion to say anything and I'm confused as to why he'd make such a big deal about giving me a ride if he had no intention of speaking to me. Not that he appears to be uncomfortable with the silence. I shift in my seat, sneaking a glance at him without moving my neck so he doesn't notice. A bruise has formed across his right cheekbone, and I suck in a breath. So he goes back to the club to avenge my ability to get hurt by just standing? My mind races and my lips are moving before I know I'm speaking.

"Why'd you go back there?"

He doesn't even flinch at my voice; his profile remains perfectly calm and focused on the road ahead. Except his jaw clenches, just slightly.

"I wasn't trying to defend your honor."

"That's good to know. You just punched yourself, then?"

He stays silent for a moment and then releases a breath, relaxing further into the car seat.

"How the fuck was I supposed to just let him get away with it? You were just getting a drink and then suddenly you're pinned down by a glass table and no one gave a shit." His voice fills the space between us, his chest moving rapidly.

"Well, you didn't need to do that," I mumble, crossing my arms in front of me in pathetic defiance. "But thank you. No one's ever gotten punched for me."

"Well, get used to it. This type of shit doesn't run when I'm around."

My cheeks burn at his insinuation that he'll have to get hurt for me again and the words spill out.

"Trust me, you won't ever have to do anything for me again. I swear."

Theo looks at me for a lingering second. "I wouldn't mind, Magdalen. I like doing things for you."

My heart leaps. "Oh," I say dumbly. "Okay."

Theo smirks, shaking his head slightly before looking back at the road. And after I realize my stupid response ended the conversation, I take a second to admire his side profile.

One hand holds the bottom of the steering wheel with ease as his other elbow rests on the center console, fingers absentmindedly brushing his bottom lip. My gaze falls to the sharp cut of his jaw, harsh and determined. The wind from the open window blows his thick hair behind his ears, curls flowing wildly around him in dark waves as he jets down the road. Despite myself, I breathe in, smelling the clean laundry and sandalwood, wanting to run my fingers through his hair to see if it's as soft as it looks. But the minute the thought crosses my mind, I banish it, reminding myself of the way he touched me last night. *Like it was painful.* Men this beautiful are dangerous. Not trusting my own hands, I tuck them underneath my legs.

I stifle a groan, having never felt this desperate to touch someone before.

Deciding that if I look at his hair any longer I'll lose my mind, my attention drifts to the finger that still brushes his full bottom lip. As if he knows I'm looking at him, his hand falls to the steering wheel, and I find myself desperate to know what he is thinking about.

This man is an actual statue. The only deviation is by the bridge of his nose, a slight bend that somehow makes him more statue-like than without it. Who looks this good at seven in the morning?

He shifts the gear and my eyes can't help but trail down his arm. The muscle in his forearm extends with the motion and my mouth goes dry, his tanned skin corded with dangerous strength.

We hit a larger bump and the car jolts forward. Suddenly, Theo's hand flashes to my knee, a mere reflex. My stomach clenches, heat trailing down to the spot he touches.

"Sorry, habit." Theo looks down to where his hand rests at my leg; his Adam's apple bobs. Despite the bump being far behind us, he doesn't remove his hand right away. For a brief moment, his thumb brushes the inside of my knee, causing goosebumps to raise on my skin. His gaze travels up from my knee to my thigh, and I look down to see my skirt has risen. Oh. He clears his throat, hand sliding off my leg and back on the steering wheel.

"Sorry. *Jesus*," he murmurs, furrowing his brow.

My heartbeat quickens. I release my breath. "Big brother reflex, right?" He straightens himself, the relaxed composure from moments ago now replaced with strained rigidity as his hands grip the steering wheel until his fingertips go white.

"Of course," he responds. "That must be it."

Trying not to be offended, I fix my skirt and stare out the window again, focusing on the street instead of his response. All the while screaming at my cheeks to stop blushing.

We enter the parking lot of the train station, which is void of any cars or people. Or trains, I quickly realize. Even the sunlight seems to have fallen back asleep. My fingers tap the armrest impatiently; the tension, alongside this sudden shift in him, is stifling. *Why did you ask to drive me, Theo?*

"This is fine." I force a smile and rest my hand on the handle of the car, eager to escape. "Thank you for the ride."

"Any time, Magdalen." He dips his head in a curt nod without looking at me. A dismissal.

Before I exit, I look back at him one last time. My eyes search his face, trying to determine the moment cocky "*get in the car, Magdalen*" Theo left and this version replaced him. He seems to notice me staring because he quickly averts his eyes to the gearshift as if silently begging me to leave. Telling me to let it go.

I can't help it. I have to ask. "Did I say something wrong?"

He pinches the bridge of his nose right by that slight bump which I now want to run my tongue over.

"No, sorry. Just had a late night yesterday." Coldness slips into his words.

This time, I don't have the strength to coax my blush into hiding. Heat prickles up to my scalp, embarrassment rushing over me.

He looks at me and I watch as the realization of his words sinks in.

"Shit, Magdalen. That's not what I meant."

The want to stand up for myself is there, as it always is, coating the back of my throat with unspoken fervor. Desperate to shout that I begged him not to help me. That I could do it by myself! That I didn't want him to look at me, that no one has ever been that close and it shouldn't have been him first. But I sit silent instead, turning my head to give myself the push to leave.

"Good luck on your errands."

"Wait, please. I just meant—"

I close the door, hearing him slam the steering wheel. Crossing my arms over my body, I walk to the platform and the echo of a train horn sounds in the distance. I feel silly and much younger than I know I am.

16

THEO

Driving through Torino was both nostalgic and nauseating. Settled at the foot of the Alps, baroque buildings in shades of beige and off-white are blinding against the morning sun. Early-rising street vendors lazily untie the tarp coverings, settling in for another day of bartering and slow selling. Faces aged by decades of laughing in the sun.

After years of this city, you stop seeing it. By the time I'd hit sixteen I could give a shit less about architectural significance. If the right person would have asked me to pour gasoline on Piazza Solferino and set it on fire, I wouldn't have thought twice. Behind the Chiesa di Santa Teresa is where we tried cocaine for the first time, and the following Sunday, I kneeled in front of the bishop for my confirmation. I got a blow job inside the archways between San Mariano and Via Tropolo, and threw up on the top of her head while I came.

I park in the spot that says "SINCLAIR," knowing that I'm not the one it's named after. A pang of jealousy settles deep between my shoulder blades, causing me to hunch forward.

I want what my father has.

The engine cuts off and I sit looking at the museum, unsure of what stops me from going in. Has it changed in the past seven years? My stomach flips when I think about the Statue of Isis anywhere but in the main floor gallery. The ceiling and floor are both black marble, creating a vacuum of onyx that she floats inside. The one truly beautiful thing my father has ever created.

When I walk into the museum, I want it to be as the person I am now, not the idiot boy who did everything so as not to miss out on youth. Heat rolls across my skin as I open the car door but I fight a shiver. A sweat breaks across my neck and the flash of those scenes into a single memory makes me understand why my father hates me. There was a time I would actively do everything he asked me not to. It was the only way I felt anything at all, watching his disappointment deepen each time I fucked up. Every punch of his fist, every lecture, was an escape—absolving me of guilt.

"Stop being a pussy," I say out loud, the only way I'll actually start walking. Putting my head down, I head toward the back entrance quickly, as if anyone would recognize me at seven in the morning in front of a closed museum.

The walk to the door feels like a funeral procession. Something has died, or ended, or maybe just been defeated. I choose the key from Anika's keychain without looking, the bite marks memorized as I run it across the pad of my thumb. Slipping the key into the lock, I turn it slowly. It used to be so easy to come here.

The door silently obeys, the frame almost opening on its own. Straightening myself, I walk in slowly. What the fuck am I so afraid of? Everything is dead inside these walls. I smooth my hair behind my ears to gain a semblance of control. It's a fucking museum, Theo. Just walk.

The long corridor to arrive at the first gallery feels achingly long. The walls are teal and clad with fragments of papyrus scrolls dating back from 2900 BC, sealed behind temperature-controlled plexiglass. The translations are stuck underneath, along with an introduction to the artifacts that visitors are expected to see. I see myself here at six years old, one hand holding a magnifying glass as the other holds *his* hand. He's so excited that I want to know more, patting my head with satisfaction.

And I was.

I wanted to know every secret my father would give me. My father is several things. *Amore*, to my mother. Daddy to Anika. Renowned archeologist and owner of the largest collection of Egyptian antiquities to the world. Accomplished businessman, dedicated historian, a generous man. A loyal father.

But to me he is only one thing.

A liar.

I reach the first gallery and since the museum isn't open yet, the room is tented in blackness. Only a single lamp glows in the far-right corner, the "ghost lamp" as Claudio Savoy likes to call it. Meant to keep the artifacts from coming to life.

"Bad for press," he said when he dragged five of them in for each floor of the museum, "if a visitor is possessed by a 3,000-year-old Egyptian king."

A pang of jealousy hits me for Dante, Jo, Lucia and Magdalen, who grew up in the company of Dr. Savoy. A true revolutionary in the field of archeology, awarded for his success in leadership of the two year-long excavations near the Pyramid of Menkaure, on the Giza Plateau. Growing up next door to him was a dream. I used to listen to them dragging in a Christmas tree after a weekend trip to the Alps. Or, every 15 August, they'd pack the car early in the morning and head to Numana for Ferragosto. Even then, when I loved my father, there was always something missing between us.

So when, one summer, Dr. Savoy announced a private excavation he was assisting AERA with, I packed my duffle bag and left the next morning without telling anyone. If my father introduced ancient Egypt to me, Dr. Savoy embedded me in it. In the deserts of Saqqara when I was seventeen years old, canvas tents and dried fish for supper. Sweaty and covered in sand, I found a mummified dog and cried from joy.

"You can hang it on your bedroom wall," he said while brushing off the excess debris and patting me on the back. "Girls love puppies."

I laughed so hard I fell down the neighboring dune and broke my right pinkie toe. Sand was falling out of my shoes for months after our trip and every time I ate anchovies, I thought of him and laughed again. The first time I left home was with him. The next was when I left for good.

I switch on the lamp and my heartbeat settles. Everything is the same; the slick black marble overwhelms the space. For a moment you think you can't breathe, that you really are in a bottomless vacuum. But soon the sensation disappears, and you're left breathless from the beauty of the space. I've visited museums across the world but it will always be this; black marble and a rusty lamp. My home. Nine statues line the walls, each spotlighted with an overhead light. Four on each side, a mixture of giant lions and panthers carved from limestone guarding the single woman on the far back wall. Eyes follow you as you make the procession toward her, cold stone glaring with heated attention. She consumes the room.

Isis. The Egyptian goddess of love. Daughter of earth and sky. She stands alone, carved in dark granite with mystic seduction. Her head is held high, eyes beckoning you toward her. I walk forward, feeling the same compulsion as I did when I was sixteen. I could destroy this entire city. But her? She was the one thing I would never touch.

I'm standing in front of her, looking at the perfect symmetry of the carved granite, and another face flashes to the front of my mind. I'm still midway down the hall. Green doe eyes follow me, mirroring the feline shape of Isis's, asking me why I went back to the club. Asking me why I left her at the fucking train station when I should have given her the keys myself and told her to drive anywhere she needs.

Wondering why I punched someone for her.

And that's the issue, isn't it? Why did I punch someone for her? Even as I think about how stupid it was to go back to the club and risk my father's wrath on my first day back, the desire to hurt someone again throbs in my knuckles.

Deep anger courses through my chest, down to the heels of my feet, and it feels like my body is on fire. I want to do it again. From how the bone crushed underneath my fist to how the blood spilled from my lip. When the pain is at its peak, I can think straight.

Her face now inches away, Isis stares at me with wonder. My whole body freezes. For the first time in twenty years, I am not in complete awe of her. I try to conjure up some appreciation for her, for this room, for anything but the sound of the passenger door shutting closed, the train approaching the station. Idiot. I stumble backward. For the first time in twenty years, I feel suffocated by this room. Needing to get out so as not to think about her and the whistle of that train, I make my way upstairs.

Fucking hell. Even the red ochre masks hanging on the wall remind me of that bloody ribbon in her hair. And, before I can suppress the thought, my mind drifts to this morning. The second she slid in the passenger seat, I became too aware of everything about her. It was a simple ride down the street, maybe ten minutes maximum. And I managed to ruin it because I wanted to kiss her. To lock the car door and lower down her seat.

Maybe it's time to pay Chiara a visit.

"Just had a late night yesterday." The words repeat again. What the fuck was I thinking?

From how silent she was when she sat down, that she didn't wear a seatbelt. How tight my hands gripped the steering wheel. How short her skirt was. Her legs were enough to set me undone.

It used to take more than just nice legs.

How, if I wasn't driving, my hand would have gratefully stayed on her knee and maybe traveled up her leg until I brushed the soft skin of her thighs and reached her—

Stop it.

My heartbeat quickens as I recall the sight of her skirt bunched up around her thighs.

Careful to not say anything I'd regret, I chose not to say anything. Which proved to be the wrong fucking choice.

But it doesn't matter, I tell myself. This is good. Let her feel scorned; it's better this way. Tomorrow will resume as normal. Yesterday was just a slight mishap in the universe. I will hang out with Dante at the club, take too many shots and dance to music I won't remember in the morning. I'll ask Chiara if she'd like to come to the wedding with me. She'll say yes.

There's no use in remembering how Magdalen looked sitting on the kitchen counter with her legs spread, hands cupping her own breasts as if she were begging me to kneel down and worship her. If I had dropped the washcloth and pressed my body into hers, slowly lowered her on the kitchen counter until her soft body was flush against mine, what would have happened?

I groan out loud, needing to expel the thought from the very cavity of my brain. My head hangs low as I walk up the stairs, trying to rid my mind of the fantasies.

No, Magdalen Savoy is not possible and you know why. Shaking off the thought, I'm walking up the steps when I hear laughter coming from the second-floor gift shop and freeze, my blood draining. My pace increases, skipping a step to reach the top of the spiral staircase until I'm behind the door. Listening to the voices: one is definitely a woman but it's muffled by the heavy aluminum, so I can't make out if the voices are familiar. When I check my watch, I see it's only 7:45 a.m. No one should be here for another two hours. Bracing for impact, I push the door in, and my eyes widen in surprise.

Dr. Claudio Savoy sits on the weathered leather chair, top button undone, and face red with laughter. Thinning gray hair sticks up in every direction. Claudio's eyes are squeezed shut, trying to compose himself, but then he breaks out in a fit of laughter again. Seeing him laugh makes me want to smile. It takes me a second, but then I see he's not alone. Turning my head, my stomach drops.

It's Magdalen.

I blink. How did she get here before me? Shame drips over me at my callousness in the car. If I'd just pressed her, or opened my fucking mouth, we could've come here together.

She stands in the corner of the small office by the bookcase, leaning gracefully with her arms crossed. Her eyes are bright and mischievous as she watches her father's fit of giggles. She is so beautiful, it hurts.

The laughter quickly dies as both their heads whip toward the direction of my intrusion. Smiles fading, Magdalen's posture stiffens as Dr. Savoy claps his hands in excitement. I try not to be embarrassed, but my heart warms against my will.

"Theo, my boy! What a beautiful surprise! What on god's green earth are you doing here so early?"

Momentarily caught off guard, I don't know what to say.

Trying to avoid seeing my father?

Couldn't sleep, I was fantasizing about your daughter without a shirt on?

Didn't you know? You are more of my home than I'll ever let anyone know.

"Just checking to see you didn't change too much since I was last here."

"Give me some credit. You know I wouldn't let your *papa* do too much damage to our masterpiece." His hands brace the table, and he grunts as he stands up. The bottom button on his shirt threatens to pop open and I wonder if he still sneaks cornetti in the bottom drawer of his desk.

Walking toward me from behind his desk, Claudio nearly knocks over all the receipts, articles and torn pieces of paper with handwritten notes that clutter his desk. There are four empty cups piled next to one another. So many pens. He keeps an extra cupful underneath his desk just in case. Claudio's desk always calmed me as a child. To know that someone so messy and so like me could be known for his brilliance. That you didn't need to lose your chaos in order to grow up. My own father's office mirrors this one, but one floor up. I picture it—organized, labeled and covered in locks.

"I should have known better. After all, *il museo è il quinto Savoy.*"

"That's where you're wrong." He hobbles toward me, brown eyes behind silver-rimmed glasses. Beard peppered with gray. "You are the fifth Savoy!" He gives a raspy laugh and reaches up to cup my face, squeezing my cheeks. It's scary to think of who I might have become, if it wasn't for this man.

"I missed you." I swallow. "Didn't get to tell you that last night."

"We missed you more, my sweet boy."

"Sure, sure." And although I have no right to ask, the question remains etched in my head. *Why did you let me run away?* A ridiculous question. But one I have found myself wondering all these years away.

He looks me over once more from head to toe, nodding with approval.

"I'm glad to see you're still handsome." He winks, his short body looking smaller than I remember. "America can make some people very ugly." He wags his finger in the air.

"Papa!" The raspy laugh across the room scolds Dr. Savoy.

I stiffen, trying not to look at her. Even in my fucking peripheral she's all I see. Ridiculous. I feel like a teenager stealing glances at a *Playboy* magazine in the barber shop. The sound of her voice pulls me in and, before I have the chance to resist, my eyes find her. I sigh. Magdalen leans against the desk, her hair now clipped up to show the sharp angles of her face. Freckles concentrate around her nose and my fingers hum to trace them. To count them.

And because I'm looking at her, it becomes glaringly obvious that she is not looking at me. "That's disrespectful, Papa. Without America we wouldn't have condensed milk! We love condensed milk."

"Condensed milk?" I ask. She looks at me, eyes spelling

out *asshole*, and then to her father, whose eyebrows are raised in amusement.

"Yes, in 1856 Gail Borden invented condensed milk." Her voice is reserved, like she's testing to see if she can continue without being interrupted. "Some would say a revelation to the modern-day baking industry." She locks eyes with me. I swallow again, holding her gaze. Even across the distance of the room, the vividness of her green eyes is startling.

"Long live condensed milk," I murmur, my throat feeling tight.

"Ah, yes! Let us say a silent thank you to dear Mr. Borden," Dr. Savoy sighs happily, looking between the two of us. "And may his contribution be remembered forever!" Smacking his hands together playfully, Dr. Savoy points at the two of us.

"My my, the two of you! So tall and grown up. You both have become beautiful before my very eyes."

"Papa, please."

"It is true, no? Theo, when is the last time you saw Magdalen? Probably when she was—"

"Thirteen." It was the last thing I thought about before going to sleep last night. She was thirteen, writing in a journal while Anika made up a dance routine in our living room. I had to walk past them to get to my room.

Magdalen snorts, dipping her head back, and my eyes find the delicate curve of her neck. I lick my lips, imagining the soft flesh beneath my tongue. If I really let myself imagine it, I hear the soft moans she would make in my ear as I sucked on the sensitive skin.

121

"Wow! So long ago. You two must have a lot of catching up to do!"

My god, I need help. *Her father is in the room.*

"Anyway, I didn't mean to disturb you both. I assumed no one would be in the museum this early. I'll leave." My hand hovers above the doorknob, ready to escape the tension in the room. Tension created by my desire to feel Magdalen beneath me when her fucking father, my mentor, is two feet away. I try to remember if I still have Chiara's number so I can resolve this teenage-like lust without Magdalen ever knowing.

Dr. Savoy settles back in his chair, arms crossed over his stomach. "No, no. My wife thinks I need to appreciate the solitude of mornings. She sets my alarm for five thirty a.m. now." He huffs and I frown, surprised.

"I thought you got your best work done at night?" I can't hide the judgment in my tone.

"This is true. But what I've learned is that it's much easier to change than we think it is. You just have to want it enough. I saw that it made her unhappy that I was always in my office at night and decided it was time I made the effort to change."

"But you love the nighttime," I repeat.

He sighs, exasperated. "I love my wife more than I love the night, Theo."

I can feel Magdalen watching us. Her brows are furrowed in confusion. We've always been in a group setting together, and it strikes me that she's never seen her father and me interact alone.

"Well, have you tried talking to her about it? Because I don't see how it's fair that you have to change who you are. I mean there are studies that literally prove that people work best at different hours, for fuck's sake. Smells like bullshit. You're not the only one who has to sacrifice for her happiness, Claudio."

The silence is deafening. I bite the inside of my cheek, looking down at the tiled floor, heat creeping up my neck. Why do I always say the wrong thing?

He readjusts the metal frame of his glasses, looking resigned. "Magdalen, perhaps you should show Theo around the museum. Show him what's changed. The new exhibit Dexter helped lead is quite a treat."

I glance over at Magdalen, who although confused does not look angry at me for arguing with her father. She shrugs, picking a piece of invisible lint from her skirt.

"*Certo, Papa.* I'll see you later tonight." She walks over to behind the leather chair, squeezing his shoulders affectionately. "Enjoy the cornetto."

"Follow me." And when she looks at me, even two meters away, I almost trip in place.

I look at Claudio one last time, whose demeanor has shifted from father to doctor. I know I've upset him.

Turning around to leave, I'm halfway through the door when I hear him say, "Dinner is at eight tonight. Under the veranda. Wear a shirt that doesn't look like it's been dragged through mud." A laugh escapes me as I take in my shirt. A single hole on the far bottom right. "Also, try to come not drunk this time."

I roll my eyes but my heart swells, feeling seen. "For you, I'll wear a suit."

Magdalen snorts and I flash a grin at her. She's so much livelier around Claudio. Waving behind my back to Dr. Savoy, I walk behind her out toward the gift shop.

"Why do boy-fights only last five seconds?" she says when the door closes, rubbing her palms together.

"That was hardly a fight. It was miscommunication between two old friends."

She pauses, analyzing my words. It makes me nervous to know how intensely she pays attention to what I have to say.

"You consider my father an old friend?"

We approach the second-floor gallery dedicated to marriage ceremonies and I pretend I'm analyzing artifacts to stall.

"I mean I've known him my entire life. He's who I was with before going to university."

"Huh. I don't think I'd ever call your father my friend."

No shit. My hands flex, trying to dismiss the memory of being eighteen and running to Claudio, begging him to the point of tears to let me leave with him. When he finally allowed me to go, I hugged him so tightly that my forearms were sore. And for those three months in Egypt, we were inseparable. Or maybe I was just impossible to get rid of, following him around everywhere he went.

"I didn't know that, how much my father helped you." Her voice is low and when I look over at her she's looking at me, fingers twisted together in confusion. The tight lines of her mouth make me feel like she has more to say, but she turns to look around the room, and we continue to peruse the gallery in silence. The only sound is her shoes against the hardwood floor, every so often stopping to stand and examining another vase or ring. Observing her profile as she takes in the artifacts, it seems she looks at me the same way she looks at these objects—cautiously.

"I'm sorry for what I said in the car. Last night, when I saw you underneath that table..." I let out a harsh breath, thinking about the hurt in her eyes. I still in the middle of the gallery, pretending to be absorbed in one of the terracotta bowls on display. "When I saw you there, I knew right then that he wasn't gonna get away with it. And if you assume it's because I feel some brotherly obligation to protect you on Anika's behalf, you're fucking wrong." I turn to her, my chest tight. "I wasn't thinking of Anika at the club or in your kitchen. All I saw was you."

For a moment Magdalen does nothing but stare at me. Her green eyes are cool underneath the dim lighting of the gallery and her mouth is a straight line, unwavering. Great. I've stunned the girl. Scratching my jaw nervously, I realize this is the most I've ever spoken to her and I've basically admitted that I'm fucking obsessed with her.

"Thank you for seeing me," she replies softly, holding my gaze. As much as I want to say more, to ask her for coffee afterward or visit the piazza to sit and watch the farmer's market set up, there are reasons Magdalen Savoy is an impossibility. So I break eye contact first, needing space away in order to remember why.

Blinking rapidly, I try to change the subject. "So, basically, they haven't changed a thing in this museum since I left." I tuck my hands in my pockets and walk down the gallery, pretending to give a fuck about any of this.

"Well, they now carry T-shirts that say, 'I LEFT MY HEART IN A MUMMY'S TOMB.'"

"I'm surprised there isn't one that says, 'GOT A SAR-COUGH-AGUS FROM MUSEUM OF TORINO.'"

She snorts. "Did you just come up with an ancient Egyptian pun on the spot?"

"No, Magdalen." I pause, turning around to face her. "I'm just a normal sarcophaguy, like everyone else. Please, don't treat me any differently."

Her mouth hangs open, shock and delight covering her face. So fucking cute. Turning back around, we exit the exhibition room and enter the adjoining one dedicated to ceremonial tombs. The quiet padding of Magdalen's shoes lets me know she is right next to me. I love it more than I should.

"Of corpse, I'm so sorry. Please forgive me for my insensitivity."

I pause, looking at her, a grin stretching across my face. Full of surprises, that girl.

Before I walk again, she nudges her hip into mine in friendly amusement.

"You and I are a lot alike."

She's looking up at me, cheeks flushed a beautiful pink.

"How so?"

"We're both insanely good at puns. Both tall, and don't say you're taller because I'll cry." A whisper of a smile threatens to break across my face. The foot separating us feels too far and my body hums to move closer.

"You're tall enough, Magdalen."

Her own smile frays. "We also both ran away from something." Prodding at the boundaries of our friendship, she again turns to look around at the items on display. My heart lurches. For a moment, I ignore her comment about me running from something and focus on her own confession. She ran away? What on earth would Magdalen Savoy have to run away from? Dr. Savoy is nothing but warmth. But love. She has no fucking right to want to leave him.

"I didn't run away."

"But you just said—"

"I didn't fucking run away." The mixture of anger, curiosity and blatant attraction for her makes my head spin viciously. But there is no conviction in my tone. I may as well sink to the floor and start crying in front of her.

She takes no time to respond, probably anticipating my denial. "So why did you leave Chivasso for seven years?"

"I was busy. I...I was working and school was intense. Lost track of time." Suddenly the lack of air conditioning makes its presence felt. A bead of sweat forms at my hairline. I need to go home and have a cold shower.

"But you didn't even come to Christmases or Easters, not Anika's birthdays or Dante's graduation. To me, that's the definition of running away."

"Are you fucking analyzing my schedule? Should I write the time and date of the next time I'll be in town?"

"Only the celestial phase and coordinates of your exact location."

I roll my eyes now, frustrated, turned on. If only she knew how twisted our fucking families really are. "This conversation is over."

I'm walking toward the exit, my T-shirt feeling itchy and tight against my skin. *Calm the fuck down.* Only twenty-five stairs to the downstairs exit. But then I hear it. Those same quiet footsteps behind me.

"Why is this conversation over? I left, too. I just wanted to compare notes. What's fucked you up so badly?"

I turn around abruptly and the suddenness causes Magdalen to slam into my chest. Our faces are inches apart and I step closer so that I'm looking down at her. My eyes find hers, seeing her searching for an answer in my gaze.

"I told you I didn't run away from anything. That's all you fucking need to know. And no offense, really, but we're not friends like this. I don't really care why you left, so if you could mind your own shit, Magdalen, that'd be brilliant." She looks at me, shocked.

Let it go, Magdalen. For the love of Christ, let it go.

Before I step back, my eyes selfishly find her trembling lips and I swallow a groan before turning around again.

Speeding down the spiral staircase, I'm about to turn left to exit the building when it dawns on me that her gentle footsteps behind me have stopped. Of course they have, you idiot. Why the fuck would she want to follow you now? Stealing a final glance, I look up to see her at the top of the staircase, hovering above the second step.

"Nice one, Theo. No wonder I never talked to you."

Mustering the final blow, I spit out, "Let's keep it that way, yeah?"

"You got it." Nodding to herself, she disappears into the darkness with a sharp turn.

"Fuck this shit." My hands slam against the handlebar of the exit, the door hitting the wall with a thud that makes me cringe. I always left the anger outside the museum. Even when I was grounded, hungover, or pissed off at Dante, once I walked inside, one deep breath could settle my nerves. I quickly look back at the walls to see if I left any indentation, but thankfully, nothing is there. Things are already slipping and it's been less than a week. I haven't even spoken to my father alone yet.

When I get outside, the bright sunlight makes me squint. I walk blindly back to the car, my hand above my eyes to try to make out the shape standing in the parking spot next to my car. *For the love of god.* It's not even 8 a.m. and this has turned into the worst day of my life.

"Just because it says Sinclair doesn't mean you can park here, Theo."

My skin crawls at the sound of his voice. Just my luck. In the bright morning light, his face looks sallow. Creases around his mouth and eyes expose his age, gray highlights weaving through his hair. But he's dressed in a crisp white shirt and fitted navy trousers, looking the part of wealthy museum owner and silver fox.

"I was just leaving."

"So what's your verdict on the museum? Up to your

standard?" He smirks and locks his car, walking toward the entrance where I stand.

"It looks the same."

He smacks his tongue. "That's it? It looks the same? Give me something more, son."

"Fine. You want my opinion? You haven't changed one goddamn thing in seven years. That's fucking lazy."

"Watch your mouth." He's next to me now, both of us 6 foot 4, each of us trying to be a little taller.

"What? You wanted my opinion, *Papa*."

"We haven't had a decline in attraction."

Why is he trying to prove the success of the museum to me?

"Good for you. What about special exhibitions? I heard Oxford just had a recent excavation. Have you reached out to them for a loan?"

"You know how I feel about Oxford."

"It's Oxford University. No one gives a fuck that you got denied tenure."

He steps closer, the smell of expensive cologne and after-shave drowning me in the open air. And then his hand is on my shoulder, gripping with force. From the outside, the motion could look endearing. A father giving his son advice. I stop breathing, a Breitling reflecting the sunlight in my eye, as he leans in to whisper in my ear.

"I don't know what's wrong with you, but you're going to cool it down with the attitude, Theo. You stay in my house for the summer, you treat me with a little respect, then you get the fuck out. Now, get your car out of my parking spot.

Last time I checked, you're not the Sinclair with the fucking museum."

Swallowing hard, I shove his hand off my shoulder and step back. He's mad about the spot. I haven't seen him in seven years and he's angry I'm in his parking spot. I laugh to avoid having to look at him. So that the crack in my voice can be masked as purposeful.

"Yes, sir." My voice is rough as I salute my father, my hand coming off my forehead to almost hit him in the nose. "I'm so sorry I've disrespected your beloved museum. Good luck." Winking, I turn to the car and get in and turn the engine on. The wheels squeal as I quickly back out of the spot and give him a final wave through the window. It's only when I'm a few blocks down that I pull the car over, my hands shaking so badly I can't hold the wheel.

17

MAGDALEN

Sitting on the leather-tufted bench in the middle of the gallery, I try not to feel bad for myself. Theo, for the second time today, has managed to make me feel worthless. Is there something about me that makes people angry? Even my own mother could find a way to hate the way I blink. And now Theo. Angry for patching me up, for driving me, for talking to me for longer than ten minutes. But as much as I want to hate him, I can feel that there is something bigger looming over him. If I squint my eyes and tilt my head, I can almost make out its shape above him.

But that doesn't mean it hurts any less.

I hear someone walking up the stairs and hold my breath, fighting my usual instinct to hide. Gripping a leather button, I relax the rest of my body and pretend to be admiring one of the coffins. At any other time, I wouldn't need to pretend. Although I'm the odd Savoy out, ancient Egypt was childhood. Sand dunes and Pharaoh statues, malachite and galena into kohl eyelines. We gathered around the fire on Fridays and listened to my father's adventures sleeping with scorpions in Luxor.

But then I read *Persuasion* at an impressionable age and

everything changed. My childhood was inherently masculine. Stories of Ra and Atum, the gods of Egypt, felt dipped in a boldness and vigor I could never relate to. Falling asleep to stories of creation and cataclysmic beginnings started inadvertently making me feel very small. What are my tears to the tears that created men and women?

But one of the books my mother came home with from the library was Jane Austen. We were fluent in English by then, but she still insisted on making me read at least one English book a month. And there it was, sitting on the kitchen table. It was a yellowing Bantam Classic edition with a portrait of a very pale Victorian woman on the front clad in black, eyes distant with what seemed like despair. Did my mother leave this book on purpose? Did she see how my eyes looked like hers? Or was it a blind choice off the trolley of unstacked books?

Either way, opening that first page felt like teenage rebellion. Anne and Wentworth's ache made me tuck my knees between my chin and sigh until I was so deflated I couldn't fathom why my stomach felt like it was burning a hole inside itself. Because even after Captain Wentworth went to sea and Anne felt old and unlovable, after a war, after death, after seven years of lost time, there was hope tucked in between the words of a letter. Enough hope for them both.

So I wanted to learn more about war. There were absences in Austen's story. What did Wentworth see those seven years? How much of him did he have to leave at sea? Needless to say, the decision was a shock to my family. Random.

Irresponsible. For weeks, my mother told me how careless it was to learn a new history when we had one at our doorstep.

"How could you do this?" She pulled at her hair. "It'll destroy your father!"

As suspected, Papa agreed with a resigned sigh. A nonchalant shrug. I didn't ask for much, so it felt like I had earned the right to choose this path. So I closed my door after dinner one night, quietly turned the key in the lock, and leafed through the pamphlets my guidance counselor thrust at me when I mentioned literature, the turning point that sent me to Oxford.

The click of shoes draws me away from my thoughts and I look up. Maybe Theo has come back to apologize. To confess. But even as I think it, I know these are wishes. The Sinclairs do not apologize. To apologize would imply they could make mistakes! And the Sinclairs do not make mistakes. I turn my head to look, and see it's definitely not Theo.

It's his father.

Dexter Sinclair, much like his son, is an enigmatic figure I was cautious of even as a child. Perhaps it was his height. Standing at 6 foot 4, it felt like he lived on beanstalks and ate children for breakfast all the way up there. Or maybe it was how his face turned red and sweaty after every family dinner from too much drink, his arm snaking around my mother's waist, a spot that I knew to be reserved only for my father's hands. His Scottish accent was harsh, brute strength in his speech. He was opinionated, loud, never seen without a suit. But as I grew up, the fear dissipated and transitioned into cautionary respect. We were proud to live next to a man that had accomplished so much and looked that good doing it. In almost every way, Theo took after Dexter's unnaturally good looks.

"Good morning, Dexter," I say from the gallery. He looks up abruptly, his face full of irritation before registering it's me and masking it with cool appraisal.

"Good morning, Magdalen." His voice is smooth, and he halts in place when he sees me. It's hard not to gawk as he sweeps a hand casually through his hair so similarly to Theo. He steps forward, one hand holding an expensive leather briefcase while the other finds the pocket of his trousers. In the dimly lit gallery, Theo and Dexter are almost identical and it makes my heart pang. So this is what he'll grow up to be. Beautiful until the end, gray hair and all.

Dexter stands right above me so I have to crane my neck to look at him.

"Did you catch Theo outside?"

His lips fall in a thin line, already failing to hide his agitation. What is it with the Sinclairs and their temper?

"Yes," he sighs, squeezing the bridge of his nose. "I forget how stubborn he is."

Bending to place his briefcase on the floor, he silently asks for permission to sit next to me. I hesitate, pushing down the sickly feeling at his edging closeness. *Don't be ridiculous,* my mind screams. *He's your father's best friend.*

I scoot over, suddenly wishing I'd never said good morning. Wishing I hadn't asked Theo about things he's too afraid to speak of. Sneaking one last glance at the stairwell,

I slip a silent plea to Theo between the time it takes for the tip of Dexter's shoe to graze the side of mine.

"He's just readjusting to Chivasso. Americans can be very different from Italians. Give him a minute." It feels like a vague enough thing to say that will both defend Theo and support Dexter.

He sighs for what feels like the tenth time since he's arrived at the museum and I begin to feel bad for him. If he were an artifact in the museum, he would be titled *Father in Pain, erected in Torino. Medium: spirit and flesh, failing heart. Loss of breath.*

Both elbows rest on his knees as he hunches forward, the movement closing the gap between us so that his knee briefly grazes mine. My leg goes rigid as the expensive fabric of his trousers touches my skin. God, here is a man in so much distress he's physically recoiling into himself, and I find a way to feel anxious. That's my issue. I never know what other people are trying to say without words.

Feeling childish and brave, rebelling against no one but the painful throb of my heart, I place my hand on his shoulder and gently rub my palm back and forth. It's how my father comforted me when I found the crab-apple pudding Anika and I made for faeries in the trash. "Life has a funny way of surprising us," and it was such a *him* thing to say that I closed the garbage lid and gave a throaty laugh.

When I touch Dexter's shoulder, the warmth and stability that I know my papa to have is absent from the cool fabric of his suit. I remove my hand, lowering it onto my lap.

"Theo has always fought me at every turn. I say black,

he says white. I want him to go to university in Sweden, he manages to go to Yale. I don't know where I went wrong. When the moment he started hating me was, I just can't figure it out." He grips the roots of his hair as if trying to physically pull the memory from his brain. "Every football game, every birthday, every award ceremony. I was there, front row, waiting and watching. I got him his first watch." He laughs, but it's forced and awkward. "It was the only thing he didn't take to college, left in the middle of his bed. Always ready to pick a fight." I could see the energy draining from him. His skin looking more translucent. The silver in his hair now a sad, dull gray.

This was new information to me. I had always assumed that the Sinclairs were a close-knit family judging by the smiles shared behind the cigarettes and *caffè* after dinner.

"Have you tried talking to him about it?" I say this because, what else do you say?

"Theo prefers actions rather than words."

I frown. What on earth does that mean?

Before I can even begin to try to muster something to say, Dexter places a hand on top of mine. The edges of his palm graze against my thigh and I stiffen involuntarily. "I'm sure he'll come around eventually. Don't worry yourself."

My mind whirls. What an odd thing for him to say. Here I was believing I was comforting him, when in reality he was reassuring me?

"Yeah, me too." I crack a smile that I hope is enough to end whatever heart to heart this is turning out to be. He briefly squeezes my hand before letting go.

"Well, I guess I should try to get some work done. Busy days before the wedding. Your mother is calling our house nonstop in preparation." He nods to me one last time and then he's gone.

My wrist twitches. What on earth just happened? One moment I was fighting with Theo, the next his father was confessing family secrets to me at eight in the morning. This entire interaction played out like I was a priest behind the confessional that Dexter offloaded his burdens to and then walked away. The spot on my hand where he touched me feels dirty. Dexter used me to forgive his own sins! My head swarms to find sympathy, replaying how his brows furrowed in pain at the mention of his son. Clearly the man is upset, and I should be concerned for him. But there's a stronger, more potent feeling of aggravation for his blame on Theo alone. It's pathetic, I realize. He's a pussy.

18

THEO

After a few days of sunbathing and driving around Chivasso, soaking up everything I had missed, I decide it's finally time to go see Giuseppe. The neon light flickers sporadically on the cafe's window, tiredly screaming L'ESSENZA when it has the energy. Once, this place used to be where we came to feel like adults. I shift my glance to the table underneath the faded landscape of the Ligurian coastline. This was where the boys from school sat every Thursday afternoon. We'd hide our uniform ties in our backpacks. Enduring the bitter taste of espresso burning our throats, silently masking our grimaces after each sip. I would lick my gums to get rid of the aftertaste while eyeing the sugar, then look away because no one else would make the first move. The tired doorbell jingles as I enter and I stifle a smile. The cafe is small, with torn leather booths and scratched plastic tables, and the smell of freshly pressed coffee is strong enough to make me pause at the front door.

A patch of light warms the table in the back right; the laminated corner is chipped, revealing a cheap plastic interior. I slide into the booth of the table when I hear the familiar throaty voice of the owner, Giuseppe, yelling at one of the waitresses.

"*Questi biscotti sono grandi come me! Nessuno vuole una bocca piena di impasto. Cazzo, cazzo, cazzo!*" *These cookies are as big as me! Nobody wants a mouth full of dough. Fuck, fuck, fuck!*

I dip my head, silent laughter causing my shoulders to shake. Giuseppe comes barrelling through the cafe, a yellowed apron tied around his stomach. He's bigger than I remember. Gray stubble covers his thick neck and face, and his cheeks are bright red, shiny from being in the hot kitchen. He coughs and the sound is painful, coming out more as a wheeze. I frown; that's stronger than I remember, too.

Hearing the bell ring, he searches the place, which is empty besides the seat I occupy, hands on his hips, and I can see the anger resurfacing as he starts to think someone is playing a prank on him.

"*Lo sai che fai il peggior caffè di Torino?*" *You know you make the worst coffee in Torino?*

His head jerks toward the sound of my voice and his big belly ripples with the sudden movement. A dirty rag appears from his back pocket and he wipes his face with it.

"*Mio dio, Theo? Il re è tornato?*" *My god, Theo? Has the king returned?*

I feel a blush creep up my neck at that word again. *King.* What the fuck about me is royal?

"All right, all right. How are you, Giuseppe?" I go to stand up and greet him but he immediately shoves me back into the booth with surprising force.

"Enough of this bullshit. You sit while I make you our new *caffè*. You're going to love it. Imported. From fucking Egypt. And the tourists love that shit, like it's part of the museum. Cost me half my dick but you've never tasted anything like it. It's like drinking from a woman's tit." He laughs and claps his hands together, his body wiggling with delight as he squeezes himself behind the counter. His back is turned, fingers grinding coffee beans while steaming milk with the other hand and the back of his shirt is covered in sweat.

"So cut the bullshit, little man. Right now, on the spot, how are the women? I've been fucking stuck here in this bullshit cafe my whole life and it looks like I'm never going to fucking leave. People want coffee on fucking Christmas Eve. Jesus Christ was born and you can't make your own cup of goddamn coffee with your family? Losers. This town is absolute trash, I'll tell you. Jesus, fuck. But from the movies I imagine the woman, you know...blonde wig, blue spandex bathing suit, long fucking legs. Did you meet anyone who looks like her?"

"You're asking if I fucked Julia Roberts?"

"Yeah, or anyone who looks like her. Giuseppe doesn't exclude."

"I was pleasantly surprised with the extra-curricular activities." A smirk pulls the corner of my mouth, recalling the long nights at Yale's resident campus bar. Well, I'm not going to lie.

"Oh, you little fucker," Giuseppe screeches. "I should poison this coffee right now, this is so unfair." His mumbles become intelligible as he begins the sacred process of assembling the cappuccino. A priest of steamed milk and espresso beans, we witness something holy when Giuseppe makes a drink.

Head bent down in concentration, Giuseppe rotates the cup several times while pouring milk from the pitcher, cursing every few seconds.

Just when I'm about to ask if he plans on putting this cappuccino on display at the museum, Giuseppe grunts happily. With a loud exhale, he leans his elbows on the bar in exhaustion, and pushes the cappuccino toward the edge, beckoning me to come look. I step across the black and white tile of the cafe and approach the cup that sits before me. Peering down at it, my breath catches in my throat.

A crown.

Giuseppe stands with one arm on his hip waiting for me to laugh or applaud his work but I can't do anything but stare. When I left Chivasso, I knew that I had cultivated a certain reputation. From the moment people started telling me I looked like my father, I knew parts of my life would be easy. I could get away with more. Like early-morning driving on the interstate with the sound of liquor bottles sloshing in the back. A makeshift ladder to the tree in front of my bedroom window for girls to leave through. I was reckless and angry but, regrettably, smart. Too smart. So, when I had to wake up those early mornings to travel an hour to school in Torino, writing essays on the back of the school bus minutes before they were due and then having those essays win awards, no one had the right to tell me I wasn't living up to my potential. They were scared. Scared that I could do both so fucking well.

Somewhere between puberty and college applications, there was never a shortage of pleasure just waiting for me to dip my fingers into. Besides my father, the only person to ever call me on my bullshit was Dr. Savoy. But even he couldn't shout *stop* loud enough. So I pretended I didn't hear, and eventually he stopped shouting.

"I'm retired from that life, Giuseppe."

I mean it to come out light-hearted but it sounds more like a plea. *Please don't call me that...I'm trying to not be that person any more.*

I can feel it coming. How easy it would be to slip back into that role, to know exactly what to say to get who I want.

Giuseppe pushes the saucer closer to me, waving his hands in nonchalance. "Kings can't retire. They can only die."

"That hardly seems fair," I say, looking down at the drink, feeling hollow.

"Nothing ever is. Now try my fucking cappuccino."

I bring the edge of the cup to my lips; the ceramic feels cool against the airless heat of the cafe. The foam is thick and warm and as I tilt the cup to reach the coffee, an image flashes of middle schoolers kneeling in pews, giggling over stupid jokes inside the echoing silence of the cathedral. This feels like a sacrament. A tiny cafe with flickering lights, coffee poured like it's the blood of Christ. The liquid hits my tongue and the heat startles me. I continue drinking, the espresso initially bitter, but like a smooth dark chocolate. And, when I swallow, I'm left with an aftertaste of pure sweetness. I've never tasted anything like it.

"Giuseppe, what the fuck." I have to actively hold in a moan.

"I know." He bows, bouncing from foot to foot.

"How the fuck did you make it taste it like that?"

"My dick, I told you. Very flavorful."

"Wow." I pause to finish the rest in a single sip, slamming the cup back into the saucer. "Give me more."

Giuseppe shrugs, obviously aware of his genius. "Coming up, your highness."

"By the way," I ask. "Does Chiara still work here?"

Giuseppe claps his hands. "She's in the back. Let me go get her."

I roll my eyes and ease into one of the bar stools. My descent has begun. The script brands itself into the back of my skull, forcing me to slip into the role I had quit. I stare down at the empty cup, a few foam bubbles popping at the edge of the bowl. It hits me that I no longer pretend to like the taste.

19

MAGDALEN

My feet begin walking before my brain realizes where we're going. Memory is a funny thing. It morphs and expands, adding colors and scents to keep the memories fresh after years of dormancy. But the foundation will always remain the same. Even if the street signs have been worn down and the fountain no longer holds any water, my body knows to turn where the splotch of yellow paint slid onto the sidewalk. That the corner I pass used to smell like baked bread. Farther down the avenue, a pink awning that has been faded by the sunlight prompts me to make another right. The coffee shop to my left with the flickering sign in the window indicates that in exactly two meters Marta's boutique will be in front of me.

My stomach flips.

I've known Marta since secondary school and yet the anxiety never gets easier. Despite being Dante's age, she wasn't afraid to talk to me and Anika growing up. Even back then, she was poking and probing at us. Trying to get us to try on something neon. My heartbeat lurches one final time as my hands close around the doorknob. I'm jealous of people who like to chit-chat.

It's warm inside the boutique. The windows haven't been opened yet and the white floors have absorbed the daylight. Smiling to myself, I see the wire rack on the far-left corner that Marta left because she accidentally spilled a gallon of glue on the floor and could never get it all the way off. Good to know some things never change.

Fabrics of tie-dye and leopard print surround the store. There is nothing but sparkles and shades of neon from what I can tell and I instantly regret coming into the store. As much as I love Marta, I will not be wearing anything bejeweled. It's simply not in my nature.

"*Cazzo.*" The nasal voice comes from behind the counter. "Who let models in my store?" A throaty laugh fills the small space and I instantly regret not wanting to come in. Marta is color. Strength in studded stilettos.

I sigh. "Marta, I know you want me to buy the zebra corset, but sucking up won't get me anywhere near it."

"First off, that would look good on a fucking horse. Second off, I don't lie. If I say you look like a model, take the compliment and fuck off."

I can't help it. A snort of laughter fills me, and I turn to look at her. The tension from this past week leaves me.

From what I learned in England, Marta would be considered the stereotypical Italian. As if she poured the sun onto herself, skin becoming so dark it's almost reflective. Layers of gold jewelry cover her neck and wrists, and her bleached hair is piled high on the crown of her head with no hair tie in sight. And, of course, she is not wearing a bra. I smirk; maybe I'm more Italian than I care to admit.

"So you're fucking back." She raises her hands in delight, her bracelets creating a cacophony of clashing metal that rings in my ears.

"Yes, and I'm in desperate need of something to wear. England is in a perpetual rainstorm, and I have nothing for above ten degrees."

"That's what you get for choosing the literal most depressing country in the entire world."

"Yes, Marta. I know."

"Does the Queen execute you if you wear color?"

"Oh my god, Marta, you're so dramatic."

She circles around me, scrutinizing everything from the color of my nail polish to my split ends, making me feel exposed and immediately less feminine. As if I'm being a woman wrong.

"You're thinner."

"Not a fan of fish and chips." I try to smile but Marta just rolls her eyes, pinching the thinning fabric of my polo. Her eyelids are dusted a bright shade of orange with two matching black hearts on the apples of her cheeks. How on earth does she have the energy to put herself together so early in the morning?

"What are you, a thirteen-year-old boy?"

"I will leave, you know."

"Shut up and let me think."

Pinching my hips, pulling my hair (even though I don't understand what hair has to do with clothing), wrapping her faded measuring tape around my thighs and accidentally groping me, Marta throws piles of clothes on the counter and for an hour I am poked and prodded until I'm sure my skin is raw. Styling people is the only time Marta stops talking and the store is eerily silent as she sighs and murmurs about my too-prominent hip bone or asking me if I ever thought about fake tanning. Only the occasional sound of satin falling from hangers disturbs the long time spent standing. After having closed my eyes and possibly blacking out for the fourth time she took my skirt off, leaving me to stand in only my underwear in the center of her store, she pats my shoulder with a reassuring, "Would I ever steer you wrong?" and lets out a comical sigh as we pass the zebra corset, her eyes practically swelling with tears at the thought of me leaving without it.

Scanning the tags of my new clothing items, she murmurs to herself, "Fuck, yeah. I'm good," and ducks behind the counter, quickly putting more clothes I can't see in my bags. I try to object but when I lean across the counter she shakes her head and shoves my face back, a bracelet hitting me in the tooth.

"Marta, don't even think about giving me anything else. I have enough clothes for the whole year."

Her jaw practically on the ground, she gapes at me. "You're really nothing like Anika, are you? I gave you like ten items, Maggie. That's good for a fucking weekend."

"Do I get a discount at least?" I try to bat my eyelashes, but it just makes Marta roll her eyes. "Since you're making me shop against my will?"

Marta narrows her eyes. "Will you let me put the corset on you?"

"Not a chance, baby." I take out my wallet and reach for my card before she grabs it and begins looking through the card holder.

"Then no discount for you, bitch," she winks, rummaging through my credit cards and, after finding one she likes, swiping it through the machine.

"Thank your daddy for me," she smirks. I try to object and tell her to use mine, but after a moment's thought, I realize my father hasn't paid for anything of mine for the past four years. He wanted me home, after all. He owes me a few skirts.

Pushing the bags toward me, Marta tucks the card back into the wallet and shakes her head. "You're thinner," she repeats.

My throat feels dry. Why is everyone in my life so perceptive? So watchful of my well-being.

I stare down at my wallet, my fingers tracing the pattern of the leather.

"Some days, I would just forget." The words feel like hot cotton in my mouth, never wanting to say it out loud to anyone. Afraid and ashamed of my own weakness. Of how such a privileged little girl could ever think she had the right to feel sad. Afraid to admit that I could stay in bed for three days straight and cry the entire time.

She reaches for my hand across the counter, her metal rings cold against my knuckles.

"We'll remind you." She takes my hand between her own and kisses it with a loud smack. The outline of bright pink lipstick stains my skin and I'm flooded with warmth. I don't deserve all the goodness I am given.

"Thanks, Marta."

"Oh, it's nothing. Thank me when you see the thongs."

My eyes widen as she begins to push me through the front doors when we both suddenly come to a standstill. Marta slams into my back, propelling us out of the store and onto the sidewalk, where we see him across the street. Faded blue jeans, a thin cotton T-shirt, and overwhelmingly manly. Theo stands tall, his lips pulled in an all-too-seductive smirk, and, just as I'm about to smile back, I realize he's smiling at Marta. Right. He thinks I'm nosy. And obsessed. And he regrets wasting his Friday evening dissecting my bloody back. When he finally looks at me, his smile disappears. My gaze dips to the cobblestone, ready to quietly go whichever direction he chooses not to. Wanting to be just a best friend's little sister again. But it's too late to pretend we haven't seen each other, and Theo is not one to hide. When my ears finally hear something past the loud pounding of my chest, I realize Marta has reached her full pterodactyl volume as she screeches at Theo to come over. He salutes her and begins walking toward us. I stare at the sidewalk, the piece of gum wedged between the cobblestones becoming extremely interesting.

Don't be a pussy.

Trying to fake confidence, I look up. But my stomach flips when I see Theo already staring at me. Piercing gray eyes giving nothing away. His gaze travels from the bags in my hand to the fading bruise on my forearm, and rather than meeting my eyes, he looks down to the sliver of my stomach showing. I hold my breath, feeling flushed. When he finally looks up to my face, he clears his throat and attempts to give me a smile, but it feels unnatural. As if he's only smiling at me for Marta's sake.

"My fucking god, you're aging like fine wine, Theo."

"Marta, we're the same age." Theo runs a hand through his hair with exasperation and I'm enveloped in his familiar scent. Clean laundry and something entirely personal, to just him. I want to breathe in, to understand what exactly it is that makes me want to bury my face in his chest and drown in it. Ridiculous. I've spent a week with him, and half of that time he's spent yelling at me. Now suddenly I'm fantasizing about his scent?

But even the fantasy makes me nervous, afraid Theo can somehow read my mind. I take a small step back for the sake of self-preservation. He's just too powerful. And I, as I've come to learn, am entirely too inexperienced to be around someone like him.

It'll always be me who gets hurt, reading into signs that aren't really there. Romanticizing the slight graze of hand.

But immediately after I step back, I know I shouldn't have. Marta and he speak in rapid Italian, throwing insults and inside jokes so I think my movement will go unnoticed. He continues to talk to Marta, feigning exasperation at another one of her flirtations, yet he looks directly at me, raising an eyebrow, chastising me with a second-long glance. Letting me know *he* knows what I did. All while claiming he doesn't remember Marta flashing him on a dare in grade twelve. Gracefully, he puts his hands in his pockets as he continues to talk to Marta, and I think I'm off the hook, but then he's asking Marta: "So what have you convinced Magdalen to buy?" His voice is deep and frustratingly suave. I roll my eyes at his ability to make me feel like a child.

"The basics. Latex corsets, lace garters. Lots of thongs."

Theo eyes the bags for a second too long and for a moment I think he's going to grab them.

"She's kidding," I interject, even though he still refuses to look at me, so instead my comment is directed at that gorgeous piece of gum on the sidewalk.

Marta snorts, "No, I'm not."

My cheeks flare. "Marta, tell me you didn't."

"Okay, I didn't." She taps her chin with her long nail, obviously lying.

"I'd be more than happy to check," Theo's voice cuts in, and I defensively clutch the bag to my chest and this time the step back I take is deliberate, wanting Theo to know he will never get to see the contents of this bag.

"No, very unnecessary," I croak.

"You and I both know that won't keep me away." He takes a step toward me and the grip I have on the bag falters slightly.

Marta clears her throat, looking from Theo to me with clear suspicion. "Okay, well, this has been great." Clapping her hands together, she winks at Theo and then starts walking back toward the shop. "Looks like you two have some catching up to do."

"We really don't," I say just as Theo says, "Thank you."

Opening the door to the shop, she turns around one final

time and looks at me, humor now gone, and nods. "Remember, we'll remind you."

And then she's gone, hands waving excitedly inside the boutique when she finds a woman browsing her mini-skirts.

"So, what will she remind you of?" The sunlight hits his hair, causing him to look radiant, and I roll my eyes at how unfair it is that he wakes up looking like that. So unfair.

"None of your business."

"Why? I'm very good with business."

"Are you stalking me? It seems I can't go anywhere these days without you right behind me."

"Yes, Magdalen. I'm stalking you."

"Oh," I say dumbly. "I'm quite boring to be stalked."

"Not when I know you have a pile of latex corsets and thongs in that bag." His eyes flash with amusement.

"Why, want to borrow them?"

"How'd you fucking know."

I don't even try to hide my laughter, my stomach cramps as I double over, a mixture of wheezes and incoherent sounds escaping me, and when I try to stop the image replaying it just begins the process all over again. A warm hand settles on my arm, squeezing affectionately. He murmurs "dork" under his breath and my heart flutters. He sighs before quickly taking the hand off and clearing his throat like he didn't mean to say anything, so I stare at the walkway, confused and not ready to look at him yet. I place my hand over my mouth to control my breathing and, when I look up, Theo's head is tilted, eyes narrowed as if trying to dissect me with his eyes. A small smile and he shakes his head, looking exasperated. I arch my back to stretch the overused stomach muscles and squint back at him.

"What?"

"Your laugh is really ugly."

I gasp, raising my hand to push his chest, but he catches my wrist before I can make contact. "Take it back!" My breath stops, unsure if I should pull it away. I'm trying to hold on to the anger, to remember how out of line he was, how small he made me feel. He looks down at our intertwined fingers, a slight frown on his brow, as if deciding whether to test out a secret desire. *What could you possibly desire, Theo?* I want to ask. But I don't.

"Can't take back what's true, baby."

My cheeks burn at the pet name. I'm too old to have a crush on my best friend's brother and the cliché makes me want to open the bag and show him the contents, to laugh about Marta's attempt to rebrand me, like friends would. But we are not friends; we are in a dark limbo between strangers and acquaintances and every time he touches me he pulls me toward a third exit that I'm unsure he even knows he's walking toward. So I stay silent, words lost as he spreads his fingers over mine and peers down at me, allowing me a final chance to retract my hand. Noticing I don't move, Theo slowly presses our hands against his heart so that my palm is trapped beneath his. I'm engulfed by his strong and warm skin and the feeling makes me dizzy, unsure of what's going on. The force of his grip causes me to step forward and, just like on the dance floor, our bodies are mere inches apart. My pulse quickens as he looks at me searchingly, fingers nuzzling my hand closer to his chest, a thumb brushing across my knuckles. A muscle feathers in his jaw as if realizing how ridiculous we must look, and he drops my hand. Why is it every time he touches me, he looks in pain?

"Are you on your period?"

He chokes on the air, eyes widening at my question. "It ended yesterday. Why?"

So this is why everyone loves him—an answer for fucking everything.

"Well, I just can't figure out your mood swings. You tell me to get in your car, you tell me to fuck off, you tell me *you see me*, you tell me to fuck off." I list each offense on my hand, and wiggle the remaining pinkie. "What's it going to be next?"

He rubs his face with his hand and stares at the boutique for a moment. Humor gone, a thick wave of tension fills the small space between us and I almost want to apologize for making him so uncomfortable. But before I have time to realize how incredibly submissive that would be, he whispers so softly I think it's the wind tickling my ear.

"I'm sorry."

"Not an answer."

"Would you like me to tell you to fuck off, Magdalen? Accept the apology and move on." His eyes darken, daring me to say anything else, and for some reason, his answer sends a wave of heat to my cheeks.

"If that's what you want to do." My voice becomes small, unrecognizable to my own ears.

"What I *want* shouldn't be talked about so early in the morning." His voice is low as his eyes lazily dip to the exposed part of my midriff before looking up at me again. Suddenly feeling dizzy and somehow naked, I can't think of anything to say. My mouth opens but I close it again and, before I have time to formulate any coherent response, he huffs.

"But hopefully, that will be resolved tonight." He is holding a torn piece of paper that shows a scribbled phone number on it. He looks at it again, shrugs, and shoves it back in his pocket.

"Like you never left," I mumble, wanting to escape this awkwardness, mortified that I thought he was insinuating anything remotely intimate with me. I'm the younger sister, and growing a few inches taller doesn't magically change that. Every time I think I am growing up, I'm reminded of how naive I can be. I reach for my bags, ready to walk back to the train station and sulk in my stupidity.

Theo eyes me while pulling out a pack of cigarettes from his back pocket. Observing me with casual indifference, I feel exposed and intimidated under his gaze. Does he enjoy making me uncomfortable?

"And here I thought you didn't keep up with what…" he pauses, lighting one of the cigarettes and letting it hover between his lips, "or who I did."

If there was any air left inside me, I would most likely choke. "More like you never even bothered to keep up with me."

"Semantics."

"Okay," I shrug. "Semantics."

Smirking, he shakes his head disapprovingly. "That's all you got, little Savoy? Okay?"

Discomfort turns into anger. "Should I show you the number of who I'm fucking so we can compare?"

The cigarette in his mouth wavers but his eyes remain fixed on me. Slowly, he plucks it with his thumb and index and exhales.

"Careful—if I find out who, I might not be the only one with a black eye."

"Is that a threat?"

"No," he shrugs his broad shoulders. "It's a promise."

I bite my bottom lip, ready to scream or maybe cry. If I'm not careful, I may just try to kiss him.

"This has been joyous, really, but I should be getting back." I shift the shopping bags I'm holding to my other hand and take a step back.

"You're blushing, Magdalen."

My mouth opens at his audacity. How dare he expose me? It takes all my willpower not to drop my bags and cover my face. "I usually don't talk about fucking before nine."

His eyes drop to my hands and he draws a deep hit from his cigarette, taking his time to answer. "Ah, I see. So when do you talk about it?"

"What?" I say, flustered. "This is ridiculous. We're not friends. We don't need to chit-chat."

"You wound me." His voice drops, and he takes a small step forward. "Am I not your friend, *Maggie*?"

I'm surprised he doesn't say anything about me blushing

again, because this time, I know my cheeks are on fire. Something about Theo calling me Maggie is oddly intimate. It's a name reserved for friends. For people who know me.

"No. I'm afraid you and I are not friends."

"Huh." He mulls over my response, blowing smoke out of the side of his mouth. "Challenge accepted."

"Excuse me?" I choke out. "What challenge? There's no challenge."

"Oh, I'm going to be your best fucking friend this summer."

"Why are you doing this?" I groan, pointing between us frantically. "*This* doesn't need to happen. We've been just fine ignoring each other all our lives. Let's go back to that."

"Now, *friend*." He says the word like a threat, taking another step toward me. "*Friends* show each other what they buy. Let's see what's in the bag."

I scoff. Does he not have a number to dial?

Confused, frustrated and in desperate need of a drink, I settle my nerves and take a step toward him so that I almost brush against his chest. "Only one man gets to see what's in this bag, *friend*. And it's not you." Before he has time to respond, I turn on my heel and walk toward the station, my hands shaking the entire way home.

20

THEO

I don't see Magdalen for another week. The wedding preparations for Lucia consume the entire town as bouquets of flowers and cakes are constantly floating in and out of their house, Vittoria's loud voice echoing between the hedgerows as she argues about how cheap the tulips look. Dante shoves me into his car and tells me his mother is forcing us to buy new tuxedos before the wedding.

"*Cazzo*, learn how to drive, you fucker." Dante slams his hand on the horn of his car and swerves to the left down the steep hill. A few branches sneak in through my open window and almost pelt me in the eye.

"Dante, can you try not to blind me before the wedding?" I grab the dashboard for any semblance of support. The idiot had cut the strap of his seatbelts back when he was trying to outsmart the police after they pulled him over for speeding while not wearing one. Dante gives a daring nod at the winding roads and then jerks the car deliberately so that my body slams into the passenger door.

"Why? So you can keep looking at my sister?"

Silence. We hit another turn and the engine roars as he

shifts gears, the mechanical purring filling the emptiness between us.

"I'm not looking at your sister."

"I wasn't born yesterday, Theo. I've known you for like, nearly twenty years, and I know what it looks like when you want to fuck someone."

Blood roars in my ears at the exposition, struggling to come up with any excuse to deny or steer this conversation in a different direction. I look out the window, watching the cloud bank move lazily across the distant mountains, the sun peeking out through the silhouette of sharp peaks and edges.

"Just because I wanted you to protect her the other week doesn't mean I want to fuck her. I would obviously do the same thing for Anika."

Dante scoffs, pressing on the gas a little harder as we cross the roundabout that leads to the main piazza of Chivasso. "You think you're so slick? Playing the loyal best friend? You're not even back a full twenty-four hours and you're dancing with her at the club behind my back."

Something about the way Dante claims ownership over Magdalen stirs a dark anger in me and, before I have a chance to calm down, to breathe and remember that my loyalty to him should supersede any sympathy for her, the words are out.

"So you're allowed to shove your dick in my sister's face, but when I dance with Magdalen for less than three minutes it's an issue? Since when do you give a shit about who she fucks?"

The car jerks to an abrupt stop at the exit of the round-about. I stifle a curse as my head almost slams into the dashboard.

"So you are fucking her?" Dante yells, whipping his head to look at me. "I swear on my mother's life, I will slit your throat. You little piece of shit. I knew it. I fucking knew—"

"Dante!" I bellow over him. "I haven't touched Magdalen. And I definitely don't want to fuck her. Now can you please look at the fucking road?"

But even the feel of those two words so close together are dangerous, holding secret fantasies between the space that separates them. I squeeze my eyes shut to erase any compromising images, focusing on the blur of coral and pale-yellow buildings that pass us by. Dante murmurs underneath his breath, revving the engine as he continues down the cobblestone road, cursing out pedestrians as we near the tailor's shop.

"Just, don't pull that shit we used to in high school with her. She's not like them. She's just a little different, a little slower than most."

I shove my hand underneath my legs and take a deep breath out, disappointment and realization settling in me as the engine turns off and we sit, neither one of us attempting to leave the car as his words echo through the small space. The words spill before I have time to catch them.

"*Certo*, you know I wouldn't do anything, Dante. It was just a dance to make some creep she knew jealous. We said no sisters, so no sisters, okay? I get it. And, not to mention that I've known her forever—why would I start anything now?" I pause, looking out at the streets and watching the crowds of people standing in front of the *macelleria*, feeling weak. "Anyway, none of this matters because I'm meeting Chiara tonight and I have a feeling I won't be thinking about your sister then."

I hope he doesn't catch on to the slip. That I think about her when I don't have Chiara to distract me. Unclenching my hands, I try to laugh but it sounds hoarse. If Dante notices, he doesn't show it. I open the car door before waiting for a response, needing to escape the sinking feeling that begins to form in the center of my chest. Of a memory unraveled before it has even begun. *It's just a crush*, I repeat as we cross the street. And again, when the bell chimes as we enter the shop. As the tailor measures the width of my shoulders and hands me back my credit card, I repeat it until they are the only words I remember in any language. *It's just a crush, it's just a crush, it's just a little crush.* I've survived worse.

At exactly nine o'clock in the evening, I'm standing outside L'Essenza, waiting for Chiara's shift to end. I check my watch, already wishing I never called her. Too late to bail? My heel shuffles against an upturned stone and, just as I'm about to make my escape, the door swings open and the sound of laughter trails through and Chiara's bright eyes greet me with delight.

"*Ciao, Theo! Come stai?*"

Wrapping her hands around my neck, she squeezes me into a hug; my hands hover at my sides, unsure of what to do with myself. When she unravels herself, peering up at me, her smile is large and promising. "I'm surprised you called. The way you looked in the cafe made me feel like I was disturbing you for asking."

Taking a step toward the cafe window, neon sign flickering as always, I spot Giuseppe behind the bar, back hunched over another coffee creation. We begin walking down the alleys of Via Roma when I spot another cafe across the street and jerk my head toward it.

Palms slick, I ask, "You want a coffee?"

Chiara rolls her eyes, a playful grin taking over her face, and she pats my shoulder. "I serve coffee all day, Theo. I didn't ask you out for more."

I roll my shoulder, feeling fucking stupid. Obviously she doesn't want coffee.

"Sorry. Why did you ask me out, then?"

She sighs exasperatedly, as if my question is boring. Since when did I get bad at this?

"Theo, don't think I don't remember us in high school. We all wanted to be the girl you chose. I gave you my number so you would choose me tonight. Call me nostalgic." A blush creeps up my neck. Her boldness is both sexy and intimidating and, before I have time to answer, she grabs my hand and drags me down the street.

"Come, I know a bar by my house that does the best spritz. Not too much orange. Come, come, slowpoke. I've got things to do." And just like that we are off, Chiara tugging me toward the quiet little bar.

"Haven't had a spritz in ages," I grunt, maybe to myself or

the city. Chiara looks back at me, that devilish smile still on her lips. We turn toward Via Georgiana, and there's a small bar with fairy lights covering the awning and wrapped around the front door, bright reds, greens and blues scattered across the floors and small outdoor tables.

"Sit, sit. Relax." She beckons me to a plastic table out front and I laugh; her directness is hot. Watching her order drinks from outside, she stands on her toes to be seen by the bartender. Her legs are bare; she's only wearing a tiny gingham skirt and cropped tank top. She's incredibly beautiful. Fair skin and freckles everywhere. Short black hair clipped back with a tortoise barrette, sharp angles. But for a brief moment, so quick it's just an image of outlines and colors, I imagine another standing at the bar. Long legs and elbows resting comfortably on the counter. Wondering what she would order and if she would like a spritz, too.

"*Ecco la qua.*"

I blink and Chiara is standing above me, leaning down to place the bright orange drinks on the table before dragging the chair and sitting next to me. Her knee brushes against my outer thigh and, just because I am sick of overthinking, I press into her further.

"Cheers to reunions and long-awaited promises." She laughs and taps her glass to mine and I can't help but laugh with her, the words ringing more truth than I care to admit.

"Thanks for the drinks." I take a sip from the amber liquid, bitter sweetness dancing on my taste buds, but I barely swallow before Chiara pipes up again.

"You were a good fuck, back in the day. You'd better not disappoint me now that you're old and boring."

I snort and almost spit my drink out. Chiara's eyes crinkle with amusement and her unapologetic motive is so fucking attractive, that any hesitations I had fade with each sip I take.

"Ah, I see, so just using me and then sending me back out to the streets?" My eyebrows shoot up in mock offense.

"Oh, Theo. A girl always knows when a man is thinking about someone else." Her tone is light but I can tell she's disappointed. Feeling fucking awful, I make the effort to rest my hand on her knee, rubbing small circles on her thigh, thinking of another girl the entire time.

"Right now, I'm not thinking about anyone but you." My voice is low, a tremor behind the last word that I try to ignore for the sake of us both. She's right. But it's all I can offer right now. She stares at me, a smile touching her lips, but the uncertainty remains. It's supposed to be fun, a night out with a beautiful woman should be the escape I so desperately need. Removing my hand, I take another sip of my drink.

"I really don't care who you think about," she says while reaching into her handbag for a cigarette, "as long as you say my name when you come." I stare at her from behind my glass, finishing off the drink before signaling to the bartender through the window for another.

"Jesus Christ, Chiara." I can't help it. I burst out in laughter, my eyes shut in a combination of mortification and amusement. "Thank you for giving me your number," I say, and now it's her turn to blush, and she leans further into her chair so that her skirt rises slightly, beckoning me to look at the smooth skin on display. "I'm honored to fulfill all your wildest fantasies."

So the night goes on and we catch up on life since high school. By the time I take her hand, warm from the summer heat, the table is left with only discarded orange peels and empty glasses. We stumble together, and I let her lazily lead us up a marble staircase toward her apartment.

21

MAGDALEN

"Anika, if you move one more time, I will honest to god slit your throat," I huff while using the back of my hand to swipe away the hair that has somehow landed on my face. Groaning, she squirms in the wooden chair that's propped in the middle of the backyard, wearing nothing but a faded orange bikini and a pair of Dante's flip-flops.

"It's too hot for this," she complains again, and I remind her that she's the one who asked me to cut her hair for the dinner party tonight. Anika's whining snaps me from my thoughts and I quickly make a show of combing her hair. "My hair is sticking to my tits and I'm all itchy." She tries to wipe away some fallen hair but I grab her wrist.

"Hold still, Anika," I sing-song, but obviously this does nothing.

"But—"

"Hold. Still." I press her back into the chair, which she once again tries to escape from, and finish the grueling process of cutting her long hair, which I have managed to only reduce a few inches. After being cursed out in Italian, English and some French dialect that she refuses to translate, I finally give up.

"All right, you're done. Please get out of my face," I sigh as she grabs the small mirror lying on the grass and looks at herself in the reflection, shaking out the freshly cut strands with her fingers.

"I look so good!" she squeals, and jumps up from the chair, shaking the excess hair off her chest and torso, screaming: "Vittoria, *guarda com'è bello Mag mi ha tagliato i capelli!*" *Look at how beautiful Mag cut my hair!*

She skips over and kisses me loudly on the cheek, while smacking my butt on her way into the kitchen to show my mother her new haircut. I exhale loudly, watching her prance through the sliding doors, their laughter fading as they ogle her hair in the bathroom mirror. Taking the broom from the garden shed, I begin to sweep the ground when I hear the wooden gate creak open.

Dante was in town playing poker with some men from the club, so I expect to see him when I turn to greet the rustling noise. But it isn't Dante. Another crisp white T-shirt that outlines the hard planes of his torso and those blue jeans frayed at the knee. Theo stands next to the tall cypress trees that line the walkway into the garden, leaves brushing his bare forearms as he halts when he sees me. Eyes widening for a moment, he dips his head in silent greeting, looking me over quickly before returning his gaze to my face.

"*Ciao*, Magdalen."

"Back to Magdalen? I was just getting used to Maggie."

"Your name's too pretty to cut short." Stunned, I can do nothing but look at him. He's been here for less than two weeks and already his skin has taken on a deep bronze, the long hair that's curled around his ears is lighter after baking in the afternoon sun.

"Thank you." I know I'm blushing. "*Buon giorno*, Theo." I nod politely and continue sweeping the area, feeling self-conscious and domestic as I do so in front of him. My hands squeeze the broom handle with a little more force than needed when he makes no effort to leave.

I look up at him again, determination not to be made a fool propelling me forward. I promise myself that I will not fall victim to the allure of someone who does not want me.

"Can I help you?" I ask.

"Either you just cut someone's hair or I am witness to the aftermath of extremely kinky foreplay."

Forcing a small smile, I rest the broom on the garden shed and wipe my hands on my torso. "Well, there's a lot you don't know about me." I mean for it to come out as a joke but my voice is too sharp, already failing at my plan to stop a crush before it has space to grow. But if Theo catches my attitude then he doesn't let it show.

"I know," he says with such ease, looking at me with those intense gray eyes so that I want to roll up into a ball and hide underneath the hydrangeas until he goes back to whatever state he came from. But I can't. So I opt for deflection and bend to pick up the towel Anika left, folding it slowly as I think of something to make him leave.

"Dante is at the club playing poker."

"I know," he repeats, this time with a flicker of annoyance in his voice. "Can't I want to see my *friend*?" Despite the warm sun across my back, his deep voice causes goosebumps to prickle my forearm, and I will myself to avert my gaze as he steps closer to me. The familiar scent of him envelops me but before I have time to process his words, that he's here even though Dante is not, he steps past me, the edges of his mouth curling up in a small smile as he settles into the chair. I blink, as if coming out of a spell, and curse myself for being so easily mesmerized by the Theo charm. *Remember, he does not want me*, I try to tell myself, but the words seem so far away with him so close to me. Crossing one long leg over the other, he rests his hands on his thighs and looks up.

"One haircut, please."

"There is absolutely no way I'm cutting your hair!" I shriek, laughing as I back away from the chair before he has time to hypnotize me again.

"Anika's hair is long—a few inches barely changes anything. But with you—I could seriously ruin your reputation! You could look like Charles the Second or an escaped prisoner." I shake my head. "I'm not going to be responsible for your scorned beauty, no way. There will be a mob of pitchforks at my front door! Do you want me to be executed?" My lungs burn by the time I'm finished, hands on my hips in defiance. But he just stares at me with that same arrogant grin, batting his eyelashes.

"I promise you that a haircut can't take away any of my beauty."

I blush again, realizing I just inadvertently called him beautiful, and tap him lightly on the shoulder. "I've never cut a man's hair before. I seriously don't know where to begin."

Rather than answering, he turns around in the chair to pick up the scissors on the rusted side table, placing them in my open palm. His fingers are gentle around my hand as he pulls me down toward him. I'm fairly certain he can hear my heartbeat by how loud it's pounding and, before I realize what's happening, he brushes his hand through my hair and gives the ends a little tug.

"Good, I'll be your first."

I open my mouth and close it again, words completely lost. My stomach clenches deliciously at his words. Standing back up, I clear my throat and decide to not overthink for once. "All right, fine, *friend*, one haircut coming up."

22

THEO

Oh, this was a bad fucking idea. Promises to Dante and myself broken because of a bathing suit and a stupid pair of scissors. I've never lied to Dante before and now I can't fucking stop. Did I know she would be here when I opened the gate to the garden? Did I wait for Dante to go into town to check if she was home? Coward. But the guilt doesn't outweigh how much I want her, so here I am.

"Is that okay?" she says as if repeating herself, and I snap out of my daze.

"Sorry?" I glance at the gate, feeling like a child caught stealing a cookie. "What'd you say?"

"I'm going to have to get your hair wet, so is it okay if your shirt gets wet?"

She stands behind me, leaning over my left shoulder to look at my face, her long hair falling in waves over my skin.

"Ehm, I can just take it off—if that's okay?"

She shrugs, tucking her hair behind her ear, and comes back around to face me, the faint smell of lavender and honeysuckle disappearing with her. Peeling off the shirt, I'm suddenly aware that I'm half-dressed while all she wears is a pair of faded tennis shorts and an agonizingly small pink bikini top. If this bothers her at all, she makes no sign of it. Her eyes scan my torso, slightly squinting to make out the tattoo that spans across my chest. I wonder if she realizes how much her eyes give away.

"Checking me out?"

"I didn't know you had a tattoo."

Giving a tight smile, I sit back down in the chair, absentmindedly brushing the symbol on my chest. "Just the two. I got them done when I was eighteen."

Memories of Egypt immediately fill my mind, the smell of kindling fireplaces and oud, aching muscles and a sleeplessness bordering on lunacy. Other memories blur and focus, fixed in black and white, hazy from the beers that seemed to grow from within the sand, the only things strong enough to flourish against the heat of Egyptian summers. I barely remember getting the tattoo. The initial sting, perhaps. I woke with a rope tied around my stomach propping me against a nearby boulder while Youssef finished the trail ending on my lower back.

"What the fuck is this?" I jerked against the rope. "I said *small*. This thing goes across my whole fucking chest!" Fear struck me unexpectedly, like sand being poured down my throat. Examining the tattoo on my chest, I could tell it was an ankh. The ancient symbol for the key to life. There could be worse things.

Youssef only pinched my bicep and patted my head. "Snooze and lose," he scolded, and continued the tattoo by the dim light of a single lantern until the first streak of orange was visible in the sky.

"Is it an ankh?" Magdalen asks as her fingers press gently on my shoulders, guiding me back against the chair. I jerk at the slight touch of her, awakened from the buried memory. She seems to realize, and her hand quickly slips off.

It's not you, I want to say, *it's that I want you to keep touching me and I shouldn't.* But instead I shrug, pretending I wasn't even aware of her touch in the first place, and roll my lips together.

"Yeah, it is, but it was done while I was unconscious, so don't read too much into it."

She snorts as she grabs the hose. Why am I being so harsh? I was the one who asked for the fucking haircut and now I'm treating her like it's a nuisance to be around her. As she adjusts the pressure of the water, I fight the urge to glance at the smooth lines of her leg while she bends toward the pipe, thighs flexing while she struggles to turn the faucet. Gripping the sides of the chair, I look forward, wondering why I would ever think this was a good idea. She lets out a frustrated moan when the stream remains weak and I close my eyes, silently cursing myself. This was a horrible idea. Truthfully, I came here to see if the night with Chiara had done the trick, satisfied these urges before I did something stupid. But with her bent over and moaning...I make to stand up and excuse myself before this gets any further, just as her gentle hands come run their fingers through my hair as she stands behind me, gripping the base of my neck to tilt my head back. I stifle a groan, melting into the chair, and I accept that I couldn't leave even if I wanted to.

174

"Tell me if it's too cold," she whispers, continuing to massage my scalp while pouring soft water onto my hair.

"No." My voice comes out strained. "No, it's really okay."

Time slows. A car drives by in the distance. A slight breeze whistles through the tree branches and for a moment I feel so content that my heart constricts. She comes around to step in front of me, wrapping a towel around my shoulders protectively, and parts my hair with a comb.

"Can you..." She bends down to my eye level, tilting my chin up to make sure the parting is even. "Ehm, can you just..." She opens her mouth and closes it again.

"Yes?"

"Open your legs, please?" She cringes at her own words, but the purity of her request makes my heart swell.

Holding a smile back, I relax further into the chair and part my legs for her. "So forward, Magdalen. First my shirt and now you're between my legs? Are you trying to seduce me?"

She steps into the opening, the summer heat radiating off her bare abdomen warms me and I'm practically clawing the chair to keep from touching her.

"Save the flirting for Chiara," she huffs, standing up so that her breasts almost graze my nose as she gathers my hair and begins to cut.

I wet my lips. She's so close that if I leaned just a few inches forward, I could kiss the space between her breasts, drag my tongue across her skin. I'm so lost in the proximity to her that I don't register what she said about Chiara.

"How did you know it was Chiara?" I pull back to find her eyes, but she gasps.

"Oh my god! You can't just move while I cut your hair! That's like haircutting sin number one."

"I don't really give a shit about my hair. How did you know it was Chiara?"

She sighs, running her hand through my hair again so that her forearm brushes against my cheek. God, this is torture.

"It doesn't take a genius to remember you two. Chiara's been talking about you since forever."

I look up at her again and this time my lips do brush against her arm. "Is that so?" I mumble against her skin, drinking in the softness, the sweet smell of sunshine and lavender that seems to come from somewhere deep inside her.

She pauses for a moment, eyes lingering on the spot where my lips connect with her arm, and takes a shaky breath in. "And Anika may have mentioned Chiara's name."

"Ah." Smiling against her arm, I give in and playfully bite her. She gasps, laughing while trying to take a step back. My foot curves inward so that when she tries, she trips on the heel of my shoe and I grab behind her knees to center her.

"That's the first time anyone's bitten me while getting a haircut," she says breathlessly. My hands remain gripping the backs of her thighs and, when I notice, I let them fall.

"Has someone bitten you in a different situation?"

I have no right to ask. No right to sound as irritated as I do. But thinking about someone else's mouth on her is torture. Magdalen clears her throat, laughter dying. I was with Chiara only five days ago, doing a lot more than biting, and here I am jealous of the idea of someone that close to Magdalen.

The soft cutting of hair fills the silence.

"I'm sorry." I clear my throat. "I shouldn't have asked."

She continues cutting my hair, a slight frown pulling in her brows. "Anika is the last person to have bitten me." She examines my hair and evens out the right side, looking unfazed by my invasive question. "I stole her push-up bra in year five." I can see the memory in the brightness of her eyes and my heart beats tenfold at the obvious love she has for my sister.

"She's the only ten-year-old I've ever heard wear a push-up bra."

Magdalen tilts her head to the side, a smile on her lips as her hand brushes my neck to check the ends of my hair. "She stole it from my mother," she continues, recalling the day with warmth. "Except she didn't know you had to stuff them, so they just looked like deflated balloons. That and it didn't fit her, so it kept riding up to her neck."

We both burst out laughing; the image of an even smaller Anika with two deflated lumps around her neck is so vivid it takes us several moments to catch our breaths. Magdalen hums with a smile and crouches to continue the haircut, so close that her breath fans my face. Sweet and floral. I should look away but it's hopeless. I'm mesmerized.

"What were you like in year five?" she asks. Freckles dust

the center of her nose in perfect symmetry, the sun casting a glow across her cheekbones that makes her appear golden and dewy. *Fuck's sake.*

"I was at the school in Torino by year three." My voice comes out rough; the sweetness of her is difficult to drag myself away from, to relive those memories. Magdalen opens her mouth in shock, and I betray myself by sneaking a glance at her lips. Her upper lip is slightly larger than her bottom lip, and I quickly look away before images of her mouth, swollen and glistening around me, threaten to make this haircut painfully unbearable. *Do not, Theo.* I grab the chair tighter.

"Oh, they told me entry was year six."

She drags me from indecency to childhood. And that's when I remember. How could I have forgotten?

"Wait, you went to that school, didn't you?"

Eyelashes fluttering against her cheekbone, Magdalen shyly smiles. "Yes. I'm surprised you remembered with how...busy you always seemed." While she was reading chapter books in the library, I was doing god knows what in the teacher's bathroom.

"I was a fucking prick back then, wasn't I?" The wind seems to have vanished; the only sound is her breathing braided with mine. My fingers ache to touch her again.

"Just back then?"

"Hey." I poke her belly button and she giggles. It's the cutest sound I've ever heard. "I saw you, Magdalen."

"Feels like you may have been the only one." Her smile falters but she seems to realize her slip and steps out of my legs to walk behind me and check the back of my head. "I always found it hard to make friends at that school. Everyone was so serious all the time," she says quietly from behind.

"Yeah, it helped if you knew where to buy weed."

"Seriously, how did they let you in that young? I couldn't imagine being in that school in year three. You were just a baby."

"My father is good at getting his way." Even though I can't see her, I feel her weighing my words and I grow nervous with her thinking about him any longer than necessary.

Quickly, I add another factor. "And I had a private tutor at the school, got to skip year six because of it, so it was kind of worth it in the end."

She pauses, her voice quiet. "Wow. That's intense, even for you. How did you do anything but study?"

I try to brush off her concern but the idea of her worrying about me is so welcome that I struggle to find the words to soothe her. "Have you met Dante?"

"So, if it wasn't for Dante, do you think you would have still been...?

"You can say it, Magdalen."

"I don't know how to say it."

"Would I have come to school drunk and fucked any girl who looked at me?" I provide.

Her hand hovers, but the corner of her mouth raises. "That's not exactly how I was going to phrase it, but sure."

I rub my eyes, feeling tired. Blaming Dante for my teen rebellion feels cheap. I made every choice without any influence. How easily I could have declined it all.

"How would you have phrased it?" My voice is gravel, still exhausted by the reminder of all that anger. Scared at how easily it can resurface.

She has stopped cutting my hair. Scissors dropped on the nearby table.

"I'm not sure." She steps around to face me again, arms crossed in front of her. I look up at her and for a moment that's all there is. Her worry blended with my anger. Confusion and something more. "I'd call them your lost years."

I run my hand through my hair, smiling to find she has only cut it a little below my ears.

"You look hot with long hair," she shrugs apologetically. "Fuck what your dad says."

"You think I'm beautiful *and* hot?"

She blinks innocently, pausing before responding. "Yes, Theo. I do."

My stomach clenches, loving how the word *yes* looks on her lips. I'm so overwhelmed by her that I can't think of anything to say. "Oh," I swallow.

"That's all the big, bad Sinclair has to say? 'Oh?'"

I know I'm going to regret it, but I can't help the words that tumble out. "You're really beautiful, too, Magdalen."

Magdalen pauses, eyebrows raised like she's waiting for me to say I'm just kidding. When I don't take it back, she just rolls her eyes and takes a step away.

"Do you want to go look at your hair? There's a better mirror in the bathroom."

Something about her dismissal doesn't sit right with me. But I don't push it, knowing she's already uncomfortable with the compliment. Standing up, I stretch my arms above my head to wake up the stiff muscles and dust off the fallen hair across my neck. "I trust you."

Magdalen snorts and tosses me my T-shirt. "You shouldn't." She winks and goes to grab the broom that stands against the shed. There she goes again, fucking winking. "Now leave before Dante asks for one as well."

"Thank you, Magdalen."

"Any time, Sinclair. I'll see you later, yeah?"

"I'll be the one with the new hair."

As I walk through the gate, I feel lighter than I have in a long time.

23

MAGDALEN

My hands shake at my sides as I hear the gate close. Taking a deep breath, I sink down in the chair that Theo had sat in moments ago, wondering what the hell just happened.

I gave Theo Sinclair a haircut, shirtless?

I'm not one to fawn and blush over men who keep in shape, but, *fuck me*. Besides, it's not like I have never seen him without a shirt. Years of going to the tennis club with the Sinclairs, swimming in the pool or watching our families play football together have familiarized me with shirtless teen boys. But Theo Sinclair is no longer a teen boy. In fact, the word "boy" feels offensive to describe him. This was different. *He* is different. Was he always this fit? Broad shoulders hardened with muscle spanning his entire body. Tanned skin stained with the dark ink of his tattoos. Painfully sculpted abdominals.

I press my fingers to my temple, trying to shake the image of the tattoos stretched taught against his chest, his shoulder blades. While he was quick to mention the ankh, he didn't acknowledge the scarab on his back. The beetle somehow belongs on him, the hard shell looking ominous and unforgiving, as if it guards him. But what really caught my eye were the wings. Spanning past his shoulder blades and hooked around his biceps, they have become a part of him, giving the illusion of movement at the slightest flex of muscle. And the ankh symbol that rests against his collarbone, historically a symbol of life, somehow looked foreboding on his body. As if warning off anyone who comes too near. *Stay away*, it seemed to scream. *Stay far away from him*. My fingers yearned to trace its outline, drawn to the parallel between the two symbols. The key to life marks his front and yet the symbol of resurrection covers his back. Another mystery. It seems I'm constantly reminded of how much I don't know about him. Dragging me from my daydream, the sliding doors jerk open.

"What are you still doing here?" Anika shrieks as she observes me in my bikini and shorts. "We've got to be at dinner in two and a half hours, Mag! You need to shower and..."

"Anika, I could get ready three times in two and a half hours!" I try to contain my laughter as she walks toward me, utter horror in her eyes.

"But... but there could be men there, Mag! Torino equals city men. Men that will pay for our drinks and date us and not look like they don't know how to do laundry!" Grabbing my wrist, she hauls me off the chair and toward the house. I steal one last look back at the chair and wonder if any of this really happened.

Steam from the shower floats through the bathroom and onto the floor of my bedroom. Shaved, scrubbed and spotless, I scour through the dresses that Marta picked out for me and groan. Tonight, all members of the Savoys and Sinclairs will be together for the first time in over seven years. Seven *years*. There was once a time in my life I thought I couldn't live without any of them. I hold the light pink slip dress and swallow hard.

Anika has picked the restaurant. As per her recommendation, we will be going to a waterside venue looking toward the Po, the longest river in Italy. University had only sticky-table quiz nights at the pub and cheeky McDonald's runs. It's been a while since I've had to actively think about how I want to present myself. Anxiety spreads into the center of my chest, a deep worry at the reunion. There was once comfort in our little quilt of a family, crocheted together with our museum, with faded scopa cards beside the hearth and Cinzia's rosemary lemonade. But now?

I slip off the towel and throw the dress on, then walk to the mirror to look at myself, my toes skimming the bathroom floor.

I grew up watching Theo Sinclair flirt. I can recite his routine, the lazy smile and slow wink, how deep his voice can get when he's in the mood for more. It was fascinating to observe from afar. He had the uncanny ability to make every girl in Chivasso feel like a real woman. He knew where to stare, how to elicit flushed cheeks and nervous laughter. Never once did I imagine being, or even wanting to be, on the receiving end of his charm. Because while those girls felt special for a few hours, blushed and giggled and fluttered their eyelashes in fascination, I also know that they hurt for days after. That something never quite heals when you're forgotten by Theo Sinclair. No man should have that power. It's disgusting and infuriating and anti-feminist, in fact, that we as a collective gender could all be burned by the same, beautiful fire.

I don't want to hurt. And I certainly don't want him to know that I've never really kissed anyone.

I'm embarrassed and ashamed and these firsts were supposed to be had with someone, drunkenly at a pub in Oxford, a place where no one needs to know who I am. For the experience. I've always thought about intimacy as something I need to just get over. Like a driver's test or gynecologist appointment. Something about Theo being the first to experience the messiness of my firsts makes acid crawl up my spine. I'm just the last girl in Chivasso available.

Despite my better judgment, I want him to want me. To be desired for a minute and maybe get to use what he teaches me with someone new, someone permanent. The thought strikes an idea in my mind that makes me pause.

He could teach me.

Is that selfish? No, no. I would be mortified to ask. I physically shake my head enough to dispel the ludicrous idea.

Wiping the steam away from the mirror, I find my reflection and gape. The dress is stunning. Dusty pink silk falls delicately over my body, outlining the shape of my hips, the dip of my belly button, enhancing the swell of my breasts—giving the complete facade of femininity. I smile, silently thanking Marta for her magic touch.

Suddenly the prospect of seeing Theo tonight is less daunting. Do I disgrace feminism for feeling more confident in a little pink dress? Brushing out the wet strands and smothering the ends in an oil Anika brought me from her trip to Nice a few years ago, I shake my head from left to right to get rid of any excess water. Too hot for a hairdryer. Once the blood has settled back into my head, I stare at the makeup bag that sits on the bathroom counter. Bedazzled with my name, it was a present from my mother when I was fifteen. A symbolic metamorphosis from girl to woman disguised in a chrome box with the letters MAG glued on with pink rhinestones. I peer into the box and feel excited for the first time seeing it. It's not so much a desire to change who I am, but a chance to show how I feel from the inside out. Taking a peach-colored blush, I sweep the shade over my cheeks and the bridge of my nose, then lightly on my eyelids.

"Not bad." I tilt my head to the side. Curiosity and a sudden power surging through me at the possibilities of what or who I can choose to be tonight. My hand dives into the chipped box.

Let's see what we can do.

24

THEO

"No jacket?"

My father looks me up and down in the rear-view mirror of the car as he shuts the engine off, turning the cufflink on his own jacket until the initial faces upward.

"Nope."

"You should have brought a jacket." He opens the car door and steps out, walking toward the restaurant, not bothering to wait for any of us. The rest of the family sit in the car in silence, his presence still lingering.

"I think you look handsome, Theo." My mum turns around, trying to find my eyes, but I let my gaze fall toward the gear shift, avoiding the worry that tries to find me in the small car. There is no need to worry, I want to tell her.

Anika shakes her head and adjusts the layers of bracelets on her wrist. "Once an asshole..." she murmurs, and opens the passenger seat on her left, adjusting the bright orange dress so that she isn't entirely exposed. "Come on." Peering her head through the open door, she smiles brightly. "Let's get drunk and chat shit."

My mum scoffs and joins her outside the car, Anika taking her hand and twirling her around. How long will other

187

people have to fill his role? Her arm wraps tightly around Mum's shoulders, so she doesn't have time to remember it should be someone else. The anger settles itself in my gut.

I follow them down an old staircase that's concealed by vines and thick hedges. The pathway is so narrow that I have to turn my foot to fit on the small steps. Humid air surrounds us once we reach the landing by the river. Anika swats a mosquito and curses under her breath while we walk to the table where Dr. Savoy and Vittoria sit beside Lucia Savoy and her new fiancé. The reason that we've all returned.

Lucia and Dante are almost identical, both dark-haired with large brown eyes. They look a lot like Vittoria. Lucia shakes her knee underneath the table energetically and it makes me smile; she's never been able to stop moving in all the years I've known her. Her fiancé, Maio, stares at her with so much fucking love I want to vomit. As she uses her hands to express something wild and dramatic, Maio tilts his head back in open laughter. Pure admiration.

There are about twelve tables along the river, so you can hear the quiet chatter from them all. Laughter filtering in and out—the chime of glasses during a toast. Imbarco Perosino is lit only by candles, which illuminate the entire walkway with a warm glow. Lanterns are placed randomly along the edges or perched on tree branches. Each table has fresh flowers in empty wine bottles with wax dripping from the side. It's pretty. Anika chose well.

Dr. Savoy stands, clapping his hands together at the sight of us.

"Ah! Dexter! Theo!" He dances in place and extends his arms to give us handshakes.

"Too handsome!" He shields his eyes in mock blindness, laughing at his own joke with such enthusiasm everyone else joins in.

"Looks who's talking, old man." I shake his hand and he squeezes briefly, making me look up to see him wink before letting go. Is that where Magdalen fucking learned it from?

I pull out my chair to sit down, and another voice enters.

"*Ciao*, everyone."

It feels like someone has dipped my head underwater, everything becoming blurry and without direction.

Looking up, I see Magdalen shimming between tables to sit near Anika. *Christ.* Is this a fucking joke? Her cheeks glow as she smiles at my mother with such adoration, it almost makes up for my father's lack. "Cinzia! You're an absolute angel!"

My fingers alternate between gripping and relaxing the chair's armrest, counting how many times I flex my leg underneath the table until my knee cracks. *One, two, three, four.* Small, meaningless motions to pretend that I'm not thinking about my best friend's little sister.

"Maggie! You look absolutely beautiful." My mum looks her up and down.

Her voice is breathless, as though she ran to be here. "Thank you. Everything you see, I owe to Marta."

"You're making me feel old, *amore*! Feels like yesterday that you were throwing empty milk bottles at your father's head and now you are…" She makes several gestures with her hands as if trying to encompass the passage of time. "And now you are completely woman!"

Nope. I can't fucking handle this. Turning to face Dante, I force myself to speak, any semblance of a sentence to distract myself.

"So, Dante. What's good with you?" It takes only the single question to trigger a stream of complaints. Settling into my chair, I let his voice dull the noise.

"Oh, only that the bank robbed me today, Jesus Christ." He puts his glass down on the table. "The fucking clerk, who, let's be real, has wanted to fuck me since year nine, decides tha—"

"Dante, language," Vittoria snaps, eyes narrowing in on him.

"I'm twenty-five, Mamma! You can't tell me what I can't say."

Vittoria nods her head as if expecting this. "Whose roof do you live under? Whose food do you eat every night? Until the day I die, I can tell you that the sky is green, *Donnie*. If I hear you take Jesus's name in vain again, you're walking home."

Anika barks out a laugh from across the table and tilts her head at Dante. "Yes, *Donnie*, listen to your mamma."

Dante's cheeks grow pink as he leans forward to address my sister. "Quick question for you, Anika. Super quick. Do you ever stop talking? I'm not sure if you know this, but just because you have a mouth, doesn't mean it has to constantly move."

"Ah, you don't like my mouth moving." Anika crosses her

arms in front of her, a symbolic gesture of a grand defense. "Because you have no experience of talking to a woman?"

"No," I chime in, feeling the need to intervene as older brother and best friend. "No, that's not true, Anika." I look at Dante. "He always talks to his mamma, of course."

Anika snorts and bangs her hands against the table, shouting so loudly the table next to us glances with annoyance. "I forgot how nice it was to have a brother!"

I wink at Dante, who mutters a string of crude curse words in a dialect only he and Anika understand. And while their conversation turns into a messy conglomeration of French and Italian, Jo, the eldest Savoy, settles quietly into the seat next to my father, loudly sighing and nodding at our fathers in acknowledgment while running his hand through his thinning hair. From what Dante's told me, Jo isn't handling fatherhood as smoothly as he does the public relations at the museum. I try to focus in on what the men are discussing but they whisper quietly to themselves, obviously not wanting anyone else to be part of the conversation. Having no desire to speak to my father, I look to my mum and Vittoria, who are occupied with Lucia's arrival. Hands flail while they bombard her and her fiancé with questions about the wedding, pinching her cheeks, and then Maio's, tears erupting at the slightest mention of the museum decorations they have chosen. I stare out at the river, trying to count the ripples of water as the ducks splash the surface.

But then I feel it, *her*.

Don't fucking look, Theo. You know how it'll end. Trying to shake the desire to look at her again, I bite down on my bottom lip until I'm sure I've drawn blood. But it's no use. Just for a second. Just to see if maybe she is thinking about looking at me, too.

I uncross my legs, shift in my seat.

I look. I look and wish that I hadn't, but it's too late now. Her eyes are wide and amused as she looks back and forth between Anika and Dante, laughing as Anika tries to stand up again. Magdalen hurriedly pulls on her wrist to keep her sitting but it's no use, Anika is too strong when she's passionate. Magdalen's arm stretches to reach Anika, causing her dress to raise a few innocent inches. Pink silk pulled taut against her body, showing the delicate shape of her waist. It feels so wrong to look at her and imagine how easy it would be to slip off that dress and watch it float in a puddle of silk by her ankles. I hear myself coughing before I realize I am, something physical to shake the thoughts out of my mind.

Dante whips his head round at the sound. "You good, bro?"

His concern causes everyone at the table to turn their heads and stare at me. And, despite everyone watching, waiting for a response, I open my mouth to find I can't answer. Magdalen shifts to look at me. Our eyes meet and because there's still a chance to pretend, I know that for as long as she lets me, I cannot look away. The familiar pink stains her cheeks but her gaze does not falter. Instead, she raises her eyebrows, silently challenging me to look away first. I sit forward, my eyes remaining fixed on her as I casually lean my elbows on the table, trying not to smile at her adorable determination. Not a chance, Magdalen.

"Yeah, I'm fine." The words release everyone from having to stare but instead of directing it toward Dante like I should, I hold her gaze. Vittoria and Mum continue to chat; our fathers shake their heads about something ancient and troublesome, no doubt. I feel everyone settle back into routine but she continues to look, head tilted in amusement, lips quirked in a tempting smile. And, just as I'm about to say something to her, Dante uses his knife to tap on the side of his wineglass loudly.

"I'd like to say something." He looks toward me and for a moment I think he caught me staring at his sister. My blood goes cold. Trying to replay the moment to see if I was that obvious, feeling guilty when he so clearly said she was unavailable to me. Turning my body away from her, I grab my wine glass so harshly it spills over the edge and onto the tablecloth. Clearing my throat, I wait for Dante to continue. He looks at me again, then Magdalen, and then breathes out through his nose before glancing at the rest of the party.

"I'd like to say that I believe love is a rare thing that not everyone gets a chance at."

Anika tries to snort but I can tell she's caught off guard. Dante is rarely serious.

"When Lucia told us she was getting married, I don't think anyone was shocked. She's always been the bravest of all of us. I think love is the scariest adventure of all," he chuckles self-effacingly. Anika smiles quietly, looking toward Lucia proudly.

"It's a brave thing to know what you want. Even braver

to seize it. You traveled the entire world and knew that your heart was always down the street." He stares at Lucia and Maio, who clasp hands tightly underneath the table. His voice cracks. "Congrats, you fuckers." He raises his glass, shrugging before downing the entire drink. "Sorry, Mamma."

Immediately as he sits down, Lucia runs around the table and embraces him from behind.

My father claps loudly, rubbing his eyes as if annoyed. "All right, enough with the sop. Why don't the kids get their food first." He gestures to the buffet up the stairs and goes back to downing his drink. How many has he had since we got here?

I shake my head and stand up with the rest of the *children*. Dante, Anika, Lucia, Maio and Jo begin walking toward the buffet that hides behind the hanging vines and up the small wooden stairs. But from the corner of my eye, I see Magdalen quickly step in front of everyone and jog up the stairs, disappearing behind the greenery. I frown. Where the fuck are you running to?

25

MAGDALEN

Smoothing down my dress, I take a deep breath and step into the buffet room. The inside of Imbarco Perosino is dimly lit by candelabras scattered throughout the small space and, while beautiful, it's almost impossible to see where you're going. In the center of the space are the two oak tables draped in heavy tablecloths with silver platters of food. But my eyes barely glance at the dishes. I brush past the couple in front of me, squinting to make out which one he is, but their uniforms are all the same. I clear my throat. He left, which is understandable. I shouldn't have expected him to wait for me when he's clearly working. Walking toward the table, I pick up a plate and stare at the food without really seeing anything. My hand extends to the serving spoon when I feel someone tap my shoulder.

"I told you to wait for me," a deep voice startles me. "I can get you the good stuff." Spinning on my heel, I see Roberto standing with his hands clasped behind his back, one eyebrow raised as he eyes the empty plate.

Setting the plate down, I turn to face him and we both look at one another for a moment before laughing in unison.

"I looked for you!" I squeal, not recognizing the high tone of my voice, of this girl who sneaks off to look for boys while at a family dinner.

"What? For three minutes? I had to restock the napkins in the back." He continues smiling, humor clear in his eyes. "I wouldn't ditch you, Mags."

"But, the food—"

"Ah, I should have known. You only haven't seen me in, what, two years? But the food, yes. The food is obviously more important."

"Are you done, Roberto?"

"Are you going to give me the hug I've been waiting for since I heard you were back?"

I sigh, feeling glad for Roberto Almeno, the only boy from secondary school I ever spoke to. He was a theater kid with the voice of a young Ezio Pinza who biked to the tennis club almost every day after school. We didn't talk much, but we saw each other enough for me to almost feel comfortable around him.

Lifting my hands up, I stand with open arms waiting for Roberto to hug me.

"Finally," Roberto grins as he scoops me into his arms, my legs dangling off the ground for a moment as he squeezes me tightly.

But as he sets me down, another voice interrupts behind us. My heart sinks. I hate how aware I am of Theo's presence. Roberto laughs about something but I can't hear anything, my mind only on Theo standing behind me. When I turn around, pretending to focus on a napkin that has fallen, I look up to see him at the far end of the buffet table. He says something to Dante but stares at me with an empty plate in his hand. I smile. What else should I do? He sighs, looking down at his empty plate for a long moment before looking back up and returning a lopsided grin. It isn't a smile with any particular layers. I remind myself that he is not jealous or even mildly interested in my conversation with Roberto, because we're *just friends*. He was curious for a moment and then his curiosity was satisfied. This is what friends do. We smile, we acknowledge, and we move on.

"Would you want to?" Roberto asks.

Embarrassed that I've not heard a single thing he's said, I nod my head quickly without knowing what I'm agreeing to. How is this possible? Just moments before, I was seeking Roberto out. And now a weird emptiness carves itself through me, painfully. Like someone is taking a blunt knife and tracing the ridges of my ribs over and over. I want Theo to care. A stupid fantasy for girls who read too many romance novels.

"How about Thursday night? I can come to Castagneto Po? Haven't been there in ages. Does that little cafe still exist down the hill?" He motions a hill with his hand, making big and obnoxious gestures to visualize the cafe. I already wish I never hugged him.

I laugh even though nothing is funny. "Yes, it's still there."

"Good." He fidgets with the strap of his apron. "I'll meet you there Thursday."

"Okay." I try to smile. Overcome with the dreaded revelation at how much I want Theo to care.

"Nine, okay?"

We step to the side as Dante reaches for a crab leg, oblivious it's me in front of him.

"That's perfect." The words feel stiff and inauthentic, but Roberto doesn't seem to notice. My mother used to tell me to think of a remote controller when I felt like crying. She would say to imagine your finger pressing down on the fast-forward button to skip past this sadness and pause on another feeling. You can go back, she would say. But you can also go forward.

"Duty calls, I'm afraid. Crab legs need serving." Roberto squeezes my shoulder and turns back toward the kitchen.

I'm aware of the muscles on my face and how if I press my teeth together and raise the corners of my mouth it could pass as a smile. I look around to see members of my family scattered about the open restaurant. Jo looks disgusted as he picks up a piece of bloody lamb with the tongs. Anika chats away in his ear about something he couldn't care less about. Lucia fixes Maio's plate for him even though he is standing next to her. Dante speaks to a female waitress with a huge grin on his face. Her back is to me, so I'm unsure if she reciprocates.

"Not a fan of crab legs?"

I turn my head to see Theo on the opposite side of the table looking at my empty plate. The tightness in my throat is so intense that I have to think about breathing in order to get air inside my lungs.

"Um, actually, no." I try to ground myself. "Never been one for crustaceans."

"Then you're probably in the wrong section."

I look down to see that I've been standing in front of the shellfish this whole time.

"Right," I start to turn. "Guess this sun is getting to my head."

"We can't have that. Your brain is worth at least sixty thousand."

"My brain is far from precious. I'm an English major."

"Agree to disagree," he says roughly while shoveling some prawns onto his plate.

Staring at the pink prawns with blurry eyes, I know I have to get away from him. "Guess I better find a table without sea creatures, then."

Just as I turn away, I hear his deep voice. "So who was the guy with the apron?"

My back stiffens and I decide to pretend I didn't hear him as I walk to the other table. It's better this way. To pretend. Fingers gripping the ceramic so tightly my joints lock in place.

Dinner drones on. It's been over three hours, and no one looks particularly eager to leave.

"Theo, you've never had a responsibility in your life. Don't try to weigh in on something you have no idea about."

My eyes shoot up to see Dexter, eyes bloodshot and ugly, waving a hand away at Theo. When he lifts his arm, his shirt is soaked in sweat.

"Nice one, Papa. Very clever."

I try to make eye contact with Theo, to let him know that I recognize Dexter's absurdity, but he's focused only on his father.

"Tell me it's not true! I mean who got you the job at the museum in New York, hmm? And the internship in Greece before that? Once you understand real life, I'm all ears to your suggestions."

Papa sighs, as if accustomed to this, and it strikes a nerve in me, his passive acceptance. It feels like his responsibility to interfere, and maybe I secretly believe it's always a father's job to intervene. But as I look around, everyone watches in silence. Vittoria, smoothing out perfectly folded napkins. Dante, playing with the stem of his wine glass. I want to rip the tablecloth off and scream while Anika clears her throat and looks toward the river. *You always have something to say! Why are you letting him talk to your brother like that?* But I realize that Anika's loudness doesn't necessarily equate to her bravery. My hands tingle with the intense desire to slap her. To shout: *LIAR.*

"I don't think you want to talk about real life," Theo says, his voice low and controlled.

Dexter's eyes dart toward Papa and then he sighs dramatically. "Aren't you tired of being the poor, broken boy who hates his father? I thought you were smart enough to not be such a fucking cliché."

"I once thought *you* were smart, but it looks like we were both fucking wrong."

"Oh god, here we go again. Why don't you leave if you hate us so much, Theo? Go. No one's missed your dramatics. We were just fine without all this."

Cinzia clutches her napkin but remains quiet, letting Dexter continue.

"I'm not fucking here for you," Theo spits out.

"Of course you're not. God forbid I forget for one fucking second that I'm the worst father on this planet."

Theo sighs. Reaching over to take the wine bottle on the table, he pours what's left into his glass. "Just wondering, you do realize that the entire restaurant has stopped talking to watch you slobber all over yourself, right?"

Dexter sniffs and runs his hand over his face roughly, as if trying to break out of a spell. Is he high? My blood chills.

"Ah, fuck off." He leans back in his chair, looking annoyingly adolescent. He waves his hand like he's stranded, waving SOS to a passing waiter. "Can we get the bill?"

Anika clears her throat in the thick silence. "So, um, well, this was supposed to be the grand surprise for Lucia and Maio," she says quietly, "but Mamma and I booked a trip to Alassio next weekend for a celebration before the wedding." Her voice is unnaturally high as she tries to pull out some measure of happiness. "Just the kids," she adds, her eyes looking toward her father. He looks sweaty and disoriented, patting his breast pocket in search of his reading glasses. He's so old he can't see the things right in front of him, I think. He can't even see Theo.

"Oh, Anika. That's wonderful!" Lucia throws her hands

around Maio and kisses him hard on the cheek. "This is exactly what we need!"

Maio blushes and leans into her kiss. "That's really sweet. Thank you, Anika," he agrees demurely.

"Oh please." Anika waves her hand to dodge the compliments away. "It's not like I did it just for you. I get a vacation, too."

Her joke falls flat as everyone keeps looking at Dexter, now squinting at the bill.

"Anika, my god, woman, you've finally done something right." Dante raises his hand in mock prayer.

"Never speak to me."

"Okay, baby girl." He stands up, stretching to look around at the families that sit nearby. After lingering too long on a child in a highchair, he shudders. "I mean, fuck, we're already in Torino. Anyone down to keep this going somewhere with a little more *je ne sais quoi*?"

Papa walks around to my mother and places the shawl that hangs from her chair over her shoulders. She looks up at him and squeezes the hand that rests on her upper arm lovingly. I blink and look away, feeling embarrassed for Cinzia after having to watch her husband ruin the evening. Sure enough, she stands up, brushes her skirt and walks swiftly away. Alone.

Before I get up, I look at Theo one more time. He sits frozen in his seat, staring at a wine stain on the tablecloth. Having no influence or importance in his life, I walk up the stairs without looking back.

Lucia, Jo and Maio decide they're tired and leave in Jo's car. My father helps Dexter into his car, walking to the driver's side. Cinzia shrugs meekly at Anika, her face soft and solemn, and decides to drive alone with my mother. Dante, Anika and I stand in the middle of the dark parking lot, listening to the distant chatter of people along the river. Dante fumbles for a cigarette; the three minutes of silence are far too intense for him. After another minute, Theo's head pops up from the stairs and he smiles awkwardly as he approaches us.

"Well, that was fucking awful." His elbow brushes against mine as he walks to stand next to Dante.

Hesitantly, Dante looks to Theo. "I'm sorry, Dexter's a dick when he's drunk."

Theo's eyebrows raise and he glances at Anika as if asking for permission. She rolls her eyes and grabs Dante's cigarette from his mouth.

"*High*," Theo corrects, shrugging his shoulders as if his father being on drugs is minor.

"No way your dad does drugs." Dante's mouth falls open in bewilderment, his eyes flickering from Theo to Anika, and I know that if he were a little drunker, he might be bold enough to say something comforting to her.

Anika snorts. "Every time he 'celebrates,' he almost always pregames with some snow."

"No shit." Dante shakes his head in disbelief. "I thought I knew everything about you guys."

Not knowing what to say, I just nod, feeling sad and

uncomfortable for Theo and Anika. For a few moments, the only sound in the parking lot is the paper of Anika's cigarette burning, stolen from between Dante's fingers. I close my eyes, breathing in the trail of smoke.

"Does your friend want to join us?" Theo says, and it takes me a moment to process he's directing this question to me.

"Who?" Using my left foot to scratch my right ankle, I hold onto Dante's shoulder to keep my balance.

"The one who hugged you over the crab legs." He narrows his eyes at me, as if he doesn't believe I don't remember.

"Who is hugging Magdalen?" Dante perks up at the drama. "Should I kill him?"

"No, Dante," I rush out. "No killing." I blink, feeling like my conversation with Roberto happened two years ago. "Oh, Roberto, yeah," I nod, happy I even remembered his name at this point.

"If that's his name, then obviously him, Magdalen," Theo replies coolly.

My eyes flicker to his and he looks back impassively. I open my mouth to respond but Anika gasps.

"Roberto was in there? Maggie! Why didn't you tell me? You know I would have said hi!"

I shift on my feet. "Sorry, it was so brief, I must've forgot," I lie. Feeling selfish for enjoying my conversation with Roberto, not wanting Anika to overpower me...*Am I a bitch?* The thought rushes through me like a brain freeze. *Am I the most selfish, cold-hearted bitch that I didn't even know that my best friend's dad was on coke and I was worried that her standing next to me would outshine me?*

"Well, does he, *Maggie*?" Theo asks again, saying my name like it's poison. He cocks his head to the side, awaiting my response, while his loafer scuffs against the pebbled flooring.

"He, um, doesn't get off until after the restaurant closes." *Liar. As if you'd ever go back in there and invite him.*

"Shame," Theo sighs. "He looked like a fun guy."

"The most fun."

"More fun than me?" Theo starts and then quickly looks to Dante. "Than us, I mean?"

Anika hoots loudly. "Brother dearest, our father just coked out at dinner and you talk less than a fucking pigeon. Of course Roberto is more fun."

"Yes, Anika!" Dante jumps up excitedly. "Berate your brother. Ruin his confidence! Tell him he's ugly next."

"Roberto is fun," I conclude, before Anika has time to come up with another insult.

"We made plans for Thursday, so he won't feel too bad about missing this," I add, careful not to look at Theo when I say it.

"Just the two of you?" Anika chimes in, her eyebrow rising so high that I count five forehead creases.

"Yes, just the two of us. Going to L'Anguilla at nine, if you need to know," I say politely. I can feel Theo's eyes boring into my face, setting my cheeks ablaze. So I keep my focus on Anika, pretending not to notice.

"Okay, as much as I'd love to keep talking about my sister's love life, can we get a move on?" Dante starts walking in the direction of town.

Embarrassed and angry, I agree quietly. "Why yes, I believe we can. I'm ready to get drunk."

Anika laughs and hooks her arm into mine. "What exactly did England do to you?"

26

THEO

A small clock hangs sadly on the mirrored wall of the bar. I watch the little hand move hurriedly around the numbers to avoid looking at myself in the reflection. It is already 1:30 in the morning, and the four of us are the only people left. Looking around the dimly lit space, I can see Dante hovering over the jukebox, the back of his head shaking as if in an argument with the machine. Anika and Magdalen play pool horribly, but their laughter is sweet against the hushed tunes of Elvis Costello. Dante must have pressed the wrong button. Anika tries to twirl the pool cue like a baton, but it hits the glittering chandelier above them, and they break out in another wave of girlish giggles.

How can Anika just move on from this? How can she separate herself from him so easily, like it wasn't also her fucking father at dinner? Taking a final sip from my fifth drink, I crush the ice between my teeth. Images of my father's flustered face feel less intense than they did after the first. Someone squeezes both my shoulders tightly, and I look over to see Dante's wide grin.

"Who wants some weed?" His breath invades the small

corner I've secluded myself in, wafting the deep smell of cigarettes and stale peanuts in my face.

I scoff, shrugging my shoulders so he stops touching me. It feels insensitive for him to bring up drugs when my father was so fucked up only a few hours ago. But then I think of all the times we've gotten high before and know I'm being irrational. It's weed. Jesus.

I bite down on the ice again. Glancing back at the mirrored clock, I'm scared I won't see who I think I am, hiding away in this bar just as he probably is in his home office. Weak. Predictable.

"You in?" He raises his eyebrows jokingly. My teeth grind into themselves, ice mixed with anger, and I desperately try to remain fun and familiar to Dante. Not wanting to slip.

"No, bro, I think I'm gonna head home."

"You're a pussy, *mate*." He says the last word mockingly. Giving my shoulders a final push, he stands beside the bar stool I sit on. "But I'll see you tomorrow, right?"

In the darkness, his glowing face reminds me of one of the masks hanging up at the museum, used to scare off demons during intense prayer sessions.

"Yeah, I'll see you tomorrow, Dante."

He gives me one last look, and in the dark shadows of the bar I see he's frowning. There's a ring of sweat around the glass of my beer, and I trace my finger through it, drawing a sad face in the wood.

"Daddy issues," I try to joke, but the truth hangs in the air between us. Taking a shaky breath, I try to give him an encouraging smile, but the muscles in my jaw are so tight

I'm afraid my whole face will break. He nods, not dwelling on it, and whistles loudly so Anika's head chirps.

"He coming?" she yells.

"No, not tonight." Dante glances at me before returning his gaze to Magdalen.

"We'll get you one of these days." Anika bounces up and down, holding the cue high above her head.

Meanwhile, Magdalen stares at him expectantly. "Aren't you going to ask me if I want any?" She tilts her head, one hand leaning on the cue for support.

"No, I actually wasn't at all." Dante stands tall, and I snort with surprise at his sudden protectiveness.

"Just so you know, Dante, if I wanted to, I could totally smoke it up with you guys. But it just so happens that I'm not in the mood, so I'm not arguing my rights."

"Yeah, whatever, Maggie. But even if you were in the mood, you still wouldn't be allowed."

Magdalen rolls her eyes and throws up her middle finger. Dante blows her a kiss and looks back at me. "You two okay to get home?" There's an edge to his voice—a test to see if his earlier suspicions will reveal themselves in how I answer.

"Take care of Anika." Pulling him in, I slap him on the shoulder, a silent understanding that whatever happens, we are both big brothers first.

"Always, brother."

27

MAGDALEN

"Bye, my little bitch."

Anika kisses me sloppily on the cheek and smacks my ass before skipping off to Dante. Even by just the posture of her back, I can tell she's happiest when walking toward him. As if he's pulling her forward, her feet settle in the footsteps he leaves behind. Thinking back on our friendship, I hope my awkwardness with intimacy didn't stop them getting together. How beautiful it would be if she was my sister in more than one way. One day I'll ask her.

Sighing, I place the cue back in the wall mount. I'm secretly happy to end the game early, as my lack of co-ordination was appalling. The bar is warm, and I take a moment to stretch my hands above my head, feeling the happy buzz of three beers trickle from my fingertips to the soles of my feet. I feel good. Almost carefree. Wanting a reason to smile, I do a little twirl when a hand catches me, finger poking me underneath my ribs, and I gasp. Spinning, Theo, arms crossed in front of him, frowns at me.

"Okay, silly girl, it's time to get you home."

The beers speak before I can, the eager smile I'd pocketed

bursting free, and I laugh openly at Theo poking me to get my attention.

"You poked me!" I say through my giggles.

"Would you prefer I tickled you?"

"No!" I shriek, taking a few steps back until the upper part of my thighs hits the cool wood of the pool table. Something shifts in Theo's gaze as he looks at me leaning against the table. His eyes lazily drift to my mouth, then slowly, deliberately, trail down to where my pink dress stops at my thighs.

"I've been told I'm very good with my hands," he says roughly, walking toward me with the stealth of a predator. Slowly. "When it comes to tickling, of course." His hands are in his trouser pockets, an unfazed demeanor. But beneath the layer of fabric, I see his fingers dig into his legs. He's holding back.

My breath catches in my throat. Fear and something else, something unfamiliar, makes me shudder at the deepness of his voice. My body feels warm and sensitive as I imagine what Theo's hands on my skin would feel like. Again. How his palms would brush against my ribcage, strong fingers gripping my hips until I'm sitting on the table.

"Mhm." I nod my head, looking up at him. "Whoever told you that was being generous."

He's so close to me that I can smell the clean cotton of his shirt. Can smell how the wind dried it on the clothesline. How his skin seems to hold the sunshine even in the dark lighting of the bar. I'm completely overwhelmed by him.

"My sincerest apologies." His knee brushes against my own, and my cheeks flood with warmth.

"Let me make it better, okay?" he whispers, tilting his head so that his hair falls to the left. Without thinking, my fingers reach out and brush through the strands, checking my work from earlier. My nails rake against his scalp accidentally, each strand curling around my fingers as if coaxing me to stay in the warmth of his head, to bury myself in his thoughts. He briefly closes his eyes, letting out a small sigh, leaning his head into my touch.

"Hair looks good," I say, swallowing before removing my hand and leaning both of them against the pool table behind me.

He opens his eyes. I stare back, lost in the silence between us. It's difficult to feel self-conscious when I'm lost in his eyes, the color of thunderstorms before a heavy rainfall.

He grunts in agreement, settling a hand at my waist, his focus falling on the soft spot underneath my ribs. Barely acknowledging that I'm here, he seems transfixed on this singular point on my stomach. In a swift move, his fingers glide across my waist, letting his thumb rhythmically smooth over the spot, back and forth, for what feels like an eternity. I don't breathe. Afraid that if I move, I'll break whatever's happening between us. So I stay silent, holding my breath.

Since we entered the bar, Theo had been sitting on the far-end stool, seemingly transfixed by the epoxy counter for the entire night. I have no idea if he's drunk. Maybe he doesn't even realize it's me that he's caressing, I think

212

happily. Maybe he thinks I'm someone else. Another girl with auburn hair and green eyes. This idea brings me relief. Like I could do anything without the risk of embarrassment. I close my eyes and memorize the press of his four fingertips underneath my beating heart, feeling thankful. His thumb presses harder into the almost hollow place above my stomach, pushing and kneading, massaging deliciously slow. I release a breath, or possibly an "oh," or maybe I moan, warmth spreading slowly down from my navel to my toes.

"Better?" His voice is dangerously low and when I look down I see that his feet are in between mine, our thighs nearly pressed against one another.

"I think I owe whoever I insulted an apology," I say to the ceiling, because looking at him feels disgustingly close to staring at the sun.

He chuckles, and it really is a luxurious sound. Like the *struffoli* Nonna used to make on Christmas Eve. Warm and decadent. He raises his right hand, bringing it to the other side of my waist, but hovers halfway. He blinks. And I know before his hand does that he's remembered it's just me.

"It's okay," I say before he can fumble an awkward apology. "I get it."

It's easier to pretend I'm not the issue if I speak first. The ends of his mouth curve downward like he wants to protest, but he stays silent, just looking at me. Trying to contain the tears that burn behind my eyes, I blink a few times and start to step away. No matter how much older I get, I think I will always feel as worthless as I did as a child. A sudden desire for Emily and rainy England, the smell of red wine and old books, consumes me. I want comfort and faded leather chairs. To never have to try new things again.

"Magdalen," he says, a roughness to his voice, but I'm too embarrassed to hear any reasoning. It would be better to feel angry. I try to muster fire, to take another step away from his proximity. But his hands are suddenly on me again, stopping me from moving.

"Shit," he says, looking at his own hands like they're not attached to him. He looks at me, brows furrowed like he wants to say something, but instead, he just shakes his head and wraps his hands around my hips more tightly.

"I get it," I mumble again, the only three words I can say without crying.

Fingers digging into my skin almost painfully, he pulls me so I'm flush against him. "No, you don't," he whispers, pushing himself further on me, lips brushing the hollow of my neck so quickly I have no time to process. My body heats with his closeness, feeling scrambled and messy.

"Well, now I certainly don't," I whisper. His fingers move to my neck, tilting it back. He comes in closer, brushing his nose against my exposed throat. I hear him take a deep breath.

And then he releases me. Quickly and efficiently, like he didn't just completely mind-fuck me on a billiard table.

He exhales through his mouth angrily. "Sorry, ehm, I'll wait outside for you. Take your time."

And then he's gone.

28

THEO

My hands tremble slightly as I pull out a cigarette, pacing in front of the bar, waiting for her. I think of her legs pressed against mine and how her neck smelled like lavender and summer. How soft her stomach was through the fabric of her dress.

"Fuck," I hiss into the empty street, my voice scratchy as it echoes down the archways. Just as I'm about to relive the memory of Magdalen against me, another memory surfaces. It catches me by surprise, as it always does. My heart beats faster as images of the attic resurface in infrared. Forcing me to remember the details. The dust settled across the cardboard boxes. How their bodies were unnaturally tangled together, all elbows and creased clothing. The tear in her skirt. Fuck me. I need another drink.

"I'm good to go." Magdalen appears beside me and the memory sinks back into the shadows.

She looks off toward the small alleyway of closed cafes and bars, avoiding my gaze intentionally. I light another cigarette. Her hair lifts in the early morning wind, and twisted pieces of dark red float around her face. I try to calm my nerves, to forget about everything. It's like I can feel her skin imprinted against my own, burning herself on me. We stay like this for a moment. Her looking away. Me looking at her. The soft sound of filtered paper burning with each drag. I throw the cigarette and watch it roll into one of the cracks in the cobblestones. Maybe one day, I'll stand right here and look at that discarded cigarette and remember that life was fucking beautiful with Magdalen against me on a pool table.

"Great, it'll be easier to get a cab at the Po," I say, staring straight ahead, and walk past her.

Magdalen stays behind me, but I can see her from the corner of my eye with her arms crossed in front of her, looking anywhere but at me. Of course she's angry. I scratch the back of my head, desperate for another cigarette, unsure of where to put my hands. Should I apologize for touching her? For making things weird? But even that feels wrong. How can I apologize for something I wish could never end?

We continue walking for ten minutes with her behind me like two ducks in a row before I hear her sigh. When I don't say anything, she coughs obnoxiously, trying to catch my attention.

"What is it, Magdalen?"

"Stop walking," she commands, her voice serious. I pause, my heels digging into the street, but my gaze remains fixed on the river ahead. Somehow, I know what's going to happen. It's in the pit forming deep in my stomach.

These years away from Chivasso, I thought I had become someone better. In the absence of my father's influence, that the good parts of me had come out. But here I am, making the same fucking mistakes I made seven years ago. It feels like I've walked full fucking circle. I remain frozen, unable to look at her. Because if I do, I know exactly what I'll do. How deeply I'll fucking consume her.

I hear her shoes against the pavement, hear her dress glide against her thighs as she walks. And then I feel it. Her body right behind me, warm and soft without even touching me. My spine stiffens, wanting so fucking badly to lean into her, for her warmth to become my warmth, to share her softness. But I don't move. I feel fingertips brush my shoulder, then press down, turning me to face her.

Magdalen stares into my eyes, her brows knitting together as she examines my stiff posture.

"What happened to you?" she questions. "One minute you were there and then it was like…" She shakes her head, trying to piece together the words. "It was like you saw a ghost."

The hand that was on my shoulder lifts and slowly comes to brush away a piece of hair that's fallen in front of my face. Her touch is so light, so careful. I stifle a moan.

"It'll be hard to get a cab at this time." My voice sounds like the gravel in our driveway, cold and small. I try to look past her, but it's impossible not to see her. Magdalen narrows her eyes, and suddenly her fingers are gripping my chin, forcing me to look at her.

"I consider myself a woman with a bit of intelligence." She steps toward me. "I'm at Oxford, you know." Her grip doesn't falter.

"Yes, I know," I murmur.

"I know what attraction looks like, or at least, what it's supposed to look like," she stutters, her vulnerability exposed. But she continues forward, and I can feel the distance closing between us, a tangible force pulling us together until her breasts barely skim the buttons of my shirt. I should step back. I should turn away. I should chalk this up to drunken flirtation.

"What do you want me to say, Magdalen?" My voice comes out sharper than I mean. Beautiful Magdalen Savoy would run back to England if she knew the things I had done, the secrets I've locked away so well.

"I don't want you to say anything." She sighs, looking up at me with a frown. Her hand slowly releases my chin, her eyes meeting mine with heat. "I want you to kiss me."

I blink. Air seeming to have left my lungs, I stumble backward and try to laugh off her request, but it comes out as a weird groan. "Excuse me?" My voice lowers. Maybe I misunderstood. Maybe she just confessed that she wanted me to *kill* her.

"I want you to kiss me, Theo." There goes that fucking idea. Her eyes are bright even in the darkened archway.

"Why me?" The words rush out: "Magdalen, you could go up to anyone in this city and they'd devour you in a heartbeat." I try to remember the reasons I should turn back to the street to look for the cab that was so important three minutes ago.

"I want *you* to devour me." She whispers it as if it were the most obvious thing in the world. "I want to kiss someone tonight, and I want it to be you." Letting my eyes fall to her

lips, I moan, gazing at the perfect outline, instantly knowing it's a mistake. But fuck it. Forgetting everything I've
promised myself not to do, I step closer. Just for a minute.
I'll stay right here for just one minute, and then I'll walk
away. Lost in the slope of her nose, the dark shadows of her
eyelashes. A minute passes. I keep staring, transfixed. Her
eyelids flutter, and suddenly, I feel her try to step back.

"Ok, I'll take the silence as my cue." Her blush is so
bright, I'm surprised I can't feel her heat from here. "Sorry,
I thought—"

It's only then I realize I've just been staring at her without
saying anything. As she tries to take another step back, I
grab the back of her neck, pulling her to me.

"Magdalen, don't you even think about walking away."
With my other hand, I slowly brush her cheek, admiring
the soft dusting of freckles across her face, the one above her
eyebrow, before pushing us both against the archway.

"You're killing me," I whisper. "You're fucking killing
me."

"I'm not the one who cornered me into a side street," she
says breathily, humor bright in her eyes.

"I'm not the one who asked me to fucking kiss them," I
counter.

She laughs, exasperated. "It's just a kiss. I'm not asking
you to fuck me in the middle of Torino."

"Now there's a thought," I murmur. Hearing her say
those words is enough to do away with the small semblance
of restraint I have.

My hips grind into her, knowing she can feel how hard I

am, but I can't find the will to care. For a selfish moment, I want her to know that I could hike her dress up and slip my fingers underneath the thin fabric and find how wet she is for me.

She started it.

"You really shouldn't say *fuck* around me." Dipping my head to her, my lips lightly graze hers, and an instant heat spreads through me, settling deep in my stomach. A hunger overpowers me. Feeling intoxicated with the humid heat and her scent of that fucking lavender, I stop myself from sinking my teeth into her neck just to taste how delicious I know she is. "I have an incredible imagination."

She moans lightly, and it's enough. My tongue licks her full bottom lip, hands wrapped around the base of her hair to get her as close as possible as I continue to explore her mouth in any way she'll let me. Our bodies are flush against one another, each of us trying to get closer, and as if reading my mind, Magdalen arches her pelvis to press against my hardness, grinding against me as I trail my mouth down to her neck, marking her with bites along her soft skin.

"Oh wow," she exhales.

"That's it," I growl, shifting so that my thigh tucks in between her legs, giving her access to the friction she wants as I continue to taste her lips. She sucks in a breath as her dress rides up her thighs; the only fabric separating her bare sex and my leg is the thin cotton of her underwear and these too-tight trousers. "Let me make you feel good, baby." Stealing a glance to look down between us, I groan loudly as I watch her hips grind against me. This should be illegal. This should be fucking illegal.

"Baby?" Magdalen laughs but I reach down, rubbing her with my finger this time, cutting her off. Magdalen bites her lip, hard. Eyelashes fluttering closed.

"Are you laughing at me again?" I say while rubbing her faster. I'm so fucking hard it's difficult to stand up straight.

In comparison to my sexual history, dry humping on a sidewalk seems relatively tame, but the sight of her so undone is enough to send me over the edge. For a moment, I truly believe I was born to make her feel good.

"Never, *baby*." She opens her eyes, taunting me. My vision starts to dot with how turned on I am.

"Don't call me that if you don't want me to come right now."

Sucking on the thin skin beneath her ear, I grunt out before thinking, "Use me, Mag, please." And snake my hands to grip her ass, helping her find a rhythm. She lets out a soft cry as I put pressure on her backside and grind my thigh harder into her.

"Fuck, that's beautiful," I pant. Watching her chase pleasure from my leg makes me think I'll come without her even touching me. Does she even realize the effect of her dress bunching up around her hips? I think back to my earlier request to have someone else devour her and I grip her harder. Wanting her pleasure and firsts to be mine. Her tanned thighs glow against the white of her panties, and the desire to sneak my fingers underneath the band and sink them into her is too tempting.

"Theo," she moans. "I think—"

But just as she's about to either confess her love for me or tell me she's coming, a car alarm goes off somewhere, followed by the sound of teenage boys kicking cans off the street. I jerk back, my knee sliding out from between her, creating a painful distance between us. While my body reacts before my mind, I'm caught in the murky in-between of my desire, drowning in a deep, utterly cold part of myself. It takes me a moment to look at her and not wish I was inside her, my fingers pumping hard as she finds release. What would she sound like if she came? Would she whimper softly, trying to quiet herself? Would it feel so good that she'd moan loudly, knowing nothing but the long pulse of release I gave her? But I blink, dizzy from the darkness of the night against the flush of her cheeks. She stares at me, breathless and flustered.

What the fuck am I doing?

I adjust myself underneath my trousers, knowing full well my erection is visible. Her eyes look down, noticing. And then I see all the bitter details that the nighttime has tried to hide. The black cracks in the marble pillars. The dirty graffiti behind the wall I've pushed Magdalen against, staining the pink satin of her dress. The ugliness of who I am never gets easier to face, and it hurts to know I've brought her down into it with me. Who the fuck do I think I am? Ravishing her on the sidewalk like a degenerate lurking the streets for a quick lay? Silver streaks of moonlight emphasize the indentations where I bit along her collarbone.

Dread sinks heavily inside my stomach, settling over me like barbed wire, cutting into the smallest parts of me.

"What's wrong?" Magdalen self-consciously lowers her dress, looking around to see the cause of my distance. I sigh, already missing the sight of her thighs around my own. Biting the inside of my cheek until the metallic sting of blood fills my mouth, I dip my tongue inside the shallow until it stings so badly my eyes water.

"What's wrong?" I repeat, my throat numb and scratchy. I feel dirty, knowing I've stolen her first time to chase a few moments of pleasure. "What's wrong is that this is fucking stupid."

A fissure has erupted between us. Hot lava seeps through the opening, spilling over me, and I feel ready to burn everything down with me. Her face contorts from confusion to deathly cold in a second.

"The only reason you're kissing me is because you're too afraid to fucking talk to anyone else," I sneer, wanting the fire to burn faster. I regret the words as soon as I say them, but I'm proud I've found something so disgusting to say when all I want to do is kiss her better. Remembering how no one seemed to notice her at the dinner table or at the club. The lava blisters my skin, lining the inside of my throat with deep lesions, begging to spill more cruelty.

"You crawl to me to get out all your sexually repressed fantasies because I'm the only man you know that doesn't need to talk to hook up." Someone in the distance pushes up the rolling gate of their store. "Humping my leg like a teenager. For god's sake, Magdalen, what part of that did you think would be enjoyable for me?"

She stares at me, her face calm, breathing deeply before tilting her head. "Are you done?" There's a slight tremor in her voice, but she seems otherwise indifferent. Her eyes pierce my skin.

"You should get a cab." My gaze stays at her collarbone, unable to look higher.

"You're a fucking coward. You say a few mean words to me so you don't feel guilty about getting with your sister's best friend, and then what? You think I'll forget that your dick was digging into my stomach after just one kiss?"

She thinks my apprehension is because of Anika. Good.

"Just because I can't control my body's natural reaction doesn't mean I like you, Magdalen," I spit out.

She opens her mouth and then closes it, blinking a few times before looking at the ground.

Bile rises in my throat. "Maybe if you had an actual conversation with a man, you'd know that." The final blow.

It's as if her hurt has manifested into a tangible barrier between us; I watch her strength finally bend into an ugly and irreversible hatred for me. *I'm doing this because I care*, I think. *Because she deserves better*, I think again, because I don't believe myself the first time.

"Oh, right," she says quietly. "I, um . . . I didn't realize that, that you didn't need to be attracted . . ." She stutters, looking at me, hurt deep in her eyes. Pain and regret, her dress cementing over her body, no longer moving with the breeze. "I forget how easily the male mind can be persuaded." She feigns a laugh. She's speaking to the floor, then in the direction where the cabs pool.

"Yup," I add. "Quite easily."

Magdalen flinches, then tries to wipe away the bruises my lips have made on her skin. I feel sorry for her reflection tomorrow morning.

"To the cabs I go." She smiles and starts toward the river. She's slow, taking her time, arms wrapped over her chest like she's cold. It's as if I've taken the heat out of her summer.

"Magdalen," I yell. *One more minute.* I just need one more minute. It's the most selfish thing I've ever done, but it's compulsory. One more fucking minute.

Turning, staring at me blankly, she asks, "Yes?" She looks fragile and delicious all at once.

My voice comes out harsh. I smirk, fueled by the pain. "Don't tell Anika, okay?"

29

MAGDALEN

"How was last night?" my mother asks from the window-sill. Her hand curls around a coffee mug, her wedding ring clinking against the ceramic as if tapping out the rhythm of an old tune only she can hear. Papa sits next to her, oblivious to the conversation, absorbed in a new report from the museum.

"Interesting." I nod my head, looking down at my own coffee. Seeing myself in the dark liquid.

"I heard Anika and Dante come home," she says in a sigh laced with accusation. With curiosity. What she really wants to say is: *Since when do you do things more reckless than Dante?*

"Cinzia didn't hear Theo come home, either," she says, and I go still, unable to think of an excuse fast enough.

"Someone was out late," she pushes. I move my gaze from my coffee to the stained oak table, not ready to look up at her yet. Last night's alcohol and this morning's regret swirl inside my stomach in a nauseating cycle. Since when the fuck does Dante come home before me?

"Couldn't sleep," I get out, as she sets the mug down.

Her ring is now tapping against the bench. I know this is a signal of impatience. Warning me to confess, or else. *Or else.* What could possibly be *or else* any more? *Else* was a terrifying threat once. But now? Hit me. Ground me. Bury me deep in the garden until I decompose and something beautiful becomes of me. I want to feel something besides this sickly shame that grows with each passing second. Give me *else.*

I crave my innocence. I want it back. A tear burns at the corner of my eye. *Use me, Mag.*

"Your dress was tight last night," she continues, not waiting for my reply. "Girls in tight dresses are dangerous for men," she tsks. "Even Dexter noticed, right, *amore*? I saw him looking."

My father huffs something unintelligible. He's very good at tuning her out when he needs to.

My mother seems to always know how low I feel and want to see more of it, prodding at my pain. I wonder what I must've done to trigger her intolerance. Was I too quiet where she was loud? Too skinny in the places she felt heaviest? She sets her cup down in the sink. A tear slips angrily off of my cheek, plummeting into my coffee. I take a long sip, gulping down my own weakness.

She groans as she rises from the bench. "Be careful, *amore*." This time she says it condescendingly. Her hand drags down against my hair, her ring getting caught in the strands, and she pretends not to realize it and tugs until I wince. I look down to see she's exposed the hickeys. I want to say something, but she's already gone, the sound of her slippers dragging against the tiles. I hold my breath until she leaves.

When I hear the lock on her bedroom door click into place, my breath stays stuck in my throat, unwilling to escape. Papa looks up at me and smiles. I hope I smile back.

30

THEO

Music blares from somewhere downstairs. A high-pitched voice whines about love and lust through melodic guitar chords, and Anika screams along with such passion it sounds like she's in pain.

"Fucking hell, Anika," I yell, palms pressed against my ears. "Who the fuck do you have to sing about?" I say less loudly, already knowing she can't hear me.

I try to continue writing, telling myself this summer, I would finish this bloody fucking thesis. "The Origins of Apotheosis in Ancient Egypt" seemed a relatively interesting topic while in Egypt, but the desire to write about men who believed in their own importance reminds me too much of my father. Divinity negating sin. Replacing error. Forgiving fault. But I told myself I would finish it without telling anyone and become the fucking doctor that he never did. And, when I have that diploma, I can say I became a doctor without complaint, that I mastered something he failed at, and I did it better than he ever fucking could. Flipping through the pages, the word *bruised* appears about some clay pot, and it causes me to stop.

Magdalen with her back against the dirty wall. What

she'll see when she looks in the mirror. My breath becomes unsteady, and I close my eyes. *In, out, in, out.*

But it begins as it always has. Images of Magdalen are replaced with the same hazy memory. It's become less clear as the years have gone on. The split wood of the attic ceiling. Was it morning or night? Yet the whole scene unfolds despite the fading details...

I try to breathe through my nose, but it's as if someone has stuffed cotton down my throat. I remember a torn, dirty skirt. A hot trail burns my cheek, and I slap it to bring myself back to reality. Am I fucking crying?

It's been ten years, you fucking pussy. Ten years to get over this same thing. Get a grip, Theo. Remember who you are. Remember to breathe. It's fine. You're fine. It'll pass, you weak piece of shit. Everyone's over it. Get the fuck over it. You fucking freak. Jesus Christ, you should have done something. You cry now, but you didn't do anything! Should've told someone, anyone. Written it down so it wouldn't fade away like it has. Was she crying? Do you remember how she shoved his face, how her nails pressed into his cheek? They were so short, they did nothing. Were your nails as short? If you would have fucking moved, do you think you could have gotten a scratch on him? Remember how his drool covered the palm of her hand as she tried to break free. Do you remember that? Of course you do! You'll never forget it; because you let it happen. You let her hurt. You let her hurt for so long. And you watched. You watched, and even if there were tears in your eyes and a tremble down your spine, you still fucking watched and left quietly through the attic door. She'll never be the same again, and you just watched.

I need help. Help. Think of how quiet she was after. Remember the zipper? How loud it was when she was quiet. Birds stopped chirping; I know you remember that. I'm fucking hurt, and I need help.

My shirt is unbearable, wrapping around my neck until I realize I'm gagging. Standing up, I pull at the neckline, faintly aware of a tearing sound, but it still clings to me so tightly. Blindly, I find scissors and try to find my neckline, but I can't fucking see. I hold the scissors by the bladed part, thinking I can just slice the shirt, but everything is fuzzy. Briefly, I think of my mum. Of her clapping on the bleachers at my tennis match. I still feel the blood pulsing through my fingertips, but now they're her fingertips, clasped together with uncontained joy. I lost that match. She's so happy. *Amore, amore, amore.* Okay, I put the scissors down. *Amore, come! You were excellent. Oh, you were so excellent.* Mamma, I lost. *Stai zitto, your swing! I almost cried it was so good.* Okay, Mamma. *You hungry?* Yes, Mamma. *Okay, let's get something to eat.* Okay, Mamma. *Gelato, I feel like a nice big gelato. Chocolate! Mhmm, I love chocolate in the summer.* Yes, Mamma. I like chocolate, too.

I wake up on the bathroom floor to someone banging on the door.

"Theo, did you fucking die in there? I need to pee and Mamma's blow-drying her hair downstairs."

"One minute," I say, my voice far away, still in the

memory. Her music has stopped. I look up and count how many rings there are in the bathroom curtain. Thirty-two. I feel very small down here.

Anika clears her throat. "You—" She starts. Tries again. "You okay?" I can see her feet shift behind the door, and I bolt upright, banging my knee against the toilet bowl.

"Ehm, yeah. One sec." I flush the toilet. Hearing any concern in Anika sends a dreadful realization that I have been here too long. How did I get into the bathroom? I remember things in blurred grayscale. Blood and chocolate. Fuzzy fingers. My head feels swollen, like someone has filled me with water. "If I told you I shat myself, would you believe me?" My voice is still not fully there, but she doesn't seem to notice.

"No, you fucking didn't!" she cackles, and I check to see her shadow bouncing from one foot to the other. I take a deep breath through my mouth: relief. Time. I have time back.

"Try not to sound too excited," I say. Wiping my face, I turn the water on and blow out a hot breath.

Her laughter slips past the door, filling the bathroom with brightness. "What the fuck did you and Magdalen do? You've been out of it for days now." Her chuckles become bubbly and uncontrollable. "Do you think Maggie is shitting herself as we speak?"

Anika stomps her heel on the ground, so amused by her own company she forgets I'm in here. "Wait, let me ask her."

"I thought you had to pee?" I call out, turning off the water after an appropriate amount of time, and unlock the door. But as I begin to turn the knob, I pause, stomach sinking quickly. "What do you mean ask Mag—"

When I open the door, Anika's head is hanging out the railing of the upstairs hallway balcony. "Magdalen Savoy, are you currently shitting yourself as we speak?" she screams down.

"I'm going to need you to repeat that," a voice yells from downstairs, and I think I might actually shit myself now.

Her voice is light and slightly winded, as if she's been running. I try not to picture what she looks like, cheeks flushed. I know that look all too well. We've expertly avoided each other for nearly a week.

Anika huffs with agitation. "I said, are you currently shitting yourself like my brother just has?"

"For fuck's sake." I bury my head in my hands and Anika snaps her attention to me and stands up from the railing. "Don't be embarrassed! I'm sure Maggie is overcome with the same bodily discomfort as you."

"No, Anika. I can promise you she's not."

"Magdalen, if you don't answer me right now, I'll assume that shit is currently leaking out of your ass."

"Must you be so descriptive?" I huff, but I'm secretly glad of this bickering.

"Yeah, I must."

I look down at my shaking hands and squeeze. The dizziness has subsided and I no longer have to focus on the beating of my heart, on how to breathe or on the thirty-two curtain rings. But the smallness lingers, the weight of the memory's shadow hovering over my own, pressing down, knotting my muscles until I feel my whole body cramp. As I stand in the hallway, Anika zooms past me, slamming the bathroom door.

The door to my bedroom is open; through it I can see my desk with the open textbook. Ancient Egypt feels impossibly far away, so I walk past the room, diverting my eyes from the spot where the scissors lie. It's almost ridiculous now. I should laugh at my own stupidity and resolve never to let it happen again.

31

MAGDALEN

Footsteps pad down the stairs as I rush toward the medicine cabinet in the Sinclairs' kitchen, looking for some pain relievers. I pause, eyeing the liquor cabinet stocked full of the hard stuff, and debate whether it's too early to get drunk. As I promised Anika, tonight I will dine and date a boy. A real-life boy who can possibly stand to touch me for longer than fourteen seconds without wanting to jump into the river and drown. Granted, he may not know it's a date, but nonetheless, I'm counting it as one. Settling for ibuprofen instead of vodka, my hands try to pry open the bottle when I hear bare feet slap against the kitchen tile and abruptly stop at the entrance. I know before I turn around.

Theo.

I close my eyes. *If you would have let me, I would have left a part of my mind for only you.*

My chest deflates, and while my heart begins to beat anxiously, I cannot find the will to be embarrassed by our fumble last week. Instead, something far more depressing unravels. I have the urge to step backward until he's right behind me. Until I can feel his heat over mine. To turn around and just stare at his beautiful face. It's addictive to look at him. Those eyes. I want them to see me. To notice the small things. I want them to see that the pain I'm in is only because I still *want* for him.

But I would rather drink cement than admit my masochistic desire to be rejected all over again. So I gather the strength of my Emily, my Anika, and return to the task of popping the ibuprofen.

"Magdalen."

I whip around, seeing him standing at the edge of the kitchen. He nods curtly, eyes darting across the room. As if subconsciously measuring the farthest points from me and judging how to approach without suspicion. *I notice everything you do, Theo. If you blink too quickly, if you lean on your heels, if you scratch your elbow, I'll notice.* Instead of saying anything at all, I give a polite, albeit awkward, smile and turn toward the cabinet once again. If there's one thing I'm excellent at, it's silence. I can hear him thinking of a polite way to excuse himself.

"You can just leave. I won't cry about it."

He laughs condescendingly, and I roll my eyes only because he can't see me.

"I didn't think you could cry," he bites back.

I flinch, surprisingly hurt by his assessment. Angry that he doesn't understand me at all. Is that what he thinks? That I'm too timid for tears? I'm ready to lash out and say something spiteful, but when I look at him I falter. He is comparatively unkempt today. Still beautiful, but there's a tiredness to him that I haven't noticed before. It feels deep. His hair is disheveled, and his neck looks damp with sweat, like he's just awoken from a nightmare. But I'm sick of people not understanding me, so I lash out anyway.

"Did you think I wasn't hurt when you humped me in an alley and then decided you didn't like me enough to finish?" The pulse in my temple throbs angrily.

"Oh please." He steps closer, quickly realizes his mistake, and steps back. "You have no emotional attachment to me. Don't act like I wasn't just the closest body that you could get off on."

Heat pours so harshly into my cheeks that I'm afraid I'll set myself on fire. "We're complete strangers," I breathe out. "You don't know a fucking thing about me." Rubbing the spot between my brows, the anger has weirdly disappeared, transforming into heavy tiredness. I remember I'm holding on to the ibuprofen bottle and try to open up the lid, but my thumb slips against the child lock and it stays closed.

"And like you know anything about me." His voice peters out as Anika's flip-flops smack loudly against the floor upstairs. He looks toward the hall, judging how much time he has before needing to act civil again.

"I know enough now," I whisper to the bottle that finally clicks open. I pour five little pills into my hand.

Anika flops in so loudly that she literally cuts the tension. Overpowers it. She hums along to Madonna, blissfully ignorant, and steps into the kitchen.

"Why aren't you changed yet?" She slaps the island countertop. Her bangles clash against the granite. "Magdalen, no
offense, but we are not going to get it right on the first try
with your limited clothing options."

Anika glances at Theo and then toward my palm filled
with pills. "What are you doing now? Are you driving Maggie to drugs?"

"Trying to tell Magdalen that that's too much medica-
tion for her body size."

"And I was just saying I know just how much my own
body needs." I smile brightly at Anika.

"Good, so, Theo, you can help us decide which outfit is
best for her!" she shrieks, guiding him to the built-in breakfast bench that sits in the corner of their kitchen. "I will
admit, I always tend to go too short, believe it or not, so it'll
be good to have a male perspective."

"Anika." Theo stops walking, and Anika almost crashes
into his back.

"Oh, come on!" she whines. "This is fun! This is what
having a sister is all about. Please, please, please, it'll be fifteen minutes max. Scout's honor."

His eyeline remains on the floor. Anika's puppy-dog eyes
could guilt a butcher into veganism.

"I'm busy, I have to go an—"

"You've been in your room all day. What's the point
of coming home if you're just going to ignore me all the
time?"

Home run. Well played, Anika.

Theo closes his eyes, trying to find another excuse besides *I actually just don't want to be anywhere near Magdalen.*

"Sit. I'll buy you a coffee tomorrow." Anika hops on one leg, batting her eyelashes.

"Gee, how can I say no to that," he huffs, but allows her to push him back onto the bench.

"Magdalen." Anika's head whips toward me. "Change. Now. I don't know how long we have him for."

"I can only stay for fifteen minutes."

"You'll stay for twenty."

"Anika."

"I'll start crying. Magdalen, move your fucking legs."

"Yes, ma'am." I grab the pile of clothes that I see she has added to. A big lump of silver jewelry has also been thrown on top.

"She's taking too long," he says and sighs, running his hands through his hair.

I walk to the hallway connecting the kitchen to Mr. Sinclair's study. "Suck my dick, Theodore," I whisper, and hear the wooden bench squeak.

"No, Theo. You just said you would," Anika whispers harshly. I pause.

"This is fucking ridiculous."

"Why are you being such an asshole?"

"Why are you making me do this?" The last line doesn't come out as a whisper. It's loud and urgent. He sounds genuinely pissed off.

"I'll hold him down," she yells out, probably realizing her version of whispering does nothing to keep a secret.

I walk slowly to the study. Hopefully, he'll grow impatient and just leave before I come out.

"Ow! Bitch!"

The chair squeaks again, and this time, I hear them laugh before I close the door.

32

THEO

"How long does she take to change?"

I tap my foot nervously on the tile. But what I really want to do is storm into the study. Close the door. Drop to my knees and beg. *Please don't let this be for a date. I'm sorry I'm being so rude, but I know it'll be better if I am. Just don't go on a date. Go to the cinema with Anika. Dressed nicely in her second-hand shirt. I'll sneak in halfway through and sit in the row behind you to watch you watch the film. I promise I won't speak. I just want to see you in the glow of the screen.*

"Anika." Magdalen's voice is calm but firm as she calls out to my sister.

The little devil snorts beside me. "Yes, your majesty?" Her foot taps excitedly against the tiles, meaning she has meddled.

"I'm sorry, did you get rid of the clothes I added? Why are these shirts for infants, Anika?" Magdalen's voice is muffled, and I almost picture what she looks like trying on clothes. Almost.

"Oh please, you weigh like, as much as a loaf of bread. Come out, I'm bored."

"You are a whore!" Magdalen groans, and I almost smile but then remember why I'm here in the first place.

Magdalen's footsteps are silent, so when I look up and see her standing underneath the archway, I'm startled.

"*Phantasma*," I say under my breath, but Magdalen's eyes narrow on me like I just called her a cunt. Obviously, she's still upset.

"Oh, fuck yeah." Anika circles Magdalen twice before grabbing her jeans and shimming them lower on her body. "And just a little...oh yeah, perfect. Now, one more thing. Gorgeous. I'm wet for you, baby."

"Disgusting," Magdalen says with false revulsion, but she tips her head back in laughter, exposing the delicate skin of her neck. I see her throat swallow, and it's so hot that I have to grab the chair to keep myself from getting up.

"Honestly don't know why Theo's even here. I'm so good!" Anika steps aside from Magdalen, and I try to think of something to say.

She's wearing dark, low-rise jeans, slightly below her belly button. My mouth goes dry. Focused on how her stomach looks when she breathes in. She has on a white T-shirt with a small pink cross in the middle of the stitching at the collar. Cropped. More stomach. More breathing. Fucking hell. She's not wearing a bra again, the curves of her chest inescapable. To avoid gawking, I try to find a distraction. A crucifix hangs on the wall above the stove. My mother brought it home from an excavation in Miglionico before I was born. I can see the dust on his head from years of neglect. Magdalen has now slipped on Anika's little heels, making her look impossibly tall. I drag my hand across my mouth to stop looking.

"Up or down?"

"Excuse me?"

Anika rolls her eyes. "Her hair. Up or down."

If she wears it down, he could wrap his hands around her ponytail and tug her toward him for a kiss. I've done it before. I would do it now, if I could. If she wears it up, he'll get to see that pretty little neck.

"I don't know. Or really care, if I'm being honest." Before I finish the sentence, I know I've made a mistake. Magdalen blinks at me for several seconds and then looks down.

"Sorry, I just mean—"

But she interrupts me before I can apologize.

"I'm sorry Anika made you endure these five terrible minutes. I can promise you, it won't ever happen again." She musters a weak laugh and turns toward the stairs. "Anika, is your makeup in the bathroom upstairs?"

Anika looks at me for too long. I can feel her disappointment, anticipating what she'll say.

"Yeah," she yells to Magdalen, who's halfway up the stairs, but keeps her eyes trained on me. "You need a belt. There's one hanging behind my door."

Asshole. But she speaks slowly. Desperately. "What the fuck happened to you?"

"I told you I didn—"

"I let you leave, didn't I? I mean I'm the one that let you go. I told you that if you didn't, he'd kill you. That you'd kill him. You'd kill each other." She pulls out one of the chairs that rests under the island and clumsily sits down. "I put the application in your fucking hand, and I sat with you

243

when you cried. I dragged you to the post office. When they said congratulations, welcome to Yale, I stole his credit card and bought you that fucking plane ticket and told you to run. I stayed up with you the night before. I put your favorite pillowcase and the fountain pen with extra ink cartridges in the side pocket. So you don't get to come back, after seven years, and put this shit on me." She takes a gulp of air. "On Magdalen. On my Magdalen. Who do you think you are?"

She slams her hands down on the island, and the glasses drying on the counter rattle. For a moment, she looks so much like Mamma it's freaky. Ferocious, but kind. Too much love for those who don't deserve it.

"I won't watch you do the same thing Papa does," she whispers sadly. Her elbows sink down on the counter as if my stupidity physically weighs her down.

It feels like she has stabbed me with one of the dirty knives in the kitchen sink. I take a deep breath in, guilt piercing my body. "You just don't understand, Ani—"

"Bullshit. I fucking understand everything."

"I'm sorry I didn't pretend I enjoyed choosing Maggie's outfit like we're at a fucking slumber party. But I don't see how that makes me anything like him."

I force my knees to extend and stand. My voice sounds soft, like putty. I slip one finger into my belt loop and tug until I feel the tip of my finger throb.

She straightens her posture, shifting in the chair, so it sits in front of the hallway entrance to the stairs, blocking me. "I know everything, Theo," she says again.

"Okay. You've made your point."

"Ask me what she's getting ready for."

"I don't really give a shit, to be honest. I'm not a girl and I'm not you guys' friend. That's why I didn't want to fucking do this. And now—" I sigh, unsure of what I'm even saying. "And now you made me look like a dick to her."

"You did that way before I got here."

"Funny." I try to walk to the hallway, but she puts out her hand to stop me.

"You don't need to ask me, is that it? Because you already know. You obviously remember." Her eyes are bright, focused on me so intensely, I feel like a teen getting caught smoking. Beneath her question is another. She knows what happened. My heart sinks, dread filling my lungs, my ears, the hollow parts of my spine. How the fuck did she find out? I try to imagine Magdalen saying anything, but it's hard to see her initiating a conversation about me almost fingering her in an alleyway.

"Don't do this, Anika. Please." Talking to Magdalen is one thing. But having to speak *about* Magdalen to someone else makes this feel too real... The fantasy I'd replayed alone in the shower ever since is not mine and hers alone any more.

"Why didn't you tell me? I wouldn't have given two shits."

"I suppose she told you, then." It feels like the right course of action. Denial, then blame. Gives me time to stall.

"You know she would rather cut her arm off than talk about anything remotely sexual. Especially if it was about you. Jesus, this is so fucked up." She pauses, staring off at the window, but then whips her head up. "Did you fucking threaten her not to tell me?"

"Can you not be so dramatic for one moment of your life? Of course I didn't threaten her."

"You haven't seen anything yet, you idiot. You know fuck-all about Magdalen. I don't bloody care if you fucked! I'd welcome it! She's as rigid as a board. But I would warn you, I would tell you that she doesn't bounce back as easily from things. They stick with her. Things hurt more. But she'll never admit it. To me, to you, not even to God. And now you've done something, I can't help her, or you. And to top it off you've driven her to going on this fucking date."

I mull over her words. *Things hurt more. She will never admit it.* What could that mean? I want to reach inside Magdalen's brain and feel how she thinks.

"What's the big deal about a fucking date?" The lie hangs in the air. Both of us stare at each other, arguing with our eyes.

Anika takes a breath. "You're right. You obviously don't care. Why don't you just leave." She extends her hand to the hallway exit to usher me out, but the growing knot in my stomach pulls taut. When I don't move, she lowers her hand.

"What do you want me to say? I obviously don't like this." My voice is whiny and tight, transparent with pain of something lost.

"Which part don't you like?"

"Does it matter?"

"Everything you do matters to me."

"I think about her," I confess, my head feeling heavy. "I wish it was me she was getting ready for. But I wish I hadn't—"

"You regret it?" Anika asks.

"I regret it *for her*," I say too quickly. "I haven't felt that good since . . . well, a while."

"So she's not as frigid as she seems, then?" Anika smirks, and I almost want to smile.

"She's incredible."

Anika chews her bottom lip. "Will you tell me what happened last week? I can't help if I don't know."

"I don't think Magdalen would like that."

"Neither would Dante." Anika stares at me expectantly.

"Anika, you can't say anything to him." The words rush out in one breath. "He wouldn't get it."

"Of course I won't. But he's not stupid. He's going to find out."

"Hopefully I'll be back in New York by then." I grimace. The thought of New York, how easy it is to lose myself in the bustling city. But now it feels like I will spend my life searching for a face I know will never be in the crowd.

"It really kills you not to be an asshole all the time, doesn't it."

"What now?" I dip my head, impatient to get away from this conversation.

"I get you for a few weeks, and you're already eager to leave me again."

"You know it's not that. But I . . . things have changed. I fucked up."

Anika sighs and glances at the stairwell where Magdalen disappeared. Slowly, she turns back to me. "You really hurt her feelings."

"She seems fine to me."

"Then you don't know her at all."

33

MAGDALEN

The nighttime air is chilly as I wait outside the small bar where Roberto suggested we meet. While it's summer for the rest of Italy, the steep mountains of Castagneto Po trap any and all residual mist, making the village perpetually dewy and wet. He's chosen a locals-only spot, even though he's not a local. I make a mental note to ask him about it and hope it's not just because it's a ten-minute walk to my house. The restaurant is hidden behind a wall of holm oak trees that crowd the hillside, with only a tiny red door peeking through the greenery. I probably should have worn a jacket. I settled for a skimpy tank top Anika chose. Hopefully, he'll see my choice not to wear a jacket and consider it flirtatious without me having to do anything flirty. I shiver, unable to help myself. Flirting already seems impossibly difficult.

Someone opens the door to exit, and warm air curls around my arms. A throaty, smoke-filled laugh fills the inside of the bar.

Briefly, I think of Theo and immediately want to cry. *The only reason you're kissing me is because you're too afraid to fucking talk to anyone else.* But instead of sulking for the millionth time this week, I crack my knuckles, stick my foot inside the door before it closes, and force myself to walk inside. The warm air smells faintly of stale body odor and beer, and I blink at the warm light. For some reason, I feel incredibly shy, and my eyes can only look at the other people's feet. I see shoes scuffing against the floor, someone tapping the heel of their sneaker. Someone's loafers are crossed at the ankles. I try to look above the calf, but my eyes begin to twitch when I do, so instead, I attempt to navigate the space via the sea of feet, hoping to find an empty space.

As I turn the corner of the bar, I hear Roberto call my name. "Magdalen, over here."

I stop walking and force my eyes to search above the calves, above the tables, and eventually to the faces.

His voice is higher than Theo's. It's not a bad thing, but I notice it immediately.

"Hey."

"Hey. You look incredible."

I shrug my shoulders, unsure of how to respond to that in a witty way, but I end up saying nothing instead.

"What can I get you to drink?" Roberto immediately fills the empty space I've made, and I feel both grateful and already very exhausted.

"I'll get a beer, thanks."

"Sure, sure. Go sit." He brushes my arm to indicate the table he's reserved for us, so I walk, thankful for being given an order.

When I sit down and settle into the seat, I watch Roberto at the bar. He's objectively very good-looking. I'm flattered that he might have asked me on a date. Cropped light brown hair gelled with military precision, bright blue eyes. I immediately think about my own hair and how messy the wind has made it. I wonder if the difference in our hair indicates something fundamental about us. When he gets the drinks, he slaps the bar loudly and, turning toward me, I notice that he's not afraid to look at me as he walks with our drinks. He flashes me a smile and keeps eye contact for the entire walk from the bar to the table. I think about how, if it was me, I would be looking down at the glasses.

"Here we are!" Roberto says excitedly.

"Here we are!" I repeat, because I genuinely have nothing else to say.

"Did you find the place all right?"

I try not to roll my eyes. As if he doesn't know that I know this place.

"Yeah. Luckily it's right near my house."

"Oh, is that right?" he says and then licks his upper lip where beads of white wine have lingered. His tongue protrudes like the amputated tentacle of an octopus, squirming frantically one last time before it realizes it's been severed from the rest of its body. I find this grotesque and try to imagine his tongue coming anywhere near my face, but I feel myself wanting to shudder. I try not to think about Theo instead. But by resisting thinking of him, I've arguably already thought about him more intensely than if I'd just thought the thought. Theo's tongue. How I found it sexy when it peeked out to moisten his lips while he was talking. I hadn't known tongues could be sexy. I wanted it all over me. I try to look at Roberto's tongue with the same perspective, but it's still revolting.

"Yeah, I think you knew that, though."

Roberto snorts into his glass. I must be funny!

"All right, you got me," Roberto says sheepishly. "I figured you'd be more inclined to say yes if you didn't have to ask for a ride."

I pause. "How do you know I can't drive?"

He looks at me like I've asked a dumb question. "Magdalen, *everyone* knows you can't drive," he says, emphasizing *everyone* as if people living on the outskirts of Pisa were aware of my driving inability.

"Oh," I say fairly bluntly.

"Yeah, so I just wanted to make sure you were comfortable." Roberto says the last word slowly, as if he's trying to seduce me with phonetics.

"That was very generous of you, Roberto."

"It was nothing."

An awkward silence settles between us and I know it's my turn to say something, but I have nothing to add to this dialogue.

"You know, you were really quiet back in secondary school," Roberto adds nonchalantly.

I sigh, annoyed but understanding there's not much else people remember me by. "Yeah, I guess I still am."

Goosebumps begin to form on my arm, and I wish I had brought a sweater. A wool jacket. A fucking parka.

"Why is that? You're so pretty."

My face heats. I realize I am deeply offended by his obtuse correlation between beauty and confidence.

But maybe I heard him wrong. Taking a huge sip of beer, I try to reword the statement, figuring out if I missed a word because of the chatter around me.

If he didn't think I was pretty, would my shyness make sense to him? My brain searches for a way to understand this, but I'm just disgusted by how different we already are. I think of Theo again. How he would obviously know the two are not mutually exclusive. He would scoff, roll his eyes, and say something smart. He'd have an anecdote lined up that would seamlessly prove his point. Right now, I can't think of anything to say and it makes me frustrated with my own intellect.

"Maybe I'm shy because I know how gorgeous I am."

Roberto stares at me for a moment.

"And because I'm so *gorgeous*, I have no need to try to talk to people who I know are less than I am."

Years ago, when Anika forced me to go to a daytime party with her in Torino, I asked her how she was so good at talking to strangers. "I just don't think of them as real people," she'd said. I always thought about that afterward, but could never get myself to think with the same indifference. But I loved it. "They're just a part of my story," she said resolutely, and paddled off to the boys with their spritzes, flipping her hair.

Looking at Roberto now, I finally begin to feel as Anika does. Whether I strip naked in front of him or throw my drink, it won't matter. He is not real to my story. I know this with certainty. In a week, in two months, in ten years, Roberto will be a nameless face with cropped hair who I went to a bar with.

"Ha, yeah, I guess that could be it," Roberto answers with no conviction. He has no prepared comeback and it doesn't make me any happier than if he did. The first date I've ever been on has been ruined by someone who's not even here.

"I guess so."

"When did you get back home?" he asks.

"A few weeks ago."

"I thought you'd be one of those who never came back to Chivasso."

"I tried, but then my sister fell in love."

He furrows his brow, making it a point to switch between looking at my left eye and right, as if he's trying to read my mind and wants me to know it. "Why don't you like home?"

God, he sounds like a psychiatrist.

"That's a tough question." I sip my beer, somehow already warm. The fuzzy ache I feel whenever I think of my childhood reappears for a moment, even after a decade. "I guess I felt a little unincluded in my own life."

I don't mean to tell the truth. Blinking away the feeling of hot tears, I try to smile, but I assume I look insane. Roberto smiles back stiffly and I feel terrible that I've wasted his night.

"That's funny you say that." He takes an even larger sip of his wine than I did of my beer, as if preparing for his speech. Is this a competition? I sip my beer just in case it is.

"I've also been grappling with identity. My last girlfriend, well, let's just say she had no room for social cognition, you know?"

I go over his words in my head and realize that I, in fact, do not know. It strikes me as odd how quickly I agreed to this date because I thought I knew Roberto, when I have no fucking clue who he turned out to be.

"Totally," I contribute.

"Thank you! I have an inner social circle that requires replenishment, and in the end, we mutually agreed that we weren't compatible—personality-wise."

Roberto's face has gone slightly clammy around the edges, and the blue outline of a vein has suddenly appeared in the middle of his forehead, throbbing with vengeance. It's not his fault. We all have veins. I suspect if I didn't spend my time memorizing Theo's face, I wouldn't have ever noticed this about Roberto.

"So what do you study at university?" I try to switch up the conversation and, surprise surprise, find out he is studying to be a psychiatrist. The conversation soon circles back to his ex, however.

By the hour mark, I truly believe I'm having a stroke. Trying to connect his words into understandable sentences, I draw a blank each time. But it seems I'm saying all the right things for Roberto to continue his monologue about his ex, Camille, whom he feels no need to stop talking about. She's studying to be a pediatric nurse in Milan. She has a cat named Sylvia, because *La Dolce Vita* is her favorite

Fellini film. She's a Gemini who does angel dust more often than Roberto likes. But he loves her. And I feel sad for both of us, out on a Thursday night with the wrong person.

After the first beer, I settle deeper into the hard, creaky chair. Familiar with the dull sensation of being talked at.

My gaze wanders to his hands, and I notice the nail on his right middle finger is much longer than the rest. Some dirt is caked underneath it, and his cuticles are sprouting like wildflowers. I stop paying attention to what he's saying after that.

34

THEO

"I know you're pissed off at me, but if we don't leave now, Anika, we're going to get there at midnight."

She turns on the hairdryer even though I know she never uses the hairdryer during the summer, and I can do nothing but sigh and go back to my room to wait.

A weekend in Alassio with Anika, Magdalen, Dante, Lucia and Maio. While normally I'd be psyched for a trip like this, I've been anxious to see Magdalen since yesterday. Do I apologize first? Do I ask her how the date went? I think about her in those jeans and wonder if he touched her leg under the table, feeling the length of her thigh. I have no right, I remind myself. No right to wonder when their night ended, or if it's continuing as I sit here, knee bouncing with nerves, waiting until it's appropriate to sprint downstairs and watch the front door for the next Savoy to leave.

Roberto Almeno, who I deduced was the fucking mystery man, went to primary *and* secondary school with Magdalen and only now insists on taking her out as soon as she's back home. Get in line, buddy.

Then a heavy knock interrupts and the brief moment with Magdalen fades.

"Busy?" My father leans against the door frame as if physically unable to enter my room.

"What's up?"

"Heading out soon?" He looks at his watch, letting me know he's disappointed. "Traffic will be congested if you wait any longer."

I sigh. "Yeah, I know, just waiting for Anika to finish up in the bathroom."

"You should have woken her up earlier, Theo." Pinching my nose, I count down from ten, trying not to blow up.

Even as the door frame hides him, I can still see myself in him. His impatience. Endless. The divot in his nose. It's painful to see exactly how I'll turn out.

"I saw your thesis." He jerks his head toward my desk. Open textbooks and the early copy of my paper lie scattered around my desk.

"I fucking told you—"

"I know."

"I told you not to—"

"Then don't leave it sitting there." He straightens himself. "I've been telling you to clean this room since you lived here."

"Sorry, I thought the verbal agreement we had the last time you tried to read it clarified that I want you to stay out of my shit."

"Again with this." He claps his hands together and sighs, lifting his foot to cross into my room, but his loafer just hovers over the divide, traversing his world and mine. Eventually, he lowers his foot back onto his side of the frame

258

and lets out a breath of relief. "Don't you get tired of always being so angry?"

A nerve in my temple pulses, and I imagine screaming so fucking hard my veins burst, and I drown in my own blood.

"Where's Mamma?" I bite.

His eyes flash for a second. Ready for a fight. "Savoys' house."

"Three a crowd?"

He glances back toward the bathroom door, and then, without warning, he's on me. I blink, unsure of how I missed the moment he even began walking toward me, but it's too late; his head is inches from mine, our noses almost brushing.

"Excuse me?" His breath is hot on my face, and up close, I idly wonder if this is what my nose looks like to others. "If you have something to say to me, say it."

It takes very little to shake my father's composure, but I've been doing it since I was a kid, and I'm still just as scared.

"How many times have I told you." He grabs my chin between his pointer finger and thumb, squeezing so hard I feel my jaw beginning to crack in protest.

"And how many times did you fuck her before I saw?" I say through clenched teeth, my breathing ragged as I look him in the eyes so he knows. So he knows I will never forget. Even halfway across the world and a decade later, I can't forget.

He stares at me momentarily before releasing my head and rolling his eyes. Absentmindedly rubbing my chin, I still feel his fingers pressing into me but I'm too exhausted to try to get him back. He walks to my desk and leafs through my thesis notes again. Knowing I won't say anything this time.

"Always so dramatic." He steps back and distractedly tucks his shirt into his trousers, then checks the time on his watch. "Put gas in the car on your way back."

35

MAGDALEN

Theo is standing outside, smoking, when I walk up their driveway. He's wearing another white T-shirt that's slightly see-through, so I can see his stomach, the faint tracing of the tattoos across his ribs making it extra painful to look at him. I try to roll my suitcase quietly to buy some time, but I barely make it a few steps before he turns his head in my direction.

He stares at me and takes an inhale of his cigarette. One arm crossed over his chest, he breathes out deeply, clouding himself in his own smoke, and shakes his head before dropping it on the floor.

"Magdalen."

That is all he says as he walks down the driveway, which makes me realize I've stopped walking completely. My cheeks flush, embarrassed that he still can cause me to forget everything, even when he's being an ass. I think of the girls at Oxford that would cry and get back with boys who broke their hearts, and how I'd roll my eyes at their silliness. I always assumed that when a man came into my life, I'd never let him affect me. But I'm no better. I would crawl on my hands and knees across this driveway to have Theo kiss me just one more time.

"Good morning." He pushes his hair behind his ear, and I squeeze the handle of my luggage to stop myself from doing it for him. "I was just thinking about you, and then you appeared at the end of the driveway. I thought I might still be dreaming. My *phantasma*."

"Are you serious right now?" I look behind me to see if this is a joke he's playing on me with Dante hiding behind a rose bush.

"I said I was just—"

"No, I heard you." I turn back around to face him. "What happened to the '*Magdalen, no offense, but I'd rather kill myself in a bath of gasoline than hang out with you for more than ten seconds.*'" I try to imitate his voice, but it comes out more like a chain-smoking bullfrog.

Theo tilts his head back and laughs freely, one hand pressing his stomach. It's such a wonderful sound that I unconsciously take a deep breath, wanting to capture it for myself. Giddy that it was me that caused his happiness. *Remember Roberto*, my brain screams. Someone who had shown me interest—took me out, bought me a drink, and told me I was pretty. But Theo places his large hand on my own, resting on the luggage, and Roberto becomes dust. My skin prickles at the contact, and I fight the urge to close my eyes and revel in it.

"You're funny." Theo looks down at our hands and wraps his fingers around my wrist, squeezing gently. "Let me, baby girl."

My stomach flutters. *Baby.* Is he drunk? I check his eyes and can't find anything to indicate a chemical imbalance, then try to mentally recall if we have already kissed and made up.

"I got it," I say, trying to tug the suitcase back.

"You should know by now that I usually get what I want."

"You lost the right to want anything from me after—"

"After what I did in the archway," he finishes solemnly. "I know."

"And your impatience with my dress-up was quite rude as well," I add.

"I know."

"Look, why don't you save the groveling for another girl. It's clear that we don't really know each other and I'm not in the mood to convince you I'm worth getting to know."

He steps closer and the scent of clean cotton washes over me. Hair as dark as ink, glimmering in the afternoon light.

"I'm getting really tired of people telling me I don't fuck-ing know you." His voice deepens. "Let me get to know you." The sun reflects off his necklace, which I now realize holds a simple gold ring. His eyes flutter to my mouth, and he sighs. "You don't know how badly I want to."

"What is wrong with you? You only come to me when you're bored with everyone else."

"That's not true."

"It feels like it."

He frowns, his grip faltering. If I were bolder, I would say something else. I would say: *When you left me that night by the river, it felt like you carved something out of me.* I let the

263

words settle at the base of my throat until I can say anything at all.

He looks down at the ground for a split second, but it's enough for his mask to slip. Suddenly, I can see all the dread and pain he's been trying to hide behind his delicate touch of my wrist. It's only for a second. He smirks again, ready to continue his façade. How silly. I want to die. I'm not the object of his affection but the distraction from his pain.

"I'm sorry you feel that way."

I tug my hand from his grip, and he takes the opportunity to reach for the luggage handle.

"Good, now leave me alone."

He arches an eyebrow, and it's so much like his father, so condescending and entitled, that I have to blink a few times to get the image out. "I miss you, Maggie."

I blanch, jerking my head back to look at him. My mouth feels dry and wooden. "Romantic," I scoff.

Looking past him, I see Dante trying to hop the fence between our houses, and I attempt to make my way to the car again.

"Does it have to be?" He glances at who I'm looking at and grabs my wrist again. "Does it have to be romantic, I mean?" His voice aims for casual, but I can see a flash of urgency in his eyes. Desperation. It startles me how completely desperate he is. Maybe I don't want to die, after all.

"We could just have fun," he suggests, and I bite my lip in order not to laugh at what a complete idiot he's being.

"This is arguably the least fun conversation I've ever had."

"I could be more fun, for you, sweet Magdalen."

"You'll be whatever anyone wants you to be, right?" I stop walking. I can feel my anger, ravenous and violent. "So long as you get what you want," I finish.

Theo stops walking. I can see muscles in his jaw tense and relax as if he's swallowing the rebuttals he wants to throw back. "You know fuck-all about me."

"And he's back!" I give a slow clap and start walking faster toward the car.

"Fuck, Magdalen. I'm complete shit at this."

"At what? Having a conversation for longer than five minutes without telling me what a repressed idiot I am?" I roll my eyes, annoyed that I've humored this conversation for as long as I have. Nothing has changed since the tennis club. Since my bloody tits and his silly haircut. Since my first real kiss.

He glances at Dante, who frowns at us before chucking the bread and preserves my mother bought into the trunk. Theo looks back at me. In this morning sun, his eyes almost glow yellow. But just as quickly, the shade shifts, and the tiredness in them reminds me of what a boy he really is.

"I didn't mean any of that," he blurts out awkwardly. "I'm sorry."

"You've said sorry before, *baby*."

He stumbles quickly and I know he's remembering the archway, too. Whispering "baby" in my ear while I grind myself on him.

Turning to him again, I ask, "How can I trust you? I know *fuck-all about you*, yeah?"

"Well, maybe I want someone to know me." He almost

lifts his hand to touch me, but instead squeezes the handle of my luggage. "Maybe I want it to be you."

"Why the sudden change of heart? I thought I was annoying and inexperienced. I thought you hated getting me off. Isn't that what you said? *What part of that was enjoyable to you?*"

"Christ, as if I haven't been enjoying that memory every fucking day since." He kicks a pebble off the driveway as we walk.

My mind whirls. What the fuck is going on?

"Listen, I'm saying sorry for the stupid shit I say. I...I can't offer you more than this. I can't give you the romance you deserve." He continues, finding his words. His voice becomes intent. Desperate. "I have no right to need you, I fucking know that, but, if you let me, I can show you what it should be like. What it can feel like. I'm sorry for everything I said. As much as I want you to know me, Magdalen..." He tugs at the roots of his hair, as if trying to pull the words out of him. "...I hate who I am most of the time, but I don't usually do anything to fix it."

Me too, I silently agree. But I opt for anger instead.

"Theo, I'm really not sure what you want me to say to any of this. You *left* me. You kissed me back and then you left me. And I'm not sure if you're drunk." I squint, trying to see if his eyes are glazed over.

He snorts. "I'm not drunk. I'm too easily seduced by you when I drink."

"So I never stood a chance sober?"

"Not what I meant."

"Then what did you mean?"

Theo breathes in deeply. "I would have been more careful with you. Would have taken my time. Would have seduced you first."

"You never had to be careful with me. Respectful would have been lovely."

"The next time I kiss you, I'll consider that."

"What makes you think I'd ever let you kiss me again? If I recall, I had to practically beg for the first one."

"I don't mind begging. I'll do it next time. This time on my knees."

I roll my eyes again, but with a smile this time. I am no stronger than any other girl. "I'll see you in Alassio."

He sighs and runs his hand through those thick curls. "Tell Anika to drive safe, please. You owe me a kiss."

"I don't owe you anything!"

"Fine, I owe you one." His smile dazzles. "Seriously, tell her to be fucking careful. I need you in one piece."

36

THEO

Dante and I arrive before everyone else. The villa is big, all stone walls and windows with green shutters.

"That's my girl!" Dante beats his hands on the steering wheel as we pull up to the place Anika rented for the weekend. "How many fucking bedrooms do you think there are?" We both try to peer up at the three-story house through the windscreen, but it's so tall we can only see the first floor.

"Shit. Six, maybe seven?"

"Obviously, we have to take advantage of this."

He parks the car by the garden and peers over at me, one eyebrow raised stupidly. I try to muster a smile but give up halfway and open the car door instead. With my back to him, I stare at the sun, the house, the permanence of a building like this.

"How do you mean?"

Dante bangs the roof of my father's car and I jerk around. "You're joking, right?"

"Our sisters are going to be in the house with us." I roll my eyes and open the trunk to start unloading the groceries and luggage, eager to divert this conversation in another direction.

"Hellooo?" he gestures, arms wide. "Big house. Lots of

268

room. Discretion. Secrecy. Hot. As long as we come home when they're all sleeping, they won't know shit."

"Oh my god, can we at least get into the house first, before we discuss ravishing the village girls?"

Dante jogs up to the front door and overturns the cement urn at the side of the entrance, per Anika's instructions. "New York has made you so boring."

"I think the word you're looking for is 'mature.' "

"Different," he mumbles, but it's loud enough so I can hear. I haul out Lucia's luggage and ignore it.

Dante wiggles the key with frustration but finally opens the door, immediately gasping. "My god, Anika. I would kiss you if you were here!"

"Despite what you may think, I don't love you talking about my sister like that, dickhead."

He clicks his tongue. "As if you're not eye-fucking my sister, too," Dante says behind his shoulder as he steps into the house. The baguette I'm holding slips out of its wrapping and onto the driveway. Dante steps back out and searches for a cigarette in his pocket. "You gotta light?" He puts the smoke in his mouth and raises his hands over his head, stretching casually.

"Eh, yeah." My mind feels melted; my hands move of their own accord to find the lighter.

"Not even gonna deny it, then?" he says between slanted lips, walking in front of me.

I find the lighter, my thumb misses the spark wheel the first time and I try again. Dante leans forward as the flame finds the end of the cig.

"Dante." My voice is hoarse. I try to muster up an excuse, an apology, anything to fill the silence. But nothing comes out.

"Yes?"

"I'm really sorry."

"For what?" He exhales the smoke, looking at me expectantly.

"I should have told you."

"You should have." He nods his head in agreement and walks past me to get more bags from the trunk.

"Nothing happened," I lie, because how can I not try to cover it up?

"Bullshit."

"Excuse me?"

"She doesn't fucking date. Never happened. Never did."

"What's that got to do with me?" I turn to face him, forgetting the baguette in my hand, and it slips to the floor again.

Dante looks at me like I'm the stupidest person alive. "Let's see." He pulls out Magdalen's luggage and throws it at my feet. "You drool every time she's around. You take her home from the club. Then you fuck Chiara the next day— *don't think I don't know what that was*. You're alone with her all night out on the streets. Then the next week she's going on a date with Roberto motherfucking Almeno. I swear to god, it's like you people think I'm actually blind."

"Listen, I didn't pla—"

"You should have just fucking told me."

My mouth opens to defend myself. To blame the gods

and the mystic power of red wine for making me want his sister.

"You're the one who said I wasn't allowed near her." My brain feels too slow, his words and mine muddle together in a thick fog that I can only seem to pluck out letter by letter.

Dante rolls his eyes and slams the trunk shut. "*Cazzo*, you complete and utter idiot. I said BE CAREFUL. I said don't pull the same shit you did in secondary school. She's my baby sister—am I not allowed one protective big brother speech? Or are you the only one fucking entitled to it?"

I bend down to pick up the beaten-up baguette, mumbling something like "of course," but I'm still so stunned I can't be sure what words I'm saying.

"You would have told me once." He rests one hand on my shoulder, keeping me bent down so I can only stare at Magdalen's luggage. His voice is low, serious. "Once, it would have killed you to keep a secret from me." Squeezing tightly for just a moment, he tosses his cigarette near the wheel of the car before releasing me with a shove.

37

MAGDALEN

When we get to the villa, Dante and Theo are nowhere to be found. Lucia and Maio's car is parked on the nearby street and when we get inside they're feeding each other olives across the kitchen island.

"Oh, this is disgusting." Anika and I ogle them through the doorway. "Can't you save this for the honeymoon?"

"To think we were going to christen this place. They beat us to it," I muse.

"Which bedroom do you think they had sex in?"

"I heard that." Lucia pipes up while wiping her mouth of excess olive oil. She eyes us with feline eyes, smirking.

"And?"

"First floor. Far right."

I gasp while Anika erupts into a fit of laughter and soon enough we're both gagging and giggling while Maio hides his head in his hands in shame.

"Maio, you've got to get used to her crude mouth," I say between laughs.

"Oh, he's used to it." Lucia smiles widely, causing Maio to abruptly get up from leaning on the kitchen island and stare hard at Lucia to convey some secret message that she's ignoring.

"When did this family get so sexually liberal? I miss the days when everyone suppressed their feelings," I sigh, walking to the counter to steal an olive.

"While this has been fun…" Maio pats down his shirt, obviously looking for something to do with his hands while he reins in his embarrassment. "…I haven't had a chance to look at the garden yet."

"That's so funny, sweetie." Lucia closes the lid to the olive container while my fingers try to grab one. "Neither have I." She swats his ass while they walk to the backyard and I hide my smile behind my hands.

"The boys have put your luggage in the rooms upstairs," Lucia calls while closing the door behind her and grabbing Maio's hand.

We walk up the marble stairs, cold stone cutting through the humid, summer air warming the house.

I peek inside the bedrooms and see Dante's swimming shorts and belts scattered across the bed in the safari-themed bedroom. There's a zebra-print cushion on the crisp white sheets and an elephant mural on the far-right wall. The furniture is dark and sleek —wicker stools and woven rugs laid carefully throughout the space. It's so Dante—chaotic and overtly masculine. It is clearly meant for him.

Anika's luggage is laid on the bed in the pink room next to his. Her curtains are frilly and fun, with a gingham tufted skirt around the bed. She lies across it, rummaging blindly for something in her luggage, humming some nameless song. I tiptoe down the hall until I spot my luggage in the corner of the bedroom diagonal from Anika's. Stepping in, I can't help but feel underwhelmed and exposed by whoever chose this room for me. Shades of various pale blues decorate the space. A simple bed with a cornflower-blue duvet. No throw pillows or vase of flowers. The only creative liberty, really, being a muted painting of the ocean above the beige headboard. It feels lifeless, incomplete. The room they made after exhausting all their efforts on the others. I throw my purse on the bed. At least there's a bed.

As I go to open the luggage, I notice a white T-shirt has been tucked into the handle of the bag. Frowning, I pull it out and go to check the size but I don't even get to the tag before a wave of his scent washes over me. It's invasive, heavenly toxic, and there's no stopping me from bringing the fabric to my nose, breathing him in. Turning scent into delusion as I wish for him here, kneeled next to me in this sad, blue room, his sunlight warming the place up. As I unravel the shirt, a piece of paper tucked between the folded creases falls onto my lap.

Looks like you forgot pajamas.
Thank god for me.

I cover my mouth with my hand to suppress my laughter. And shake my head—ashamed, happy, confused, anxious. Wanting more.

A few words scribbled and all that anger following our rendezvous in Torino bleeds away with a little pen to paper. I sigh. He'll be back in New York soon enough. Why not have some fun in the meantime?

Opening my luggage, the sound of my own gasp startles me when I find the contents completely rearranged.

"Theo, this is a major invasion of privacy," I grumble through a smile as I take in what he's done. My pajamas are definitely gone. Instead, the lingerie Marta supplied me with sits neatly on top of my clothes. Lavender thong. Lavender bra. White socks with lace lining, oddly enough. A uniform for the sexually repressed.

"Oh my god." My head falls into the open luggage as I process Theo seeing me in this. "Oh my god," I say again, because what else is there to say?

"Should I ask?"

My head jerks up to see Anika, clad in her bright orange bikini and tiny sarong, looking at me through the door frame.

"Oh, it's nothing." I quickly shut my luggage and stand up. But it happens in slow motion, the paper falls onto the floor and Anika's eyes dart to it and the white T-shirt in my hand.

"Don't you da—" I start, but Anika dives to the floor before I can even get my knees to bend.

"Is it from Roberto?" She crumples the paper tightly in her hand, rolling across the carpeted floor so she's out of reach.

"No! You know how it went with him."

"So who's it from, then?" Her breathing is fast, paper still held tightly in her hand.

"Anika, don't open it." I crawl toward her but she kicks her tiny feet out, stopping me.

"Tell me!" She wiggles her toes, almost touching my forehead before I back away.

"I can't."

"Why not? Are you fucking a priest?"

"Anika!"

"A rabbi?"

"Okay, you've made your point," I huff, lying down on my back. The ceiling fan humming is the only noise in the room for a moment. I take a breath out.

"My brother?" she says, a slight edge in her voice. I roll my head to look at her, unsure if she's joking or not. My heart stammers. A million denials, justifications, confessions at the ready, but I remain silent, remembering Theo's words.

Just don't tell Anika, okay?

"Please, be serious." My voice cracks at the end and I try to smile to make up for it but my lips feel numb and I'm unsure if I said anything at all.

"I am." She throws the crumpled paper at my stomach, the paper bouncing off my hip and landing between us. It lands closer to her than it does to me. "I know something happened."

I sit up, resting on my elbows as I continue to stare at her, at a loss for words, for excuses.

"I know because Theo told me," she interrupts before I

even get the chance to speak. *Just don't tell Anika, okay?* Did I mishear?

"What do you mean?"

"I mean he told me something happened between you two after Lucia's engagement dinner."

"Oh." I frown, feeling both hurt and relief. His parting words were a lie to get me out of his sight. Did he sit down and gossip about me with Anika over drinks? Maybe he met up with her and Dante right after. Maybe they laughed together.

I see his snarl, how his canine tooth poked out when he was telling me off. It was so sharp, so predatory, and it was inside my mouth. I remember wishing he had made me bleed.

"Maggie, you don't need to hide shit like that from me."

"Oh," I sniffle. "Okay."

"He didn't tell me everything." She crosses her legs and inches closer to me, concern welling in her eyes. "I basically had to force it out of him."

"He told me not to tell you." How could I have listened to him so religiously? So afraid that she would find out and he would be disappointed that I broke his cardinal rule.

"Don't do that, come on." Anika crawls on her knees until she's draped over me like heavy mink. Warm. Cozy. She's slightly sticky from all the sunscreen lathered on her body but she wraps her hands around my shoulders, embracing me so tightly, I'm lost in vanilla and Coppertone 8.

"I'm so sorry." I don't register I'm crying until she's

rocking me back and forth, soothing me, whispering gently between comforting coos. "It's okay, Maggie. Please, it'll always be okay."

"He was so mean," I hear myself saying in a heavy exhale, snot and tears now dripping down my face. The words feel hooked inside me; saying them out loud feels like tearing apart pieces of me.

"Fuck him." Anika curls around me, squeezing, squeezing, squeezing, trying, without knowing, to stitch the puncture together again.

"He's your brother!" I sob even more.

"That doesn't mean he's always right. Listen, Mag, Theo was born good, there's no denying that. But, shit, man. There's so much you don't know about him. There're things even I don't know about him. Things that eat him up all the time. He cried, the day before he left for Yale, did you know that? Sobbed all night. It went on forever, and I thought he was going to pass out from crying so much. I stayed with him the entire time and thought that gorgeous face was permanently tear-stained. But not once did he tell me why he was crying. I begged. I begged for hours, Maggie. Not a peep. So what I'm saying is . . . What the fuck am I even saying?"

I sniffle, looking at Anika lost in the memory of herself and Theo. "I didn't know that."

"Of course not, no one does. He'd literally kill me if he knew I was telling you."

"Do you have any idea what it could have been about?" My own sadness feels far away. Tucked in the luggage across the room. I'm desperate to know more about Theo.

"Whatever it is, I'm sure my father is to blame."

"Yeah, we don't talk about him a lot, do we?"

"We shouldn't have to," Anika answers sharply. "He's only been friends with your saint of a father for twenty years. You would think..." She stops mid-sentence, lost in thought. "You would think just a little of that would rub off on him."

"My father's not perfect."

"Mag." She turns her head to me, her eyes burning into mine. "Your father is *absolutely* perfect."

This time, I don't try to deny it. "Why did you never tell me how bad he got?" I search for her hands, wrapping them tightly in my own.

"Because," she says, and sighs, settling her head on my shoulder, "all shall be well, and all shall be well, and all manner of things shall be well," she singsongs.

We sit there on the floor of the blue bedroom, her prayer ringing in our ears. I think of Theo crying again and shut my eyes.

"Mother Julian of Norwich?"

I feel her nod against me. "Found a postcard with that quote a few years ago in one of the euro bins at the market. I really liked it. Helps me when things get tough."

Tough? I swallow hard. Knowing if I try to broach the subject she'll spook, the only way she knows how. Deflect with a joke or turn the radio on and dance the question off.

"You know, I tried to make her my confirmation saint," I say instead.

"No way." Anika's head pops off my shoulder to look at me, eyes lit up.

279

"Very much way. My mother said she didn't count, so I went with Saint Angela."

"I never knew that!"

"That's why it's freaky!" I giggle despite myself. Amused that we're geeking out over saints.

"I love being freaky with you." She rests her head back on my shoulder, nuzzling her temple against my skin. "It makes me feel like everything will be all right."

"You're my favorite freak. I love you so much." My throat tightens, tears threatening to resurface if I think too hard about her. About how often I avoided calling during university. How little I wondered if she was okay. I make a mental note to worry more for her. To remember that she can dance and be sad, too.

"Me more. And because I love you, I need you to know that Theo is . . . Theo is more like my father than he cares to admit."

"Anika—"

She stops me. "Don't let him take advantage of you." She unravels her hand so she's now holding mine, as she's always done. "Don't let him get away with shit," she says with a final huff.

We don't talk any more after that. She doesn't offer any further information about Theo and neither do I. We sit on the floor instead, the radio in her room streaming into the quiet of mine. Raf's voice whispers, *"Sei la più bella del mondo. Sei la più bella per me."* Anika unconsciously hums along.

It's unsettling to know that Theo's goodness is eclipsed by a darkness none of us can make out. It hides behind broad shoulders and witty banter. *Don't let him take advantage of you.* I chew my lip. But I *would* let him. The thought is terrifying and exciting. I *would* let him.

38

THEO

Dante slams the payphone against the telephone box. "Fuck off, you piece of Sicilian shit." Despite the booth covering him, his voice is loud and clear.

"Jesus," I mumble, rubbing the back of my neck as I try to apologize with a lame smile to the beach-going passers-by. They glance at Dante with disgust and I shrug: *Run along. You don't want to be here for this!*

Dante shoves the door open and sniffs loudly. "Well, she's a fucking cunt."

"No luck?"

We cross the street to enter *il budello di Alassio* and I instantly smile. Small shops with their doors wide open, shades of coral, yellow and teal crowding the tiny streets. Beach balls with Italian flags and fishing nets spill onto the pathways. Mini electric fans drone in the stiff heat of summer, doing nothing but providing white noise to an already obnoxiously loud fucking environment. We enter the first walkway into the market and immediately the scent of hot, fresh *piadine* hits me. *Fuck me, that's heavenly.* Roasted peppers dripping in olive oil, *prosciutto di Parma* layered in a cool blanket of burrata. I almost drool, searching for the shop to devour one.

"You would think an orgy would warrant some sort of loyalty. It's not like I'm asking for fucking meth. It's shrooms, for crying out loud."

My hand reaches out to stop him in the middle of the small street, *piadine* eviscerated from my mind. "You've had an orgy?"

Dante falters a moment. "Who hasn't, you know what I mean?" He digs his elbow into my ribs and tries to continue walking but I put my hand out again, pausing him.

"No, eh, crazy thing, but I don't actually know what you mean, Dante. I've never had a fucking orgy."

"Guess not every Sinclair is as fun as Anika."

My fists clench; it's my turn to stop walking. "You motherfucker. Did you have a fucking orgy with my sister?"

"What happens in Paris, stays in Paris, brother. And that's all I can say on that."

I grip his shirt so tightly I hear the fabric ripping. Pushing him out of the crowd of tourists, we go into a shaded empty corner and I shove him forcefully against the bricks.

"You're on my dick about even thinking about Magdalen and you go and have a fucking orgy with my sister?" The last words come out louder than expected and, when I peer over to make sure no one heard, a small boy with gelato dripping down his wrist stares up at me.

"Clearly, our sisters are *very* different," he whispers, and winks at the ice cream boy, who's watching us, completely mesmerized.

"I'm going to punch you," I growl.

"No, no, you're not." He tries to wiggle out of my grip but I press him against the wall again until he winces.

"I could."

"Of course you could, you're so strong and agile." Dante tries to pat my shoulder but I swat him away so his hand hits the concrete wall behind him.

"Ow, ow, okay. Listen, it happened years ago. Seven consenting adults gathered in an exclusive Parisian brothel and created something really magical that night. Some would call it an act of God."

"Seven?" I push again, my brain trying to compute how seven naked bodies could even attempt fucking in sync, and my mind immediately blanks when I remember my sister was one of them.

"Not the point. Shouldn't have said that. That's on me." Dante squirms in my hand, bracing for impact.

"I'm going on a fucking date with Magdalen," I spit out.

"Theo," Dante starts, but I slam him back into the wall again, rather enjoying this now. "Okay, okay," he wheezes out, his face grimacing with each subsequent hit to the wall.

"And maybe I'll even give her a kiss goodnight," I say more calmly. Flashes of Torino, late at night, hands tangled in her hair, in her skirt. Remembering the hesitancy of her lips at first. How she sighed into me when our lips brushed. I bite my tongue to snap out of the memory.

"Ew. Please, that's my sister," Dante says, and then hesitantly smiles. I scoff, mouth open to retort, but he cuts me off. "Fine, all right. Jesus. Take her on a date. Give her flowers. Buy her a small plot of land in Scotland and make her a Lady."

I release him with a final shove that sends him into a coughing fit. "I really fucking hate you."

Dante brushes his shirt off and readjusts the collar and I turn around to eat the shit out of a *piadina*. "No, you really fucking don't."

I turn around quickly and he flinches. Unable to hide my smile, I bend forward and cackle loudly.

"Not funny," he murmurs, smoothing his brick-hard hair. "You're the one who said you'd hit me. Now that we'll have to find shrooms the old-fashioned way, I'll need to seduce the streets."

"Oh, you should have seen the look on your face. You thought I was going to do it!" I say, still bent over.

"Ha ha. 'Look, I made Dante flinch!' Good one. Are we ever going to leave this damp corner you've sequestered me in or are you planning on spanking me also?"

I stand straight and sigh happily. Am I going to ask Magdalen on a date? My stomach clenches at the thought. I imagine kissing her shoulder at the dinner table and immediately I know. I imagine finishing what we started underneath that archway.

"Lead the way, *signore*."

"Okay, but we're getting some *piadine* before the beach. All this fighting has exhausted me."

"Just start walking, Dante."

"Okay, okay." He opens his mouth to say something else but decides against it and just smiles before turning around and walking off.

39

MAGDALEN

After our fifth time around *il budello*, I'm obligated to speak up. Anika has already changed my bathing suit top, bought us matching beaded sarongs and purchased a professional ear-piercing gun.

"You like books, right? Let's go into the bookstore," she chirps as we approach a quiet side street. There's a single lamppost at the end of the alley. We start walking down farther and I see a wooden sign hanging on top of a bright green door. It swings in the breeze and the rusty hinges squeak with the movement. *LIBRI USATI.*

"Anika, we're not wearing shirts. They're never going to let us in," I whisper harshly before she opens the door.

She rolls her eyes and grabs my wrist with the hand not occupied with her dozen shopping bags. "It's Alassio, not the Vatican, you idiot. Everyone is in their bathing suits."

The doorbell chimes as we enter and instantly the smell of old books floods through. It's a heady and nostalgic scent, so peaceful that my eyes almost close. When the door shuts behind us, the noises of Alassio's busy streets disappear, the store suddenly hushed. Like finding a damp cave during a rainfall, I'm overcome with calm from such a noiseless space.

"*Buonasera*," says an old woman sitting behind the counter. Only the top of her head pokes out from over the desk and when she speaks I see that the front row of her teeth are missing.

I nod hello and walk deeper into the aisles of books. Anika and I split up, and I begin to make my way down to the nineteenth-century literature section. The store is dark and cool, the lack of windows in the back keeps sunlight from heating up the place, and I sigh happily.

The floor creaks behind me in the Russian literature section and I flinch, momentarily startled. I turn right and walk down the aisle when I hear footsteps behind me again. The footsteps are too loud and far-apart to be Anika's. *All right, don't get ahead of yourself, Magdalen.* I casually continue down the aisle and turn left this time. When I'm halfway down the next aisle, the footsteps halt.

I look up to check what section I'm in and catch a scribbled MYTHOLOGY AND FOLKLORE note on the top shelf. Turning around to track my way back to the nineteenth-century literature aisle, I suddenly slam into something hard and lose my balance when two hands grip my shoulders, keeping me from falling over.

"Mhm," a deep voice says, close to my ear. "If I didn't know better, I'd think you were running away from me."

I know before I look, by the hard planes of his chest.

"Stalking me again?" My eyes can't seem to meet his. I think of Anika's confession. Of his eyes red and swollen. I think of his words: *The only reason you're kissing me is because you're too afraid to fucking talk to anyone else.* I flinch unwillingly and take a step back. Theo must notice my change because he instantly drops his hands from my shoulders.

"Sorry." He rubs the back of his neck. "I wasn't trying to scare you but I couldn't think of anything to say when I saw you come in the bookstore."

"It's okay."

He tries to smile, but only one side of his mouth raises and he gives up instantly.

"This feels awkward," I manage to say. "*I* feel awkward."

"Magdalen, you don't have to feel—" He takes a step forward and I flinch again, retreating down the aisle.

"I want to forgive you," I whisper. "I want to be fun and flirty." My throat is oddly tight and the tears from earlier pool in the corner of my eyes. I try to blink a few times but everything is just blurrier.

He opens his mouth but I cut him off before he can say anything, feeling brave in the mythology section of this bookstore. I speak slowly, saying the words as if I'm reciting from one of the books off the shelves.

"The only reason you're kissing me is because you're too afraid to fucking talk to anyone else." I repeat the words that have haunted me since that night and it's the first time I've said them out loud. It's Theo's turn to flinch, his face falling. But instead of stepping back, of pushing me away, he pushes toward me.

"You have to know..." His hands hover over my shoulders again but at the last second he drops them. "Shit. I'm

so sorry. You have to know that I only said that because I—"
He cuts himself off and it's my turn to step closer.

"Because you didn't want Anika to find out?"

"Magdalen, I couldn't give a fuck about Anika knowing."

"Then what?" I search his face for any clue but his eyes are closed off, careful to not give anything away. "If not Anika, then Dante?"

He sighs and shakes his head. I step closer and brush my pinkie against his wrist. It's the most I can offer, but his eyes immediately look down at where we're touching. He turns his hand so that his fingers brush against mine slowly and, taking his own pinkie finger, he curls it so that it's holding mine.

"You think I'd let Dante stop me from having you?" His voice is strained, sounding utterly distraught.

"Then what was it, Theo? What did I do wrong?"

His eyes shoot up to mine, brows furrowed in confusion, in anger. He blinks. "You think you did something wrong?"

"How could I not when you basically said as much?"

"Magdalen, I haven't stopped thinking about your body in my hands since that night," he says, voice low. His eyes are dark as he releases my little finger and snakes his hands around my hips and up my sides, squeezing for a moment before settling them on my neck, his thumb absentmindedly brushing against my throat. "I think about your lips; about how delicious you taste." He lets out a small, almost involuntary groan and presses his forehead against mine. "My god, I have thought about being inside of you every morning since, *amore*."

My body flushes at the thought of Theo thinking about me by himself and, for a second, I let myself believe him. To leave my hurt in Torino. But as much as I want this, as much as I want him, I think of how dirty I felt the morning after. Stained.

"What was it, then?" I repeat, refusing to let this go.

He stills, lost in his own words, the memory flush between us. I watch reality settle in his eyes again and he grimaces. "I can't." He steps back. "I know that's not what you want to hear but I can't, I can't—" He swallows hard, releasing his hands from my neck but still almost pressed against me.

"Please," I beg, reaching for his hand. "I need to know why."

Theo winces. "If it meant I could have you to myself, believe me, I would tell you in a heartbeat. But you have to trust me, Magdalen. I know, I know, you shouldn't, but just promise you'll be with me this summer. I won't let you down."

You'll be with me this summer.

"Okay," I sigh. "I'll give you the weekend." I don't know why I agree. Emily screams in my subconscious, furious I'd let someone seduce me with blatant secrets on the table.

"Summer," he corrects.

"We'll see if you want me that long."

"I want you for as long as you'll have me."

I roll my eyes, unable to help myself, looking off to the side to get a respite from his intensity.

"I'm quite serious. I think about you more than I fucking should." He raises his hand and grazes his knuckles against my cheek gently. My eyes flutter closed at his hands on my skin.

"How much?" I nuzzle further into his touch.

"Fuck off." I hear him smile. "Don't make me say it out loud."

"I think about you, too." I open my eyes. "More than I fucking should."

His knuckles still for a moment, soaking in my words. And then Theo's face erupts in the most blinding smile I've ever seen. It's so intense that I lose my breath, so taken by his utter beauty.

"You're warm," he muses, resuming his gentle strokes against my cheek.

"It's summer," I reply. "That tends to happen."

"No." His voice is gruff. Unsteady. "It's this hair. There's so much of it. Turn around for me." I look at him a second, confused before turning around so that I'm facing the rows of book spines. His chest brushes against my back with each breath.

"When I saw you the first night I got back to Chivasso, I couldn't see your face properly in the dark because of all this hair. Couldn't see that cute freckle above your eyebrow." His breath fans the side of my face, making me shiver while his hands continue exploring, fingers combing through the strands before splitting it into three sections.

"I've been meaning to get it cut." I feel him overlapping the pieces in a continuous pattern until he tugs on the end. Is he braiding my hair?

"Your hair is beautiful." His voice is deliciously deep

as he pulls on the braid, tilting my head until my neck is exposed to him. "But I've thought about doing this since the moment I saw you." He lowers his lips to my neck and kisses me lightly at first. I stifle a moan, lost in his scent of clean laundry and sunscreen.

"Anika is in the store somewhere."

"Baby, she left almost the minute she walked in."

"What?" He continues kissing down my neck and, when I go to bend my head forward, he pulls the braid again, kissing me until he reaches my shoulder.

"The second you were far enough into the store, she walked right out."

I laugh loudly and he covers my mouth with his large hand, muffling me. Then, without warning, he bites down on my shoulder.

"Mhm," I moan into his hand, feeling the bite all the way down my spine. My body heats deliciously, and I squirm, needing more of him. Needing all of him. But he keeps himself at a distance so the only parts of us that touch are his hand on my mouth and my back pressed against his chest.

"Magdalen, you should know better than to yell in a bookstore."

"That rule only applies to libraries." My voice is still slightly muted from his hand over my mouth, so I tentatively graze my teeth across his palm and bite down, mumbling into his skin. "You're not the only one who can bite."

"Fuck," he growls and drops his hand to my throat, loosely holding it there, running that thumb over my neck again. "Do you have a hair tie?" he asks. It takes a moment for my brain to remember he had braided my hair. That we weren't just biting each other in a bookstore. My mind is whirling between the heat of his body and hearing him curse in my ear to now being asked to speak.

"On my wrist," I swallow.

"My good girl." He dips his finger underneath the hair tie on my wrist and slides it off.

As he ties the ends together, I tentatively ask, "So where did you learn to braid?"

Pausing a moment, he doesn't say anything right away. When I'm about to tell him it's okay, that I don't need to know, he whispers, "Had to do Anika's hair some mornings." I mull over his words as I feel him securing the band in place.

"Why? Where was Cinzia?" It feels like a dangerous question, but my curiosity gets the better of me. Desperate for anything he'll give me.

"She had a hard time for a while," he says softly, twirling his finger around the loose strands at the end of the braid. "Mornings were the hardest. Something about having hours of darkness to then facing the daylight, she couldn't always do it right away."

"She was depressed?" I press.

"Probably still is. I don't talk to her enough to know."

"Why don't you? Talk to her, that is."

He plants a soft kiss on my shoulder, then leans his forehead on me, letting the weight of his head push down on me. "Because I'm afraid she'll tell me I'm right. I don't like thinking about her sad."

"I understand," I say, and I do. I've missed a lot about the Sinclairs.

"It was either learn how to braid or let Anika go to school with a bird's nest growing in her hair."

"You're a good brother." I say it without thinking.

He tenses behind me, dropping the braid. "I could be better."

"We all could. But you're better than most."

He sighs loudly and I turn around to look at him again. "Why can't we ever just be young and flirty together?" He tilts his head, moving a piece of escaped hair out of my face and tucking it behind my ear.

"That's Anika and Dante's job," I reply. "We are obligated to maintain an air of misery and hopelessness."

"That seems bloody unfair."

"Can't choose the cards we're dealt." I shrug my shoulders. "I'm afraid we're stuck with it."

"I reject that. I'm going to be so fun you won't even remember how to brood."

My eyes go wide and I inhale with a smirk. "Impossible. I've been brooding since before I could walk."

He takes my hands in his and squeezes them reassuringly, pausing a moment before the words rush out, eyes ablaze. "That first night back, you were lying in the grass. When I saw you, I couldn't move. I had to look down at my hands to make sure there were ten fingers." My heart beats faster at his unprompted confession. "I still think I've dreamt you into my summer." I stare at him, breathless and surprised. "I keep waiting to wake up."

"Stay asleep." My eyelashes flutter, feeling flush from his words. "I'll wake you up when summer's over."

A brief flash of an unknown emotion flickers over Theo's face. "Deal," he says softly, his warm breath fanning over my face, causing me to shiver again.

"Was that your version of fun and flirty?" I ask teasingly, but my insides feel deliciously heavy from his words.

Hand relaxing in mine, Theo lazily grins. "Sorry, should I have said I've thought about fucking you since that little pink dress?"

"Theo!" I screech, covering his mouth without thinking. "You can't say things like that in public."

Dragging my hand to his mouth, his tongue traces the center of my palm, and he moans into my hand. "And how much I want to see you come?"

"Oh my god." My insides melt, stomach tensing with desire, and I drop my hand. Needing space from his carefree sex-talk. Who is this man? "You definitely can't say that."

"No?" he muses, smile devilish. "You don't want me to make you come, *Maggie*?"

"We're going to get arrested if anyone hears you." But my voice trembles; there's no conviction in my tone. Imagining how Theo would touch me leaves me frozen with need. If he asked, I'm certain I'd let him undress me in the middle of this aisle.

"They can listen." He dips his head so that his lips brush mine and he gives me a light kiss. "I don't mind."

"Can we go now?" I say against his lips, feeling flushed

and uncomfortable with how much I want him, unsure where to put all these feelings. "I think I need some air."

He chuckles, pressing a kiss to my forehead. "Fine. Let's go back to brooding."

Theo drags me down the aisles back to the entrance, where the old woman still sits happy and toothless at the front desk. Theo salutes her and then opens the door for me, bowing as I pass him. Outside, the sun has started to set, casting the whole city in a golden hue. Theo holds my hand, my stomach flips, and I resist rolling my eyes at my own happiness.

He turns to face me, backlit by the dimming summer light. "I wasn't going to come back here. Ever. But I felt something." He drags both our hands to the space underneath his heart, outlining the rib, pushing with emphasis. "I felt something here. Pulling me." He winks. I think I die again. "Maybe it was you. Tugging on that telephone wire."

"You remember that?" Two tin cans held together by a string between our houses. Weaving between rose bushes and tall cypress trees dividing us. Looking back, we were obviously mimicking our mother's kitchen phone calls, curious to see what it was like to talk aimlessly for hours, to speak through silences, breaths through the microphone.

"It's hard to forget anything about this place." We walk across the cobblestones together toward the beach. Theo's fingers are still entwined with mine, swinging evenly with the pace of our footsteps. I mull over his words and can't help but think he didn't mean it as a good thing.

40

THEO

A fight has broken out on the beach. Anika and Dante dance demonically around Lucia and Maio, who are sitting rigidly on a picnic blanket with a bottle of white wine between them. They don't even see Magdalen and me approach them, too busy shaking their shoulders and smoking to pay any attention to us. Lucia eventually spots us, and instantly her eyes go wide and pleading.

"Ah, Theo!" She crawls up to her knees and squeezes her hands together in prayer. "For the love of god, please get these two away from us. They've been dancing like this for twenty minutes."

"We're blessing your marriage!" Anika drops her head between her legs so that her hair drags in the sand and starts bouncing her knees sporadically. "This is an important marriage ritual to ensure peace and sexual gratification for both. Please let us do our thing!"

"Dante," I call out, understanding why Anika would do this but surprised by his participation.

He whips his head toward us, and instantly his eyes glance at our hands. I watch his face go through a series of emotions. Brows raised in surprise, then furrowed in

297

annoyance. He takes a long drag of his cigarette, nodding to himself. "She promised to buy dinner if I did this with her," he explains, and continues to side-step around Maio, who looks like he is seconds away from throwing up.

"The space feels thoroughly cleansed, Anika." Magdalen drops my hand and jogs to them, ushering them away. "Let the lovebirds do their thing."

When everyone concedes, Anika leads us along the beach. She and Magdalen walk together, arms linked, cackling loudly while kicking up sand and stopping every so often to pick up a shell.

"That took literally no time at all," Dante says, hands shoved in his pockets.

"Sorry, bro," I shrug. "Guess I'm trying something new. Gotta not be afraid, right?" I bite down on my tongue, regretting the words instantly.

"What the fuck do you have to be afraid of?" Dante sneers, and starts counting with his fingers. "Too many opportunities thrown at you? Too many girls? Too much love from everyone?"

"All right, all right," I say laughingly to stop him from continuing, but it stings.

"No, seriously, tell me what you're afraid of."

"Dante, it's nothing. I don't know why I said it." Shrugging, I suddenly become aware of how high my shoulders are. Locked in place, the tension falls down my spine and I will myself to fucking relax.

"You obviously have something you're afraid of. I want to know what it is. Did I do something?"

"Of course you didn't do anything. Seriously, leave it alone. I'm an idiot."

"You're not a fucking idiot," he spits back. "That's why everyone loves you, *genio*."

"Can you just leave it alone?" My voice raises, breathing harsh. Magdalen and Anika turn back to look at us so I offer them a small smile, a shrug, *just boys being boys.* Anika's eyes travel to Dante, frowning at him and then back to me.

"Of course." He raises his hands innocently. "Don't go running back to New York now that I've fucking upset you. I'm sure now you're here for Maggie you can manage to stick it out a little longer than two months," he murmurs, and trudges ahead of me.

"Dante," I try, but it's too late. He jogs toward the water and strips down to his underwear.

Anika shakes her head when we get to the shore. "I don't even want to know." She runs toward Dante and dives headfirst into the ocean.

I close my eyes and sigh, filling my lungs with salty air. I picture us as teenagers, Dante showing up with an old, beaten-up Lambretta that he stole from the museum parking lot. "Look at this shit!" He bounced excitedly on the torn seat. "Come on! There's even some gas left. Let's go down the hill." I picture the day I told him I was leaving. I hoped my being here now was enough to forgive my decision to ever leave, but I see the resentment boiling in him.

"Want to swim?" Magdalen asks. I open my eyes, squinting at the sunset. Every time I look at her, hunger pangs in my chest. I'm terrified by how much I want her.

299

"Come here," I say.

"Demanding." She smiles and steps closer.

I graze my finger across the knot of her sarong. "Can I take this off?" I try to clear my throat, noticing how rough my voice sounds, almost trembling with need.

"Yes, please," she says, but there's a hesitancy; her smile flinches.

Taking my hand off her, I look at her intently. "Magdalen, you'll tell me if you're not comfortable?" I mean it to come out as a question, but it's too hard, abrasive.

"Yeah, course I will."

"I mean it. You know that, right? We don't need to do anything you don't want to. I'd be happy drinking coffee with you, watching you read until sunrise, and be thankful for it."

"Theo." She steps toward me and takes my hand, guiding it to the knot of the sarong again. "I want to. You know I've never necessarily done a lot of this." Her voice wavers and it takes everything in me not to wrap her in my arms until the doubt that I selfishly planted is flushed out.

I untie the knot and dip my finger underneath the linen until the cloth falls to the sand. "Don't apologize, please. You don't need to explain anything."

"Okay. Noted. Now take off your shirt."

"Excuse me?" I try to hide my smile at her boldness and she gasps, hands flying to her hips.

"Excuse you? I'm standing here bare-ass and vulnerable and you're fully clothed."

"Magdalen, it's a beach, baby. Look around. You're probably the most covered person here."

"Okay, *baby.*" Magdalen steps closer and tentatively runs her fingernails across the skin exposed at the bottom of my shirt. I shiver, leaning my hips forward unconsciously to get more of her touch. "Then get this off."

I lift my hands up above my head and wait. "I'm afraid I'll need help." My voice is tight, full of need. Not wanting to scare her off, I clear my throat to lessen my blatant desire for her, but it does nothing.

Magdalen giggles and that familiar hunger grows. For all her giggles.

"Okay, I think I can help." Her hands explore underneath my shirt, fingers running gently along the seam of my shorts. I let out an exhale, willing myself to control the hardness already forming. Trying to find the will to be embarrassed, but I find I'm too entranced by her to care. Her fingers remain low and after a moment she dips one into my waistband.

"Ehm." I force my eyes upward to not look at her hands inside my shorts, almost positive that if I do look, Magdalen will definitely be able to see how hard I already am. "Shirt is the other way," I gasp, trying to adjust myself discreetly.

"Oops, sorry." I hear her smiling and find myself joining her. "This is why I don't drive. My direction skills are fucked."

"It's a common mistake. Up, down. Could happen to anyone."

Her hands are everywhere. First taking the fabric of my shirt, she wanders up my stomach, then drags it farther up to my ribs. I take a slow breath out, never having such a reaction to someone just touching my skin. But everything

301

feels different with her, new. Her touch means more. She steps closer, our toes overlapping in the sand, hips brushing against one another briefly, and I thin my lips to stop from moaning.

"You're too big," she says while trying to tug the shirt over my shoulders. Her words cause a spike of adrenaline to shoot down my spine and directly to my dick. Jesus Christ.

"You're doing this on purpose," I mumble through the shirt now stuck over my mouth, certain my erection is entirely visible through my shorts.

"No! It's really stuck," she says, laughing, her stomach pressing up against mine as she continues to try to pull it off.

"My god, Magdalen. Stop talking." I think of anything to not think of her underneath me, squirming and naked, whispering those same words for something very different.

"Okay, okay. I got it." The shirt slips off my head and while she's turning it inside out, I take the opportunity to adjust myself again. Am I fifteen fucking years old?

When she looks up from the shirt debacle, her eyes zone in on my hands trying to hide how hard I am and she bites down on her lip.

"Sorry," I say, feeling guilty for my blatant display of arousal on a public beach.

"I did that?" She tilts her head, examining my body like a statue at the museum.

"Eh, yes, Magdalen. That usually happens when the girl I like slips her fingers near my dick."

"Huh," she muses. "I never thought I'd be able to seduce anyone."

"You should give yourself more credit, then. You do it all the time to me."

"You're right." She smiles cheerfully, looking like she's made of magic. "I really should."

She throws my shirt on top of her sarong and begins jogging down to the water. I give up trying to hide myself when I look at her ass moving as she runs.

"Shit," I say, taking a deep breath before running after her.

41

MAGDALEN

I dip my head in the warm water, listening to the steady acoustics of the ocean. I try not to think about Theo's disgustingly beautiful body, how easy I was to forgive and indulge in him. I try not to think about how I'm going to have sex with him, but it's a futile attempt. I always assumed my first time, at this stage in my life, would be out of necessity. Because I've reached unacceptable virgin territory. I had a plan to finish Emily's secret gin that she hides in her underwear drawer and have her set me up with someone who was only interested in a one-night thing. I would close my eyes and think of England, resigning myself to the inevitable pain and discomfort of that night, the ultimate regret the next morning.

But now things have changed. The pain I've been preparing for is rearranging itself into giddy anticipation. Into curiosity. A dark part of myself thinks that if Theo is the one hurting me, I'll enjoy it more than I won't. When I come up for air, I realize I've swum farther out than I thought. Anika and Dante are far away, just two dots bobbing in and out of the waves. Turning around to find Theo, I squint through the salt water to see him close behind. His biceps look intimidatingly contoured in the water as he paddles toward me and I gulp, nerves anchoring me in place.

"Trying to swim away?" he says through strokes, and it's all too effortless for him, swimming and talking. God really does have favorites.

"Don't think I could ever out-swim you, to be fair."

"I'd let you, if you wanted me to," he says, only a few feet away from me now. If he reached out his hand he could touch me. But he stays in place, treading calmly in that spot.

"I don't," I say shakily. He swallows hard and just stares at me with a smirk.

"Good. Because I'm happy swimming to you." He slowly swims closer and I feel his fingers curl around my elbow, pulling me gently toward him. His other hand finds my waist and then dips to grab the back of my thigh. "Open," he says gruffly, and I realize he means my legs. I will my heart to stop beating as fast, and comply, latching my thighs around his waist. Without hesitation, his hands travel to my ass, pushing me fully against him.

"The fish will talk," I mumble, raking my fingers through his hair, pulling slightly at the nape of his neck.

His eyes flutter shut for a second, his voice catches. "They're probably just jealous."

I settle my hands on his shoulders and then, hesitantly, I explore farther down, keeping one hand near his collarbone while the other runs down the length of his torso. Theo inhales sharply and shifts under me, grinding his hardness against my leg.

"Is this okay?" I whisper. The waves lap gently over our bodies, rocking us slowly.

"Yes, yes." Dipping his head toward me, he brushes his lips against mine. "Is this okay?" He repeats my question now, and I tilt my chin up to give him access to my lips, memories of our last kiss warming me.

"Yes," I breathe, too happy in his proximity to be embarrassed. "Yes."

Theo lets out a small groan and captures my lips between his, dominantly. I feel his hand come up to hold my head, his thumb grazing against my cheek as his tongue dips into my mouth. It's as if we both sink into one another, his breath becoming mine, my hands becoming his. I lick his top lip curiously—his breath hitches, and he dives deeper to bite down on my bottom lip.

"Ah," I exhale, and he rests his forehead against mine, our breaths rapid. His pupils are so dilated, the irises are practically black, and I'm unable to look away.

And then I try something.

I move the hand resting on his lower back to his taut stomach, hesitantly outlining the edge of his boxers.

Theo stills but doesn't say anything, so I continue touching him, dipping my hand underneath his waistband.

"Is this oka—" I start, but he tilts his head back and rasps, "Yes, fuck. Yes, it's okay."

I smile to myself, his loss of control making me bolder. Less afraid of doing this wrong. Carefully, I wrap my hands around him and begin with a gentle stroke, feeling his full length. Wow. He tilts his head back to me, looking in my eyes as I stroke him again, this time a little firmer.

"I want you to feel good," Theo hisses between his teeth. "You shouldn't have to do this for me."

"I want to," I supply. "I want to see if I can seduce you even more."

"As if you don't already know what you do to me," he groans as I continue stroking him, staring at me with hooded eyes. *I know nothing about you*, I want to say. *I want to know everything.* He doesn't look away the entire time, but instead he seems desperate to meet my gaze. His eyes dart from my lips to my breasts and back up to my eyes, head tilted as if memorizing me. I'm mesmerized by him undone, unable to keep from staring into his gray eyes. The piece of wet hair that dangles in front of his face, the drops of sea water falling down his temple. He begins to rock his hips at the pace of my hands and I find it difficult to breathe. He's fucking fluent in sex. Unashamed, relentless, even in the middle of the sea. He's all breath and wonder, whispering heady praise. *Just like that, yes. I didn't know it could...* he doesn't finish that one. *Please, Magdalen, you're going to embarrass me.* I realize I haven't breathed in a long enough time that a burning pain flutters in my lungs. To feel so wanted by another, by Theo, is terrifying. I gently brush my thumb over the tip and he jerks forward, gripping my thighs to support himself, his wet hair buried in the crook of my neck as he exhales harshly.

"Magdalen. You can't do that."

I freeze. Embarrassed. Of course I would find a way to fuck up a hand job.

"Oh, okay. Sorry." My hand loosens, instantly cringing.

He chuckles slightly and grabs my hand under the water to put it back on him. Feeling him under my palm and his calloused hand guiding me to how he likes to be touched is too much; I feel like I'm drowning above the water. "Oh, baby, that's not what I meant." *Baby.* He says it like I've been his for years. I never thought I'd be anyone's and here I am, owned by Theo in a matter of minutes. He squeezes my hand hard and when I do it again, brush my thumb over that same spot, he groans deeply. "Like that. Fuck," he pants.

"So, when you say 'don't do that,' you really mean...?"

"You weren't supposed to see me this undone so quickly."

"I like you undone." And I really do. "It's sexy." Did I say that out loud? I feel his body tensing beneath me, his movements becoming more ragged, less careful with me; one of his hands wraps around the back of my neck, holding me while he thrusts into my hand.

"I'm going to," he says in a harsh exhale. "Ah, yes, I'm going to—" My stomach flutters, heat spreading across my body as if his pleasure were my own. Moaning every crude saying under the setting sun, with a few final thrusts, Theo bites down on my shoulder while his whole body shudders for what feels like ages. He melts into me, stomach pressed against mine, biting turning into licking, into kissing. He sighs, so I sigh back. "Well, fuck." He laughs. "I'm feeling shy." The apples of his cheeks are tinged pink, and he splashes his face with water.

"That's my job," I grin, releasing my legs from him and floating on my back, arms spread out like a sedated starfish. I feel him stare at me as I bob in and out of the water, and I have to hold back my smile.

"You're not shy; you're selective."

"You think?" I'm honestly curious about how he sees me.

"Sometimes, it feels like I know everything you're thinking with one look. And other times I can't understand you at all."

I tilt my head to look at him, water filling my ear so I can hear both the sounds of the ocean and Theo's breathing.

"You and me both." I look back at the now darkened sky. "I'm terrified about how much I don't know myself. It's a constant point of tension between me and my mother."

"Who does she think you are?"

I huff out an annoyed breath. "Is this normal post-hand-job talk?"

Theo laughs loudly and splashes me with water. I wish for seashells to capture that sound, that beautiful laugh, so when I hold it up to my ear, I can hear him instead of the sea.

"No one's ever given me a hand job in the middle of the ocean. I don't know the rules."

"Really?" I muse. "This is my fifth. You'd be surprised how popular they are at Oxford." Theo doesn't say anything back so I peer over at him cautiously.

"Oh, you shouldn't have said that." He dips his body so that the water covers his shoulders and only his head is visible. He stalks forward and I squeal.

"Theo!" I try to swim backward but within seconds he grabs me by my foot and pulls me toward him. Kicking my ankle is useless but I try anyway, flailing dramatically.

"Mhm, want to redact that, Magdalen?" His hand rests on my stomach, running the pads of his fingers all over me, and I squirm unconsciously, pushing my hips outside the water into his touch.

"Fine, only four," I breathe, enjoying a jealous Theo. His mouth pulls in a predatory smile.

"Funny girl," he says, voice low. His hand mirrors mine minutes before as he brushes against the waistband of my bikini bottoms, mouth slightly open as he watches my stomach contract at the touch.

"Funny, beautiful girl." And then, without warning, Theo grabs me from underneath the water and tosses me in the air. I yelp loudly and land back in the water with a crash. His laugh is loud enough for me to hear underwater, and I secretly gush. Who knew I was so funny? Just as I'm about to swim back up, I feel Theo's hands tracing the scars scattered across my back and I tense, staying underwater a moment longer before lifting my head. Rubbing my eyes slowly, I open them to find Theo looking at me, frowning a bit.

"What's wrong?" I ask, though I feel his question from here.

"You never told me what those scars are." He lifts his chin toward my back casually, but I see the tension in his eyes.

"Oh." My gaze stays trained on my hands dipping in and out of the ocean, watching the water flow through my fingers. "It happened a while ago. It was just an accident."

Theo stares at me for a beat, and I watch him try to accept the answer, but his tongue rolls across his gums and he frowns again. "How'd it happen?"

The giddiness of giving my first hand-job is slowly fizzling. It's the way he's looking at me, as if he already knows and wants to check if I'll be brave enough to say it. A wave of something close to annoyance threatens to seep into my answer. *You know nothing about me.*

"It was so long ago, I hardly even remember."

"Sure, but you must remember something about it. Where were you when it happened?"

I bite the inside of my cheek, looking toward the slight outline of the moon. Clouds move lazily across the sky. I search for a star; maybe if I find one soon enough I can wish this moment away.

"Theo, what are you doing? It was a stupid accident; I just don't remember."

"You said that already." His voice has changed and our eyes meet, challenging one another. No longer playful and fun. No longer flirty. He tries to reach out to touch my back but I flinch away.

"So accept that as my answer," I retort.

Theo immediately drops his hand and looks at me painfully. "Who the fuck has a back full of scars and doesn't remember how they got them, Magdalen?"

"I guess I do," I sigh, swimming closer to the shore. Feeling disappointed by how quickly this turned bad. It must be me, I think, resigned. I must bleed out this blueness. Me and my fucking blue bedroom. Hugging myself underwater,

311

I draw my chin tight toward my neck, trying to cover up a shiver, but Theo sees and immediately swims closer to me. I pretend to cover up another flinch and start swimming faster, just a few feet away from the sandy beach, but his jaw tightens, looking at me sadly, nodding to himself. My throat constricts and the words stick to my throat. *Give me a second*, I want to say. *How can you want me to show you my ugliest parts when I just got you?*

He looks up. "It's getting dark. And you're cold."

"I'm fine," I shrug, still putting distance between us. *Just give me a fucking second.*

"You're not." He swims past me, careful not to touch me as he walks out of the water.

He passes my sarong to me when I near him and we both dry ourselves in silence. What felt romantic moments ago now feels dirty, sand and sea water coating my skin. While he makes no move to say anything first, Theo stares at me the entire time I dry myself.

"I can feel you staring," I say while tying the sarong.

"I can see your goosebumps from here," he says gruffly. "Take this." He holds up his T-shirt between us and, when I don't take it, he steps closer. I stay still, staring at him, so serious and brooding. So concerned about the temperature of my body. Suddenly, this is all very funny to me. I try to hold the laughter in, press my hand against my head to center myself, but it's useless.

"What?" he asks, annoyed when I continue laughing, still holding the shirt between us.

"You're offering me your shirt after giving me the 'you're not fine' speech?" I say, bewildered.

"I wasn't trying to make a speech. But it's clear that you're not fine."

"Oh, thank you so much for that astute observation. How profound! No one's fucking fine, Theo. That's the human condition. News flash: you're not fine! You need to back off. Don't expect more from me than you're willing to give."

Theo steps toward me and this time I don't step back. Instead, I lift my chin and look at him as he walks forward, not stopping until he's standing right in front of me with the fabric of the shirt gathered by the collar.

"What are you—" I start, but Theo places the shirt over my head, momentarily blinding me before it falls around my neck. He doesn't let go of the shirt but holds it by the collar.

"You're cold." He's so close that I can smell the salt water on his skin, see the patterns of his curls already drying. "And you're not fine. And I'm not fucking fine, sure." Even in the darkness, his eyes pierce through mine. He's all tension and concern, and my throat goes dry as I'm about to say something, anything to keep him right here, to confess. *Theo, how can I possibly be cold when you've swallowed the sun?* Then a voice calls from down the beach and I blink the thought away.

"*Niente cazzo modo. Theo, sei tu?*"

It takes me a moment to register that the voice isn't Anika's or anyone I know. There's only a single streetlamp on the boardwalk and I squint, trying to make out the shape of the mystery girl. Short. Chin-length hair. Theo curses quietly when he realizes who it is and drops the shirt that hangs from my neck. For a split second, his eyes are wide, afraid. His mouth twitches a little, a nervous tic, and then I watch the fear completely drain from him, replaced by the usual cool calmness. Yet now it comes off as artificial, like a coating around himself to hide the cracks. My gaze remains on him, forgetting about the girl for a moment. How did he do that? Finding his emotions like a puzzle he needs to settle into the right groove.

One moment the world was ending for him. I saw it. The fire and brimstone might as well have burned through his eyes. But now, it's as if he's never known pain. He scratches the tattoo on his chest as we wait for her to come closer, and he looks almost bored.

"Theo! What are the chances!" She throws the towel hanging from her forearm on the sand and jumps into Theo's arms, holding him tightly around the neck. He stays still at first, his whole body stiff and unresponsive before he eventually wraps his arms around her small frame, rubbing gently on her upper back. Should I leave? I glance around to see the string of cafe and restaurant lights behind us a few hundred feet away and consider stepping quietly away to let them reconnect.

"What are you doing here?" Theo asks as he sets her down. I try to not linger on his hands still wrapped around her waist but it's the only thing I see.

"I'm here for the weekend with some friends! We're

staying at Hotel Regina down the road," she replies happily, her black bob bouncing as she speaks.

"Ah, not following me, are you?" Theo jokes, and my eyebrows shoot up before I remember to control my face.

"Don't worry yourself. I've got plenty of pretty boys to distract me."

"Yeah, like who?"

"The usual crew. Carmine, Jacobo. Samuel's coming in later tonight."

I stare down at my feet, digging them farther into the cold sand, cementing myself in place to endure this. Am I being too sensitive? I think back to our conversation in Torino, how happy I was to have him alone for a few minutes. Proud that I spoke at all. *Not stalking me, are you?* I resent him stealing my line but am also ashamed by how much better it sounds coming from him. He's playful, completely confident in his effect on her. I feel myself becoming too aware of my body, of how I breathe, that I'm wearing his shirt around my neck as I stand awkwardly next to them.

"We're all going out for drinks tonight—you two should join us."

This makes me look up at her. Allowing myself to take her in, my stomach fills with dread and something like teenage angst. She's absolutely beautiful. Delicate, obnoxiously feminine. Her hair seems immune to the unrelenting wind of the beach as it sits like a halo around her face.

I was never jealous of other people's beauty before. But now I stare at her and feel only the absence of my own. The parts of me under-saturated and overly pronounced claw

315

their way to the forefront of my mind. So much so that I almost miss Theo's response.

"Maggie's pretty tired. I think she's going to turn in for the night." He doesn't look at me when he responds. I try to meet his eyes but he doesn't budge. My face must reveal my surprise because mystery girl supplies a quick laugh. What the fuck just happened? *He must like her.* And then the world seems to tilt on its axis.

This is Chiara, the one he fucked. It makes too much sense. It never occurred to me that he was being fun and flirty with others and then coming back to me for a new challenge. Willing myself to stop overreacting, I play with the knot in my sarong, but the idea persists loudly in my head. *He likes her.* We never agreed to an exclusive *you take my virginity and only make sexy eyes at me* pact. This is fair game.

"Yeah, swimming for twenty minutes is just *so* exhausting." My voice is dull. Theo still won't look at me. Instead, he stares only at Chiara and her perfect hair, effectively excluding me from their conversation.

"What time?" he says. I chew on the inside of my mouth, thinking of anything to suppress the hot sting of tears threatening to surface.

She checks her watch. "Nine-ish? Maybe Mag can relax beforehand and meet us if you're up to it? No pressure."

She's nice *and* pretty. This is all too much. I unbury my feet from the sand, blinking faster as the tears viciously try to spill.

"Theo's right," I hear myself say, and it surprises me how

perfectly normal my voice sounds. Happy even. "I actually really am tired."

This seems to get Theo's attention. He casually turns his head to look at me and the moment our eyes lock, he looks away. "I'll drop you home."

"No, no. Go hang out with..." I begin, but realize I can't exactly disclose that I know who she is. It seems remarkably funny to me how much one girl's name could ruin my life.

"Ah, Chiara!" she beams and sticks out her hand to shake mine. "So nice to meet you, *Mag*."

My heart sinks so low that I'm afraid I'll step on it if I move.

"You too. Your name is beautiful," I say, and her mouth splits in another soul-shattering grin.

"Thank you!" Her hand is warm and pleasant as she takes mine, guiding the handshake. I think about how cold and limp my hand is in hers and wonder if she notices it, too.

When our hands drop, I offer a small smile and go to take Theo's shirt off my neck.

"What are you doing?" he asks, now completely turned to face me. Now you notice me, Theo? All it took was giving you the shirt off my back.

"Giving you your shirt back." My voice is too cheery for the exchange of a shirt, but it's the only way I can speak right now without crying. Better off being overly cheery than having a tantrum in front of the lovebirds.

"I gave it to you."

"You can't go out drinking shirtless. Think of the scandal." I hand him his shirt back and he looks at me harshly.

317

Don't test me, he says silently.

Please let me go, I say back.

He doesn't take it but lets my hand hang useless in the air between us.

"It's Alassio, Magdalen. I'll be fine."

Before I can answer, Chiara shrieks and the sound of her hand slapping against her forehead startles me. "Ah, Magdalen! I should have known. You're Dante's little sister, right? I didn't realize! You've grown up so much!"

Theo stiffens noticeably and I can't hide my confusion.

"You know me?"

"*Certo*. Dante told me all about you back in the day. My god, you turned out to be stunning."

Despite the sadness, a faraway part of me is happily surprised that Dante has ever talked about me.

"This makes so much sense now." She points at the two of us by way of explanation and I shrug.

"Yes, Theo's just doing his big brother due diligence." Patting him on the shoulder, I then place the shirt against his chest. His hand comes over mine as he reaches for it and I get a flash of us in the ocean, our hands intertwined underwater, heavy breaths and fluttering eyelashes. *Yes, it's okay.* His heart beats in equal, measured pulses. So unaffected by all of this, by me, that I have to jerk my hand away for self-preservation. A muscle in Theo's jaw tightens as he looks at where our hands met, but he's silent otherwise and finally takes the shirt. *Good.* If Chiara notices that there's any tension in the air, she ignores it and swiftly moves the conversation along.

"Oh, I think you'll really get on with the boys. You should come out with us and tell Dante, obviously. Please! It'll be fun, I promise. If there's one thing I know, it's how to party."

"You sound like Anika," I say lamely as Theo snarls at the same time, "She won't be able to make it tonight."

"Magdalen can make up her own mind," Chiara fires back as my mouth opens stupidly, shocked by how quickly she is able to defend me. She knows nothing about me and yet her instinct is to protect against Theo. I wonder how well she knows him, to take my side over his.

I know I should speak up, but I'm afraid that if I open my mouth, the only thing that will come out is a sob. Instead, I stay silent and feel Chiara staring at me. I know before our eyes lock that she's aware something is off between Theo and me. Call it woman's intuition. She smiles again, but this time it's forced.

"Magdalen, do you want him to take you home?"

"No, I can find my way back. It was nice to see you. Really. Have fun tonight."

"Yeah, you too," Chiara says. "Get home safe." Theo opens his mouth but Chiara smacks him on the shoulder and then shoves him in the direction of town.

As I make my way toward the houses along the beach, I can still hear Chiara and Theo's hushed whispers. "What did you do now?" she screeches, half-jokingly. I'm too far away by the time Theo answers and I'm grateful for the distance. The sobs claw their way up my throat and the sound of my own crying scares me. My hands fly to my mouth to muffle the sounds, but it does nothing, so I push against my lips so tightly I feel the strain of my front teeth, how they scrape against my palm in protest.

He's nice to me for ten minutes and I forget everything he's done.

By the time I reach the front of the villa, I've left a trail of tears behind me. My hand shakily finds the front door-knob but when I go to twist it doesn't move. *You've got to be kidding me.* I try again, but the door must be two hundred years old and made of elven-blessed oak, because it doesn't budge an inch. I stumble to the garden to see if Lucia left the back door open, but it's sealed tight and I groan. *Of course,* I mumble to myself. *Of course she decides to be an adult today.* After thirty minutes of searching, I am back at the front of the house, my trail of tears all dried up. Shivering slightly, I curse myself for giving Theo his shirt back and walk to the small chair tucked by the front door. Anika and Dante are sure to be home soon. Settling into the cushioned seat, I wrap my sarong around my shoulders and make myself as small as possible. The tiredness floods through me force-fully. I close my eyes, salt water and dismissive gray eyes pull me into unconsciousness and I drift off to sleep.

42

THEO

"What the fuck was that?"

I shrug out of Chiara's grip and stop walking before we near the bordello entrance.

"Excuse me?" she says with a laugh. "You can't be fucking serious?"

"You just stormed in between us and basically demanded she go home alone. She's Dante's little sister. I'm supposed to watch out for her."

"Oh, she's Dante's *little sister*?" Chiara cackles. "Give me a fucking break. She was on the verge of tears. I was saving her."

"Who the fuck do you think you are, Chiara? You always do this, act like you know everything." My voice is cold.

Chiara's eyes widen slightly but she spits out, "I'm a woman. And I know what it's like to be fucked over by you."

My breath hitches and Magdalen's face enters my mind. I stare at the walkway to the beach, wishing her into existence. How did this happen? My head tries to wrap around the sudden shift from the ocean. Questioning her. Probing her for answers that I'm not willing to give. And then Chiara. Out of all people, it had to be Chiara.

"I'm sorry, I just...I don't know why I did that." I squeeze my eyes shut, running my hands through my hair until my scalp burns. "I don't know why I did that."

"Yes, you do," Chiara says and shrugs. "You didn't want her to find out that we fucked." Her tone is light but I can tell she's disappointed.

"No, that's not...Chiara, I'm not ashamed that we slept together."

"But she's who you were thinking about." Chiara looks at me. "She's the reason you called me."

"It's not like that," I start but I have no excuse ready. Of course it's that.

"And yet you almost had an aneurism when I mentioned Carmine, Jacob and Samuel?" Chiara snorts and rummages through her purse until she pulls out a cigarette and lighter.

"God, I'm sorry." I slide down against one of the houses and sit down on the sidewalk, closing my eyes. "I keep doing this shit."

Chiara takes a long inhale and I can hear her heels pace slowly in front of me. "She'll forgive you."

"This wasn't the first time I've..." I struggle to find the words that can capture what I'm doing. The cycle I've been digging myself into since I saw her lying in the grass that warm night.

"Been a dick?" Chiara fills in the silence. I groan and open my eyes to find her looking at me. She takes another inhale and then extends her hand, offering me the cigarette.

"I guess that sums it up." Taking a puff, I think about

Magdalen in the ocean and inwardly groan. I think of her hands on my stomach, trailing down until—

"Come have a drink with me." Chiara interrupts the flashback. "Give her some time alone. We'll figure out what you can say."

Anger swells in my stomach, burning me up until I notice I'm pulling at the collar of my T-shirt and I jerk my hand away, taking a deep breath. "Chiara, I'm twenty-five years old. I shouldn't need help with telling a girl I like her." What the fuck have I done?

"Oi!" Chiara claps loudly in front of my face and my head bangs against the wall.

"Ow. What the fuck?"

"Would you be upset if she was sleeping with someone else? Or is this a casual thing?" She bends down, squatting in front of me.

"Why would you say something like that?" The words come out rushed. Picturing Magdalen even *wanting* someone else is difficult, let alone fucking them. I think about Roberto, his hands over her body, buying her a drink. I pinch the end of the cigarette between my fingers and Chiara smacks her lips and grabs it out of my hand.

"That's not an answer."

I breathe out, annoyed by her and the turn of this night. "Yes, obviously."

"Well, the girl on the beach didn't know that." She points to where we left Magdalen and then looks at her watch.

"Maybe I don't know if she likes me," I retort. Eight

tear-shaped scars, still raised and red against her olive skin, come back into my mind.

"Oh, come on. Look me in the eye and tell me you don't know that she's practically in love with you." My mind slows. Love? I want to laugh and cry, to go back into the ocean and breathe in. There'll never be fucking love.

Standing up, I brush the dirt off my shorts. "Are we getting this drink or not, Chiara?"

My knee bounces so fiercely that the plastic table we're sat at lifts for a moment and the drinks almost spill. "Jesus, Theo. Can you relax for one second?"

"We've been here for two hours—four drinks down and you've been utterly no help." I finish off my last drink and abruptly stand up and shove my hands in my pocket to find some cash.

"Are you kidding me? I've given you, like, thirty ways to apologize!" Chiara bops her head to the disco music playing loudly in the restaurant and takes a sip of her drink, ignoring my pacing entirely.

"You've given me literal shit." I throw the cash on the table and wipe the beer from my mouth, needing to leave immediately. "I'm going now."

"Toodle-oo!" she calls out, and immediately gets up from the table to go sit down with a group of people at a table nearby.

"Remember, tell her you had amnesia and forgot who I was!"

As I go to walk out onto a quieter street, I hear another voice call my name.

"Theo!"

I groan silently and slow my pace down, deciding right now that I hate this fucking city.

When I turn around, I see Dante and Anika with linked arms strutting toward me.

"Where's Mag?" Anika immediately asks when she sees me alone.

"She was feeling tired," I say, unable to look her in the eye. Thinking only of Magdalen now, and the mess I've made.

"She was feeling tired?" Dante repeats and steps forward, releasing Anika and putting his hand on my shoulder firmly. *What did you do*, his tightening grip seems to say. I scoff and shrug his hand off me, thinking of his indifference to Magdalen when she was at the club.

"Yeah, Dante, she was feeling tired. Maybe if you weren't so far up Anika's ass you'd know that."

"Theo." Anika's voice spikes, even with the loud music playing, and maybe it's the drinks, or the anger, or Chiara's horrible advice, but I roll my eyes at them both and start to walk off.

"What? You've never given two shits about her before. And now suddenly because I like her, you start acting like the scary big brother?"

Dante grabs the collar of my shirt and yanks me back toward him and I stumble backward.

"You really want to talk about who is a better fucking brother? Where were you for the past seven years, huh? Riddle me that." His grip on my shirt tightens, pulling me closer to him until our faces are only inches apart, his words spitting across my face.

"We all gave you a fucking pass because Dexter's an ass-hole, sure. But seven years? Seven years without a fucking word?" He's screaming now, the vein in his forehead bulging angrily with every word, and his eyes begin to water slightly. My eyes blur, mirroring his unshed tears, and I don't fight him as he shoves me hard into a wooden hostess stand behind me.

"You don't know who I am any more. You don't know Anika. And you sure as fuck don't know Magdalen. So don't lecture me on who the fuck is a better brother."

A sharp sting rushes down my spine from where my back hit the stand and I bend forward, laughing. Enjoying the distraction from his words.

"Being a good brother means fucking talking to her every once in a while, yeah?"

The moment I raise my head a white flash of pain shoots through my nose and I stagger slightly. "You piece of shit," Dante says with little conviction. They have no fucking idea.

When I touch my face, I discover it's covered in some-thing warm and wet, and realize I'm bleeding. The blood trickles evenly out of my nose and down my neck until my shirt sticks uncomfortably to me. He's fucking ruined my shirt.

"Dante, what the hell do you think you're doing?" Anika rushes toward me but I shake my head, putting my hand out to stop her coming any closer. He's right. She shouldn't have to fight the battles I've been running from all these years.

"I'm fine," I spit, looking straight at Dante. He shakes out his hand and looks down at it like he's surprised he hit me, and I have to smile. Seven years ago, Dante Savoy would never dream of risking an injury on a street fight. Maybe I really don't know him any more. "He's wanted to do that for a long time." I roll my neck out and groan slightly.

"You're not even going to deny it?"

"Deny what?" I say with a tired breath, trying to wipe away the blood that seems to be everywhere now.

"Don't play stupid, okay? You left cause of your dad, right? You left Anika all by herself because you're too chicken shit to say anything to him and you hoped she would fix this by the time you decided it was safe to come home."

At the mention of Anika's name, something in me snaps and, before I know it, my hands are wrapped around his neck so tightly I feel his blood pulsing beneath my palms. I'm aware of people stopping to watch us, probably thinking this is two drunken idiots fighting over nothing, but I don't care. I squeeze harder and Dante gags, choking pathetically as I cut off his air supply. When his face starts turning bright red, I squeeze harder.

"Why I left is none of your fucking concern," I whisper in his ear so only he can hear. "But just know, I will always be a better brother than you. I would fucking kill anyone for her, including you, you selfish prick. Can you say the same for your sister? Have you ever spent a minute protecting Magdalen?" I release him harshly and back away from them both. He coughs roughly, sputtering incoherent gasps as Anika grabs him and hauls him up before he falls to the ground.

"Anika, be safe tonight. I'll leave the key underneath the

fern," I yell, and begin to jog out of the cluster of people now gathered around us.

"Crazy," I hear Dante mutter. "Batshit crazy asshole."

"What the fuck, Theo!" she yells. "You can't bloody choke Dante and then tell me to be safe, you idiot."

Chuckling slightly, I pick up my pace, eager to see Magdalen. Although nothing's changed, and it's going to be a hard fucking graft getting her to accept my apology, I feel better, closer to who I want to be. My blood has dried by the time I make it back to the house.

I fumble with the key, the darkness watching as I aimlessly probe the elusive hole. Not a single lamp outside this villa and it's a guessing game that I am pathetically losing as the tip of the key scrapes the door. Cursing loudly, I slam my foot into the door but immediately cringe at my stupidity. This can't be fucking happening. I tap the door with my head in gentle knocks.

"Theo?" a voice whispers from somewhere to the left of me. "What are you doing here?"

"*San Antonio.*" I jump at the sound and try to squint through the darkness, though I'd recognize that voice anywhere. "Magdalen, what the hell are you doing outside?"

I remember nothing as I fall to my knees in front of her. After a few moments in the darkness, my eyes adjust and I can see her curled up on the chair, hugging herself with the sarong wrapped tightly around her. Touching her ankle, I inhale sharply at her coldness.

"You're fucking freezing," I hiss and instinctively go to pick her up, but then remember how she flinched away last time, so I pause, shoving my hands in my pockets to keep from touching her. "Have you been outside this whole time?"

"I didn't have a key." Her teeth chatter slightly, and dread fills me instantly. How long has she been here? Freezing while I was having drinks with another woman and strangling Dante against a wall.

"Magdalen, let me take you inside. Please, let me take you inside." It comes out as a whisper.

In the darkness, I see her nod and it's all I need. I rush to scoop her up, bringing her tight against my body.

"It seems like you're always saving me," she says weakly, embarrassed. White noise fills my mind and I fight down the rage that claws its way up.

"Oh no." I press her to me closely. "You've saved me just by existing."

Magdalen leans herself into me, already her skin feeling slightly warmer, and miraculously the key slides in. "You left me."

My heart breaks. I'm surprised I can still fucking walk. "I know."

"I thought things were different now."

"They are."

"You left me. Everything's the same."

Unable to stand this for one more moment, I can do nothing but hold her together.

"Hold on to me," I say while opening the door. When we get inside the entryway, Magdalen shudders from the temperature difference but soon enough sighs in relief, unconsciously snuggling further into my arms.

"Okay, you can put me down now." She squirms a little and I release her from my grasp, feeling desperately bare without her. We stand in the dark living room for a moment and Magdalen clears her throat.

"Let me turn the light on," I say, to stall, to have a few more minutes with her just near me. "Go get that blanket on the couch."

Flicking the lamp on in the corner of the room, I brace myself to see her again, afraid that she might've already disappeared. A trick of the light. I stare at the lightbulb, my eyes adjusting to the warm orange glow. *Magdalen. I think I've dreamed in darkness for so long because I was meant to wake up for you.* Turning around, Magdalen stands there, barefoot and wrapped in a blanket in the middle of the wooden floor, so overwhelmingly perfect that I have to look away for a moment and adjust to reality. She's not mine to make warm.

"What the fuck happened?"

Magdalen's gasp makes me jump, and I look at her, confused. "What?"

Eyes wide with horror, she lets the blanket drop in a pool around her. "It looks like someone drowned you in blood." She starts toward me, but I stop her with a shake of my head, remembering that I must look like the lead in a slasher.

"No, no, I'm fine."

"Here we go again," she huffs, hands on her hips in

annoyance. "Fine, you said?" It's so cute, so utterly Magdalen, that I bite my lip not to smile.

"If I recall, you were the one who was fine last time."

"And you were the one who walked away with some other girl." Her voice comes out raw and my skin prickles with guilt at trying to lighten this. Eyes piercing into mine, her pain is on full display. Seeing her so hurt is fucking devastating. I step closer, needing to explain everything, but I have no idea where to start.

The silence of the house magnifies the shakiness of my breath. "I'm useless at this. At liking you. I'm terrified of how much I need you."

Magdalen's eyebrows crease in confusion. "You literally dismissed me. You didn't want me anywhere near you."

"I slept with Chiara." The words tumble out. "The day I ran into you shopping, I called her right after and had sex with her that evening."

I watch as Magdalen tries to process my words but she still looks confused. "Yeah, obviously you slept with her."

"You knew?"

"Isn't that why you didn't want me around? So you could pick up where you left off?"

I blanche, stunned at her conclusion. "You think I wanted to have sex with her right after you gave me a hand job in the ocean?"

Magdalen's eyes widen and she quickly glances at the front door as if someone will mystically appear inside the house. "Theo! Don't say that word in this communal area." She waves her hands frantically around the living room.

"You said it at the beach! That's the definition of a communal space."

"Ah, semantics." She looks at me closely, eyes observing the blood crusted around my nose and chin.

"What happened, really?" she asks again, but the idea that she thought I was on a date with Chiara this whole time is so painful that I struggle to answer.

"I didn't want you to find out that we'd fucked from Chiara. Saying you were tired was the quickest way I could get you out of there before she said anything."

"You made me feel really ugly." Magdalen looks down at herself and a stab of shame courses through me. "Like I was this leech, sucking up your fun while you flirted with another girl."

"Stop," I croak. "Stop, Maggie."

"Then stop hurting me."

A wave of déjà vu hits me, at how my father would box up my mother's pain so he could ignore it, walk over it, shove it far inside a closet and forget it was there at all.

My hands ball into tight fists at my sides to stop myself from reaching out and holding her. Where do I begin? I settle for words, for the truth, and hope she understands.

"I see you in everything," I whisper. "I look for you around every corner, hoping for just a glimpse so that I can endure the rest of my day." My voice catches on the last word and I sigh, looking at the ground for a moment before meeting her eyes again. "I keep trying to stay away, Magdalen. Because you're Anika's best friend and because you're Dante's little sister and your father means the world to me.

And my papa…" I swallow, keeping my breathing even and slow. "Sometimes I think I'm more like him than I want to be."

The truth, even the sliver of it I'm admitting, seems to drain any energy I have left. It would be the right moment to confess everything, right here, say it all now and pray for forgiveness later. But as much as I try, the words won't fucking come out. I bend down in front of her, so close that my nose can graze her knee if I just lean forward an inch, the heat of her skin warming me as I reach around her, gathering the fallen blanket.

"You're nothing like him." Her voice breaks as she looks down at me. "But you need to stop running away from me."

I stand up, bringing the blanket with me so that it runs behind her calves, her thighs, and eventually, as I stand up, I lay it onto her shoulders, cloaking her tightly in the knitted wool.

"I've been running to try to save you," I say and smile tightly.

"I didn't think it would be this difficult to get you to sleep with me."

We stare at each other and, within seconds, both of us erupt in laughter.

"Stop laughing!" she says through her giggles. "I thought you would be an easy lay!"

"God, Magdalen," I close my eyes and groan miserably. "If you want me to fuck you, you can't say 'lay' again. Grossly unattractive." My heartbeat slows, happy to have these small moments. She gasps, shoving me playfully on the chest, and it's easy to forget what's waiting back in Chivasso when it's this quiet, just the sound of her laugh and the rose bushes gently tapping against the window. I say a quick prayer.

"You want to talk about unattractive? Your entire face is soaked in blood."

Touching my nose, I cringe slightly at the blood caked under my nostrils and am genuinely terrified to look in a mirror. "Point taken. Not going to ask me more about this?"

"Betting my life and Anika's George Michael CD that it was my brother."

"How did you—"

Magdalen sighs and just reaches out her hand for me to take.

"How did you know?"

"The brooding bromance at the beach? The no talking? It was bound to happen sooner or later. Dante's experimenting with his new-found masculinity. Come," she adjusts the blanket around herself and starts walking toward the stairs, looking back at me with a shy smile.

"Already did."

She gapes. "Grossly unattractive." She shakes her head disapprovingly, but her eyes are warm. A vibrant green just under the glow of a single lamp. I'm scared by how easy it is to want to follow her. "It's my turn to clean you up, lover boy."

43

MAGDALEN

"By the way," I go to ask while walking along the upstairs hallway toward the bathroom, with Theo following close behind, "did you happen to go through my luggage?" I hug the blanket tighter around me, trying to suppress the residual guilt I have about forgiving him. Thinking about telling my Emily what he's done, what he's said to me, and still walking with him, makes me slightly queasy. I should fight harder, forgive less. But I think of him bent underneath me, whispering desperately.

I look for you around every corner, hoping for just a glimpse of you so that I can endure the rest of my day.

My heart aches. No one has ever said anything like that to me before.

I open the bathroom door and stand against it, ushering him in. But he stops in front of me, smiling wickedly. "I may have rearranged it for practical purposes."

"Of course. The thong is a practical summer staple."

"I thought so." His hands reach to touch me but I see him hesitate, asking me with his eyes if it's okay. I nod shyly, wondering if he knows how much I appreciate the consent, the relief of knowing that it's me who decides. I never knew I needed it until someone asked.

"But only for me." His hands are warm against my neck as his thumbs drift lazily across my cheekbones; it's so natural to be undone around Theo that I wonder if this is what it's like for other people all the time. I used to tense at the idea of someone seeing me when I wasn't prepared. Even in class, I'd think about how I looked while thinking. I'd wonder what I looked like from the side, writing notes across the page. Sometimes I'd think so hard about others looking at me that I'd end up not writing at all and eventually spend the night relearning the lesson once I got back to our flat. But it's all different with him. It's addictive to be brave.

Theo leans closer, towering over me in the bathroom doorway, his shoulders looking obnoxiously broad as he holds me in his hands.

My throat is dry as I try to speak when he consumes the space around me so intensely.

"Oh. Should I call Roberto and tell him not to come?"

Theo tsks, rubbing the sensitive skin behind my ear so that my neck tilts up to face him, and my grip on the blanket falters.

"Mhm, only if you want me not to drown him in the ocean." His thumb catches my bottom lip, and he stares at my mouth, looking so desperate that my heart flips.

Just as he begins to bend his head to kiss me, I remember his bloody nose and squeal. "You're covered in blood!"

"What?" He blinks, still staring at my lips.

"Your face! It's disgusting. Let's save the ravishing for when you don't look like a bloodthirsty Jacobite."

He chuckles softly but settles for a kiss on my forehead. "Okay, *dottoressa*," he murmurs into my skin, lips lingering on me. "Clean me up."

After a quick shower, Theo sits on the edge of the bathtub, watching me through the fogged mirror as I wait for the tap to warm before filling the basin and wetting a washcloth to clean up the blood the shower didn't wash. I've swapped the blanket for one of Dante's sweatshirts and my ratty pajama shorts I snuck into the luggage before Anika could stop me.

"Why did you choose Oxford?" he asks as I look at him in the reflection of the mirror.

I frown, never having had to justify or explain my choice. "I don't know. I know our parents went there." I think about the four of them in the same city, studying in the same library as me before a big exam. "But it wasn't just that. Sure, I'm happy to know that I'm just as capable as them. Just as smart." I run my finger underneath the tap but the water is still too cold. "But it was better that I could do it my way. By myself, I guess. I could not talk or not leave my bed for days and they wouldn't know, which was fun in the beginning. They check up on me less because they went there." I check the water again and this time it's warm and I dip the cloth underneath the tap.

"And you like that they don't check up on you? You don't feel lonely?"

As I turn around, Theo's looking at me contemplatively.

He's so obviously trying to figure me out that I start to feel self-conscious.

"I've always preferred being lonely." Theo silently opens his legs for me to step between and immediately starts stroking my calves, the backs of my knees, my thighs. I fight the urge to sigh and fall into his touch but focus on cleaning him up, gently scrubbing the blood off his chin.

"Interesting. I grew up constantly surrounded by noise. When I first got to Connecticut, my roommate was a week late, so it was just me in the dorm. I felt like I was going insane."

My finger brushes under his chin and he looks up at me, his eyes somehow grayer in the fluorescent lights. The salt water has made his hair curlier and he looks so perfect that I train my gaze only on the bottom half of his face.

"I've been this way since I was a kid." When I say that, Theo looks down.

"What's wrong?"

His head stays tilted downwards so I can only see his hair, curls in a messy halo around him, and, just when I'm about to ask again, he looks back up at me, a small smile on his lips. "Nothing. We just never spoke much before. As kids, I mean. I would have liked to know that." His tone is off, and his jaw hardens a little.

"You seemed so much older back then," I say. "I was always hiding behind a corner when you came around." Theo flinches when I try to clean the blood around his nose, and I wince. "Sorry. I see Dante put all his effort into this punch."

He responds by sliding his hand up my legs, playing with the edge of my shorts, and my stomach tightens. "I can take a little pain, Magdalen. So, anyway, you were scared of me?" he probes.

"Scared?" I make my way down his neck until I reach the edge of his shirt, focusing on dabbing the blood off his collarbone and not how his voice seems to lower each time he talks. I press my lips together as his fingernail grazes lazily across my thighs, feeling the need to grip his shoulders to steady myself from his touch. "Intimidated," I conclude. "Even as a teen, you were just . . . *big.*" I dip the towel underneath his shirt, massaging him in slow circles, and feel his breath quicken.

"Why didn't you ever call me across our telephone wire?" he asks, and it sounds so earnest, so genuinely curious, that my hand stills underneath his shirt. I try to think of a way to explain how small I began to feel by the time he left, but everything sounds so pitiful.

"I was intimidated by you even across the street and over the phone."

How could I ever think that the brightest star in Chivasso would want to talk to me across the telephone wire? A line reserved for secret confessions and after-school gossip. For the nights when we were grounded. A little tug to wake the other up. *Did you hear? Yes, I heard. But tell me anyway.*

"Dante spent our childhood trying to ignore my existence," I shrug, the words stinging even after living through it for the past decade. "I figured you wanted to, too."

Theo's demeanor changes at the mention of Dante. "We're not the same person."

"You could have talked to me." The idea of him initiating conversation with a seven-year-old version of myself is laughable. By then, he was already hanging around girls and drinking *caffè*. I had just learned how to use scissors to cut my sister's headbands in half.

"I was scared of you."

Rolling my eyes, I make my way back to the sink and toss the now red washcloth in the laundry basket. "Scared I might ask you to read me a story?" I turn the tap back on to wash my hands as Theo strips off his shirt, throwing it in the basket, too. I try not to stare at him in the mirror but he's just so beautiful that I give up and watch as he stretches his hands above his head. He's all sharp contours and biceps. No one should look this fucking good after having been beaten up.

Theo rests his hands on his hips as he examines me, eyes traveling up my body so intensely that I feel lightheaded.

"Maybe I was scared of how young you were. Like you were another person I could easily mess up."

I turn the sink off and rest my hands on the basin as Theo walks up close behind me so that my back lightly touches his chest.

"Anika came out fine. Arguably better than me, some would say," I say, but my throat is dry. He slowly leans further into my back and moves my hair to the right side before covering my hands with his on the basin, squeezing me gently beneath him as he cages me tightly against him.

I suppress a shudder as he continues, settling his chin in the crook of my neck.

"Mhm," he breathes, running his nose through my hair before going back to staring at us in the mirror. "So lovely." He licks his bottom lip, taking it between his teeth, and it's enough to make me arch against him. He inhales sharply as my ass becomes flush with his groin. I watch in the mirror as his eyes fall to where our bodies meet and he groans.

"Look how well you fit." He says it absentmindedly, and this time when I grind against him, his hands snake around my stomach possessively, fingers sliding down until they hook between where my thigh meets my pubic bone, making it impossible to move.

"No, no." He curls his fingers tighter, looking at me in the reflection. "My turn."

Theo grabs my hand and pulls me into the blue bedroom. It's stifling in here with the window shut but I'm so nervous that walking all the way across the room feels impossible. I almost pat myself on the back for not throwing up yet, but I hold off. There's still time. A single seashell nightlight plugged in the far-left corner of the room dimly illuminates the space, but besides that it is dark and it takes my eyes a moment to adjust.

"Lavender," he hums after closing the door behind us, and I walk into the middle of the room, feeling clumsy.

"Magdalen, actually," I supply while smoothing out my sweatshirt, feeling increasingly unsure of where to put my hands.

"You smart-ass." He comes closer to me, and this time

I'm convinced I will throw up, so I keep my mouth shut and try not to breathe. The moonlight tries to peak in through the sheer curtains, creating an effervescent glow throughout the room. Theo stands shirtless in front of me, a crooked smile on his lips. "You smell like lavender." He gathers my fidgeting hands and gently raises them above my head. "Honeysuckle," he continues to whisper, and runs his fingers along the edge of the sweatshirt. I look down at his hands that begin to raise the sweatshirt off, my heart stammering uncontrollably. In anticipation, or maybe pre-paredness, when I'd flung on the sweatshirt and shorts, I'd also put on the undergarments Marta picked out. Coincidentally, also lavender-colored and completely sheer.

"Why, thank you," I say shyly. It feels oddly intimate to be recognized by scent alone. The face I have now will change, age, droop. But in twenty years, he could smell lavender while in a park in New York and think of me.

"Fair's fair," he murmurs, and goes to pull the thick fabric off me, his hands running up my torso as he does so. Once he reaches the edge of my breasts, he stays there for a moment and takes a sharp breath when he sees the bralette.

"Before, in the kitchen," he says, voice rough, "when I was cleaning you up, I had to leave the room because of how beautiful you were." I'm mesmerized by him as he retells the story. "There you were, sitting on the counter with blood fucking everywhere, and I was trying to control my erection from seeing you touch yourself." His knuckles graze over my nipples and I gasp.

"Mhm, fuck, when did you put these on?" he asks, mesmerized. His knuckles graze over them again and I let out a small groan as they harden underneath his touch.

"Couldn't disappoint Marta," I manage to say, despite feeling like I'm going to die.

"Thank god for Marta."

44

THEO

The feelings I've tried to bury finally escape when I take her in. I let myself feel the ache. For her. For this.

Her eyes lock with mine and I become dizzy with the intimacy. She licks her lips, looking expectant, anxious.

My hands move of their own accord over her breasts and stomach and then I push her shoulders so she falls back onto the bed. Her nipples are completely visible underneath the sheer fabric, desperate to be released. As she sits there with her legs slightly open and breasts exposed just for me, it's impossible not to want all of her.

She rolls her eyes, trying to close her legs, but I sit down on the bed next to her and rest my hand on the inside of her thigh. She stiffens slightly and I look up to find her staring at my hand, her mouth slacked as if transfixed by the sight of me holding her open. My grip tightens, inching up the inside of her leg, and I'm already so hard I should be embarrassed. Her legs are paler here, and I have a vision of sinking my teeth into her softness. Licking and sucking the untouched skin until she whimpers my name.

"You have enough innocence to save us all." I repeat

Anika's warning aloud from that first night in Chivasso and I look down at my hand, loosening my grip.

"Excuse me?" Magdalen abruptly sits up, and I curse myself for saying that out fucking loud.

"Shit, I'm sorry." My head whirls. "Anika, she—"

"Oh, I know Anika says that. Says it to me every morning, in fact."

Her palm presses against her forehead and she takes a quick glance at the window. She bites her lip as though she's debating whether or not to say something.

"I'm not as innocent as Anika thinks."

My stomach lurches and I must look sick because her eyebrows furrow.

"I didn't mean to offend you." I edge closer to her, wishing I could tell her that innocence is better than whatever the fuck I am.

"I'm not offended. Just clarifying." She shrugs, parting her legs further.

The image of seeing her for the first time since I came back appears in my mind. Toes in the grass, overalls barely covering her ass, being so surprised at how tall she was when she stood up.

I let myself think the thought I've been holding back since the moment I saw her.

I want to be inside her.

I slowly turn my body and kneel on the bed so that I'm over her. We're the same height like this, our heads inches apart. With only that tiny thong and sheer bra, her nipples taunt me, peeking through the semi-transparent fabric. How has she resisted being with anyone for so long? Images of her and Roberto flash to mind and I inwardly groan. I try to breathe slowly but the nightmare begins again. The noise of ripped fabric is so loud, I shut my eyes.

"Hey." She brushes a piece of my hair behind my ear and I lean into her touch. The need to touch, to be touched by her, is so bad my hands shake.

Opening my eyes, I find Magdalen's staring back at me, wide and green, full of concern. It's like she knows. She scoots closer, nodding her head, whispering comforting things that make my eyes prick. Pathetic, I look down. *I should tell her.* The shame of having his shadow follow me, even at night in a bedroom with Magdalen, miles away, is so heavy that I think about walking out.

But then her fingertips hover next to my cheek, slowly, as if testing whether I'll run. *Never again, Magdalen*, I want to say. *I only ran because it would scare you how badly I want to stay.* I blink slowly, my chin dipping in a short nod, hoping she can see what I'm too afraid for her to hear. She sighs, still looking at me with those beautiful doe eyes. The worry dissolves as her fingertips graze my jaw. I release a breath, my head leaning into her palm.

"Magdalen," I whisper.

"You're scaring me," she answers, but she's smiling.

"Why?" I lick her cheek, basking in the warmth of her body.

"I've never seen you this way."

"You've never seen me at all," I correct. "But I'm okay.

I tend to overthink a little sometimes." *But I've seen you*, I want to add.

"I've seen you since the moment Titziana Benedetto asked me if she could fuck you," Magdalen says, and I'm caught off guard by the memory of uncomfortable sex in that car. Trying to recall that scene, it scares me when I can't remember her there. Why would Titziana ask her? I feel sick knowing she knew what was happening that night.

"I threw up after that," I confess, the words slipping out before I have time to hide them away.

Her smile disappears, replaced once again with concern. "Why?"

"I...I never wanted to have...I just—" I take a deep breath. Try to balance the throbbing in my dick with the awful memory of the smell of stale fast food in that car. Her perfume that reminded me of my grandmother. "I wasn't ready and I did it anyway."

"I'm sorry you felt you had to do something before you were ready to."

Every time she speaks, I feel it on my skin.

Swallowing hard, I open my eyes to find hers pouring into mine. Emotion swirls in the dark green and I grimace at the idea of her pitying me for fucking someone at sixteen. "I don't want to talk about Titziana," I say, my hands wrapping about her hips tightly, needing to feel as much of her as I can before I have to let this fantasy go. My head leans into hers and the feeling of her hair brushing my neck is enough...

Hasn't it been obvious, Magdalen? I want to shout. *Don't you know I've touched myself to the thought of you?*

My fingers trace her neck and she sighs. The sound alone is enough to make my hardness increase tenfold, painfully pressing against my shorts.

My lips brush against her jaw and my hands slide down her body. I grip her ass through the thin fabric, squeezing her closer to me. A groan bubbles in my throat, the feeling of her body against mine is beyond any fantasy. She arches closer toward me until our bodies are flush against one another and I push my hips into hers, wanting her to feel, for her to know she has the control.

My hands slide up her spine to grip the back of her neck, forcing her to look at me. Teeth grazing her cheekbone. A deep hum of pleasure escapes her and I'd do anything to hear that sound again.

I break away for a moment to look at her. Her lips are parted, her pupils wide.

My lips devour hers in one fluid motion. She freezes at first, not expecting the intrusion, but within seconds her lips soften, opening for me, kissing me back. My fingers wrap in her hair, gripping tightly. The fullness of her lips is intoxicating. I can't help myself; my teeth bite her bottom lip and I stifle a moan. My legs are moving before I realize as I blindly settle between her open thighs.

"Theo," she moans, and I almost come at the sound of my name from her mouth.

"Since the moment I saw you in the grass."

She laughs again and when her mouth opens I kiss her again, wanting her laughter to be a part of me. Her lips instinctively part, allowing me entrance with no hesitation this time, and her tongue brushes against mine.

Holy fuck, I think. It's never felt like this before.

Her hands travel down my chest, fingers gliding across my bare stomach. I press closer into her, needing her to touch me. Magdalen moans and it sets my skin ablaze. I swallow her kisses, devouring her mouth until it is swollen and marked by me. Kissing always felt like a stepping stone, to get what I really wanted. But as I grab her face to bring her closer to me, I realize I want to claim her, brand her with myself, the same way she's branded me.

Heady silence falls between us as my tongue dips into her mouth to find more, feeling like more will never be enough. There is hunger in this kiss, and she responds with equal demand, looping her fingers into the belt buckle of my shorts, drawing me in. I grind into her, aching for relief from the pressure that begins to build at the bottom of my spine. She breaks the kiss, breathless and blushing. Searching my eyes, she extends her hand, from my belt to the front of my shorts, cupping my hardness between her fingers. I inhale sharply, the slight contact enough to send me over. She looks down and then back at me, eyes glossy. As she goes to reach for me again, I grip her wrist and turn it over, planting a light kiss on her palm. If anyone is going to touch first tonight, it's going to be me.

45

MAGDALEN

He's everywhere. One moment I was asleep outside and now, here I am, having almost-sex with Theo Sinclair. Alassio is a fantastic city.

"I want to feel you," he whispers as he grips my wrist, stopping me from touching him. His eyes are dark and impenetrable, and I know there is nothing I can say for him to change his mind.

I pout. "No fair. I started first." I take a step closer, pushing myself into his hardness. For someone who has never done this before, my body seems to know exactly what it wants.

His cheeks flush and he tips his head back in laughter, pinching my bottom lip between his fingers endearingly.

"We have time, baby," he smiles at me, his eyes glazing over every part of my face as if trying to memorize it before the sun rises. "But right now, I need to see what you look like when you come."

Just when I think I have a handle on dirty talk, Theo says the unthinkable.

"Say it," he demands when I don't answer, a slight edge to his voice.

"Say what?"

"Say I can."

"Okay, Theo," I say for the first time in my life. "You can."

An exhale escapes him and he smiles so brightly I stop breathing. Taking his time, he gently palms my right side, and I inhale sharply, unused to this feeling. Looking up, he smirks. Am I an easy lay?

Almost as if forgetting that his every movement is making me achy, he circles my breast with his fingers, watching as my nipples harden beneath him. And then he takes my nipple in between his fingers, pinching slightly and I gasp, the feeling shooting down through me.

"Does that feel good?" He smiles knowingly. Words are still lost and I can only manage another nod.

He moves his hand to my other breast and continues the same, agonizing pattern, trailing his fingers in slow, deliberate circles. My breath quickens, the sharp pain of his fingers making me want to sink into the bed and float in this feeling. And then he pinches me again, kneading my aching breast until my back reflexively arches against the bed.

And all the while, he's watching me. Watching me squirm as my body tries to find relief from the uncomfortable feeling that is building in the pit of my stomach.

"Does that feel good?" His voice is taunting. Of course, he knows how good it feels. I've practically melted.

"Tell me how good it feels." He pinches me again and I moan, the ability to keep my eyes open getting harder the more he touches me.

"It feels good," I whisper, locking eyes with him. Wanting him to know that what I want to say is: *"You are good, Theo. You are so good."*

His lips part, his heavy breathing mirroring mine. "My Magdalen."

He lets go of me and I almost whimper at the loss of contact and need to check myself.

"Now I'm really going to touch you, *zuccherina*," he whispers, a smile tugging at the corner of his mouth.

My knees tremble, body aching with anticipation, feeling lost and needy all at once. "Please, I want you."

"Not as much as I want you."

His fingers dip beneath the elastic, his nail grazing across my pelvic bone. "My good girl." He smiles again and dips his finger lower, touching me fully, and I moan out loud.

"Oh god."

In slow, deliberate circles he touches my center, while his other hand fists my hair, making me look at him as his fingers explore, gliding up and down, achingly slow. His fingers are wet and slippery, giving away how badly I want this.

"Fuck," he hisses, looking down at where his hand circles. My hips balk at the intensity of his touch and I look down to follow his gaze. Oh wow. Watching his fingers press and play with me is beyond anything I've ever experienced. I rotate my hips again, reveling in the pleasure his fingers create.

"Look how wet you are for me," he says, so low that I almost think I made it up.

And then his middle finger is tapping at my entrance,

making small circles around my rim, dipping half his finger into me, exploring the boundaries.

Even with only a finger, the fullness of him is foreign. "You like me inside you, sweet girl?" he says in my ear.

"Yes, yes," I pant, unaccustomed to the need in my voice. "But I want more of you."

He releases a breath through clenched teeth, pumping his finger slowly inside me. "God, Magdalen, you're fucking perfect." His eyes are focused on my center, mesmerized by his own fingers inside me. He pushes his finger more and I wince at the slight pinching sensation.

But Theo catches my eye. "Just like that, yes." His gaze searches mine as he curls his finger to rub against the walls of my insides and now I'm wincing for a different reason. My body clenches around him to find relief, testing the pleasure. Theo hisses slightly and pulls his finger out to circle my rim again before diving back in, pulsing his finger slowly in me. God, this can't be legal. This is what I've been missing? How is he destroying me with one single finger?

Just when I'm feel myself tightening around him, Theo removes his finger, leaving me to feel empty. "You're gonna come with me inside you," he says gruffly, pulling my underwear down and tossing it across the room. "Is that okay, Maggie?"

"I think so, yes," I say shakily. "I'm on birth control, by the way."

"Is that so?" Theo grips the back of my knees and pulls me farther down on the bed. "So I get to feel you bare?"

I try to close my legs, desperate to control this building

ache inside me from the way he's looking at me and hearing those filthy words. Theo must notice and keeps my legs open, blatantly staring at me, eyes hooded as he kneels off the bed, undoing his belt in one motion, and his shorts fall to the floor.

"I'm trying to savor you," he says, palming himself over his now tight boxers, his hardness visible underneath the black fabric.

"You get this entire weekend, remember?"

"Summer," he says darkly. "I get the summer."

I hope, I think, but don't say anything. Coming back onto the bed, I lean up and take the opportunity to slip my fingers beneath his boxers, tugging them off.

"There you go, undressing me again," he chuckles, but when my hands touch his length the laugh turns into a heady sigh. My eyes widen when I really take him in, having only felt him in the ocean, I didn't realize... *Wow.* I lick my lips, trying to picture all of him inside me. How on earth will he fit?

Noticing my apprehension, Theo lifts my face, plants a chaste kiss on my lips and smiles. "I'm gonna take care of you." Slowly, he lowers us back onto the bed and positions himself so the tip of him brushes against my entrance. "Now, you tell me if it's too much." Slowly, with a shaky breath, Theo pushes himself inside me, taking his time, pausing every so often until he's completely there. I squeeze my eyes shut, my hands reflexively gripping his biceps as I wait for the slight pinching sensation to lessen. He stays still, letting me adjust, whispering gently. "You're doing so good, Magdalen." Tentatively, I try to move a little, pushing my hips up to get more of him.

"One second," I whisper with a shaky breath.

"Take your time," Theo says tightly as I continue to move, exploring the boundaries of my own body, grinding a little faster as the pinching subsides. While it's certainly foreign, there's barely any pain after a few minutes. Must be Theo's magic touch. Eyes still shut, I gyrate my hips and immediately a spark of pleasure floods me. "Oh."

When I finally open my eyes, Theo's looking at me, biting down on his bottom lip, cheeks stained red.

"Do I feel good now?" he asks, hands traveling to my hips, flexing himself inside me so that I involuntarily shudder. "Let me make you feel good."

I nod. And that's all Theo needs to start moving, steadily increasing his pace...

"That's right." He's still looking at me, his eyes dark and cloudy, and I can feel his desire in the tight grip he has on my waist and the quickening pace of him inside me. I can't help as I arch closer, my hips circling as I meet his pace, continuing the motion until our rhythm increases. His breathing is erratic, every so often a small groan escaping him as he watches me sink onto him.

"Ride me, Magdalen. Just like that, yes."

I can't hold it in. I moan out loud and my hips undulate, finding the rhythm of Theo. His thumb presses against my center, circling and tapping slowly as he continues to pump in and out of me.

"I can't—" I begin, but I don't even know what I'm trying

to say. Gripping the back of his hair for some sort of stability, I grind myself on him and he lets out a harsh exhale.

"Maggie, you're so fucking tight."

I press my head further into the pillow. Feeling how he flexes himself inside me is enough to make me understand why Mary had to stay a virgin. How could she have done anything else?

"I'm not going to last long," he whispers, his eyes on my lips, my neck. The hand on my waist moves to my head, fingers digging into my hair, pulling deliciously.

"Theo." Was that my voice? I didn't even know I could whimper.

"Come for me," he demands. "I need to feel you come around me, Magdalen."

I bite down on my bottom lip hard to contain the loud moan trying to escape as something inside me quickens. Hot pulses of pleasure tighten everything inside me until I feel like I'm going to shatter.

"Ah, that's it," Theo growls, his pace getting faster, it's so intense that I cry out loudly and rest my forehead on his shoulder to keep from collapsing. "You have to look at me, baby." A hand snakes up the valley between my breasts before he reaches for my neck to tilt my head up. And I know the moment he looks at me, eyes hazy with desire, that I don't stand a chance. With a few more deep thrusts, his thumb rubs me again and I can't contain it any more. I quiver uncontrollably and my vision goes black as I pulse harshly, a flood of pleasure running through me for what feels like an eternity as my insides clench rhythmically around his length.

Theo continues to massage my walls, his pace slowing down, and he groans in my ear, "Yes, Magdalen. Fuck," and then I feel him shudder above me, his movements becoming sloppy as he jerks one final time and stills, spilling into me. "Fuck," he repeats, and I giggle, feeling warm and happy with him on top of me. After a few moments, I try to regain any semblance of normalcy. It feels appropriate that men would wage wars over love and sex. I get it now, I really do. What's a lifetime of trauma for ten minutes of absolute bliss? Theo laughs gently and I realize I've not said anything, too busy coming down from the euphoria.

"What?" I say, my smile mirroring his. Theo takes himself out of me and I wince slightly, immediately miss being filled with him. He shakes his head slightly and then touches his fingers to my entrance, making me quiver, bringing his fingers to his mouth.

"Theo—" I try to stop him but it's too late. He dips his fingers into his mouth and sucks, staring at me the entire time.

"You're delicious." He says it seriously. No smile any more. "I can't believe no one has tasted you before."

My cheeks flush. "I'm feeling shy," I say, and Theo laughs freely while scooting down to lie on his side, resting his head on one hand. "Touché."

I lift my hands over my head and stretch, my body feeling warm and relaxed.

"What was your favorite book growing up?" Theo asks, his finger gently grazing my stomach, and I tilt my head to look at him.

"Excuse me, I'm trying to bask in my first post-orgasm." Theo raises his hand and bops my nose playfully. "You're so fucking cute."

"Trying to sweet-talk me?" I ask, turning my body to mirror his. "You already got me in bed."

"I just want to know everything about you."

"Kiss-ass," I smile, but my heart warms and I ponder his question. "I really liked *The Shadow*." Tucking my head into my elbow, I think about my mother. "My mother read to me every night till I was ten."

"You read that as a kid?"

"Options were limited on English books. And I never minded; when she read them they never seemed as scary."

Theo sighs and reaches out to take my hand, bringing it to his chest. "Does it ever make you nervous how connected our families are?" His voice is quiet, curious, almost prodding me to ask more.

"It made me feel really safe for a long time. To know I had two families to always look after me." Theo doesn't say anything but I see it. The color has drained from his cheeks.

"Why did she stop reading to you? After you were ten?" he asks, just as quiet as before.

"I'm not sure." It's all I can say, my tongue feeling numb. I don't like where this conversation is headed and I try to clear my mind to avoid thinking about anything too serious. "Uh, yeah. I'm not too sure," I repeat.

We both lie there in silence, looking at one another, listening to the waves, an occasional seagull flying close to the window.

After a minute, Theo interrupts. "*Sir Gawain and the Green Knight*," he says, and I have to roll my eyes at his audacity.

"You're questioning me reading a Hans Christian Andersen tale while you're lounging around reading a fourteenth-century Middle English poem?" Theo hooks his ankle around my calf and it's such a casual display of comfort that my heart sings.

We stay there for the next few hours asking each other questions, each of us testing the boundary the other one has drawn.

The night continues with questions, laughs. Favorite movie? First kiss? Have you seen a ghost? *Kiss me, please. Gladly.* Do you believe in fate?

At around midnight, we hear the front door open and both freeze.

"He'll actually kill me," Theo whispers, and just as he prepares to rise we hear Maio singing loudly up the stairs. Very un-Maio like. We turn to look at each other and our laughter comes out in quiet wheezes. "Shh, shh." Theo's hand comes over my mouth and mine over his.

"Maio's singing!" I say between gasps and his palm against my skin.

"He's in love," Theo whispers, leaning forward to kiss the back of his hand. "We all sing when we're in love."

Pulling me onto his chest, Theo rubs my back in gentle circles. Tiredness, the happy and full kind, envelops us and I rest my head on his bare chest, closing my eyes at the sound of his steady heartbeat and the smell of his skin. I really hope this can last.

46

THEO

The next few days are spent in a lazy terra-cotta haze. I sneak into Magdalen's room after spending the day at the beach with Dante and Anika. We come back home around five, all of us sleepy with too much sun and the ever-flowing spiked granitas Anika keeps shoving in front of us. Stumbling through the front door, we'll shake the sand off our feet and they'll run to see who can get to the big bathroom first. I'll walk slower than the rest of them, letting Dante go to the fancy bathroom so I can find Magdalen upstairs and join her if she's in the shower. She'll tell me about England and her friend Emily, naked and covered in soap, and I'll try to control my erection because she's naked and covered in soap and thinks I'm paying attention to a story about her friend. But I love it so much when she speaks. She massages herself with the loofa and I ask about her favorite literary theory.

The nightmares have stopped. I don't want to say it's all because of her, but it's hard not to feel like I've saved all my truths so I can share them with her. Things about home I couldn't think about without panicking, don't feel as bad. Tennis on the beach. Talking through my dissertation. She can talk about Jane Austen for hours. At dinner I'll sneak a glance and she'll graze my ankle with her toe. I'll refill her glass when I notice it's empty. There's an openness to her that I have only seen when I watch her talk to Anika, and I know I'm acting the same way. She'll sneak out of my room when the sun rises, or we hear Dante and Anika unlock the front door after their night out. She wears my sweatshirt now when she's cold.

Dante and I haven't spoken one-on-one since the fight, but after a day, we are both wearing down. We're speaking through other people's stories. Like when Anika asks me how my face feels, Dante will blow air through his teeth and throw some sand around. He's desperate to say something. And, when I ask Magdalen about the scariest dream she's ever had, Dante will interrupt with a story about how he once stuck his dad's finger in a bowl of water to make him pee while he was sleeping but it didn't work and Dr. Savoy ended up catching a cold instead.

Our fights have a very temporary shelf life. We'll start like this and eventually one of us will ask a neutral question. Like, "Do you know the time? Oh, and by the way, is this thing over yet? I've been dying to tell you about what's been happening."

Tonight is our last night in Alassio and the wedding is in two weeks. I watch Magdalen walk back from the gelateria with Anika, wearing overalls and a turquoise scarf around her chest—she's sunburnt on her forehead and nose. My daydreams now consist of putting sun cream on her shoulders and washing salt water out of that beautiful fucking

362

hair in the shower. She licks the gelato dripping down the cone and I audibly mutter under my breath.

"Jesus." I try to look anywhere else to distract me and end up catching two men with thinning hair chain-smoking cigarettes near the entrance of the gelateria ogling at Magdalen with no shame. But she's completely oblivious. Anika narrows her eyes at the men, immediately shutting them up. But my Magdalen still doesn't look, doesn't even know what's happening as she continues to lick her gelato. There's something about her lack of awareness that makes me inexplicably fucking sad.

Coming up to my table while Anika looks at keychains outside one of the shops, she plops down in the furthest chair from me.

"Excuse me?" I ask. "What do you think you're doing?"

"Munching," she says, and wraps her lips around the tip of the ice cream.

"Magdalen," I say, my voice inexcusably low.

"Yes?" She flutters her eyelashes, and this time when she licks the dripping cream, she stares directly at me.

"Are you flirting with me?" I ask, turning my chair slightly to face her.

"That depends." She wipes some of the ice cream on her lips with her finger slowly. Achingly slow. And it's such a beautiful sight, innocent and seductive, I'm scared of what I would do to keep her always looking at me. "Is it working?"

"It always works with you."

Unable to stand the distance, I reach out my foot and hook my toes underneath her chair, pulling her toward me.

She yelps and almost drops the cone, but recovers quickly enough when my hands slide up her thighs to steady her.

"I'd like to taste," I say when she's close enough, and lean forward in my chair, wanting to put my mouth where hers was. To lick the ice cream with the taste of her still on it. Her eyes are wide, and the sunburn on her cheeks makes them greener.

"By all means," she says, and puts the gelato between us. I wrap my hand around the one holding the ice cream and she sucks in a breath. "Déjà vu," she whispers, and I know she's remembering the ocean, my hand over hers, guiding her as she touched me.

I gently squeeze her hand and bring the ice cream to my mouth, looking closely at her while I dip my tongue to the top and rotate our hands to get a full taste.

Magdalen squirms in her seat and I'm immediately hard when I think about her being turned on by me. "How is it?" she asks shakily, her eyes trained on my lips. I lean back in my chair to keep myself from throwing the ice cream on the floor and ripping that bandanna off her.

I muse over the question. "I've tasted sweeter."

She smiles that smile where her upper lip almost touches the top of her nose, and I grip the chair to stay seated. "Now you're flirting with *me*."

"Always am, sweet girl."

A plastic bag is thrown down on the table, breaking the trance between us, and Anika coughs loudly. "The sexual tension between you two is radiating through the entire fucking town." She pulls up another chair and sits between us. "I know Dante and I gave you our blessing, but for the love of god can you not give the poor ice cream a joint blow job in the middle of the street?"

"Anika!" Magdalen slams her back against the chair to create some distance between us and looks around worriedly for Dante.

"Don't worry. He's trying to flirt with the lady at the *tabaccheria*."

"Isn't she like seventy years old?" I ask, wondering if it's the woman I'm thinking of.

"Yeah."

"And we're not going to acknowledge that him flirting with a seventy-year-old is a little weird."

"Nah," Anika says, and bites down on her cone. "He's done much worse."

"True," Magdalen and I say at the same time.

Anika stares at us for a moment before rolling her eyes and says, with a mouth full of gelato, "Oh, gag me. They're speaking at the same time now. Listen, I know I'm the one that inadvertently pushed you two together, but I'm going to need you to not be this disgusting. You're turning into Lucia and Maio."

"So sorry, it won't happen again." Magdalen places her hand on her heart. "I swear."

"As long as Dante's not here, I can't make that promise." I shrug.

Anika gasps loudly. "Excuse me! Aren't you afraid of my wrath? I could punch you, you know!"

"My god, Anika, I'm literally begging you to try to punch me."

"Oh, what? Because you're obnoxiously tall and your biceps are the size of my calves, you think I can't do it?"

"It has nothing to do with my calf-sized biceps. I just know you—you're happy!"

I leap forward and take the last bite of her ice cream cone before she can stop me and she shrieks helplessly.

"No, you did not just do that." She stares at her empty hand, stunned.

"It unfortunately looks like I did."

"You better walk away right now or, I swear to god, I will punch you so hard your liver will come out of your mouth."

I chew the cone loudly, smacking my lips. "Mhm, only if Magdalen can come with me."

"Ugh, get out of my face, you complete and utter swine."

I chew louder, gulping the last bit of the sugary wafer down, hands mockingly on my hips as I stand. "Magdalen," I ask, turning to her, "would you accompany me for a drink? I'm feeling particularly parched."

"Why, I'd love to. That is if Anika doesn't want to join?"

Anika covers her mouth with her hands as her eyes bounce from Magdalen to me in horror.

"Oh god, what have I created...?"

"So is that a no?" Magdalen gets up from her chair, gracefully ignoring Anika's distress.

"Is it too late to be Lucia's best friend instead?"

"You little bitch!" Magdalen gasps and goes to swat Anika, who moves away before she reaches her. "I was going to let you finish my gelato!" She pouts, waving the cone.

"The one you gave a blow job?"

"Anika!"

"Fine! Gimme!"

The two argue happily in circles, so I walk away and let them settle, how sisters do. But it's funny, I'm just as content watching Magdalen happy across the street with Anika as I am when it's me making her smile. It reminds me of what Dr. Savoy was on about that morning at the museum—how it doesn't feel like you're sacrificing anything when you make the woman you love smile. I completely fucking get it.

The ogling men at the next table nod at me as I pass them.

"Fuck off," I say, and one of them jerks his head up but doesn't do anything. How unsurprising.

I continue down the alleyways of Alassio, the faint yellow glow of a few streetlights illuminating the pathway. When I look up, I see an old couple sitting on their balcony, sipping out of teacups. One of them notices me and waves with a polite smile. The iron railing is lined with fresh tulips and there are too many terra-cotta pots scattered around the small opening for it to be safe. Life's small pleasures—flowers and fresh basil. The loud noise of tourists has tapered to quiet conversations between locals and even in the dark night I can see the old man's hand wrapped around his wife's, holding her palm in his lap. Her cardigan is wrapped tightly around her shoulders as she leans into his warmth and in the shadowy night, they almost look like they're connected to one another.

I sit down on the concrete steps in front of the old couple's flat and wait for Magdalen. When I'm left alone, my mind immediately flashes to the night in her room under the same moonlight as now, watching her body respond to me. My knee bounces anxiously and I fumble for a cigarette. I'm not used to this. These periods of raging desire for someone. It feels insane to be in a constant state of need for one person.

"Penny for your thoughts?"

A pair of sandals with shells glued along the thick strap stand in front of me. Jesus, I know her even by her toes.

"Trying to remember how to be a gentleman." I exhale and look up at her.

"Fun and flirty, remember?" Magdalen bends down so she's squatting in between my legs, holding onto my knees for support. I stop fidgeting.

"No need for gentleman-approved behavior. I'm a cool girl." She shrugs.

"Oh really?" I say, testing out her pseudo bravery when it comes to talking about anything involving sex. Let's see how much she can take.

"Try me. What are you *really* thinking about?" She holds my gaze, humor deep in her smile. She thinks I'm bluffing. I weigh the odds of me going to hell and conclude that I've already dug my way down at this point. How much more fun would it be if she's down there with me?

"I want to taste you again, sweet girl."

Magdalen doesn't flinch, but it's as if I can see the wires in her brain crossing, trying to understand what I mean. She opens her mouth and closes it again.

"You don't mean—"

"Yes, I do."

"How chivalrous." Her long hair brushes against my

knee and I reach out to run my hands through the auburn strands.

"I assure you; this is completely selfish."

"Should we do it here?"

I have to stare at her for a second before bursting out in laughter, completely taken aback. "Yes, Magdalen, please let me go down on you so the nice elderly couple can watch."

"What? Maybe they'll throw money if we do it well enough." She joins me in laughing joyously, her eyes closed shut as she snorts and giggles. Magdalen tries to cover her mouth with her hand to silence herself, but I wrap my fingers around her wrist to pull her down to where I sit.

"I lied before. You have an incredible laugh," I whisper when we've both calmed down enough, our breathing still fast with unspent laughter.

"Mhm." She leans forward so that her nose brushes softly against mine. "I know."

I scoff. "That's when you're supposed to tell me I have a great laugh, too."

She stays close to my face, nuzzling me in slow and delicious motions, eyelashes fluttering against my forehead, down the bridge of my nose, my cheeks.

"But I'm not a liar," she says, and plants a soft kiss on my cheekbone, lips still cool and sugary from the gelato. I lean my head back and smile lazily and then dip my head to kiss her. Her lips part, licking her bottom lip, and, just as I'm about to press my mouth to hers, I tilt my chin up and bite down playfully on her nose instead.

Magdalen erupts in another fit of laughter and pushes her hands into my shoulders. "What was that for?" she gasps.

"For insulting my laugh," I muse. "I am very offended."

"You just bit a chunk of my nose off!"

"You're pretty enough to go nose-less. No one will even notice."

"I'll be the laughingstock of Chivasso!" she says, smiling and standing up, holding her hand to her nose. I stand up and begin stalking toward her with my teeth bared.

"You know I'd kill anyone who laughs at you," I snarl, and Magdalen shrieks giddily and begins to walk backward away from me.

"Theo," she warns, and I continue my pursuit, crouching low as I track her steps. And then I launch at her. She yelps and runs down the alleyway lined with bars, sandals smacking loudly against the cobblestone street, and people watch curiously, sipping their spritzes as Magdalen dashes past them.

"Come here, *phantasma*," I yell, and chase her through the streets, laughing happily. "You know I'm always going to catch you."

47

MAGDALEN

He does catch me eventually. I lasted three minutes behind a rusty fountain before strong hands grabbed me by the waist, hauling me into him.

"On my back," he commands when he lets me go.

"What?" My heart is still pounding from the small race across town.

"You heard me. On my back."

I sigh and walk around him, placing my hands on his broad shoulders before jumping on his back and wrapping my legs around his waist. "Am I allowed to ask why this is happening?" I question when he starts walking, hands protectively gripping my calves as he turns toward the path to the beach houses.

"Because I like being beneath you," he supplies, leaving my throat dry. Even taking the piss, Theo makes anything he says lusty and outrageously attractive. It's sickening. As he walks us to the villa, I can feel the powerful muscles of his back move beneath me, and every so often he'll grunt when he readjusts me on him. Heat spreads down my body, craving his sounds. Wanting to climb across him so that I'm straddling his front and watch him the entire time.

God, what the fuck is happening to me? I'm spending too much time with Anika. I submit to being carried, on his back, and sink down so my chin nestles into the space between his shoulder and head, my hair swinging over the both of us as he steps over the uneven sidewalk.

"Crude," I whisper.

He stops walking and turns his head slightly so that his lips brush against my cheek when he talks. He breathes in, voice low. "Only for you."

When we arrive at the villa, Lucia and Maio are sitting out in the garden, drinking beers and eating olives.

"Fuckers," Theo moans. "Shouldn't they be out doing almost-married shit?"

"We can try to sneak past the sliding door. I don't think they've noticed us yet," I offer, and Theo intertwines his fingers with mine.

"No, no. Let's chat with your big sis. It's her wedding week, after all."

We only take one step in the kitchen before Lucia's head turns and eyes us through the sliding door.

"Ah, lovebirds. Can you bring the wine before you come outside? It's in the fridge."

"How do you know we were even planning on coming outside?"

"Because I'm telling you to?" she says and waves her hand at me like I've asked what color the sky is.

"Brat." I stick my tongue out and Theo goes to grab the wine as I open the sliding door.

"There she is," Lucia says happily, patting the empty chair next to her. She's wearing a white sundress that drags across the floor even with her legs crossed.

"Are you drunk?" I ask, counting the five empty bottles on the table in front of her. Knowing Lucia has probably drunk a minimum of three.

"What? I can't be excited to chat with my little sister without being drunk?"

"I mean, you're never happy to see me." I mean for it to come out as a joke, but the words sound accusatory instead, too much truth weighing them down.

"You think I don't like you?" Lucia turns to face me better, ready to fight.

"Lucia..." Maio tries to calm her down but she swiftly ignores him, turning even farther toward me.

"Answer the question, Maggie."

"Obviously you like me, Lulu. We've just never been close."

"We're not close because you choose not to be," she fires back. "You were always weird growing up."

My heart sinks at being caught, at being judged by my own sister. "I'm sorry."

"No, don't fucking apologize. Just tell me why."

"How am I supposed to know why I act the way I act?" I spit back, the pressure in my temples getting increasingly harder to ignore. My left pinkie goes numb and I try to hit it underneath the table without anyone noticing but the whole table ends up shaking and one of the empty beer bottles falls over.

"I think you know why," she says and my brain goes quiet. It's funny, she's done this before. Two times, actually, always making sure to confront me with someone else present. Last time, I was eighteen and she dragged me out for drinks with Marta. After each time, I promised myself I'd come up with something striking to say back but never wanted to think about it long enough to actually come up with anything. I look at Maio, who stares at his fingernails, pretending he's not here. Marta had tried to comfort me, smothering me with soft words and misphrased motivational quotes. *Be the product you want to change,* she said. I think she meant, *Be the change you want to see.*

"I'm not doing this now." It's the exact same thing I said the two other times.

"You said that before."

"Sorry I don't like being attacked like this, Lucia. You never want to just talk to me, do you? You want to talk *at* me. Don't think I don't know what you're doing."

"What, I'm not allowed to be concerned about my baby sister?"

"You just want to know if you're right! If Mum told you the truth! Don't play stupid."

She stays silent but looks at Maio, who finally meets her gaze, and any adrenaline or anger I have leaves when I watch them talk through their eyes. She's told him.

Lucia turns back to me. "How do you know Mum told me?"

"Because you started watching what you said around me. You used to joke around me all the time and then one day,

374

it just stopped. You were so scared to say anything wrong that you just stopped saying anything at all." My throat closes, and I try to swallow down the residual sadness of these memories. This is the most I've ever talked about it. My head throbs violently and the gelato sits heavy in my stomach. It feels like someone is scraping my brain with a knife, peeling thin layers off until all that's left is the smell of oil sizzling on skin. *Calm down.*

The sliding door opens behind us and I freeze, completely forgetting Theo was in the kitchen.

"Couldn't get this fucking cork out of the bottle," he says, placing the wine on the table with four glasses.

But Lucia stands up. "Sorry," she says with a giant smile splayed across her face. It's so tight her face looks like it's about to crack. "I underestimated how much I drank." She begins to gather the empty bottles from the table. "You two have at it."

Maio stands up clumsily from his chair. "Sorry, man. We'll catch up tomorrow morning."

He pats him on the shoulder and, just as they're about to walk through the sliding door, Theo speaks up. "Wait, Lucia." He slides a glass in front of me and begins pouring the wine.

"Yes?" Her voice is sharp, like a schoolteacher anticipating a stupid question from one of their students.

"You called us lovebirds before." Lucia's eyes look from Theo to mine. "How did you know that we were...?"

"Because," she responds, her eyes softening, adjusting the bottles in her hands before Maio silently takes three of them

375

from her and walks inside, "I've never seen her like that before."

"Oh," Theo says, and my palms sweat from Lucia's exposing observation. Am I different than I usually am? I feel oddly defensive, like I need to explain my smiles, why I laughed as many times as I have. Knowing how closely Lucia is watching me is surprising. I always assumed I fell just behind her peripheral.

"And not to mention the fact that you were thirty seconds away from murdering poor Roberto when you saw Maggie talking to him at *my* engagement dinner." Lucia winks at Theo and turns to look at me one final time. "Goodnight," she nods.

"Goodnight." There's nothing else to say. As much as I hate her for trying to expose me, part of me will always miss my big sister. *If you promise not to ask me any more, you can sit with us here a little longer.* It hurts to know that she's carried this burden with her all these years. She is shackled to my pain simply because she is my sister.

"See you, Lucia."

Theo looks at me while he fills his wine glass and I think I see him frown, but it's gone before I have time to ask.

48

MAGDALEN

Wine is a blessed drink. After three glasses, the anxiety of my conversation with Lucia subdues to a manageable discomfort that I can tuck away behind the peeling label on the wine. Cicadas hum loudly in the hyacinth bushes behind us, and we sit quietly together, breathing in the smell of honeysuckles and snapdragons that grow around us. My head leans on the backing of the wrought-iron garden chair, and I stare peacefully at the stars while my feet rest on Theo's lap.

"Are the stars this clear in Oxford?"

When I lift my head, Theo is staring at me. His head tilts lazily, making no effort to conceal his blatant perusal of my body.

"I don't look at the stars," I say, stretching my ankles on his thighs until they crack. "I'm too busy trying not to be the dumbest person there."

"Even if half your brain was missing, you'd be smarter than most people there."

I scoff. "That's something a genius would say."

"I'm not a genius." Finishing the last sip of his wine, he places the glass on the table, and then squeezes my foot reassuringly. "I just knew how to cheat the system."

"You went to Yale! And *Columbia*. And a gifted secondary school. Won every award a student could. Went on an excavation with my father when you were seventeen. And were the only first-year on the varsity football team. Should I keep going?"

"You keeping tabs on me, Savoy?" The hand on my foot moves up to my ankle and he pulls me closer to him. Between the wine and the feeling of his hands on me, I feel utterly intoxicated.

"I wasn't immune to the Theo Sinclair charm," I smirk. It seems odd that he'd even have to ask. His talent traveled through the steep hills of Chivasso like wildfire. Hooking his foot underneath my chair, he pulls me even closer so that my legs are almost straddling his. I gulp, eyeing the wine for any charitable drops, but the bottle is empty. Why am I still nervous? How long before he's tired of my body and wishes for someone else's legs around him? These are lame girl thoughts, I know.

Theo runs his hands up my legs, firmly gripping me, touching me everywhere. His nails graze gently across my skin and it immediately sends goosebumps up my spine. When his hands dip underneath my overalls and start massaging my thighs, he moans as he seeks more of me but the chair stops him. He raises his head to look at me, his eyes practically black in the nighttime. He squeezes me again and I feel it in my core this time.

"I wish I got you sooner." His voice is soft. Intense. When I raise my body so I'm no longer leaning on the base of the chair, Theo immediately takes the opportunity to pull me up so I'm sitting astride him.

"Should have come back last summer." My arms loop around his neck, my fingers playing with his already over-grown hair.

"Yeah, I fucking should have." He groans and dives toward my lips, his hand snakes underneath my chin and hungrily pulls me closer to get better access to my mouth. My head feels light, floating on waves of wine and the feeling of his strong thighs beneath mine. "Come here, please," he begs and dips his tongue into my mouth. I instantly sigh, tasting the dry wine and his distinct sweetness.

Once, when Lucia came home from a research trip to Saint Catherine's Monastery, she tried to explain to me what kissing should be like. The conversation was awkward, rushed, brutally revealing our distance before we knew it ourselves. We were in the museum and she was telling me about her latest fling with someone on the research trip.

"He told me that humans invented kissing to try to breathe in each other's souls. Because words and hugs and even sex weren't strong enough to symbolize needing another person so badly. Wanting to be bruised by them. Needing to communicate between the shapes and curves of each other's lips their desperation."

My mind tried to attach features to this mystery boy, wondering what kind of person captured Lucia's attention for long enough. I hope he's found someone's soul worth searching for.

Theo's hands slide down from my cheek to fiddle with the button of my overalls and the cool metal touches my skin. I shudder involuntarily; the heat of his breath combined with the coldness is electric, and I arch my back to get closer to him.

"Are you trying to undress me in the middle of the garden?" I smile as he unhooks the button so my left strap falls down my shoulder.

Breaking the kiss, Theo looks down at my bare shoulder and leans down to kiss it while skimming the top of the bandeau. "I would never."

Theo's hands travel to my back, where the scarf is knotted. I feel one finger drop into the center of the knot and pull it so the fabric loosens. He tugs gently and the knot comes undone and he brings his hand to the front of my chest to keep it from falling down completely.

"My sister and her soon-to-be husband could be watching!" I gasp as his hand runs over my breasts, only the thin fabric between his hand and my hardened nipples.

"Their room faces the west side of the beach. And I closed the blinds of the sliding door. You think I'd let anyone but me get to see this?" he asks darkly and curls his fingers around the scarf. Some feminist proverb tries to snake its way to my consciousness, but I shove it back, loving the possession. Theo pulls the scarf off completely, so I'm exposed apart from the right buckle that keeps one side of my overalls up. I gasp, instantly trying to cover myself, but he holds down my wrist.

"No, no, I want to look at you." I fight the embarrassment.

Somehow being half naked outside is more intense than being completely naked with him in the shower. But the way he's staring at me lessens the mortification slightly—him leaning back while biting down on his bottom lip so hard I think he's going to draw blood. He adjusts me on his lap and I instantly feel his hardness press against me, making the last of my embarrassment disappear.

"But what if I want to look at you?" I retort, and rest my hands on the buckle of his belt, grazing his stomach with my nail.

"Eager, sweet girl," he hisses, reflexively rocking his hips into mine, and I almost cry out from the contact. He wraps his hand around the bunched-up denim around my waist and rocks his hips again, and this time, I have to hold onto his shoulder for support.

"Use me, Magdalen." Those words. I look up at him, wondering if he remembers, and he gives a small smile. "I never got to see you come like this."

His hands squeeze my hips and fingers press into the bottom of my spine, guiding me to grind on him slowly. The friction of my denim combined with his erection is almost too intense and I close my eyes, fingers gripping his T-shirt as he lifts his hips again, making contact with my clit so that I moan loudly.

"Fuck," he murmurs, and when I open my eyes his mouth is open, watching me closely.

"Again," I whimper, not recognizing the neediness of my own voice, but too entranced to care. My plea seems to awaken a new hunger in him because he instantly flexes himself against me again, but this time he doesn't stop; instead he leans closer to me, wrapping his arms around me, one hand around the back of my neck while the other is pressed firmly on my hip. He holds me so that I'm flush against him and grinds onto me again.

"Make yourself feel good on me, Mag. You know how." He breathes harshly, and I suck in a breath as I match his rhythm, grinding into him with abandon. Another moan leaves my lips and Theo flips the hand at the back of my neck to my mouth, covering the whimpers and unintelligible words coming out of me.

"You have to come quietly," his voice whispers in my ear, not once stopping the flex and roll of his hip. "Come quietly just for me, that's it." Our pace quickens and I bite down on the center of his palm, unsure of where to put all this building pleasure inside me if not through a loud scream.

"God, I can't get enough of your fucking sounds." Theo shifts so that we're on the edge of the chair, and I feel the familiar tightening in my core. I hold onto the arm of the chair and rock harshly into him, almost delusional with pleasure.

"Oh, Theo." My voice is muffled in his hand, unsure of what I'm even trying to say.

"You're doing so good," he says, the last word coming out as a groan desperate enough to shatter the building tightness. My eyes squeeze shut as I pulse violently, shuddering as the waves of pleasure continue to fill me as Theo rubs against me.

"Ah, yes," he says, and I open my eyes to look down

at where our bodies are connected. His erection is visible through his shorts now and I cup him as my orgasm continues to overtake all my senses.

"You need to feel good now," I hear myself say, looking up at him through my eyelashes and squeezing him gently.

"I'm already so close." He sucks in a breath and covers my hand to stop me from touching him further. "But I want you in my bed, now."

Without warning, Theo stands up with me still straddling him. My overalls swing down, the metal hitting the leg of the chair, and he begins to walk us inside the house.

49

THEO

Closing the bedroom door, I allow her to slide off me, her bare breasts pressing against my chest as her feet reach the ground. The overalls immediately fall off her, landing in a pool of denim around her feet so she's only wearing light blue underwear. I lean back against the door, just looking at her for a moment. Wanting to memorize it all. Her long legs, thighs rubbing together. The fabric of her panties so thin that I can see the outline of her underneath. I release a breath, my vision going dark when I think about burying my face in her until the only thing she can remember is my name.

"You're staring," she whispers, head tilted and hands behind her back like she's observing a piece at the museum.

"You're staring," I croak and start to walk to her, but she puts out her hand, stopping me.

"It's my turn to taste." Her voice is stern, almost demanding, and my hand drops to my erection, massaging briefly to ease some of this ache. There are a few moments of my life that I consider perfect. But the sight of Magdalen walking toward me, breasts moving perfectly with each step as she reaches for my shirt, is fucking sinful. Her hands run up and down my stomach, causing my abdomen to seize. They travel up until she grazes my right nipple, curiosity clear in her eyes as she looks up at me. She pinches me gently and I exhale harshly through my nose.

"Does that feel as good as it does when you do this to me?" She pinches me again and a sharp trail of pleasure shoots to my groin.

"Ehm, yes," I choke out and she smiles wickedly, clearly proud of herself. My heart warms, infatuated with her mind and body. It's difficult to explain how much I want to understand her.

"Good to know." Her hands move from my chest, then she hooks her thumbs around my belt. As she brings her head close to my pectorals, she tentatively draws a circle around my left nipple with her tongue. "What about this?"

I press my hands against the door behind me, blinded with a need to be inside her. "Magdalen, please. I don't know how much more I can take of this." My skin feels hot and tight; I've never felt this much desire for someone. She hums against me and I feel it deep in my chest. She licks and bites all the way down, and I close my eyes until she kneels in front of me, looking up at me. Her doe eyes are mesmerizing, soft and innocent, and I can't help but brush my fingertips against her cheek, scared of how much I'm beginning to need her. Her long fingers shakily undo the belt buckle and, when she fumbles with the bar inside the hole, I grip her hand, trying to steady it, but I realize my hands are shaking even more than hers.

"Shit," I laugh. "This feels very new to me." Slowly, we

both release the bar and she slides it off, tossing it to the side.

Magdalen looks up at me skeptically. "Don't tell me you've never gotten a blow job."

"Not from someone I care about," I answer honestly.

Her mouth falls open and it takes everything in me not to sink to my knees and kiss her. But I can tell she's nervous already. I don't need to ask to know she's never done this before. She smiles sweetly, nodding, understanding—undoing the button of my shorts. When she pulls them down, her eyes widen slightly at the sight of me hard against my boxers and I bite down on my lip to hide my smile.

"You're so much bigger down here," she says, eye level with my crotch, and takes a deep breath before slipping her fingers beneath the fabric and feeling me. My head instantly hits the back of the door, as she pulls down the boxers so that my erection springs out, swollen and eager.

"You don't have to do anything you're not comfortable with," I rasp as her hands grip the base and she slowly begins to rub me.

"Shh," she says and, before I even get the chance to laugh, her mouth wraps around the tip of me and I instinctually reach for her head. She's cautious at first, dipping her tongue down the length of me, tracing the veins that pulse greedily. My exhale is harsh and she must take this as a signal of doing it right because she squeezes me harder, and begins sucking me firmly, testing how far she can go. When I feel myself hit the back of her throat, I jerk, thrusting my hips in a frenzy to feel that again.

"Fucking perfect," I lift my head from the door to watch her take me. Her lips are impossibly full and the sight causes me to jerk again. She looks up at me while I'm still inside her, and the combination is physically too much to handle. My thighs begin to shake as she continues to suck and lick, soft moans coming out of her mouth that cause my tip to swell painfully. "You're doing so good." My breathing is labored as her hands twist and rub the length she can't fit inside her mouth. "Mhm, just like that. Just like that." My vision begins to blur and I wrap my fingers in her long hair, not forcing her deeper, but just needing to be close. To feel her warmth. Magdalen moans again, her tongue swirling around my tip, and, just when I think I can't handle any more, I see one of her hands dive into her panties, unconsciously touching herself. My body roars, needing release and needing to make her feel good. "Magdalen, I'm going to come, so if you don't want me to do it in your mouth—" I hiss, but she hollows out her cheeks and the feeling is so intense that I flex deeply in her throat. "God, I'm not going to last. Fuck." I watch her fingers circle around herself faster, and I can't hold it in any longer. Hot release makes my whole body shudder, and Magdalen whimpers as I thrust sloppily into her mouth, the vibration of her throat causing me to spill even more than I thought possible. "Christ," I huff, my erection still half there when she releases me from her mouth, wiping her lip with her middle finger. When she looks up at me, she places a gentle kiss on the tip of my dick and the noise that comes out of me is almost inhuman.

"Ah, you can't look at me like that while kissing my dick. It's too much."

She smiles happily. Her lips are red and plump and it's only after a few moments of looking at each other that she realizes her hand is still in her panties.

"Oh my god." She takes her hand out. "I've become insatiable."

"Watching you touch yourself is what sent me over the edge," I reveal, already starting to get hard again when I think about her trying to pleasure herself.

"Oh really? Is that your kink?" She leans both her hands back so that her breasts are on full display, hair brushing the floor, and my mouth waters hungrily.

"Get on the bed," I rasp.

Magdalen frowns. "But we both already—"

"Please, get on the bed."

Her eyes darken and she nods, walking toward the bed. When she's at the edge she bends over, putting her hands and knees on the mattress, crawling toward the headboard. I run a hand across my mouth, having no words to describe the sight of her round ass on display in front of me.

"Stop," I croak, and Magdalen freezes, whipping her head to look at me. "Stay just like that." I stalk toward her, fully aware of my once-again erect dick between us, and can't help but graze my finger down her center. I hear her suck in a breath, and selfishly, I find myself gripping her hips, and pressing myself against her entrance. As I glide a hand down her spine, her back arches. "I'm gonna slip myself in, okay?" Magdalen nods. "It might be a little more intense this way, so tell me if it's too much."

"That's okay," she says eagerly, and I smile. My Magdalen. Parting her with my thumb, I massage her entrance before slowly entering her.

The second I'm inside her, I know I'm doomed. She's so fucking tight.

"Wow," she groans, bucking slightly as I set the pace and feel her tighten even more around me.

"So... fucking... good... Maggie." My head tilts back as I push further inside her, basking in how perfectly we fit.

"You're everywhere." Her legs spread wider, and I wrap my hands where her ass meets her hips, grinding myself harder into her.

"You can take it, baby." Unable to stop myself, I bend forward to find her clit, rubbing her bare sex in slow circles as I continue thrusting inside her.

"Oh god." Her hands fist the bedsheets and her back arches reflexively, rotating her hips to find her own pleasure. "Yes, Theo," she croaks. Her thighs begin to tremble against me and I know she's almost there.

"You gonna come soon?" My pace quickens, movements becoming more ragged, and I know I'm close again. Shit, she is too fucking good. But I refuse to come first, wanting to feel her finish around me.

"Ah, yes," Maggie gasps as I bend lower to get better access to her, wanting to hit that spot that will make her scream out my name. She writhes beneath me, ass gyrating hypnotically, taking my full length easily now.

"I need you to come now, okay?" I bite back a moan, rubbing her faster.

"Oh, fuck." Her head drops to the mattress, and I have to suppress the urge to laugh, so happy I'm making her curse. *I feel like fucking singing*, I want to say. *Every time I see you, I feel like singing.*

After a few more deep thrusts into her, I feel her begin to tighten, her body pulling me deeper than I fucking knew possible. "Let go," I hiss between my teeth, feeling the familiar pressure begin to build. My words seem to unravel her, her movements becoming needier.

"You feel so good," Magdalen cries out, and then I feel it, she pulses sinfully around my cock, her tightness so intense that I only manage one more thrust before I'm already spilling inside her.

"Fuck," I growl, pulling her down so she's sitting between my legs, my cock still buried in her as she writhes against me, helping me find my release. When she rotates her hips so fucking slowly on top of me, I don't stand a chance, I come loudly, sliding my hands across her stomach, up her breasts, squeezing her gently as I continue to ride this high. "How are you this good?"

She leans the back of her head onto my shoulder, a slow smile across her lips, and I wrap my arms around her, holding her tightly against me. Turning her head to me, she kisses me lightly on the cheek, eyelashes fluttering closed.

"I have a very hands-on teacher," she says, stifling a yawn.

"Am I boring you, sleepy girl?" I chuckle, nuzzling into her hair. "I'm literally still inside you. I might be insulted."

Magdalen hums peacefully. "I'm interested in everything you say. I think you just fucked the life out of me." She turns again to look at me and we both burst out in laughter, tumbling onto the bed, our bodies braided together, smiling until our faces are too tired to do anything but rest against one another and fall asleep.

And the night continues like this.

50

MAGDALEN

I don't dream tonight. Too loose-limbed and happy. Around 4 a.m., I hear a loud crash and my eyes fly open. Disoriented for a moment, I look around the dark room to see I'm still in Theo's bed, but when I turn my body he's not next to me. Letting my eyes adjust to the darkness, I notice the imprint of his body isn't even on the mattress any more, making me think he left some time ago. For some reason, the happiness from the night tries to drain away, but I sit up quickly, desperate to keep it in, rationalizing my absurdity. *We fell asleep laughing*, I remind myself. *We fell asleep laughing.*

But, when minutes pass and he doesn't come back, I scramble to get out of bed and go back to my room, the feeling that I'm an intruder in his space growing stronger the longer I sit here. I put on my underwear, buckle my overalls and walk to the bedroom door, when I hear Lucia. I pause, checking the clock again to be certain it's 4 a.m. It is. And Lucia speaks again. Who is she talking to? I can't hear anyone else's voice, but I think of the bed again, cold and devoid of Theo, my stomach sinking.

"You're being ridiculous," I whisper to myself. Needing to hear the words out loud. He went to the bathroom, maybe ran into Lucia, who also needed the bathroom. Perhaps they're exchanging sleepy pleasantries at this very moment.

"You can go first," Lucia is saying.

"Thanks," Theo replies.

I don't think about the fact that Lucia's room is downstairs with her own ensuite. And that there's also the hall bathroom across from the kitchen. These things happen. Maybe the plumbing is broken downstairs, or all the toilet paper has been stolen by the neighbors. I stay behind the door for another few minutes and then I hear it. Theo clears his throat. The door is too thick for me to make out any words but, when I wait another few seconds and hear Lucia sigh, I know with a sad certainty that there were never any sleepy pleasantries. I focus on getting out of the room. On the feeling of my hand on the doorknob, twisting it until the stiff lock leaves the keyhole. When I open the door, I peer into the hallway and frown. No one's here. I step out fully, digging my feet into the carpeted floor, and pause again, waiting to see if they're still somewhere I missed. A few minutes go by, and no one makes a sound, so I decide it's safe to go back to my blue bedroom. Now I understand why I was given this room. It was a precaution. Theo's way of patting my shoulder and giving me a space for when it all inevitably fell apart. He knew. Of course, a genius always plans ahead.

I sprint quietly down the hall and open the door when something in the corner of my eye moves. My heart leaps and I take one step in. I could just not look. I could go into my room, close the door behind me and pretend I needed to start packing. But the feeling of something wrong nags at me. I turn my head slightly and the object on the ground looks like an elbow. I take a cautious step back from my door, making sure I'm hidden by the table in the center of the hallway, and peer over it. And that's when I see them. Theo and Lucia, sitting on the top step of the stairs. One of his elbows is leaning on the floor, and the other hand is on her knee. He gives Lucia a gentle squeeze and keeps his hand resting on her. It looks tender and intimate. The corners of my mouth begin to drag down, and I know I'm on the verge of tears. There's no time to process what they could be speaking about. To rationalize. I just feel cold and naive. To think I could have held his attention! Before I leave them, I notice on the step where their feet are resting, an empty wine bottle has broken. Ah, I understand. They were drinking wine. He woke up to drink wine with Lucia and it dropped and smashed on the stairs.

I lock the door, feeling cold. The open luggage sits in the corner of my room, the lingerie scattered on top. How cruel. Do I crave being hurt? I must have known this would happen.

My teeth start chattering and I will myself to get it together, but the coldness seems to have washed over my brain, my hands. The bed seems so far away and that smell comes back again. Oil sizzling on skin. I try to cover my nose, my mouth, but my hands are too cold to move so I sink to the floor. I press my head into the ground and try to breathe but the smell follows me. It's trapped inside the carpet, penetrating me, and because I can't move, I start gagging. *Freak!* Amid this, another image comes to mind. Maio silently taking the empty beer bottles from Lucia. Another wave of nausea hits me, and I think about having to tell him about Lucia and Theo.

This hasn't happened since last year. It's odd to be conscious of your mind disconnecting from your body while it's happening. So I do what I did then. I say my prayer between the choked breaths. *My eyes, my ears, my mouth, my heart.* I gag again but as the words spill from my throat, my head feels lighter and I roll over so I am lying on my back. *My whole being without reserve.* My hand rests on my face and it's only then that I feel the tears, warm and wet down my cheeks. I breathe out. The smell lessens. *Guard me, as your property and possession.*

I am so small compared to this universe, curled in this tight ball on the floor of a villa in Alassio. The smell is gone. *Amen.* I should be grateful it stopped when it did, I remind myself. People have it much worse. I say another prayer for them, before everything goes dark.

51

THEO

My suitcase stands in the corner of my bedroom, packed and ready to go. Magdalen wasn't here when I got back, every trace of her gone so efficiently I had to check the garden to see if her scarf was still there. I play with the frayed edges and check the clock for the fourth time in the past ten minutes to see if it's still too early to go and knock on her door again. It was locked the first time. I tapped gently to see if maybe she was still awake, maybe she was changing and wanted to make sure no one was going to barge in— either way, I got no response. I try not to overthink it but between the silent getaway and the locked door, my nerves grow taut.

It's fine. I jump up from where I am sitting and fumble for a loose cigarette at the bottom of one of Dante's shopping bags. *Everything's fine.* Putting it in my mouth, I yank the handle of my luggage out the door and start to rush downstairs. My body betrays me, though, my luggage abandoned in front of my room as I stand inches away from Magdalen's bedroom. I press my fingers to the knob, twisting slightly. But it doesn't budge. The sun is up, Magdalen. You're always up when the sun is.

* * *

Lucia and Maio leave before everyone else. She nods at me when they get into their car and I think I give a small wave.

"You have to tell her," Lucia had said last night. "She'll be devastated, mortified, and she'll either start crying or stop talking altogether. But, if she finds out another way, it'll be the end. You'll never stand a chance."

Dante comes down next, luggage and a halfway-deflated beach ball under his arm.

"You ready?" he asks when he sees our trunk open and my luggage already inside.

"Are the girls up yet?"

"Say what you really mean." Dante rolls his eyes and throws his belongings inside. "I fucking punch you and you still don't get it?"

"Jesus Christ, all right. Is Magdalen up?"

Dante slams the trunk closed and points at me accusingly, snickering, "Ha! Pussy! My punch made you my literal bitch."

"Get that finger out of my face, Dante," I growl, and stand up off the car, taking a step toward him.

Dante flinches and slinks to the passenger side of the car. "Right, sorry. All in good fun, all in good fun."

We look at each other over the roof and, though I want to smile, happy to see we're back to normal, the anxiety of what I have to tell Magdalen weighs my muscles down.

Dante shrugs. "Her door was closed when I walked past." Seeing I'm not satisfied, he adds, "Everything all right between you two?" And for the first time, he doesn't ask critically. Almost concerned. It feels like I've been kicked in the stomach, when the one fucking time I want to tell him everything, I spit out a lie.

"Yeah, just wanted to say goodbye is all."

"Cool." He opens the door and shouts from inside, easily accepting my answer, "We'll see them in a few hours, anyway. Let's go before the traffic."

"We have to put gas in the car before we get back," I mumble as I get in, starting the engine.

52

MAGDALEN

"Papa?" I knock on the office door at the museum. "You here?"

I hear scuffling and an inarticulate noise that I know to be my father when he's eating something he shouldn't be. I push the door open to see him, thinning gray hair and gold-rimmed glasses, furiously wiping crumbs off his sweater vest.

"*Cara mia!*" He stands up and more crumbs fall down his torso. "My baby is back!"

He hops from one foot to the other while I walk around the desk; I can't help but laugh at his childish excitement to see me after only two days away.

"You're eating suspiciously." I narrow my eyes at the trail of crumbs from his desk to his vest. He ignores me, waving the question away before squeezing me to his chest. I close my eyes, wrapped in the smell of faint cologne and firewood that stays on his clothes even in the hottest month of the year. Burying my face in the itchy fabric of his sweater, I swallow the growing lump in my throat when I think about how much I love him and feel ashamed for accepting anything less than this.

"How was the trip?" he asks as he releases me.

I pretend to look around his desk, playing with the embossed leather handle of a letter opener he got on a trip in Madagascar. I cast my eyes down, knowing that if I look at him, the tears will follow instantly.

"Good, good," I say to the desk. "Lucia…" I see the broken wine bottle underneath her legs. His stupid hand. I grip the handle of the letter opener tight, feeling the hard edges of where the leather is sewn together press into my skin. "Lucia and Maio looked very happy."

"That's wonderful." My father sits back down at his desk and opens the drawer in front of him to reveal the half-eaten cornetto resting on a napkin. We look at each other and I raise my pinkie to him, and he follows, wrapping his pinkie around mine. "Your secret is safe with me."

"How was your trip?" he asks again, not letting go of my hand.

"I just told you." I frown. Does he not remember just asking me that?

"You told me how the trip was for Lucia."

I stare at him, unable to think of anything to say. *I'm in love. I gave him all I could offer and it still wasn't enough.*

"Fine. Fun," I manage to say. "You know Anika always makes everything exciting."

"Good. I'm happy you have Anika." He pats my hand, giving me a small smile before picking up his cornetto again.

"How was everything at home?" I ask. "Mother ban sweets again?"

"Your mamma doesn't understand that sweets are the

reason our marriage has been successful for thirty years. She's never known me without my sweets!"

I laugh, happy he's found a way to his cornetto. "Did you do anything with the Sinclairs?"

Chewing slowly, he picks up the handkerchief on his desk to clean the cornetto left on his beard, and swallows.

"We see the Sinclairs less and less." My father shrugs. "Since most of you left, we have no reason to get together any more."

"But you're best friends. How can you say you don't have a reason to get together?"

"Listen, I respect Dexter professionally. He's a hard worker and extremely intelligent. But, *amore*, he was never my friend. I never liked the way he treated his children, never understood the recreational activities. And I hear the rumors,"—he looks at me knowingly and my skin prickles— "about the women." He sighs. "But your mother and Cinzia are inseparable, have been since college. Who was I to ruin that?"

I stand there completely baffled. To think of my father as someone separate from my mother, as someone with a *before*, someone with hidden feelings and things that keep him up at night, is difficult to process. Has he sacrificed his friendships, his Saturday nights, for the sake of our family? It feels like someone has gone into my memories and erased the best parts. My entire life, our families were stitched together like a quilt, catching me whenever I fell. You couldn't tell where the Sinclairs ended and the Savoys began; we were a singular unit.

"But we did everything with them growing up. You always went off to the side and talked and drank the grappa and, hello? The museum!" I smack my head in dismay. "You run the museum together!"

My father's deep green eyes stare into mine. "It was fate that we were both passionate about the same things."

"How can you call it fate when it made you unhappy?"

"Because she took it as fate. And she's who I listen to." *She*, meaning my mother.

I smack my lips together, instantly angry that she's found a way into this conversation without being here.

"You can't always treat her like she's God, Papa. She's not perfect."

"Oh, but she's perfect for me. You'll understand when you find your person."

My stomach flips, acidic rage burning at my father's naiveté when it comes to her. My papa's brilliance shines through every corner of the world. We could be walking through the desert, flying in a cloud bank, ankle-deep in the Ganges river, and he would know something about it. My mother is the one thing he'll never fully understand. And he fucking loves the chase.

"We both know that will never happen."

He stops chewing the cornetto and looks up at me, the surprise evident even behind his glasses. "Magdalen." Shock and disappointment run through every letter of my name.

"You know it, Papa. Mother thinks it, too. Dante, Lucia. I see the way you all look at me. It's like..." The words feel thick and rotten in my mouth. "I feel like I've been running my whole life just to look up and see I've been in the same spot the whole time." Tears blur my vision, and I try to blink them away before he notices. *I ran away just to come back to this same town and be used again.*

"Ah." He sits back in his chair, resting his elbows on the arm piece and nodding his head, calculating my problems to formulate the correct response. Even now that I'm twenty years old, my papa can unravel my problems and give them back to me tied with a neat bow.

"You sound scared." He smiles. Only he could smile while it feels like my heart has been hollowed out.

"Why would I be scared?"

"Don't cringe when I say it..." He shakes his finger at me and I concede by sitting on the corner of his desk, hands tucked underneath my legs to prevent any cringing. He smiles again and strokes his beard twice before speaking. "I think you may have found your person."

"Papa..."

"No," he interrupts before I have time to even blush. "I have had the privilege of watching you stretch tall through growing pains. I have watched you dance in the hallway with awful bangs flopping across your forehead and watched proudly when you wobbled down the hill on a tricycle. Jo, Lucia, Dante—I love them more than words. Of course. But the day you were born, I swear—you were a beacon of light. Like it was inside your skin, glowing so brightly it had to come out through you somehow. I told your mamma, God captured starlight and swaddled you with it. I was blessed. *I am blessed.*" His eyes glisten with unspent tears and I know mine look the same. Taking a long, shaky breath, Papa rolls his chair closer to me.

"But as the years went on, there were times when it felt like I had lost you. Moments that this beautiful face—it was still you, still my too-tall Magdalen, but you became empty."

My chest hurts, pain and embarrassment striking my body when I think about my father watching me grow up. You're so concerned with becoming an adult on your own that you forget others are also concerned. That papas will always worry. Here I was thinking I was the unproblematic child. The one who braided her own hair, remembered to turn the lights off when leaving a room.

"I'm sorry," I croak. "I never wanted you to worry about me."

He shakes his head. "You could be swaddled in bubble wrap and I'd still find a way to worry. But this summer, watching you glow, it's like you're not afraid to laugh any more. Not afraid to snort!"

I smile broadly, untucking my hand from my lap to reach out and hold his hand.

"Should I tell you who it is?" He raises his eyebrow, shaking my hands playfully.

"Shouldn't I be the one telling *you* who it is?" I ask, feeling lighter after talking to him. Who cares if Theo doesn't like me any more? At least I had him for a weekend.

"Ah, but you know I am a good guesser."

"Fine, guess away, *il dottore*."

He smiles, the lines around his eyes branching out toward his temple as he does so. "I think it's a boy I once knew."

"Interesting assumption."

"I think he's trying to be a man but cannot even face his reflection without wincing."

"Are you defending him? How do you know he even messed up in the first place?"

"Magdalen, do you forget that you are half of me? Half of all your pain is felt by my whole heart. I know when you're upset, angry, scared, in love. I get a tug right here." He points to his heart, rubbing his chest in a circle like he can feel my pain as we speak. "And I know that you love him, so don't try to deny it. I am a doctor, remember! But I also know that Theo will fight to avoid feeling anything at all, in case those feelings turn him into Dexter."

I lean forward, pressing my palms into my eyes until the urge to cry mellows.

"And if I get hurt in the process of this fight with himself? Is that fair, Papa?"

"Well, that's for you to decide. You can teach him there are other ways to patch up his pain. Tell him it's okay to ache. To hurt and sob, to stomp around, and kiss, yes! Kiss it better! But you tell him that you do it together. Sit knee by knee and you hurt with his heart and stomp with your foot and kiss together, equally. You show him it's okay to ache with you. And, in turn, you can share your hopes with him."

"That sounds lovely. But I think it's too late for us. I . . ." The words struggle to come to the surface.

My father looks at me, love pouring out of him so that I instantly feel better, because I know I've done something right if Claudio Savoy loves me. He adjusts himself in the big leather chair, clearing his throat and stroking his beard one final time before answering.

"Theo Sinclair is scared by how much you consume him."

I thought I'd spent this summer learning everything I could about Theo. The pattern that his curls form when touched by salt water. The sweetness of the skin across his chest, painted with the ankh symbol. That *Sir Gawain and the Green Knight* comforted the child in him.

But what I hadn't known was that he'd been confiding in my father. Sneaking to the museum early in the mornings, telling him about us. About his confusion. His pain. His desire to learn just a little bit more about me. Should I be angry? Embarrassed? Upset that he spent hours with my papa, the man who saw through gap teeth and teenage posters on the wall, talking about me?

Ever loyal, my father refused to confess any secrets. But I sat on the train back to Chivasso with his voice in my head.

Theo Sinclair is scared by how much you consume him.

My father's use of the word *consume* makes Theo's feelings seem archaic, like loving me is rooted in an ancient and immovable tradition, like it's beyond him. I watch the blur of deep green rolling hills through the window, thinking about that night in Alassio. The faint trace of salt water still left on his skin, the taste of him in my mouth, how he sighs right before he falls asleep. How perfect a moment can be until you notice a loose thread and soon its unraveling is the only thing you can focus on. My stop is announced, and the memories of Theo fade away with the faint sound of the train horn. Rubbing my eyes tiredly, I drag my feet as I exit the station, something my mother would scold me for, but I have no energy to care. Right as I'm about to begin my ascent of the hill, I freeze.

Theo leans against the wooden fence of a house near the station. He doesn't see me, so I take a few selfish moments to just stare. To forget about Lucia, about confronting him and hating myself for loving him. I love him. Denying it is so exhausting. But admitting it is piteous! Because he hurt me and I still pine for him. Desperately.

Wearing a white T-shirt again, and those light blue jeans that are torn near the ankle. Red Adidas sneakers. He is the type of beautiful that people write songs about. His beauty could start wars, I think.

A dog barks from a backyard behind me and Theo turns his head toward the noise, to find me instead. His eyes widen and immediately, he hops off the fence and runs his hands over the front of his jeans and then waves. Waves! My hand betrays me. I wave back. He then shoves his hands in his pockets and gestures with his head for me to walk to him. So I do.

"I haven't seen you," he says when I'm close enough.

"Why are you here?" I try walking up the hill but he immediately reaches for my arm, stopping me. Even this, his fingers around my wrist, is enough to make me want to close my eyes and bathe in his touch.

"What's going on?"

"Really?" My voice comes out surprisingly angry. Good! I should be yelling. "Nothing you want to tell me?"

Theo searches my eyes, confusion clear in his gaze. "If there's something I did, just tell me, Magdalen," he says roughly, letting go of my hand. How dare he be angry with me? When it's been him throwing darts at me the entire game.

"Fine, if you want to play it that way," I breathe out. "*Lucia?*"

He stills, and it's enough of a reaction to know my suspicion was right. I blink away the tears and take another deep breath, my father's voice giving me strength.

"You were with Lucia in the middle of the night, drinking wine on the stairs." It's all I can say without feeling the familiar lump in my throat. Unable to look at him, I begin walking again, leaving him standing there behind me. "And you've been talking to my father," I add. Might as well get everything out in the open.

"Magdalen," he calls out, and I walk faster, his footsteps chasing after me. "Maggie, I promise you, I wasn't trying to do anything behind your back."

The audacity of men! Hands all over my engaged sister and he has the nerve to speak. I whirl around. "So, when you were touching my sister just after we fucked, you were thinking of me?"

"I was not *touching your sister*." He rolls his eyes as he says the last words, like I made it all up.

I start walking again. "I watched."

"Well, you watched wrong."

"Don't tell me how I watched!"

"We were talking about you, Magdalen!" Theo appears in front of me, his chest moving rapidly as he blocks my path. "Don't you realize that I only ever want to talk about you? With Lucia and your father, it's always just you."

"I'm supposed to believe you were talking about *me* with my ethereal-looking sister at four a.m. with a bottle of wine in hand?"

"Yes, because it's fucking true. I couldn't sleep, but you looked so fucking peaceful that I just stepped outside instead to get your scarf from the garden." He looks at me like I'm the dumbest person alive. "And then I found your sister on the steps, with the wine."

"With the wine," I repeat.

"She was upset because of how your conversation ended."

"Oh." A pang of regret for how I acted. Another person I have given a sleepless night.

"She kept saying she was scared for you."

"Oh," I repeat, unable to process Lucia speaking to Theo about me, about my secrets. My skin prickles and that compulsion, the one that screams to divert the conversation, rings violently in my head.

"Why is she scared for you, Magdalen?"

"What was the crashing noise?" I ask, needing time to think of a response. Accepting that I'm in love with this stupid boy makes it so much harder to keep things from him. Maybe it wouldn't be so bad to be weak with someone, *to ache together.*

"My big foot knocked over the bottle." Theo taps his

sneaker against my sandal and I stare at our feet touching, still unable to look at him.

"Why couldn't you sleep?"

"Come with me." He holds my hand, bringing it to his lips, and kisses me before tucking it into his elbow. "I need to tell you something."

53

MAGDALEN

We walk in silence as we approach my garden. The back of my hand still hums with the impression of his lips.

"What do you need to tell me?"

Theo inhales deeply and stops walking, letting go of me. He guides us underneath the veranda, the smell of hydrangeas and rosemary enveloping us as he sits on top of the table. I stand in front of him, unsure of what's going on and suddenly, Theo turns to me. Grabbing my face in both his hands, he brings me to him and kisses me, devouring my lips, licking, sucking, massaging his tongue against mine until I think my head is going to fall off. He breaks off the kiss and presses his forehead against mine, catching his breath.

"It's like lightning," he murmurs, running his lips against the bridge of my nose. "Every time I kiss you, it's like swallowing lightning."

And then he's gone, stepping back, running his hands through his hair. It's only when he looks at me that my heart sinks. Preoccupied with my own anger, I didn't realize how upset he looked before. How dark the circles under his eyes are, having nothing to do with the healing bruise from

Dante. His tiredness is potent and he sits back farther onto the table, beckoning me to join him.

"You know, I saw you around eleven o'clock at night once; I heard the back door open because of that creaking sound it always makes." It's like I can see his body cave inward the more he talks, so I sit down quietly, afraid that if I make any noise, he'll spook. "I would get so excited when I heard that sound, because it meant that wherever that person was going, I could go with them. No one ever said no. Anyone in your family, I would run out the back door and go with them. And it was late, and I heard the door, and I thought that it was odd because Dante would have told me if he was going out. So I was in the shower, and I looked through the little window above the soap shelf to see who it was, and it was you." He looks at me, eyes wide and so vulnerable, but his gaze never wavers. Brushing a piece of hair from my forehead, he continues.

"It was you, and your hand was covering your mouth like you were trying to be quiet, and I thought, *Isn't that weird?* You rarely used that door. And here was the quietest girl I'd ever known, trying to be *even more quiet*. But I kept watching. I remember absentmindedly washing the shampoo out of my hair long after it was gone because it made that squeaky noise against my palm, you know? And my fingers were all pruned but I didn't...I didn't realize, I didn't feel anything, so I was still scrubbing because the streetlamp across from us had a spotlight on your face and I could see that you were crying." He turns his shoulder away from me, so absorbed in the memory it's almost as if he forgets I'm here.

"You were crying. And it was so awful to watch. When I think back, I still don't remember ever getting out of the shower. But one second, I was under running water and the next, my hand was on the front doorknob, so ready to turn it, to run out and see if you were okay. Even though we never talked, that you think I never noticed you, it hurt me to see you so upset. It felt like a razor burn across my chest. So I was about to unlock the door when I looked down and... and I was, I was naked."

He laughs, and I flinch. His voice is hoarse, and the sound is painful against the quiet of his story.

"I forgot to put clothes on or even a fucking towel because when I saw you were upset, I forgot everything. Nothing mattered. You, you were family." He breathes deeply, facing me now.

"And now, you're my lightning, my summer." His eyes are red, and slowly he walks toward me, hands cupping each side of my face, fingers tangled in the knotted waves of my hair.

Exhaling harshly, he searches my eyes and whispers, "I'm going to tell you something that I know will end whatever the fuck is happening between us."

I blink, confused by the shift. "You want to end this?" I try to remove my head from his hold, but he doesn't let me. His fingers cradle my head, and his thumb glides against my cheekbone in absentminded strokes.

"Why I left." He squeezes my face between his hands so tightly that for a moment I can't hear anything but the rough pressure of his palms against my temples. Tears rim the edges of his eyes, his breathing becoming sporadic, yet he looks at me with a wildness I've never seen before. The words rush out.

"I'm sorry, *mi dispiace.* I'm so sorry." He releases me and stands up, stumbling against the corner of the bench.

"Theo, you're scaring me." His back faces me, strong shoulders slumped in defeat. I want to reach out and touch him, but I'm scared to disrupt his thoughts. I can tell he's pinching the bridge of his nose with his fingers, steadying himself even now.

"I went back upstairs, to put jeans on." It takes me a moment to remember his story, to recall my own tears from that night.

"To find you and see what was wrong." The memory begins to creep back and for some reason, I begin to feel sick. Knowing he never found me, knowing I slept in the grass of his backyard that night because Anika wasn't home.

"But when I came back outside you were gone. I looked everywhere and even called Anika to see if you were with her."

"I wasn't," I whisper.

He turns around to look at me, sighing before agreeing. "No, you weren't." Slowly, he walks toward me again, tilting my head to look at him. "So I went into your house."

The finality of his words causes a cold sweat to break across my back. How close we were to finding each other that night. Who knows if I could have turned out different if Theo had found me that night?

"Okay."

"So I went into your house because I thought maybe you went back in there. But, obviously, you weren't there. And for some fucking reason I went upstairs." He squeezes his eyes shut as if to escape the memory. "Your mamma was there."

"Of course she was; she's the one who—" Suddenly, the memory floods my mind so intensely it feels like my skull expands to accommodate the details I'd forgotten. I remember the red plastic chair. The unopened tomato jar sitting on the island. The smell of oil. But even now, after everything I have shared with Theo, I cannot make myself say it.

"She what?" His voice is cold and, when I don't answer, he bends down, opening my legs to fit himself between them. My cheeks burn, embarrassed, still, by the intensity in his eyes.

"I can't. Please," I whisper, looking only at his lips. My limbs feel like lead, not a part of my body any more. With a heavy breath, I try to block the unwanted images from resurfacing, but it's too late. I'm there, in the kitchen.

"What did she do, Magdalen?" His elbows rest on my thighs, fingers brushing my chin to get me to look at him. Humiliating. I shouldn't have to tell him anything. I should be able to have this secret, to bury it beneath the veranda where only I can watch it die. But he presses on, keeping my chin locked, so I must look at him. And then I see the anger fade, melting into pure concern, into overwhelming worry, and the desire to ease his comfort surpasses the need to keep my secret. The words bubble out before I realize I have ever wanted to tell someone.

"I have a few burns," I begin, unsure where to start. "Underneath my ribs and across my back, on my right side. There's about six or seven—"

"Eight," Theo interrupts, his voice rough. "There are eight."

"Right. There are eight," I blush, forgetting that Theo has seen every inch of my body. "Well, I was in the kitchen reading—I...I can't remember what I was reading." I try to recall the cover of the book. A name of a character. But my mind draws a blank. For some reason, this makes me more upset than remembering just what happened. If I can't remember the book, then it surely wasn't worth shattering the fragile bond between mother and daughter.

"And my mother asked me to watch the garlic to stop it from burning and I swear, I don't even remember saying yes, I was that obsessed with the book—whatever it was. And I guess I didn't end up watching it at all and, when she came back into the kitchen with the jars of tomato, the garlic was burnt in the oil. Completely charred. Like ashes." Theo's fingers flex against my legs, pulling me closer to him and settling his hands on my thighs. Anchoring me to reality, maybe knowing I don't want to enter into the folds of this memory alone.

"Well, of course she wouldn't stop screaming. Telling me I'm selfish and stuck in *la la land*, which she says so often that I don't even hear it any more. And the book was so good, that I just took it off the island and started walking to the dining room table while she was yelling. Obviously, that was rude. I should have apologized, but I just got so sick of being the one she yells at that my head went silent. But I guess I tuned everything out too well, because then all of a sudden I just fell over."

The memory doesn't make me sad, but replaying the scene in my head—the absence of time, and the darkness from those few moments of staring at words in a book to the grout in the tile—my stomach drops. A sick feeling crawls up my throat.

"You fell?" His eyebrows furrow in confusion.

"Well, she threw the pan of hot oil at me, so yeah, I fell."

Silence. He takes a breath in. Then out. Closes his eyes. And, when he opens them, there is nothing. I try to recall feeling pain. But it's so distant. I can only remember the oil seeping into the dips in the floor and thinking how difficult it would be to clean up. Anger seeps off his fingertips. I see the slight tremor of his Adam's apple as he swallows. I begin to worry. Worry for my mother, oddly enough. That this will ruin how he sees her.

"Jesus, fuck, Magdalen." Theo grips my waist, fingers splayed across my stomach as he presses his forehead against my ribs.

"The pan, it must have hit my head or something. I woke up alone, burned. Smelling this awful smell. And then there they were, just me and my new burnt flesh." I laugh softly, running my fingers through his hair, but he jerks his head to stop my hand and stares back up at me, the darkness now directed at me.

"How can you fucking laugh?" The disgust in his tone is palpable, and a wave of anger fills me.

"What else should I do? Cry? Throw something back at her to get even? It happened years ago. I don't care any more."

"It's abuse."

"It's life," I say, louder than I mean to. "And she apologized the next day, of course." I feel compelled to defend her. She is my mother, supposed to be my *mamma*.

"Don't ruin this for me, Theo. Don't tell me that my mother abuses me."

"You're seriously fucked if you don't see that."

"You're not allowed to come here after years and tell me my mum hates me."

"Well, Magdalen, what the fuck do you call someone who scars their daughter over tomato sauce?"

"You're foul."

"And I guess you're delusional." He stands back up, grabbing his chin with his hand, biting down on his index finger.

My voice is quiet; I'm trying to think of a way to make him understand. Angry that I've betrayed my mamma to this boy.

"She was always there for me. She just messed up one time."

"Those scars are permanent, Magdalen." He whips his head toward me. Everything about him has changed. He's harsh, all hard edges and rigid.

"You made me tell you. I didn't ask for your opinion. I could say a lot of things about your dad. You have no right to lecture me about perfect parenting."

"That's not what I'm—"

I cut him off. "What happened after you went upstairs?"

"What?" He stares at me blankly, consumed by a memory he wasn't even there for.

"I told you. Now it's your turn. What happened after you went upstairs?"

"This was a mistake. The upstairs part, that doesn't fucking matter. It's before." He paces around the dark garden nervously and even when I hate him, I feel drawn to protect him.

I reach out my hand, an olive branch of understanding. I hear myself whisper, "Our parents' mistakes do not have to bleed into us." My fingers stay wrapped in his, hoping that, for now, this is enough. "Please, tell me."

54

THEO

I stare at the garden around us, little cherub statues poking out like they're listening. Cursing myself for confessing it all out here, in this sacred place of happy memories. She laces her fingers in mine, pulling me to her through the tips of our touching hands.

"I'm so sorry," I say first. Why am I the one who has to hurt her?

Movement, purpose, direction are all impossible because I'm paralyzed by the sudden possibility of losing Magdalen before she's even mine.

"You need to stop saying that." Her tone is light but the pressure of her hand around mine gives away how nervous she is. *I'm sorry,* I think again and she squeezes my hand. *Can you feel it? Can you feel how scared I am to lose you?*

I let go of her hand, tugging at the collar of my shirt, and for the first time in seventeen years, I coax the memory to come back.

I wasn't kidding. Going upstairs that day to the Savoys' was nothing compared to what happened years before.

* * *

The attic was dingy and smelled like stale onions because it was right over the kitchen. When Mamma cooked, the smell floated to the top of the house and became trapped in this dusty room with only the one small window in the corner. There were always spiders above the door, which is why I didn't like coming up here. Unless of course it was to use the homemade telephone across the wire and talk to Dante. I usually ran through the door quickly, hating how thin those spiders were. It looked like they were made from pieces of Anika or Mamma's hair left in the bathtub and it gave me the creeps.

I was eight years old. My favorite movie was *E.T.*, which I saw with both my parents and it made all of us cry. When the lights came on in the theater, I looked at my mum and dad, both their elbows brushing against my own, and felt so safe. The three of us, connected by a little alien named E.T.

That week, I was trying to save up money to see the movie again with Dante, and I followed the trail of bronze coins all the way to the attic. I could have asked Papa but I wanted him to be proud that I was resourceful. That's how I ended up there. We usually never go to the attic; the spiders were a really big deal. I remember feeling surprised by how little dust there was on the doorknob. Each time I had been there, there was always a pile of dust by the entrance and some more coating the doorknob. But it was gone, almost like it had been cleaned. Mamma complained about how the extra eleven stairs hurt her knees so it wasn't worth cleaning the space unless my grandparents were coming to town. I thought, *Are Nonna Gina and Nonno Canio coming to town?* Surely Mamma would have told me; usually their visit involves her screaming at all of us to clean our rooms and getting out the solid gold rooster Nonna Gina bought them for one of their anniversaries. So I made a mental note to myself that Papa might say no to me going to the movies because I'd have to clean my room.

Approaching the door, I heard a muffled noise escape from behind the wood. Despite the pounding in my chest, curiosity egged me on, pressing my ear against the keyhole to make out the sound. For a second, I thought it could be an animal, trapped in our little attic, maybe a bird that'd snuck through the terra-cotta tiles of the roof and couldn't find its way back. But my thought was interrupted, the sound becoming clearer now: breathier and distinctly human. It sounded like crying, but not quite. The air felt thick in my throat but I willed the muscles in my fingers to push lightly against the door. Through the darkness, that's when I saw Papa.

Red in the face and biting down on his bottom lip, so hard that it was almost white. I could tell even from the doorway. Jaw loose, and my little arm still against the wood of the door, I actually felt myself wobble. My stomach hurt really fucking bad and I thought I was going to be sick right there, on the spot. My father's trousers were down to his ankles, the metal buckle of his belt hitting the floor over and over again as a woman with her skirt above her bottom was bent over in front of him. One hand was wrapped tightly around her waistline yanking her to him, hard so that the skirt tore all the way down, and I saw the curve of her butt. She says, "Yes, yes," and my father laughs happily. His other hand was holding her head down, tangled in the messy curls. I looked away, and I guess that's when I made a noise because, suddenly, he's looking at me. My father's body continued to move back and forth behind the woman, teeth still biting down on his lip as he finds my eyes. Through the dark I could make out that the woman had black smeared under her eyes, but most of her hair was covering her face so it took me a second to realize that I knew who she was. That I saw her every day.

"Came to watch, Theodore?" my father mouthed, Mrs. Savoy still unaware I was there as she intertwined her hand on top of my father's, throwing her head back with a grin.

"Dexter," she breathed, and then he yanked her head farther back, exposing her neck and bending forward, planting a loud, wet kiss. A horrible, unforgettable sound.

"Hurry up, Vittoria." He continued bumping into her behind faster and Mrs. Savoy shut her eyes and cried out, really loud, and she tried to lift her head up but he forced it down.

"Dexter," she said through strangled breaths. "I love you, Dex."

"Yeah, me too." When he spoke, he spat a little on the top of her head, a little drool dripping down his chin.

I hear myself screaming for my papa, my eyelashes wet and heavy, but he cuts off my scream. "You'll thank me later, son."

"What'd you say?" Mrs. Savoy asked, a little dazed.

A few moments later, he pushed Mrs. Savoy away and exhaled harshly, running his hand through his hair. She stumbled forward, losing her footing, trying to reach for one of the cardboard boxes but instead toppling forward against the wall with the window.

"Papa?" I said, confused, because what else can you do but call for your father when you're lost?

"We were just playing, Theo. Don't tell you mother— it's our..." He bent down to pick up his trousers, huffing loudly. "It's our little game."

"Oh my god." Mrs. Savoy finally sees me and desperately tries to lower her skirt, but it's torn.

"A game," I repeat after him, looking over to Mrs. Savoy, who sat huddled underneath the window, her head in between her legs. She massaged her hair, rocking slightly like a mother rocking a child. Except in this case, she was both mother and child.

It was the first time I saw an adult that looked smaller than a child.

"Mamma can play, too," I said, taking a step back, but Papa was on me before I even knew what was happening. His hand, the one that had been tangled in her hair, was now wrapped around my neck and he squeezed so tightly, I could hear my heartbeat in my own throat. I thought about how he'd connected all three of us now through the curl of his fingers against my throat. A month ago, it was my elbows tucked safely between my mum and dad at the movie theater, and now my father looks down on me, dried spit at the corner of his mouth and eyes black, alien, but with nothing like the kindness of E.T., and I felt something sever between us. He gripped me tighter, my vision dotting black, and I was only faintly aware of Mrs. Savoy sobbing next to us.

"Mamma doesn't play this game with me, you understand?" His breath was heavy and rancid. "She's no good."

"Yes, Papa," I choked out. The words felt rotten in my mouth. It's what I said when he taught me how to cross a busy road, and when he asked if I wanted to learn more about Heliopolis during Christmas break. And now I said it as a plea.

It was at this point that my papa stopped being my papa. He became a shadow of someone I once knew to be filled with love, now empty and dark in the center. If I reached forward a little, I was sure my hand would go right through him.

My neck ached, and I gagged in his palm. Looking back, it was clear he was on some drug. Maybe cocaine—I think he's always been partial to cocaine. And, when I looked over at Mrs. Savoy, she was now standing up, pacing, hands still in her hair. She kicked something beneath her that she sat on when she fell. My father let my throat go, shoving me back against the door, and I gasped, gagged, bile rising in my throat. I wanted to run away. But where to go? Here was the man I'd spent my youth chasing, only to find I'd been running the wrong way.

"Fucking hell, Vittoria. If all you're going to do is cry in the corner, you can leave." He stretched his hands above

425

his head lazily and then zipped up his trousers. The noise serrated against the silence, making me flinch.

Vittoria ran past us, her hands covering her face. "I'm sorry," she whispered in my vague direction. I looked over to where she had been standing a moment before and saw the tin can, our telephone across the wire, crushed flat. The string attached to the end hung limply from the windowsill. Connection severed.

I have kept the secret for seventeen years. It has hurt. My first introduction to sex was through my own father's brute force. I still feel my tiny neck, my little bones, crushed underneath the weight of the hands that he once embraced me with. And now my neck, bigger, responsible for holding my head up high, still feels the strength of his grip for the rest of my life. So, until now, I've kept my head low. Unable to stretch tall just yet. But one day, I hope I will. For me. For Mamma. For my Magdalen. For my dreams at night. I really hope.

55

THEO

By the time I am done telling her, it's dark outside. The crickets chirp wildly in the overgrown grass around us. Someone is having a party in their backyard, and we can hear a bottle of champagne pop open and people cheering. Magdalen is silent the entire time but I see her eyes move frantically, watching her process the story in real time.

"My mother?" she says first and dips her head low. "Your father?" Pressing her lips together tightly, her eyes leak with tears. I feel horrible that it's me, again, making her this upset.

"You were eight." She covers her mouth, and she lets out a guttural sob that breaks through the crickets' chirp, and I feel my own eyes brim with tears.

"My dad? How could they do this to him?"

My knees shake as I go to sit down on the bench again and I try not to notice how her body shifts slightly away from me. *You knew this would happen, Theo. It would always end with her farther away.* I stay parallel to her, careful not to touch.

"I think..." My voice feels drained after reliving the memory. "I think they've been doing it since university."

I find myself relaxing into the relief that someone finally knows, that this weight can sit across two pairs of shoulders, and, selfishly, I'm relieved it's Magdalen. Fuck, they could still be doing it now, but I don't tell her this. I haven't been back to the attic since that day, haven't checked to see if the dust has settled back in place since.

"Oh my god." Magdalen runs her hands through her hair, shaking her head, and I can tell she's trying to put the pieces together from the past seventeen years. Every glance. Every family outing, shared meal, movie night in our living room. Who knows what they've done in the dark around us? I watch as the secret stains every holiday, birthday, celebration. While it felt nice for a second to have her underneath this veranda with me, knowing I've disturbed treasured memories makes me regret every word.

"Why haven't you told anyone?"

Why? Why don't I speak to my mum just as much as I don't speak to my dad? Why did I abandon everyone because I was running from a ghost in the attic? Why did it take me seventeen years and the green eyes of Magdalen Savoy to finally unravel this burden?

"I think he choked the words out of me." I shrug in defeat, my eyes watering at the truth. "Every time I want to say it, to confess to my mum or Anika or even your father, I'll get this panic attack. Like I can't remember how to breathe any more or my lungs turn into concrete and, fuck, it was easier to keep pushing it back. Even when I think about it by myself, I'll wake up somewhere I don't remember walking to. It's all so fucking weird." I shake my head, mortified at how this one little moment has manifested into a lifetime of isolation. "So I just stopped trying to say it."

Magdalen continues to look out at the dark backyard but then looks to me, sorrow deep in her eyes. "No one that young should have to carry such a heavy secret," she whispers.

When a cry breaks through the still of the night, I don't realize it's me until Magdalen wraps her arms around my shoulders, rubbing the length of my back tenderly. Closing the space I left between us. My hand covers my mouth, trying to hold it in, trying to shove the memory back inside.

"It's okay, Theo. It's okay." She holds me tighter, her cheek pressed against my shaking shoulder.

"I should have told someone." I'm heaving. Salty tears pour down my cheeks, my neck, and I'm sure they coat Magdalen's arms, too.

"Yes," she agrees, the heat of her face warming the crease in my shoulder. "But you shouldn't have had to. You keep doing things you shouldn't have had to."

For the next hour, we both sit on the bench until my cries turn into hiccups and soon, I can't even lift my head. So I drop my head in my hands and tell her about finding her mother upstairs the day before I left, after she maimed Magdalen. That she was crying on the floor of her bedroom when I walked up those stairs. That I fucking comforted her, the wrong Savoy. My face is swollen; my skin feels red and itchy.

The last time I had seen Vittoria cry was in the attic that day. I suppose she remembered that because she broke out in another fury of tears and loud sobs and kept apologizing to me.

"If I had known she just fucking abused you, I would have never forgiven her."

Magdalen stills at the mention of her mother. "You forgave her?"

"I was leaving. It felt like I could at least forgive one person."

Her hands slip off me, a coldness stretching around me, and I instantly ache for her body around me again.

"How could you forgive her?"

"If it was between forgiving your mother or my father, the choice felt obvious."

"My mother—" she starts but stands up abruptly.

"Your mother what?" The same feeling I got when we were together in the ocean descends on me. Of her omitting. It's like I can see her burning holes in the photos, wanting to alter her own memories for self-preservation. Still, I don't push.

"You idolize my father," she says. "And you watch your father fuck my mum and then go on a three-month excavation in Egypt with him, where he talks about how perfect his fucking wife is, and you say nothing?"

What do I say? Yes, I've learned to forget. To shut up and listen to Dr. Savoy explain the origination of monogamy, of giving your soul to another human, even when it's with the woman who has stolen away my childhood. How do you interrupt and say, "Excuse me, but your wife has been giving her soul to my father while taking yours."

She has taken out parts of him so slowly that it'll be too late before he realizes he can't stand straight if she doesn't remind him how. Dr. Savoy, for all of the accolades and discoveries, would crumble without sitting down with Vittoria at the kitchen table every day when he gets home. So you don't say anything. You stay silent and hope you'll eventually forget seeing the black mascara smudged under her eyes, and how she rocked herself sadly.

"We all have to forgive eventually," I say lamely. "It's easier than carrying this shit all the time." Do I believe this? In theory. But knowing about Vittoria's abuse of Magdalen makes it difficult to keep my promise of forgiveness. My hands ball into tight fists until the wooden bench scrapes the skin of my knuckles raw.

Magdalen whirls her head. "This is bullshit." Her voice is barely above a whisper, but the weight of what I've told her is heavy in every word. "I don't see you forgiving your father *ever*, right? But just because my mum can cry a little, it doesn't make her any more redeemable than him."

"My father and your mother are not the same."

She dips her head and pulls at her hair. "You don't know anything about my fucking mother," she says harshly. "All these years of us claiming to be these successful families, here we are. Selfish, broken, abused." The last word slips out and I know she regrets it by the way her body tenses, as if feeling the aftershock of her admission.

"I am so sorry for what you had to witness, Theo. But to know that my father has been living underneath the shadow of her mistakes all these years..." She shakes her head. "And that you *knew*." She angrily wipes away the tears that have resurfaced and I can feel her leave me before she even says the words. I don't try to wipe the tears away, because this is the end. I should let myself cry at the end.

"You knew and you ran away." To think that I found the love of my life. I should have known it could never be that easy. I say goodbye in my mind before she does, and this time I know she cannot read my thoughts. Connection severed. A limp string lying between us.

"You knew and you fucked me."

"I know." I knew every time I kissed her, touched her, breathed her name and thought of being inside her, that it would eventually end because I knew and continued to want her anyway.

"I should go inside." Magdalen stands up. I want to scream.

"I should, too." I stay seated, my body unable to process such a heavy loss. It happened so quickly, no time to mourn. I try to stand up but it's like my bones have been hollowed out. They're still here but they're less.

"You should hug your mum," Magdalen says.

"Will you tell anyone?" I ask dumbly. *How could I lose you before I even told you that I love you?*

"I don't know," she says and sighs. "The wedding is in two weeks. I don't want to ruin everyone's excitement."

"Of course. I understand."

"I'm going to leave now."

"Sure." *Stay.*

"I'm sorry for you, but I have to go."

"Stop apologizing, Magdalen."

"Sure," she says in defeat. "I'll see you at the wedding."

All the years of panic attacks are nothing to the emptiness of watching Magdalen go back inside her house, away from me. Because of a secret from seventeen years ago. If I had known that this is what Dr. Savoy spoke about, I would have come home to her every weekend. I would have read her favorite books and sat next to her at dinner. We could have had time. I used to think that the more time between me and that awful memory meant it would consume me less. But now? My hands clasp tightly together, my muscles shaking in exhaustion. To think, people get lifetimes of this love, and all I have to cherish are a few summer nights.

56

MAGDALEN

The wedding comes. Two weeks without exchanging a smile, let alone a word with Theo. Marta drops off my dress. It's pale green, she says, to match my eyes.

Oxford mails the course catalog for next semester. Am I excited to go back? Excited to be alone, yes. To stay in the bathroom for two hours and not have anyone knock on the door. I'm excited to drink heavily without someone asking if I'm okay.

I consider dying on Monday. Anika pats my shoulder when I start crying at the tennis club. I told her that things just didn't work with Theo and she didn't probe me for more, probably suspecting that it would end quickly. I drink four beers on Wednesday. When I see Theo at the cafe in Torino on Friday with Dante and two other guys, he just stares at me through the glass. No half smile, no frown, nothing. I feel like I'm at the zoo, watching Theo through this clear cage between us. I'm not sure which one of us is the animal but I suspect it's me. Except, I realize I crave entrapment. I desire confinement. So we'd be forced to coexist. Surrounded only by the strong smell of freshly ground coffee and his beautiful mind.

I want to forget that I know what he knows and curl

around him tightly until we can both push out this memory. I stare back through the window and continue walking down the street.

On the day of the wedding, my mother ignores me and I spit at her heels when she turns around. She cries when Lucia comes down the stairs into the kitchen, wearing a robe, holding the silky white dress in her hands. Lucia's gaze goes past my mother and she smiles at me. She looks radiant. I smile back. My mother yells for my father to get the camera and my mind spins.

I look down to see I'm standing in the same spot my mother hit me all those years ago. How funny. Should I remind her about that? Remind her how she used to poke fun at me for being shy around boys. When she rolled her eyes because I said I was scared to kiss Romeo on stage. I rush to the bathroom, pretending to need my lip gloss, and close the door behind me. My fingers curl around the basin. *Just breathe.* My father's footsteps, in his brand-new shoes, click loudly against the tile of the kitchen floor.

The medicine cabinet is slightly open so I peer inside. An expensive jar of face cream, two hair ties with a loose piece of hair tangled around them, and an eyebrow razor. When I reach inside to pick up the eyebrow razor, the base of the cabinet is sticky with dried-up toothpaste and I grimace. My mother is the worst cleaner in the world. She only pays attention to the surface. I hold the razor out and look at the edge of it, where the metal meets the plastic holder. It's beginning to rust. She must run it under the water and put it directly back in the cabinet.

It's still difficult to breathe, so I reach for something to distract myself, spotting the jar of expensive face cream tucked in the cabinet. I unscrew the lid, staring into the white pillowy cream. I remember Theo's words and I spit inside it.

57

MAGDALEN

The museum has been converted into a beautiful venue for Lucia and Maio. Long tables draped in lace tablecloths nestle elegantly between the giant sphinx statues. Papyrus paper name cards sit at each person's chair, along with hundreds of candelabras, dripping with wax, placed perfectly at each table. A cellist sits next to one of the mummies in the adjoining room, where the middle has been cleared to create a dance floor. Lucia and Maio glow as they say their vows, cut their cake and dance for the first time as a married couple. I am so proud that my sister has been brave enough to find the love of her life, and I feel blessed to welcome Maio into the family.

I spend the whole night talking to strangers I'm supposed to know. They ask me a million questions and I don't remember a single one of my answers. By the time I sit down, a large portion of the guests have already left. Thank god I wasn't the maid of honor. My stomach growls angrily, reminding me I haven't eaten since yesterday, during the rehearsal dinner, sans Theo. And while I knew he was here during the ceremony, I refused to look at him. But that doesn't mean I didn't *see* him. He was wearing black and ignored me the entire time. I try to be proud that I walked away. He waited until after I had given most of myself, but at least I had the nerve to stand up before he took the rest of me. Still, a part of me wished that he would have stood up, too. Maybe even took a step and whispered for me to stay.

I shake the thought away. It's too late for yearning. In another week, I'll be back in rainy Oxford. Anika has bought a ticket to visit me in October, so my two sisters will finally meet. I came to Chivasso a virgin who did not believe in love. And I'll return to Oxford with a ravenous ache for someone I might only see in my dreams. My stomach growls again, but when I look down at the food I feel nothing. No desire to reach my hand to the fork. The thought of chewing is tiring.

Nestling myself into one of the chairs near the dance floor, I'm happy to be alone for a moment. Dexter stands off in the far corner with a shorter man, his face sweaty as he talks aggressively close to him, and it's now so obvious that he's on something. I glance at Cinzia Sinclair, who chats on the other side of the museum with a cousin of Maio's, and I wonder if, the entire time she's speaking to this woman, her mind is on Dexter. How exhausting it must be to not trust your person. To wonder if their eyes will wander, even after two kids and decades of marriage. Then I look over at my own mother. She stands underneath the moss-covered tombs with one arm draped lazily over my father's shoulder as he points wildly at the *Ancient Book of the Dead* papyrus hanging on the wall. This is how I will always remember them, lost in their own world of ancient Egypt and loud laughter. But now a secret hangs over them alongside the pretty moss.

I sip the champagne and close my eyes as the cellist begins a new song and my mind drifts to Theo. If I had known leaving him that night would lead to unplanned absences and active avoidance, would I have ever asked him to kiss me? Anika claims it was because he wasn't feeling well but even she couldn't hide her disappointment. Less than three months home and I've cleaved our family's bond like chopping firewood. Hacking away until the pieces of us are unsalvageable, too small to even burn. But I think about a tiny Theo, having to endure his father's humiliation, and I feel selfish for even considering him having to hold that secret alone. I wish it were me who had seen them in the attic. Is that love? Wanting to endure someone else's pain? It's a scary thought. To realize I would cut my wrists and bleed out if it meant that Theo would never be hurt again is a heady revelation. Would I do the same for Dante? I know the answer, but I brush it away before it lands.

Downing the last of the champagne, I hear a fantastic laugh and turn to watch Anika hastily grab one of Maio's many cousins, dragging him to the dance floor. Her dress is tangerine orange with intricate beading of pinks and yellows, making her glow in the dim candlelight of the museum. The cousin's face is bright red as she takes his hand and places it on her lower back and, when she readjusts it so that he's cupping her ass, I snort with laughter to myself. The combination of expensive champagne and Anika's eternal confidence makes it impossible not to smile.

"Hello, Magdalen."

My eyes close. Immediately the smile slips. I would know it was him by the shape of his shadow, by the echo of his footsteps against the granite floor, but I blink up to be sure. When our eyes meet, my breath catches in my throat. Cold gray eyes stare intensely at me, his gaze lingering over my body, my face, my hair, and I know mine do the same as I take in the sight of him in a tux. Yes, he's wearing all black, but he dominates the color, looking tall and broad in the fitted jacket. My hand stings with the desire to fix his bow-tie but I remain seated, my knees shaking underneath my dress.

His casual hello is disturbed by the clench of his jaw and how tightly his fists are shoved in his pocket. His lips. Impossibly soft. I reach for another glass of champagne, downing it in three sips, willing myself to remember what else I thought about before Theo Sinclair.

"Hi."

"You're beautiful." He exhales harshly. "It shocks me every time I look at you. How beautiful you are."

Now it's my turn to exhale, completely caught off guard by his confession. I want to lie down on the table and sob. Beg him to take it back. To say it again.

"Thank you. You look beautiful, too."

"So Anika tells me you're going back to Oxford next week," he says dejectedly.

"Our own little Cupid. She tells me you bought your plane ticket for New York."

"Yeah, they're quite worried about the state of my thesis."

"Who's they?"

"My fucking father called his friend at Columbia and told him about my lack of progress. I think my presence here makes him nervous."

"You must be tired."

"I've had seven years to rest. It shouldn't still surprise me."

"Will you talk to him before you leave?"

"No." His lips thin. "No, there's nothing more to say. I'd rather spend my last days talking to you. Anika. Dante. Who needs fathers anyway?"

"You'll always have mine."

He taps his foot impatiently, eager to stop talking about this, and glances nervously at the dance floor. And I know before he asks. *Yes.*

"Dance with me?"

"I've never slow-danced with anyone. I might step on you."

Theo bends forward to take the glass out of my grip and some of his hair falls in front of his face. "I'm sorry I keep taking these firsts." I can feel his breath on my neck and I struggle not to close my eyes at his nearness. I can smell the clean laundry, the sandalwood, the last night in Alassio. If I lean forward just a little, his hair would brush against my cheek.

"Why are you sorry?" *Why did you let them get away with it? Tell me again, so maybe this time, I'll understand.*

His fingers wrap around mine, pulling me up, and immediately his hands are around my hips, gripping tightly. "Because I want them all."

After his first night back, it was clear I had been waiting for him. Waiting to give him all my firsts. The truth is easier than trying to deny my feelings. "I think you already took all I have to offer."

His eyes search mine painfully and he takes a step closer so we're almost flush against each other. He dips his head so that his lips brush against the high point of my cheekbone and he sighs sadly before whispering, "He knows."

Frowning, I try to look at him, to understand what he means, but he turns his head and leads me to the dance floor.

"What are you talking about?" There are three other couples on the floor, so he chooses an empty spot before whirling me around, snaking one hand around my waist while the other takes my hand and places it behind his neck.

"I should have told you in the backyard."

"What? Dexter knows that I know?"

Theo shakes his head. "No, no. Your father." He looks toward my papa, who sits at the head table, watching us while eating a slice of cake. When he sees us both looking at him, he drops his fork and waves, smiling happily. "He's known for some time."

If it wasn't for Theo's arm guiding me as we dance, I'm not sure I'd still be standing up straight. The lights of the candles begin to blur and I'm aware of a faint ringing in my ear. *He's known. He's known. He has known.*

"What do you mean, he's known?"

"I lied when I said you're the only person I told. I told him, the night... remember the night I got these bloody tattoos in Egypt? I told him everything. About the attic, Vittoria, *E.T.* I said it all to him. At this point, the guilt was consuming me and that trip was the first time I had stepped out of Chivasso—it finally felt like his hand wasn't around my throat any more."

I swallow the tears as I look to my father again, still staring at us with smiling eyes. "And what did he say?"

"He said don't worry. And that he was sorry. He apologized to me—I couldn't believe it. This man's business partner and wife are fucking behind his back and he's apologizing to me." Theo shakes his head, his voice far away, and I know he's back in Egypt, next to my papa.

"'How special it is that I love her enough to forgive the both of them. You will not understand. My children will never understand. But as long as she and I can still sit side by side at the kitchen table, I am happy to be loved this way.'"

The song ends, and another begins.

"That is not love." My voice is hoarse, ruined.

"To him it is."

"So I'm not supposed to say anything?" How devastating. To know my one example of true love was doomed from the start. I think back to being a child and watching them kiss on lazy Sundays, and it makes me want to scream. Deep down, did I know their kisses were poisoned?

"My sweet girl." He lets go of my waist and cradles his

fingers around the base of my head to look at him. "Our parents' mistakes don't have to bleed into our choices, right?"

I sniffle. "Are you quoting me?"

His thumb brushes against my upper lip and he smiles crookedly. "I've spent most of my days thinking about things you've said this summer."

If love is the kitchen table, a bowl of softening fruit, knowing when to hug instead of kiss, then it seems obvious that I must confess. Even if he'll never reciprocate. It's time to be brave.

"I love you, Theo."

His face crumples and he tries to look away, but I bring my fingers to his chin, keeping him looking at me.

"No." Theo blinks rapidly a few times and lets go of my neck. His eyes instantly fill with tears. Our gentle dance comes to a pause, just us now standing on the dance floor. "Magdalen, no. I mean, fuck. I have done *nothing* but hurt you. I'm really not worth loving."

"How can you say that?" I step forward where he has stepped back, determined to show through the trembling of my fingers in his hair that *this is love.*

"You have changed summer for me," I whisper. "Instead of sunlight, I'll now think of you."

"Magdalen." He breathes out my name, dipping his forehead to rest against mine. "Since the moment I saw you in the grass."

"I know," I smile. The cellist drags his bow softly against one of the strings a final time. I look back to Theo, who stares at me, desperate, frozen. And I know he loves me.

"One day, I'll come back to this museum, and I'll see you here." His voice shakes, and he clears his throat. "And I'll know it's you because of your stupid overalls and faded old T-shirts. I hope by then I'll have finally talked to my dad, sat him down and told him what that day fucking did to me." I let the tears spill out of me, not caring that I'm crying at my sister's wedding. I know he loves me, yes. But I can feel the end coming.

"But maybe then I'll be whole. Less afraid of him," he laughs, and a tear falls down onto the white shirt underneath his jacket. I watch it expand and settle in the fabric. My palm comes to his cheek, tears falling between the divots of my fingers.

"And there will be so much room for you in here." He takes my hand and lays it on his heart, pressing hard. "There will be so much room. For you."

"One day," I whisper back.

58

THEO

ONE WEEK LATER

"We are gathered here today to celebrate the Summer of Return."

Dante, Anika, Magdalen and I sit on the cool stairs underneath the bell tower in Chivasso. It is 3 a.m. and the town is asleep, with only the moon to light the piazza. In a rare occasion, there are no crickets—just silence and Dante's loud fucking breathing.

"The return of my baby sister and the king of Chivasso." He has an open wine bottle in his hand, and points to Magdalen and me before taking a swig. "Who are now fucking."

Magdalen gasps and covers her eyes. "Dante!"

"The truth will set you free, sister. We're in front of a church, do you really want to deny your sin on Theo's last night here?" Even as a joke, my heart lurches when I think about leaving them again.

"Objection." Anika reaches across Magdalen to take the wine bottle from Dante. "They haven't fucked."

Yes, we fucking have.

446

"This is not happening." Magdalen buries her head in her hands further.

"Yes, good Magdalen, cover your ears," Dante says. "Theo? Is this true?"

"Not talking about this."

"Okay, you'll tell me later."

"No, I really won't."

Anika stands up and shoves the bottle into Magdalen's lap, holding up a small black plastic bag.

"Enough of this. Whether the two consummated the union is irrelevant. Let's consummate the summer."

Before any of us have time to ask what she means, Anika pulls out a small teal gun and Dante screams.

"What the fuck, Anika? Is this some sort of *Romeo and Juliet* murder-suicide?" I let their chatter fill my head so I don't have to think about my beautiful *phantasma*. She's a meter away. I can smell her from here, honeysuckle and lavender, and I lean closer, breathing deeper. Memorizing.

Anika stares at Dante, dumbfounded. "I'm genuinely afraid to go away with you."

Magdalen perks up, and I realize I've been staring at her, so I clear my throat and try to focus on Anika's words.

"Go where?" she asks.

Dante groans, annoyed. "Fuck, Anika. Way to go ruin the surprise."

"What's going on?" Magdalen looks between Anika and Dante, who stare at each other anxiously.

Annoyed, in love, I yell loudly for Magdalen's sake. "Tell us right fucking now!"

"Well, we were going to wait until it was all ready," Anika starts and sounds genuinely nervous. "But we bought a space."

"A space?" Magdalen asks, clasping her hands together. "Like *the* space?"

"We're officially the owners of a wine bar!" Magdalen jumps up, screeching happily, running toward Anika. "Well, technically it's just a dilapidated hole in the South of France, but it was cheap and Dante and I are excellent on a budget." She grunts as Magdalen squeezes her tightly.

"Oh my god! Oh my god! How could you both keep this from us all summer?"

"We were *supposed* to wait until it was ready to tell anyone," Dante complains, but I see him try to suppress his smile, happy with Magdalen's response. "But I guess this is fine, too."

"I'm so proud of both of you." She wraps her arms around Anika, hugging her tightly, and one of her hands squeezes Dante's wrist. I pat Dante on the head, trying to scruff his gelled hair, but it doesn't even budge.

"While you two were drooling over each other, Anika and I were building a motherfucking business." He shrugs, winking at me.

"Proud of you," I mouth.

"You too," he smirks.

Anika sniffles happily, unwrapping herself from Magdalen, and my heart clenches. My little sister and best friend: business owners.

"Anyway," she wipes her eyes. "Of course, you two are required to come to the opening."

"Of course," Magdalen agrees, her eyes shining as she looks at me. "We'll be there."

"Good." Anika reaches into the bag, taking out a small clear box with metal pieces in it, and shakes it excitedly. "Now we're piercing our ears!"

"Oh no, I am not. No. No. No." Dante swipes the bottle from Magdalen as she sits back down and takes a long swig. "I don't know what kind of back-alley dealer you got that from, Anika."

"It's an ear-piercing gun, Dante. Not a pound of cocaine."

"Ever heard of an ear infection? Who's the idiot now, dumbass?"

I raise my hand to Dante, gesturing for the bottle. "I'll do it." My voice is bleak and I take a long glug of wine, closing my eyes as it warms my throat. I want to be happy for them but it's hard, knowing their life is beginning together. And ours is . . .

"Only if Magdalen pierces me," I hear myself say.

"Poetic. A romantic till the bitter end." Dante grabs the bottle, taking a quick sip before handing it over again. "This is why the ladies love you."

Magdalen tries to look at me, but it's becoming increasingly difficult to pretend this isn't our last moment together for a long time.

"I could barely cut your hair, let alone pierce a hole through your flesh!"

"I'd be honored to be hurt by you." The wine has made my voice rough, exposing my growing sadness.

"Gross," Dante chimes in behind us.

"Only if you pierce mine." Magdalen walks over to me and sits down, her leg brushing against me. Her hair bounces wildly down her back as she scoots onto the step next to me. I am trying to not feel sad. I think of the seasons, how they come and go—leaves shrivel, we buy scarves and decorate trees and eventually, with enough time, summer returns. The cycle is inevitable. I try to think of Magdalen as my summer, to remember that she can return.

She props up her head on one hand, our eyes lock and it hurts so much that I almost believe I'll cry in front of them all. It hurts not to be whole. My hand is moving her hair away from her face before I remember that I shouldn't touch her any more and I brush my thumb over her earlobe. She shivers.

"Pierceable?" she asks lightly, green eyes dancing across my face.

"I don't want to hurt you."

She stares at me knowingly. *Too late*, she seems to say, both of us recalling the night at the wedding a week earlier. My eyes burn and I drop my hand, going to look away, but her fingers lace through my hair before I have the chance, tugging slightly so I'm forced to meet her eyes. She traces my ear gently and I lean into her touch, wondering if this can be enough between us. Did letting her go mean letting him win? It's difficult to know.

"You know, I'll look for you everywhere," I whisper, my voice barely audible.

"I know." Magdalen smiles and takes the bottle from my lap, putting it on the step behind us. She then takes my hand in hers, bringing it to her lips, and kisses my palm softly.

"I'll be the one in overalls."

Acknowledgments

I feel giddy as I write these acknowledgments. As an avid reader and a nosy person, I'm always curious to gain insight into the author's process when I finish a book. It's surreal to know that, by writing this, I've really completed my first book.

I'd like to thank my mom first. She taught me everything I know about what it means to imagine. Between the Madonna CDs on shuffle and *I Love Lucy* playing in the background of all our childhood dinners, I was constantly immersed in noise and color. It's not hard to find creativity when surrounded by such a force of nature. Love you, Mamma. I'm so proud to be your daughter.

I'd like to thank my sister—my best friend—who paved the way for us to choose these unconventional careers. I've spent most of my life hoping to find similarities between us in my reflection. You're so smart, it's infuriating. The only person I trust with my deepest secrets. I love you, Juju, even from 6,187 miles away. If I don't say it enough: goodnight, love you, too. Woof.

To my papa: just because I'm putting you in the acknowledgments, doesn't mean you can read this book. A very logical and methodical man who lets me gush over my latest celebrity crush without so much as a wince, he's what tethers me to Chivasso, driving too fast down the winding roads of Castagneto Po. Our trips to Italy together are some of the happiest moments of my life.

To my little TikTok and Instagram community: I could never have done this without you. If it weren't for your endless support, this book would still be sitting sadly in my drafts, unfinished. This book is as much yours as it is mine.

To Kinza, at Pan Macmillan. What were the chances of meeting at a busy coffee shop in London? You've made all my dreams come true, transforming this book into something I'm proud to have written. Your talent is unmatched. I feel entirely indebted to you and your suggestions for more sex scenes.

To Lauren, my agent, who received a frantic email from a complete stranger and graciously replied—you're a force to be reckoned with. Thank you for having my back.

To Bernadette, to Gab—girlhood is glorious with you both by my side.

To Magdalen and Theo, who overtook my dreams one summer night and compelled me to write down their story. I have learned so much about myself through these fictional characters. I'm a different person after having created them.

About the Author

CAMERON CAPELLO is a content creator from New York City. She graduated from St. Joseph's University with a degree in English. An avid reader and writer, she often daydreams about romance tropes and explains them to her sister, who increasingly worries about her imagination.

When she isn't writing, she can be found lounging around with her English bulldog, Malfoy, scarfing down Korean food and drinking an alarming amount of coffee (with too much vanilla).

You can find out more at:

CameronCapellobooks.com
TikTok @chamberofsecretbooks
Instagram @thechamberofsecretbooks